LAWRENCE SANDERS

"A masterful storyteller…"

—*KING FEATURES SYNDICATE*

"A writer who has matured into one of our great ones."

—*PITTSBURGH PRESS*

THE THIRD DEADLY SIN

"One of his best…a fast, furious read!"

—*JOHN BARKHAM REVIEWS*

"Sanders has built another high-voltage thriller with the skill that made THE FIRST DEADLY SIN and his earlier books best-sellers!"

—*PUBLISHERS WEEKLY*

Lawrence SANDERS

The THIRD Deadly Sin

BERKLEY BOOKS, NEW YORK

This Berkley book contains the complete
text of the original hardcover edition.
It has been completely reset in a typeface
designed for easy reading, and was printed
from new film.

THE THIRD DEADLY SIN

A Berkley Book / published by arrangement with
the author

PRINTING HISTORY
G. P. Putnam's Sons edition / August 1981
Berkley edition / August 1982

ISBN: 0-425-05507-8

A BERKLEY BOOK ® TM 757,375
Berkley Books are published by Berkley Publishing Corporation,
200 Madison Avenue, New York, New York 10016.
The name "BERKLEY" and the stylized "B" with design
are trademarks belonging to Berkley Publishing Corporation.
PRINTED IN THE UNITED STATES OF AMERICA

The THIRD
Deadly Sin

1

Some days lasted forever; some were never born. She awoke in a fury of expectation, gone as soon as felt; the world closed about. Once again life became a succession of swan pecks.

Zoe Kohler, blinking, woke holding a saggy breast, soft as a broken bird. The other wrist was clamped between her thighs. She was conscious of the phlegmy light of late winter, leaking through drawn blinds.

Outside, she knew, would be a metal day, no sun, and a sky that pressed. The air would smell of sulfur. She heard traffic drone and, within the apartment house, the dull thumps of morning doors. In the corner of her bedroom a radiator hissed derisively.

She stared at the ceiling and sensed herself anxiously, the auguries of her entrails: plump organs, a living pulse, the whispering course of tainted blood. A full bladder pressed, and deeper yet she felt the heavy ache that would become biting cramps when her menses began.

She pushed the covers aside, swung her feet out of bed. She moved cautiously; something might twist, something might snap. She sat yawning, hugging herself, bending forward.

"Thursday," she said aloud to the empty room. "March thirteenth."

Her voice sounded cracked, unused. She straightened up, cleared her throat, tried again:

"Thursday. March thirteenth."

That sounded better. A huskiness, but strong, definite. Almost masculine.

Naked, she stood up, stretched, knuckled her scalp. For

an instant she swayed, and grabbed the headboard of the bed for support. Then the vertigo passed; she was steady again.

"Like a dizzy spell," she had said to Dr. Stark. "I feel like I might fall."

"And how long does this last?" he inquired. He was shuffling papers on his desk, not looking at her. "A few minutes?"

"Less than that. Just a few seconds."

"How often?"

"Uh . . . occasionally."

"Just before your period?"

She thought a moment.

"Yes," she said, "that's right. Before the cramps begin."

Then he looked up.

"Nothing to worry about," he assured her.

But she did worry. She did not like that feeling of disorientation, however brief, when she was out of control.

She padded into the kitchen to switch on the electric percolator, prepared the night before. Then into the bathroom to relieve herself. Before she flushed the toilet, she inspected the color of her urine. It appeared to be a pale gold, but perhaps a little cloudy, and she wondered if she should call Dr. Stark.

Back to the bedroom for five minutes of stretching exercises, performed slowly, almost languidly. She bent far over, knees stiff, to put her palms flat on the floor. She reached far overhead, flexing her spine. She twisted her torso side to side, arms extended. She moved her head about on her neck. She thrust pelvis and buttocks forward and back in a copulative movement she had never seen in any exercise manual but which, she was convinced, lessened the severity of her menstrual cramps.

She returned to the bathroom, brushed her teeth, massaged her gums. She stepped on the scale. Still 124. Her weight hadn't varied more than three pounds since the day she was married.

Because her period was approaching, she took a hotter shower than usual. She lathered with a soap advertised to contain a moisturizing cream that would keep her skin soft and supple. She believed this to be true.

She soaped her body thoroughly and carefully, although she had showered before going to bed the previous night. While she was drying herself with one of the blue-striped towels stolen from the hotel where she worked, she looked down and regretted her smooth, hairless legs for reasons she could not comprehend.

And while looking down, inspecting, saw, yes, the glint of two gray pubic hairs, the first she had ever found. She uttered a sound of dismay, took manicure scissors from the medicine cabinet and clipped them away. She stared at the kinked hairs lying in her palm. Silver wires.

In the bedroom, she turned on the bedside radio, tuned to WQXR. The weather report was not encouraging: overcast, chance of showers, temperature in the high thirties. The announcer's voice sounded something like Kenneth's, and she wondered if her alimony check would arrive on time.

She dressed swiftly. White cotton bra and panties. Not-too-sheer pantyhose in a mousy color. Low-heeled brogues. White turtleneck sweater, tweed skirt with wide, crushed leather belt. Her makeup was minimal and palish. She spent as little time as possible before the mirror. Her short brown hair needed only a quick comb.

In the cabinet over the sink in the kitchen, Zoe Kohler kept her medicines and vitamins and minerals, her pills and food supplements, painkillers and tranquilizers: a collection much too large for the bathroom cabinet.

Taped to the inside of the kitchen cabinet door was a typed schedule of what items should be taken each day of the month: some daily, some every other day, some semiweekly, some weekly, some biweekly, some monthly. New drugs were occasionally added. None was ever eliminated.

She poured a full glass of cold grapefruit juice, purchased in quart bottles. On this Thursday morning, March 13th, sipping and swallowing, she downed vitamins A, C, E, and B_{12}, iron and zinc tablets, her birth control pill, a Midol tablet, the capsule for her disease, half a choline tablet, two Anacin, an alfalfa pill, a capsule said to be rich in lecithin, and another of kelp, a single Librium, and an antacid tablet which she was supposed to let melt in her mouth but which she chewed up and swallowed.

She then had a slice of unbuttered whole wheat toast

with her first cup of black, decaffeinated coffee. She put an ice cube in the coffee to cool it quickly so she could gulp it down. With her second cup of coffee, also with an ice cube, she smoked a filter-tip advertised as having the lowest tar content of any cigarette in the world.

She rinsed the breakfast things in the sink and left them there for washing in the evening. The kitchen was a walk-through, and she exited into the living room, moving a little faster now, a little more purposefully.

She took a coat from the foyer closet. It was a chesterfield in black wool with a gray velvet collar. She checked the contents of her black leather shoulder bag: keys, wallet, this and that, a small can of Mace, which was illegal in New York City but which had been obtained for her by Everett Pinckney, and her Swiss Army folding pocket knife, a red-handled tool with two blades, a file, an awl, a tiny pair of scissors, and a bottle opener.

She peered through the peephole of the outside door. The corridor appeared empty. She unbolted the door, took off the chain, turned the lock and eased the door open cautiously. The hallway was empty. She double-locked the door behind her, rang for the elevator, and waited nervously.

She rode down to the lobby by herself, moved quickly to the outside doors and the sidewalk. Leo, the doorman, was shining the brass plaque that listed the names of the five doctors and psychiatrists who had offices on the ground floor.

"Morning, Miz Kohler," Leo said.

She gave him a dim smile and started walking west toward Madison Avenue. She strode rapidly, with a jerky step, looking neither to the right nor the left, not meeting the eyes of pedestrians who passed. But they did not give her a second glance. In fact, she knew, not even a first.

The Hotel Granger, a coffin on end, was pressed between two steel and glass skyscrapers on Madison Avenue, between 46th and 47th streets. The entrance to the hotel, framed by stained marble columns, seemed more like the portal to an obsolete gentlemen's club where members dozed behind *The Wall Street Journal* and liveried servants brought glasses of sherry on silver salvers.

The reality was not too different. The Granger dated from 1912, and although occasionally refurbished, nothing had been "modernized" or "updated." In the gloomy cocktail lounge, one still rang a bell to summon service, plastic and chromium were abjured, and over the entire main floor—lobby, desk, lounge, dining room, and executive offices—lay the somber, sourish smell of old carpeting, musty upholstery, and too many dead cigars.

For all of that, the Granger was a successful hostelry, with most of its 283 rooms and suites leased on an annual basis to midtown corporations for the use of executives staying overnight in the city, or for the convenience of out-of-town visitors. Those accommodations available to transients were frequently reserved a year in advance, for the rooms were large and comfortable, the service genial, the rates moderate, and the dining room was said to possess the third-best wine cellar in New York.

The Granger also offered the last hotel billiard room in the city, although there was only one table, and the faded, green felt was torn.

In its almost seventy-year history, the Granger, like all hotels, had its share of tragedy and violence. Heart attacks. Strokes. Two murders. Eight suicides, three of which were leaps from upper floors.

In 1932, a guest had choked to death on a fishbone in the dining room.

In 1949, two gentlemen sharing a suite on the 8th floor had taken an overdose of barbiturates and died, naked, in each other's arms.

In 1953, in a particularly messy incident, an enraged husband had smashed open the door of Room 1208 where his wife and her lover were singing "God Bless America" in bed. The husband had not harmed either, but had dived headfirst from the nearest window, hurtling to his death on Madison Avenue, badly damaging the frosted glass marquee.

In 1968, there had been a shoot-out in a large 3rd-floor corporation suite. One man had been killed, one injured, and a room-service waiter present in the suite had suffered the indignity of a bullet wound in his nates.

The management, of course, had immediately canceled the lease, since a morality clause was an important part of all long-term agreements with the Hotel Granger.

But despite these isolated occurrences, the Granger was essentially a quiet, staid, conservative establishment, catering to old, familiar guests, and frequently their children and grandchildren. The Security Section was not large, and most of its efforts were devoted to quietly evicting drunks and derelicts who wandered in from Madison Avenue, politely asking obvious hookers to move from the cocktail lounge, and keeping a record of lost-and-found articles, a task that bedevils every metropolitan hotel.

Zoe Kohler, having walked uptown from her East 39th Street apartment, entered the Hotel Granger at 8:46 A.M. She nodded at the doorman, the bellhops, the day shift coming on duty behind the reservation desk.

She went through a door marked "Employees Only," down a short corridor to a small suite of offices housing the Security Section. As usual, Barney McMillan, who worked the 1:00 to 9:00 A.M. shift, was asleep on the leather couch in Everett Pinckney's office. She shook him awake. He was a fleshy man, not too clean, and she found it distasteful to touch him.

"Wha'?" he said.

"Get up," she said. "You're supposed to be on duty."

"Yeah," he said, sitting up, yawning, tasting his tongue. "How about some coffee, babe?"

She looked at him.

"No," she said stiffly.

He looked at her.

"How about some coffee, Zoe?"

"That's better," she said. "A Danish?"

"Why not? Prune—or whatever they've got."

"Any excitement?" she asked.

"Nah," he said. "A couple of drunks singing on the ninth floor. That was about it. Quiet night. Just the way I like it."

She hung her coat away in an open closet. She put her purse in the bottom drawer of her desk, and extracted a japanned tray from the wide top drawer. She went out the way she had come, through the lobby and cocktail lounge, into a side corridor that led to the kitchen.

They were busy with breakfast in there, serving in the dining room and making up room orders, and no one spoke to her. No one looked at her. Sometimes she had a fantasy that she was an invisible woman.

She poured two black coffees for Mr. Pinckney and herself. Barney McMillan liked his with two sugars and two creams. The Danish and strudel didn't look especially appetizing, so she selected a jelly doughnut for Barney. He'd eat anything.

She carried her loaded tray back to the Security Section offices. Everett Pinckney had arrived; he and McMillan were sitting on opposite sides of Pinckney's desk, their feet up. They were laughing loudly, but cut it short and took their feet down when Zoe entered. Mr. Pinckney said good morning and both thanked her politely for their morning coffee.

When she went back to her own office, she heard their laughter start up again. She suspected they might be laughing at her, and looked down to make certain her sweater and skirt were not stained, her belt was properly buckled, her pantyhose without runs. She could see nothing amiss, but still . . .

She sat primly at her desk in the windowless office, sipping her coffee. She listened to the drone of talk of the two men and the bustling sounds of the hotel about her. She wondered if she *was* invisible. She wondered if she did exist.

Zoe Kohler was neither this nor that: not short, not tall; not fair, not dark; not thin, not plump. She lacked the saving grace of a single extreme.

In their final argument, just before Kenneth had stormed out of the house, he had shouted in fury and frustration: "You're not definite! You're just not *there!*"

Her lusterless hair was cut in a short bob: a straight line of bangs across her brow, a center part with thick wings falling just below her ears. She had not changed that style since college. Her hair fitted as precisely as a good wig and was all of a piece, no tendrils or curls, as if it could be lifted off, revealing the pale scalp of a nun or collaborator.

Her face was triangular, dwindling to a pointed chin. The eyes were the same shade of brown as her hair, and without fire or depth. The eyeballs were slightly distended, the lashes a lighter brown and wispy.

Her lips were not pinched. Clever makeup could have softened them—but for what?

At work, in public, her features seemed immobile, set. She rarely smiled—and then it was gone, a flicker. Some thought her serious, solemn, dull. All were wrong. No one knew.

She would soon be thirty-seven, and though she exercised infrequently, her body remained young, with good muscle tone. Her stomach was reasonably flat, buttocks taut. Her thighs were not slack, and there was a sweet indentation between ribcage and hips.

Dr. Stark assured her that, other than the controllable disorder and menstrual cramps, she was in excellent health.

She knew better. She was unloved and incapable of inspiring respect. Was that not an illness?

Dim she may have been, even blank, for there was nothing robust, vital, or assertive in the role she played. The dowdy clothes. The sensible shoes. The subdued eyes, the quick, tremulous smile.

That was the lark, you see. It was all a grand hustle. Now, after so many years, she was swindling the world. She was making her mark.

Barney McMillan left, giving her a wave as he passed her office.

"Ta-ta," he said.

She planned her work for the day: drawing up the Security Section's employment schedule for the following week, writing letters to departed guests who had left personal property in their rooms, filing petty cash vouchers with the bookkeeping department.

It was, she acknowledged, hardly enough to keep her busy for eight hours. But she had learned to pace herself, to appear constantly busy, to maintain a low profile so that no executive might become curious enough to question her value to the Hotel Granger.

She felt no guilt in taking advantage of this sinecure; her take-home pay was less than $200 a week. She was able to live comfortably only because of her alimony and the yearly checks of $3000 each from her mother and father. She had a modest savings account, a checking account, and a small portfolio of tax-exempt municipal bonds.

She did not waste money, but neither did she deny herself. Anyone who might glimpse the gowns concealed in the back of her closet, or the lingerie hidden in the bottom drawer of her dresser, would agree to that: she did not deny herself—what she wanted and what she needed.

Everett Pinckney stopped by. Because there was no extra chair in her tiny office, he put one thin haunch on the edge of her desk and perched there, looking down at her.

He was a tall, jointed man, balding, a bony crown rising from a horseshoe of gray hair. His bare scalp was freckled and there was a sprinkle across his nose and cheekbones.

His eyes seemed constantly teary, his lips moist. He had the largest ears Zoe Kohler had ever seen: slices of drooping veal. His voice was hoarse and raspy, which was odd because he had a Boston accent, and one expected a tone more elegant and precise.

He wore vested suits with small bowties and, occasionally, in his lapel, a fake flower made of feathers. His cracked shoes were always polished to a high gloss. If he was a man on the way down, there was no bitterness or self-pity in him.

It hadn't taken Zoe long to realize she had been hired by an alcoholic. You could not judge from his manner or speech, for he moved steadily, if slowly, and his words were never garbled. But even in the morning he exuded a faint but perceptible odor: sour, piercing, musty. Whiskey had soaked into his cells, into the lining of his stomach, and bubbled up to seep from the pores of his skin.

He was never obviously drunk, but she had heard the drawer of his desk slide open, the clink of bottle against glass, the closing of the desk drawer: a steady and never-ending series of sounds that got him through the day in what Zoe imagined to be a constant glow, a buzz, a dulling of whatever gnawed at him so that he could function and face the world with equanimity and charm.

And he *was* charming, with a crooked smile, endless patience, and sympathy that seemed without limit. He was invariably cheerful, always obliging, and knew how to endure fools. Zoe had heard gossip of a bedridden wife and a son who had gone bad, but she had never asked, and Everett Pinckney had volunteered no information about his life outside the Hotel Granger.

Nor did he ever question Zoe about her private life.

They respected each other's pain. It brought them closer than confessions and confidences.

"Sergeant Coe called me last night," Pinckney told her. "At home. His wife is pregnant."

"Again?" Zoe Kohler said.

"Again," he said, smiling. "So he'd like all the work he can get. Naturally. You're going to make out next week's schedule today?"

She nodded.

"Can you use him?"

That was the way Everett Pinckney was. He didn't *tell* her to find work for Sergeant Coe, although he had every right to. But the employment schedule of the Security Section was one of her duties, so he asked her.

"Could he fill in for Joe Levine?" she asked.

"I'm sure he could."

"I'll check with him before I show you the schedule."

"Fine. Thank you, Zoe."

Pinckney, Barney McMillan, and Joseph T. Levine, the three security officers, worked eight hours a day. Each had two days off a week (Pinckney, the chief, on Saturday and Sunday). To fill in on their days off, or during vacations or illness, temporary security guards were employed.

Most of the temps were moonlighting New York policemen and detectives. The Security Section had a list of a dozen or so officers who might be available, and had little trouble keeping a man on duty around the clock.

Pinckney told Zoe Kohler he was going to check at the desk and then he was going to inspect the new locks on the steel doors leading to the roof.

"Be back in about an hour," he said.

She nodded.

He slid off her desk. He stood a moment, not departing, and she looked up inquiringly.

"Zoe . . ." he said.

She waited.

"You're all right?" he asked anxiously. "You're not ill? You seem a little, uh, subdued."

His concern touched her briefly.

"I'm fine, Mr. Pinckney," she said. "It's that time of the month again."

"Oh, *that,*" he said, relieved. Then, with a harsh bark

of laughter, "Well, I have to shave every morning."

He smiled, and was gone.

Yes, he shaved every morning. But you didn't get back pains and cramps from shaving, she should have told him. You didn't see the dark, gummy stains. You didn't imagine the ooze and flow. The constant crucifixion.

The longer she lived, the more vulgar life seemed to her. Not society or culture, but life itself. Breathing, eating, excreting, intercourse, bleeding.

Animal. Crude. Disgusting. Those were the words she used.

She worked slowly, steadily all morning, head bent over her desk, a silent drudge. She didn't look up when Everett Pinckney returned from his tour of inspection. She heard him in his office: desk drawer opened, clink of glass, drawer slammed shut.

She was not bored with her job. To be bored, she would have had to think about it, be conscious of it. But she moved mechanically, her hands, eyes, and a snippet of brain sufficient for the task. The rest of her was away and floating.

At 12:30 she took her japanned tray and went into the kitchen. One of the chefs fixed her a tunafish salad plate with lettuce, tomato and cucumber slices, a single large radish cut fancily to resemble a flower. She carried the food and a pot of hot tea back to her office.

Pinckney never ate lunch.

"Got to keep this down," he would say, patting his sunken stomach.

But she heard the sliding of his desk drawer . . .

She ate her lunch sitting erect in her stenographer's chair, her spine not touching the back. The cramps were intensifying, the pain in the lumbar region beginning to glow. It seemed centered just above the sacrum, but internal. The pain was a sun, spreading its rays.

She picked delicately at her salad, taking small bites, masticating thoroughly. She sipped her tea. When she had finished the food, she lighted a cigarette and poured a second cup of tea.

She kept a small pharmacopoeia in the middle drawer of her desk. She washed down two Anacin, a Midol and a vitamin C tablet. Then she patted her lips lightly with the linen napkin and brought the used dishes back to the scullery.

It was a rackety, steaming room, manned by two youths, a black and a Puerto Rican in sweat-soaked T shirts. They worked at top speed, scraping plates into garbage cans, filling racks with china, glassware, cutlery, pushing the racks into a huge washing machine.

They looked up when she came in, gave her scurvy glances. The Puerto Rican winked and shouted something in Spanish. The black roared with laughter and slapped his thigh. She emptied her tray, turned, and walked out. Their laughter followed her.

She called Sergeant Coe at his precinct, but he wasn't on duty. She called him at home. Mrs. Coe answered, and Zoe identified herself.

"Oh yes," Mrs. Coe said anxiously. "Can you hang on a sec? He's working in the basement. I'll call him right away."

When the sergeant came on the phone, breathless, Zoe informed him that she had him down for Joe Levine's shift, 5:00 P.M. to 1:00 A.M., on Monday and Tuesday nights.

"Great," he said. "Many thanks."

"If for any reason you are unable to make it," she said formally, "please let us know as soon as possible."

"I'll be there," he assured her. "Thanks again."

She took the employment schedule into Mr. Pinckney's office and stood by his desk as he read it.

"I checked with Sergeant Coe," she said. "He told me he'll be able to fill in for Joe Levine."

"Good," Pinckney said. "It looks fine to me, Zoe. You can type it up. Copies to the desk, front office, and bookkeeping."

He said that every week.

"Yes, Mr. Pinckney," she said.

She had just started typing the roster when her phone rang, an unusual occurrence.

"Hotel Granger," she said. "Security Section. May I help you?"

"You sure can, sweetie," a woman's voice said briskly. "Come to a great cocktail party Harry and I are throwing this afternoon."

"Maddie!" Zoe Kohler said happily. "How *are* you?"

"Full of piss and vinegar," Madeline Kurnitz said. "How they hanging, kiddo?"

The two women chatted awhile. Mostly, Maddie chatted, rapidly and loudly, and Zoe listened, smiling and nodding at the phone.

It seemed to her she had been listening to Madeline Kurnitz all her life. Or at least since she had shared a room with her and two other girls at the University of Minnesota. That had been in 1960–1963, and even then Maddie had been gabbling a blue streak.

"A four-year vacation from the realities of life," was her judgment on the value of a college education, and her scholastic career reflected this belief. It was one long party studded with dates, escapades, affairs, unexplained absences, threats of expulsion, and an endless parade of yearning boys and older men that awed her roommates.

Maddie: "Listen, the only reason we're all here is to snare a husband. Right? So why don't they teach us something useful—like moaning. The only reason I got all these guys calling is that I've learned how to moan realistically while screwing. That's all a woman has to know to be a success: how to moan. This place should have a course called Moaning 101–102. Then the second year's course could be called Remedial Moaning."

Maddie: "Look, there are men, and there are husbands. If you were male, would you want to be a husband? The hell you would. You'd want to charge through life banging everything in sight. Men fuck, husbands have sex. Men smell, husbands use fou-fou. Men drink whiskey, husbands drink beer. Men are hung, husbands have hernias. Shit, I don't want a husband, I want a *man*."

The three roommates, from small towns in Minnesota, Wisconsin, and Iowa, listened to these pronouncements with nervous giggles. It wasn't the way *they* had been brought up. Maddie, from New York City, was a foreigner.

They worshiped her, because she was smart, funny, generous. And she passed along the men she didn't want or had tired of. In return, they loaned her lecture notes, coached her, covered up her absences, and finally got her through the four years to a BA degree.

She didn't show up for graduation, having taken off for

Bermuda with a Yalie. But her diploma was mailed to her.

When Zoe Kohler came to New York from Winona, Minnesota, after her divorce, her first phone call was to Maddie. She was now Madeline Kurnitz with her own number in the directory. Harold Kurnitz was her fourth husband, and Maddie took Zoe under her wing as an experienced combat soldier might comfort, advise, and share his know-how with a raw recruit.

Maddie: "A divorce is like falling off a horse. You've got to get right back up and ride again or you'll be spooked for life."

"I don't think I want to marry again," Zoe said timidly.

Maddie: "Bullshit."

She had done her best—cocktail parties, dinner, blind dates—but finally she realized Zoe Kohler had been telling the truth: she didn't want to marry again, not at that point in her life.

Maddie (wrathfully): "That doesn't mean you can't *screw,* for God's sake. No wonder you have cramps. If I go two days without a bang, I sneeze and dust comes out my ears."

Now, listening to Maddie natter on about all the beautiful people who would be at her cocktail party ("A zillion horny studs!"), Zoe Kohler caught some of her excitement and said she'd come over from work, just for a few minutes, but she had to get home early.

Maddie: "That's what they all say, kiddo. But they come and they stay and they drink up all our booze. There's a guy I want you to meet . . . ."

"Oh no," Zoe said. "Not again."

"Just meet him," Maddie urged. "That's all. Just shake his paw and say, 'How ja do.' Is that so awful?"

"No," Zoe said faintly, "I guess not."

Maddie finally got off the phone and Zoe went back to typing the Security Section roster for the following week. She guessed that she had been invited to the cocktail party at the last minute because Maddie had realized that she would have a preponderance of male guests and not enough women. So she was calling friends and acquaintances frantically, trying to redress the balance.

Zoe wasn't offended. That was the way she received the few invitations that came her way. At the last minute. To even up a dining table or take the place of a reneging guest. She was never first choice.

The empty afternoon wasted away. She distributed copies of the Security Section's employment schedule. She typed up four letters to departed guests who had left personal property in their rooms, and took the letters to Everett Pinckney for his signature. She delivered petty cash vouchers to the bookkeeping department.

She spoke briefly and coolly to the other Hotel Granger employees she dealt with, and they replied in kind. She had rebuffed their attempts at friendship, or even light-hearted companionship. She preferred to do her job swaddled in silence.

Back in her office, she spent the last hour at her desk, idly leafing through the current issue of a weekly trade magazine devoted to the hotel business in New York City. It contained articles on current occupancy rates, conventions scheduled for the coming months, predictions on the summer tourism season.

The most interesting section, to Zoe, was that dealing with hotel security matters. Frequently the names and addresses (undoubtedly fictitious) and physical descriptions of deadbeats were given. Numbers of stolen credit cards were listed. Crimes committed in hotels, especially swindles and cons, were detailed.

A regular column titled "WANTED" gave names, aliases, and descriptions of known criminals—robbers, burglars, prostitutes, pimps, professional gamblers, etc.—working New York hotels. In addition, unsolved hotel crimes were listed, with the name and phone number of the New York Police Department officer investigating the crime.

The last item in the column read:

"Homicide at the Grand Park on February 15th. Victim of stabbing: George T. Puller, 54, white male, of Denver, Colo. Anyone with information relating to this crime please contact Detective Sergeant Abner Boone, KL-5-8604."

That notice had been in the magazine for the past three weeks. Zoe Kohler wondered if Detective Sergeant Abner Boone was still seated by the phone, waiting . . .

Madeline and Harold Kurnitz lived in a high-rise on

East 49th Street. The apartment house was just like
Maddie: loud, brash, glittering. Five people crowded into
the self-service elevator behind Zoe Kohler. She huddled
back in a corner, watching them. They were laughing,
their hands on each other. Zoe guessed they were going to
the party. They were.

The door of the seven-room duplex was open. Sound
surged out into the hall. In the foyer a uniformed maid
took hats and coats, hung them away on a temporary
rack, and handed out numbered checks. That was the way
Maddie did things.

The party was catered, with two bartenders working
behind counters and liveried waiters passing trays of hors
d'oeuvres and California champagne. Maddie was lost in
the throng, but her husband stood near the doorway to
greet guests.

He was a big, hairy man, tufts sprouting from his ears.
Zoe knew he was in yarn, fabrics, linings—something like
that. "The rag business," Maddie called it. He had a slow,
dry manner, ironic, amused and amazed that he found
himself married to a jangling, outgoing, capricious
woman.

Zoe liked him, and kissed his cheek. He seemed very
solid to her, very protective, as he steered her to the
nearest bar and ordered a glass of white wine for her.

"You remembered, Harry," she said.

"Of course I remembered," he said, smiling. "Of all
Maddie's friends, I like you the best. I wish you'd see
more of her. Maybe you can calm her down."

"No one can calm Maddie down."

"That's true," he said happily. "She's something, isn't
she? Isn't she something?"

He moved away to greet more guests. Zoe put her back
against the bar, looked around. A typical Maddie stand-
up party: crushed, smoky. A hi-fi was blasting from
somewhere. People were shrieking. She smiled, smiled,
smiled. No one spoke to her.

She had never seen so many beautiful men. Some were
elegant in three-piece Italian suits, gold aglitter at cuffs
and wrists. Some were raffish, with embroidered Greek
shirts opened low, medallions swinging against furred
chests. Some, many, she supposed, were homosexuals. It
didn't matter; they were all beautiful.

White, flashing teeth. Wicked eyes. Jaws bearded or shaved blue. Twirled mustaches. Hair slicked, dry-blown, coiffed, or deliberately tangled. Wet mouths in motion. Hands waving: long, slender fingers. Sprung hips. Sculpted legs and, here and there, jeans tight enough to show a bulge.

She thought of their fuzzed thighs. The satiny buttocks. Coil of tendon, rope of muscle. Most of all, their strength. Physical strength. The power there.

That was what had astounded her about Kenneth. He was not a stalwart man, but when he first gripped her on their wedding night, she had cried out in shock and surprise. The force! It frightened her.

And that—that thing. That reddish, purplish, knobbed thing poking out, trembling in the air. A club. It was a club, nodding at her.

She looked dazedly around the crowded room and saw the clubs, straining.

"Zoe!" Maddie screamed. "Baby! Why aren't you mingling? You've got to *mingle!*"

A bouncy ragamuffin of a woman with a snarl of long black hair liberally laced with gray. Silver wires didn't bother *her*. She couldn't be slowed by age or chastened by experience. She plunged vigorously through life, kicking up her heels.

Her face was a palette of makeup: black eyebrows like carets, shadowed eyes with fake lashes as thick as feather dusters. A whitened face with a bold, crimsoned mouth. Sharp teeth, feral teeth.

Her plump, unbound body capered; everything jounced, bobbed, swung. Diamonds sparkled at throat, ears, wrists, fingers. Her smart frock of black crepe was stained with a spilled drink. She smoked a thin cigar.

"He's around here somewhere," she shouted, grasping Zoe's arm. "David something. How are you, kiddo? He's wearing some kind of a cheesy velvet suit, but on him it looks good. My God, you're pale. David something. A mustache from here to there, and he smells of pot. You've *got* to take care of yourself, sweetie. Now get out there and *mingle*. You can't miss him. David something. Oh God, he's gorgeous. A young Clark Gable. If I see him, I'll grab him and find you. They say he's hung like Man-o'-War."

Then she was gone, diving into the mob. Zoe turned her back to the party, pressed against the bar, asked for another glass of white wine. She would sip it slowly, then slip away. No one would miss her.

This city had a rude vigor she could not countenance. It swirled her, and she felt adrift. Things were always at high tide, rising and rubbing. Noise, dirt, violence. The scream of sex everywhere. She could not endure the rawness.

A shoulder touched her; she pulled away, and looked at him.

"I beg your pardon," he said, smiling timidly. "Someone bumped me."

"That's all right," she said.

He looked at what she was drinking.

"White wine?" he asked.

She nodded.

He asked the bartender for a glass of white wine.

"Quite a party," he said to Zoe.

She nodded again. "Noisy," she said.

"Isn't it. And crowded and stuffy. My name is Ernest Mittle. I work in Mr. Kurnitz's office."

"Zoe Kohler," she said, so softly that he didn't hear and asked her to repeat it. "Zoe Kohler. I'm a friend of Maddie Kurnitz."

They shook hands. His clasp was tender, his smile fragile.

"I've never been here before," he offered. "Have you?"

"A few times."

"I guess it's a beautiful apartment—without the people."

"I don't know," she confessed. "I've only been here for parties. It's always been crowded."

She thought desperately of something more to say. She had been taught to ask men questions about themselves: their work, ambitions, hobbies—whatever. Get them talking about themselves, and they would think you interesting and clever. That's what her mother had told her—several times.

But the best she could do was: "Where are you from?"

"Wisconsin," he said. "A small town. Trempealeau. I'm sure you've never heard of it."

She didn't want to tell him; she wanted him to think her

a Manhattan sophisticate. But then her smile flickered, and she said:

"Yes, I've heard of it. I'm from Winona."

He turned to her with the delighted astonishment of a small boy.

"Winona!" he cried. "Neighbor!"

They moved a little closer: explorers caught in a dance of savages.

"Listen," he said excitedly, "are you here with anyone?"

"Oh no. No."

"Could we go someplace and have a drink together? Some quieter place? You're the first person I've met in New York who even heard of Trempealeau. I'd really like to talk to you."

"All right," she said.

No one noticed them leave.

In the lobby, he stopped her with a light hand on her arm, then jerked it away convulsively.

"Uh," he said, "I was wondering . . . Could we have dinner together? I know a little Italian place not far from here. If we're going to have a glass of wine, we might as well . . ."

His wispy voice trailed off. She stared at him a moment.

He was no David something in a velvet suit, smelling of pot. He was Ernest Mittle, a dusty young man who would always be an outlander in the metropolis.

There he stood, stooped, eager, as anxious to please as a cocker spaniel. The cheap tweed overcoat was too tight in the shoulders and strained at its buttons. About his neck was a plaid wool muffler. He was hatless, but carried a pair of clumpy, fleece-lined gloves.

He seemed inoffensive and washed-out to Zoe Kohler. Faded eyebrows, blond lashes, eyes of milky blue. His complexion was fair, his haircut an atrocity that left his pink ears naked, isolated by clipper and razor.

But still . . . His smile was warm and hopeful. His small teeth were even and white. He was as tall as she, and if he straightened up, he would have been taller. But he seemed to crouch inside himself, hiding.

She was ever so careful. He appeared harmless, not pushy in the New York manner, but she knew as well as anyone the dangers that awaited the lone woman in the

cruel city. Mugging. Burglary. Rape. Violent death. It
was in the newspapers every day. And on TV in color.
The chalked outline. The congealing blood.

"Well . . . all right," she said finally. "Thank you. But I
have to get home early. By nine at the latest. Uh, I'm
expecting a phone call."

"Fine," he said happily. "Let's go. It's not far; we can
walk it in a few minutes."

She knew the restaurant. She had been there twice
before, by herself. Each time she had been seated at the
same small table near the door to the restrooms. The food
was good, but the service had been execrable, although
she had left generous tips.

This time, with a man, she was escorted by a smiling
maitre d' to a comfortable corner table. A waiter came
bustling to assist in removing her coat. A table candle in a
ruby globe was lighted. Glasses of white wine were
brought, menus proffered.

They both ordered veal piccata, spaghetti, and salad.
They each had two more glasses of wine with their food.
Service was prompt and flawless. They agreed the dinner
was a success.

And she did enjoy it. Ernest Mittle was well-mannered,
solicitous of her wants: "More bread? Butter? Ready for
another wine? Dessert? No? Then surely espresso and a
brandy? Fine!"

She had an uneasy feeling that he could ill afford this
splendid meal, but he seemed delighted to be dining with
her. When their brandies were served, she murmured
something about paying her share, but he grandly waved
the suggestion away and assured her that it was *his*
pleasure. He sounded sincere.

During dinner, their early conversation had been about
their childhood in Winona and Trempealeau: the hayrides
and sleighrides, skating on the river, hunting and the taste
of fried squirrel, illicit applejack, and days so cold that
schools were closed and no one dared venture forth from
home.

They spoke of college days (he had attended the
University of Wisconsin at Madison). He had visited
Minneapolis, both had been to Chicago. Once he had
gone to New Orleans for the Mardi Gras, and once she

had been as far west as Denver. They agreed that one day they would journey to Europe, the West Indies, and perhaps Japan.

She learned more about him:

He was thirty-five, almost two years younger than she. He had never been married, or even engaged. He lived alone in a small studio apartment in the Gramercy Park area. He had a small circle of friends and acquaintances, mostly business associates.

He entertained rarely, went to the movies, theater, and ballet infrequently. He was taking courses at the New School in computer technology. His current job with Harold Kurnitz's company was in a small section called Inventory Control, and he hoped some day to persuade Mr. Kurnitz to computerize the entire operation.

All this came pouring forth with little prompting from Zoe. Ernest Mittle seemed happy to talk about himself, and it suddenly occurred to her that he might very well be as lonely as she.

When they came out of the restaurant a little before 8:00 P.M., the sky was blotchy. A moldy wind gusted off the East River, and the air smelled rawly of snow.

"We'll get a cab," Ernest Mittle said, pulling on his clumsy gloves.

"Oh, that's not necessary," she said. "I can get a bus right across the street."

"Where do you live, Zoe?"

She hesitated a moment, then: "East Thirty-ninth Street. Near Lexington."

"But you'll have to walk from the bus stop. Alone. I don't like that. Look, it's only about ten short blocks. Why don't we walk? It's still early, and there are a lot of people around."

"You don't have to do that. I'll just get on—"

"Come on," he said exuberantly, taking her arm. "In Minnesota and Wisconsin, this is a nice spring evening!"

So they set off, walking briskly southward. He adjusted his stride to her, assisted her up and down curbs, led her carefully around dog droppings and sidewalk obstructions, including a man slumped in a doorway, his legs extended. He was drinking from a bottle in a brown paper bag.

"That used to upset me," Ernest said. "When I first

came to New York. But you get so you hardly notice it."

Zoe nodded. "Once I saw a well-dressed man lying on the sidewalk on Fifth Avenue. People were just walking around him."

"Was he drunk or dead or what?"

"I don't know," she confessed. "I just walked around him, too. That happened almost eight years ago, and it still bothers me. I should have done something or tried to do something."

"You know what New Yorkers say: 'Don't get involved.'"

"I know," she said. "Still . . ."

"Zoe, I've been babbling about myself all evening, but you've hardly said a word about yourself. Do you work?"

"Oh yes. In the Security Section of the Hotel Granger."

"That sounds interesting," he said politely.

"Not really," she said, and then perhaps it was the wine and brandy, but she began speaking of herself, she who was usually so secret.

She told him she had been married for three years, and was divorced. She told him she now lived alone, and the moment she heard her own words, regretted them. A divorced woman living alone; she knew how men reacted to *that*.

She told him that she lived a very quiet life, read a lot, watched TV. She admitted that New York frightened her at times. It was so big, so dirty and noisy, so uncaring. But she had no desire to return to the Midwest, ever.

"I know what you mean," he said. "It's everything bad you can think of, but it's—it's exciting. And fascinating. Things are always happening. Unexpected things. Nothing unexpected happens much in Trempealeau."

"Or Winona," she said. "It's a kind of love-hate relationship. With New York, I mean."

"Love-hate," he said wonderingly. "Yes, that's very true."

They turned onto her block, and she began to worry. It had been a pleasant evening, better than she had expected—but what now? Would he demand a good-night kiss? Would he insist on seeing her to her apartment door? Would he suddenly turn angry and importunate?

But when she halted outside the lobby entrance,

he stopped too, drew off a glove, and proffered a white hand.

"Thank you, Zoe," he said smiling. "It's been a fine evening. I really enjoyed it."

"Thank *you*," she said, surprised and shaking his soft hand. "The dinner was wonderful."

"Can we do it again?" he asked anxiously. "Can I call you?"

"Of course," she said. "I'd like that. I'm in the book."

"I'll call," he vowed, and she hoped he meant it.

She stopped to get her mail, including, thankfully, her alimony check. At the elevator, she turned to look back to the sidewalk. Ernest Mittle was still standing there. He waved. She waved back, but didn't feel safe until she was upstairs, inside her own apartment, the door locked, bolted, and chained.

She turned on all the lights and walked cautiously through the rooms, peering into closets and under the bed.

She made certain the venetian blinds were tightly closed. She was convinced there was a man across the street who stood in a darkened room with binoculars, watching her windows. She had never actually seen him, but his shades were always up and occasionally she had glimpsed flashes of white and moving shadows.

She went directly to her medicine supply in the kitchen, and swallowed a vitamin C pill, a B-complex capsule, and a magnesium tablet. Her premenstrual cramps had become increasingly severe, and she wanted to take a Darvon. But in view of what lay ahead, she settled for a Midol and two Anacin.

Dr. Stark could not understand her monthly cramps. She was on the Pill, and that usually eliminated or alleviated the symptoms. A complete examination had revealed no physiological cause, and Stark had suggested that the cramps might have a psychological origin.

He had offered to recommend a counselor, psychologist, or psychiatrist. Zoe had indignantly rejected his advice.

"There's nothing wrong with me," she said hotly.

"*Something* is wrong," he replied, "if what should be a

normal, natural, healthy function causes you so much pain."

"I've had bad cramps all my life," she told him. "Ever since I began to bleed."

He looked at her queerly.

"It's your decision," he said.

She started the tub, then returned to the bedroom to undress. When she was naked, she palpated her breasts tenderly. That morning they had been soft, saggy. Now they seemed enlarged, harder, the nipples semi-erect. But at least she felt no sensation of bloat and could see no indication that her ankles had swollen.

She poured perfumed oil into the tub and eased into water as hot as she could endure. She lay motionless, melted, the back of her neck on the tub rim. She closed her eyes and soaked blissfully. The cramps seemed to diminish.

After a while she roused, and began to lather herself with scented soap that she bought from a Madison Avenue apothecary. It cost $2.75 a cake, and smelled subtly of frangipani. She cleansed herself thoroughly, her ears, vulva, rectum, and between her toes.

She did not masturbate.

Zoe opened the tub drain and stood cautiously. She turned on the shower and rinsed the suds away. She sniffed at her armpits, but smelled only the flowery fragrance of the imported soap. She dried thoroughly and inspected herself for more gray pubic hairs, but found none.

She returned to the bedroom. She turned on the bedside radio, switching from WQXR to a station that featured hard rock. Sitting on the edge of the bed, listening to the driving music, she painted her toenails and fingernails a glossy vermilion. Then she walked about the room, waving her hands in the air to dry the polish and moving her body in time to the music.

Taking care not to smudge her nails, she opened the bottom drawer of her dresser and lifted out stacks of sensible underwear and earth-colored pantyhose. In the back of the drawer were concealed her treasures. Her precious things.

She selected a brief brassiere and a bikini of sheer black nylon with small appliquéd leaves that concealed the nipples and pudendum. The lingerie came on with a whisper, weightless and clinging. She applied Aphrodisia behind her ears, within her armpits, on the inside of her thighs.

In the back of the bedroom closet, behind the rack of practical, everyday clothes, were her secret costumes. They hung in plastic bags from hooks screwed into the wall. There were five gowns, all expensive, all new. The red silk had been worn once. The others had never been used.

She donned a sheath of black crepe. When the side zipper was closed, the dress clung like paint. A second skin. Décolletage revealed the swell of her hardened breasts. Her slender waist was accented, the lyre of her hips. In back, firm buttocks pressed.

Then, seamed black silk hose with rosetted garters. Evening sandals of thin straps with three-inch spike heels, the tallest she could manage. She wore no jewels, but around her left wrist she fastened a fine chain supporting a legend of gold letters. It read: WHY NOT?

She combed her short brown hair quickly. Then went into the living room, to the closet. In the back, concealed, was her trenchcoat and a large patent leather shoulder bag. In the bag, wrapped in tissue, was a black nylon wig and a makeup kit.

She spent a few moments transferring things from her workaday bag: cigarettes, matches, Swiss Army pocket knife, the small can of Chemical Mace, keys, coins, wallet with slightly more than forty dollars. Before she transferred the wallet, she removed all her identification cards and hid them on the top shelf of the closet.

Then she shrugged into the trenchcoat and buttoned it up to her neck. She buckled the belt loosely so the coat hung like a sack. Slinging her shoulder bag, she sallied forth leaving all the lights in the apartment burning.

Bathing and dressing had taken almost an hour. Never once during that time had she looked in a mirror.

The night doorman was behind the desk and tipped his cap to her as she passed. She teetered over to Third Avenue on her high heels. She looked about nervously for Ernest Mittle, but he was long gone.

There were sudden swirls of light, powdery snow, and she had to wait almost five minutes for an uptown cab.

She told the driver to take her to Central Park West and
72nd Street.

"The Dakota?" he asked.

"That corner," she said crisply. "It's close enough."

"Whatever you say, lady," he said, and then drove in
silence, for which she was thankful.

She gave him a generous tip when he let her off. She
stood on the windswept corner, lighting a cigarette slowly
and not moving in any direction until the cab pulled away,
and she saw its taillights receding west on 72nd Street.

Then she, too, headed west, walking rapidly, her heels
clicking on a sidewalk already dusted with snow. Men
passed, but she did not raise her eyes. She bent against
the wind, clutching her shoulder bag with both hands. But
she was not cold. She glowed.

The Filmore was a residential hotel. Downstairs, one
flight from the sidewalk, was a dim restaurant featuring a
"continental menu." The restaurant seemed to be lan-
guishing, but the connecting bar, brightly lighted, had
several customers, most of them watching a TV set
suspended on chains from the ceiling.

Zoe Kohler had been there once before. It suited her
needs perfectly.

She sat at the bar in her trenchcoat, holding her bag on
her lap. She ordered a glass of white wine and finished it
quickly. Very calm. Making certain she looked at none of
the single men. The bartender was not the one who had
been on duty during her previous visit.

"Where is the ladies' room, please?" she asked, just as
she had before.

"Back there through the hotel entrance," he said,
pointing. "You go up the stairs and through the lobby. It's
to your right."

"Thank you," she said, paid for her wine and left a tip.
Not too large a tip, she judged, and not too small. He'd
never remember her. No one ever did.

The lavatory was tiled in white with stained fixtures of
cracked porcelain. Disinfectant stung the nose. There was
a middle-aged woman at one of the sinks, inspecting
herself in the streaked mirror, moving her head this way
and that. She turned when Zoe came in.

"Hullo, dearie," she said brightly, smiling.

Zoe nodded and walked down the row of five toilet

stalls, glancing under the doors. They all appeared to be unoccupied. She went into the last stall, closed the door and latched it. She waited patiently for two or three minutes, then heard the outside door open and close.

She exited cautiously. The restroom seemed to be empty, but to make certain, she opened the doors of all the stalls and checked. Then she went over to one of the sinks and began working swiftly. Finally, finally, she looked at her image.

She removed the wig from her shoulder bag, shook it out, pulled it on. The nylon was black and glossy, with feathered curls across her brow and thick, rippling waves that fell almost to her shoulders. She smoothed it into place, turning this way and that, just as the middle-aged woman had.

Satisfied, she began applying makeup. She darkened her brows, mascaraed her lashes, brushed on silvery-blue eye shadow, powder, rouge, a deep crimson lipstick with an outer layer of moist gloss.

She worked quickly, and within fifteen minutes the transformation was complete. Even in the dulled mirror she looked vibrant, alive. She was a warm, sensuous woman, eager for joy. Glittering eyes challenged and promised.

She opened her coat to snug the wool crepe dress down over her hips, wiggling slightly to make certain it fit without a wrinkle. She tugged the neckline lower, took a deep breath and, in the mirror, showed her teeth.

Then she wrapped the unbuttoned trenchcoat about her, cinched the belt tight, and turned up the collar in back. Her neck and the top of her bosom were exposed.

She examined herself. She licked her lips.

She exited through the hotel lobby, bag swinging from her shoulder. Men in the lobby stared at her. Men passing on the sidewalk outside stared at her. She lighted a cigarette, smoking with outsize, theatrical movements.

She waited under the marquee for a cab, humming.

The Hotel Pierce, Manhattan's newest hostelry, occupied the entire blockfront on Sixth Avenue between 56th and 57th streets. It had 1200 rooms, suites, penthouses, banquet rooms, meeting rooms, a convention hall, a nightclub on the roof.

Below the main lobby floor was a concourse with three dining rooms, a coffee and snack bar, gift shops and boutiques, the offices of travel agents and a stockbroker, a bookstore, men's and women's clothing shops, and four cocktail lounges. "You can live your life at the Pierce" was the advertised boast.

Zoe Kohler had selected the Pierce because she knew it was currently hosting three conventions; the concourse cocktail lounges were sure to be crowded. She chose the El Khatar, a bar with a vaguely Moorish theme, walls hung with silken draperies, waitresses dressed as belly dancers.

She stood a moment just inside the entrance, looking around as if expecting to be met. When the hatcheck girl came forward, she surrendered her trenchcoat and made her way slowly to the bar, peering about in the dimness, still acting the role of a lady awaiting her escort.

Most of the small tables were occupied by couples and foursomes. The bar was crowded: singles, doubles, groups. There were a few seated women, but men were standing two and three deep, reaching over shoulders to take refills from perspiring bartenders in fezzes.

The room was terribly overheated, smoky, smelling vilely of cheap incense. Shriek of conversation. Shouts of laughter. Tinny blare of piped Eastern music. Zoe wondered how long she might endure this swamp of raw noise.

She stood a moment near the bar, chin up, spine straight.

A red-faced man, hair tousled, tie askew, spluttering with laughter at something his companion had just said, made a sudden lurch backward and bumped her roughly.

"Whoops!" he said, catching her arm as she staggered. "Beg your pardon, lady. Any harm done?"

"No, no," she said, giving him a rueful smile, rubbing her arm. "It's all right."

"Not all right," he protested. "I'm sorry as hell. Buy you a drink? Then you'll forgive me?"

"Thank you," she said, still smiling, "but I'll pay for it. But I'd appreciate it if you could order a glass of white wine for me. I can't get near the bar."

She fumbled in her bag. He made a grand gesture.

"Put your money away, sweetie," he said. "This is on the house—my house!"

He and his friend found this a remarkably humorous sally. They heaved with merriment, bending over their drinks. In a few minutes, Zoe had her glass of wine.

"Come join us," the red-faced man urged. "Me and my pal here have been boring each other all night. He's a sex fiend, but I'll protect you from him!"

More loud guffaws.

"Sounds like a lot of fun," Zoe said, "but I'm waiting for my boyfriend. Maybe some other time."

"Any time at all," the friend said, speaking for the first time. His lickerish eyes traveled slowly down the length of her body to her strapped sandals, then up again. "You name the time, and I'll be there, I guarantee!"

They were still laughing, nudging each other with elbows when, smiling faintly, she moved away from them, down the bar. She didn't want two men. She wanted one man.

Searching, she saw a woman seated at the bar gathering up purse and gloves. Her escort, standing alongside, had just received his bill and was counting money onto the bar.

Sidling swiftly through the press, protecting her glass of wine with a cupped hand, and saying, "Pardon. Pardon. Pardon," Zoe Kohler succeeded in claiming the barstool a second after the woman slid off.

"Got it all warm for you, honey," the brassy blonde said. Then she took a closer look at Zoe, and said, "Good luck!"

"Yes," Zoe said. "Thanks." And turned swiftly away.

To her right was a noisy group of five men engaged in a loud debate on professional football teams. It was the single man seated to her left who interested Zoe. He was staring straight ahead, hunched over what appeared to be a martini-rocks. He was apparently oblivious to the hubbub around him.

"Pardon me, sir," Zoe Kohler said, leaning toward him. "Could you tell me what time it is, please?"

He turned his head slowly to look at her, then glanced down at his gold wristwatch.

"Almost eleven-fifteen," he said.

"Thank you, sir," she said, then swung partly around on her barstool to search the room with anxious eyes. As she swung, her knees brushed his fat thigh.

"What's the matter?" the man said. "He didn't show up?"

She swung back, then turned her head to face him, looking into his eyes.

"What makes you think it's a man?" she said. "Maybe I'm waiting for my girlfriend."

"No way," he said, his eyes lowering to her bosom. "A beautiful woman like you, it's got to be a man. And he's a fool for being late."

"Well," she said, giggling, "to tell you the truth, it's me that's late—by about an hour!"

Five minutes later, he had become more animated, had bought a round of drinks, and they knew all about each other—all they wanted to know.

His name was Fred (no last name offered), and he was in New York to attend a convention of electrical appliance marketing managers in that very hotel. He was from Akron, Ohio, and couldn't wait to get back. Zoe judged him to be in his early fifties.

She was Irene (no last name offered), and she was originally from Minneapolis. She had come to New York seeking a career as model and actress. But now she was executive assistant to an independent TV producer who made commercials and educational films.

They had swung around to face each other. Their knees rubbed.

"Why are you sitting here alone?" Zoe asked. "A convention and all that. Why aren't you out with the boys, tearing up the town?"

"Oh, I was," he said. "Earlier. But then things got a little raunchy. They wanted to go down to Greenwich Village and see the freaks. That's not my idea of a good time. So I cut out."

"What's your idea of a good time?" she challenged, but when she saw the flicker of fear in his eyes, she wondered if she was moving too fast.

"Oh," he said, looking down, "you know . . . A nightcap, and then up to my room to watch TV. I'm really a very quiet guy."

"You say," she scoffed. "You quiet ones are the worst. Hell on wheels when you get rolling."

He laughed, chest swelling with pride.

"Well . . ." he said, "maybe. I guess I've sowed my share of wild oats."

He was heavy, heavy. His florid face was pudgy, neck thick, torso soft. Collops flapped at the corners of his mouth. He had the sandpaper cough of a heavy smoker. In addition to the gold wristwatch, he wore gold cufflinks, a pearl tie tac, a pinkie ring set with a square diamond. He was not drunk, exactly, but he was on his way: a little dazed, beginning to slur.

He ordered another round of drinks. She reached for her wine, and he grabbed her wrist and turned the chain so he could read the words: WHY NOT?

He raised his eyes to stare at her.

"Why not?" he said hoarsely.

She leaned close to him, her cool cheek against his hot, sweated jowl. She whispered into his ear:

"I told you that you quiet ones are hell on wheels. Can we go to your room? Have a little party?"

He nodded dumbly.

They drained their drinks. He paid his bill from a thick wallet. They pushed their way through the throng. She gave him her coat check and he paid to reclaim her trenchcoat.

"I left my coat in my room," he said. "I'm on the thirtieth floor."

"Way up in the sky," she said.

"That's right, girlie," he said, staggering and catching her arm to steady himself. "Way up with the birdies."

"It's your own room?" she said in a low voice. "Or do you have a roommate?"

"It's all mine," he mumbled. "Yours and mine."

They had to jam their way into a crowded elevator filled with laughing, yelling, drunken convention-goers. Another couple got off on the 30th floor, but turned down the long corridor in the opposite direction. Fred led the way around one turn to Room 3015.

He halted before the flush door.

"Take a look at this door, Irene," he demanded. "Tell me what you see. Or don't see!"

She knew immediately what it was—she had read about it in the hotel trade magazine—but she could not deny him his moment of triumph.

"It just looks like an ordinary door to me," she said, shrugging.

"No keyhole!" he said. "Just that thing . . ."

He pointed to a narrow, metal-rimmed slot directly under the knob. Then he took a white plastic card from his jacket pocket. It was no larger than a credit card.

"Magnetic," he explained to Zoe. "The printed code is between two pieces of solid plastic. You can't see it. And no way for your friendly neighborhood locksmith to copy it. Not yet there isn't."

"That's wonderful," she said.

"Great security," he said. "Practically eliminates break-ins. Who can pick a lock that doesn't show?"

He fumbled a bit, then got the plastic card inserted into the slot. The bolt slid back, he turned the knob, opened the door and stood aside.

"Welcome to my castle," he said.

The room was certainly larger, cleaner, and more attractively furnished than the rooms at the Hotel Granger. But it had the impersonality of all hotel rooms: everything designed to repel cigarette burns and glass stains, to require minimal maintenance. Pictures were bolted to the walls; the base of the TV set was anchored to the floor.

"Make yourself at home," Fred said. "I gotta see a man about a dog."

He went into the bathroom, closed the door. Zoe moved slowly and cautiously. She removed her coat, folded it once, placed it carefully on the polished bureau near the door. She sat down slowly in a high-backed armchair. She touched no surface.

She heard the toilet flush. In a moment he came out of the bathroom, smoothing strands of rusty hair across his white scalp.

"Well now," he said heartily, "let's get this show on the road. How about a shot of the world's best brandy? I never travel without it."

"You know what they say about alcohol?" she said archly. "It increases the desire and decreases the performance."

"Lotta bullshit," he said. "You won't have any complaints, little lady."

"Well . . . maybe just a sip."

"Atta girl. This'll put lead in your pencil—if you had a pencil!"

They both laughed immoderately. She watched him take a pint bottle from the top dresser drawer. He poured her a small drink in a water glass and a larger one for himself.

When he brought the drink over to her, she was deliberately busy with a compact mirror, poking at her wig. So he set the glass on the endtable next to the armchair. Then he sat on the edge of the bed. He turned to face her.

"Say," he said, "you wouldn't mind if I smoked a cigar, would you?"

"Of course not, honey," she said. "I just love the smell of a good cigar."

"You sure, babe?" he said doubtfully. "My wife doesn't."

"I do," she assured him. "Go right ahead."

So he stripped the cellophane from a cigar and lighted up, puffing contentedly.

He took the pillows from under the bedspread, propped them against the headboard. He removed his jacket and vest, took off his shoes. He loosened his tie, unbuttoned his collar. The fleshy neck, reddened, bulged free.

Then he sat back against the pillows, his feet up, ankles crossed. He held his cigar in one hand, brandy in the other.

"Oh boy, oh boy, oh boy," he sighed. "This is the life. Daddy told me there would be nights like this, but he didn't tell me how few and far between. Hey, sweetheart, why don't you make yourself more comfortable?"

"I thought you'd never ask," she said, giggling.

She stood, moved closer to the bed. She locked his eyes, but when she began to draw the side zipper of her dress slowly downward, his gaze followed that movement. The brandy and cigar were forgotten. He watched everything she did.

She pulled the dress over her head, being careful not to dislodge her wig. She smiled at his expression, turned, walked away with an exaggerated wiggle. She folded the dress atop her trenchcoat.

She turned to face him, hip-sprung, hands on her waist. She sucked in her stomach, thrust her bosom forward. She tilted her head to one side.

"You like?" she said coquettishly.

"Wow," he said shakily. "Oh wow, you're really something. Old Fred really grabbed the brass ring tonight. Come here."

She stood next to the bed. He put his brandy on the bedside table. He touched the band of smooth white skin between bikini and stocking top. She turned back and forth, letting him stroke.

"You're driving me crazy," she said throatily.

She leaned over the bed, her face close to his. He reached up to touch the wig. She drew back.

"Why don't you take off all those clothes?" she whispered. "I have to go make wee-wee and then I'll come back to you. I'll do anything you want. And I mean *anything*."

He made a grunting sound and reached for her. But she laughed, moved away. She picked up her shoulder bag, went to the bathroom door, turned. He was staring at her. She waggled her fingers at him, disappeared inside.

She locked the door, worked swiftly. She took off sandals, garters, stockings, lingerie. She relieved herself. When she flushed the toilet, she used two sheets of toilet paper to press the tank lever, then watched as the tissue went swirling away.

She opened her bag, made her preparations. Then she just waited, staring at her image in the medicine cabinet mirror. After a while she recognized herself.

She stayed in there until she heard his call:

"Irene? What's keeping you?"

She unlocked the door, opened it a crack, peeked out. He had turned off the overhead light, turned on the bedside lamp. The bedspread and blankets had been thrown off. He was lying back. The sheet was pulled up to his waist. His naked torso was haired and puffy. His plump breasts made almond-shaped shadows. He was smoking his cigar.

She draped one of the hotel bath towels over her right forearm and hand. She switched off the bathroom light.

"Ready or not," she said lightly, "here I come."

He turned to stare at her naked body moving into the cone of lamplight.

"Ah Jesus," he breathed.

She went around to the right side of the bed, away from the table and the lamp. She bent over him, smiling tenderly.

He turned to the left to put his cigar in the ashtray. She lowered her arm, let the towel fall away.

Handling the Swiss Army knife like a dagger, she plunged the big blade into the left side of his fat neck and sawed back toward her.

He made a sound, a gargle, and his heavy body leaped convulsively from the bed. Blood spouted in streams, gobbets, a flood that sprayed the air with a crimson fog. It soaked the bed, dripped onto the floor.

Zoe Kohler threw back the sheet, exposing his pulpy abdomen, veined legs, his flaccid penis and testicles, half-hidden in a nest of grayish-brown hair, tangled.

With bloodied, slippery hand, she drove the knife blade again and again into his genitals. No triumph or exultation in her face. Not grinning or yowling, but intent and businesslike. Saying aloud with each stab, "There. There. There."

2

Former Chief of Detectives Edward X. Delaney had two methods of eating sandwiches.

Those he categorized as "dry" sandwiches—such as roast beef on white or what he termed an interracial sandwich, ham on bagel—were eaten while seated at the kitchen table. The top was spread with the financial section of the previous day's *New York Times*.

The meal finished, crumbs and newspaper were crumpled up and dumped into the step-on garbage can under the sink.

"Wet" sandwiches—such as potato salad and pastrami on rye, with hot English mustard, or brisling sardines with tomato and onion slices slathered with mayonnaise—were eaten while standing bent over the sink. Finished, Delaney ran the hot water and flushed the drippings away.

Both methods of dining were anathema to the Chief's wife, Monica. She never ceased in her efforts to persuade him to adopt more civilized eating habits, even if it was only a midday snack.

Delaney tried to explain to her, as patiently as he could, that he had spent thirty years of his life with the New York Police Department, most of them in the Detective Division. He had become addicted to sandwiches since, considering the long, brutal hours the job demanded, sandwiches consumed while working were usually the only sustenance available.

"But you're retired now!" she would cry.

"Habits are habits," he would reply loftily.

Actually, he loved sandwiches. One of the recurring fantasies of his increasingly onerous retirement was the dream that he might one day compile a slim volume, *Chief Delaney's Sandwich Book*. Who had a better right? Who but he had discovered the glory of cold pork and thinly sliced white radish on pumpernickel?

On the evening of March 19th, Monica Delaney, with the assistance of Mrs. Rebecca Boone, wife of Detective Sergeant Abner Boone, was preparing a buffet for fourteen members of her women's group. The dinner was to be preceded by a psychologist's lecture followed by a general discussion. Then the buffet would be served.

"We're having avocado and cottage cheese salad," Monica said firmly. "Bibb lettuce, cherry tomatoes, cucumbers, little green peppers. There's plenty for you. And if you don't like that, there's a cheese-and-macaroni casserole ready to pop in the oven, or the cold chicken left over from last night."

"Don't you worry about me," he advised. "I ate so much yesterday, I'd really like to take it easy tonight. I'll just make a sandwich and take that and a bottle of beer into the den. I assure you, I am not going to starve."

In his methodical way, he began his preparations early, before Rebecca Boone arrived and the women got busy in the kitchen. He inspected the contents of the refrigerator, and built two sandwiches from what was available.

One was white meat of chicken with slices of red onion and little discs of pitted black olives. With a small dollop of horseradish sauce. The second was a crude construction of canned Argentine corned beef, the meat red and crumbly, with cucumber slices. On rye. He wrapped both sandwiches in aluminum foil, and thrust them in the back of the refrigerator to chill.

When Rebecca arrived, and soon after that the front doorbell began to ring, Edward X. Delaney hastily retrieved his sandwiches, took a bottle of cold Löwenbräu Dark, and hustled out of the kitchen. He retired to his den, closing the heavy door firmly behind him.

The desk in the study was covered with papers, receipts, letters, vouchers, open notebooks. For the past two weeks, Delaney had been spending a few hours each day working on his federal income tax return. Actually, the Chief was doing the donkey work, assembling totals of income, expenses, deductions, etc. The final return would be prepared by Monica, his second wife.

Monica was the widow of Bernard Gilbert, a victim of

Daniel Blank, a random killer Delaney had helped apprehend. The multiple homicides had been brought to an end right there in the room where Delaney was now seated, headquarters for Operation Lombard.

A year after his first wife, Barbara, had died of kidney infection, the Chief had married Monica Gilbert. He had two children, Edward, Jr., and Elizabeth, both now married, Liza with twin boys. Monica had two young girls, Mary and Sylvia, now away at boarding school, preparing for college.

Monica's first husband, Gilbert, had been a CPA and tax accountant, and she had taken courses to enable her to assist him in what had started as a kitchen business. She had kept up with annual changes in the tax laws. Delaney was happy to leave to her the task of preparing the final return that each year seemed to become longer and more complex.

Since he didn't want to disturb the papers on his desk, Delaney drew up a wheeled typewriter table. He removed his old Underwood, setting it on the floor with an effort that, he was pleased to note, didn't elicit a grunt.

He then lifted the leaves of the table, locked them in position, and spread the wide surface with newspaper. He unwrapped his sandwiches, uncapped the beer, and settled down in his worn swivel chair.

He took a bite of the corned beef sandwich. Washed it down with a swallow of dark beer. *Then* he grunted.

He donned his reading glasses and set to work, oblivious to the sounds of talk and laughter in the living room outside his door. When you had worked as long as he had in a crowded detective squad room, you learned the trick of closing your ears. You can shut your mouth and your eyes; why not your ears?

He worked steadily, doggedly. He added up their total annual income, for Monica had brought to their marriage an annuity her deceased husband had set up, plus investments in a modest stock portfolio that yielded good dividends although prices were down.

Edward X. Delaney had a generous pension, income from investments in high-yield, tax-exempt New York City bonds which—thank God—had not defaulted, and he had applied for early Social Security. Between them, husband and wife, they were able to live comfortably in a wholly owned refurbished brownstone right next to the 251st Precinct house.

Still, a combined income that would have allowed them to live in comparative luxury ten years ago was now being cruelly eroded by inflation. It had not yet seriously affected their way of life, since neither was profligate, but it was worrisome.

Delaney, going over his check disbursements, saw how much had gone in cash gifts to Eddie, Jr., to Liza, and to Liza's children. And how much had gone to clothing and educating Mary and Sylvia. He did not regret a penny of it, but still . . . By the time the two younger girls were ready for college, in a few years, the cost of a university education would probably be $50,000 or more. It was discouraging.

He finished the corned beef sandwich. And the beer. He listened carefully at the door to the living room. He heard the voice of a woman he believed to be the lecturing psychologist.

Judging the time was right, he darted out the door leading to the kitchen. Moving as quietly as he could, he grabbed another beer from the refrigerator, a can of Schlitz this time, and hurried back to his study. He pushed his glasses atop his head. He popped the beer, took a swallow. Took a bite of the chicken sandwich.

He sat slumped, feet up on the corner of his desk. He thought about the children, all the children, Monica's and his. And he thought sadly of the one child they had together, an infant son who died from a respiratory infection after three months of fragile life. The coffin had been so small.

After a while, munching slowly and sipping his beer, he heard the sounds of conversation and vociferous debate coming from the living room. He guessed the lecture was over, the general discussion period was concluding, and soon the avocado and cottage cheese salad would be served. He had been wise to avoid *that!*

The door to the living room opened suddenly. A young woman started in. She saw him, drew back in alarm and confusion.

"Oh!" she said. "I'm sorry. I thought this was . . ."

He lumbered to his feet, smiling.

"Perfectly all right," he said. "What you're probably looking for is out in the hallway, near the front door."

"Thank you," she said. "Sorry to disturb you."

He made a small gesture. She closed the door. He sat down again, and to reassure himself, to convince himself, he tested his skills at observation. He had seen the woman for possibly five seconds.

She was, he recited to himself, a female Caucasian, about thirty-five years old, approximately 5′ 6″ tall, weight: 120, blondish hair shoulder-length, triangular face with long, thin nose and pouty lips. Wearing gold loop earrings. A loose dress of forest-green wool. Digital watch on her left wrist. Bare legs, no stockings. Loafers. A distinctive lisp in her voice. A Band-Aid on her right shin.

He smiled. Not bad. He could pick her out of a lineup or describe her sufficiently for a police artist to make a sketch. He was still a cop.

God, how he missed it.

He sat brooding, wondering not for the first time if he had made an error in resigning his prestigious position as Chief of Detectives and opting for retirement. His reason then had been the political bullshit connected with the job.

Now he questioned if the political pressures in such high rank were not a natural concomitant. The fact that he could not endure them might have been a weakness. Perhaps a stronger man could have done all he did while resisting the tugs, threats, and plots of a city government of ambitious men and women. And when he could not resist, then compromising to the smallest degree compatible with survival.

Still, he was—

His reverie was interrupted by a light, tentative tap on the door leading to the kitchen.

"Come in," he called.

The door opened.

Edward X. Delaney struggled to his feet, strode across the room, shook the other man's proffered hand.

"Sergeant!" he said, smiling happily.

A few minutes later, Detective Sergeant Abner Boone was seated in a cracked leather club chair. Delaney moved his swivel chair so he could converse with his visitor without the desk being a barrier between them.

The Chief had made a quick trip to the busy kitchen to bring back a bucket of ice and a bottle of soda water for the sergeant, who was an alcoholic who had not touched a drop in two years. Delaney mixed himself a weak highball, straight rye and water.

"I dropped by to pick up Rebecca," Boone explained, "but they're still eating. I hope I'm not disturbing you, sir."

"Not at all," the Chief said genially. He motioned toward his littered desk. "Tax returns. I've had enough for one night. Tell me, what's the feeling about the new PC?"

For about fifteen minutes the two men talked shop, gossiping about Departmental matters. Most of the information came from Boone: who had been promoted, who transferred, who retired.

"They're putting the dicks back in the precincts," he told Delaney. "The special squads just didn't work out."

"I read about it," the Chief said, nodding. "But they're keeping some of the squads, aren't they?"

"A few. That's where I am now. It's a major crime unit working out of Midtown North."

"Good for you," Delaney said warmly. "How many men have you got?"

Boone shifted uncomfortably. "Well, uh, a month ago I had five. Right now I have twenty-four, and they're bringing in a lieutenant tomorrow morning."

The Chief was startled, but tried not to show it. He looked at Boone curiously. The man seemed exhausted, sallow loops below his eyes. His body had fallen in on itself, shrunken with fatigue. He looked in need of forty-eight hours of nothing but sleep and hot food.

Boone was tall, thin, with a shambling walk and floppy gestures. He had gingery hair, a pale and freckled complexion. He was probably getting on to forty by now, but he still had a shy, awkward, farmerish manner, a boyish and charming smile.

Delaney had worked with him on the Victor Maitland homicide and knew what a good detective he was when he was off the booze. Boone had a slow but analytical and thorough mind. He accepted the boredom and frustrations of his job without complaint. When raw courage was demanded, he could be a tiger.

The Chief inspected him narrowly. He noted the slight tremor of the slender fingers. It couldn't be booze. Rebecca had married him only after he had vowed never to touch the stuff again. Delaney couldn't believe that Boone would risk what was apparently a happy marriage.

"Sergeant," he said finally, "I've got to tell you: you look like death warmed over. What's wrong?"

Boone set his empty glass on the rug alongside his chair. He sat hunched over, forearms on his bony knees, his long hands clasping and unclasping. He looked up at Delaney.

"We've got a repeater," he said. "Homicide."

The Chief stared at him, then took a slow sip of his highball.

"You're sure?" he asked.

Boone nodded.

"Only two so far," he said, "but it's the same MO; no doubt about it. We've kept a lid on it so far, but it's only a question of time before some smart reporter puts the two together."

"Two similar killings?" Delaney said doubtfully. "Could be coincidence."

The sergeant sighed, straightened up. He lit a cigarette, holding it in tobacco-stained fingers. He sat back, crossed and recrossed his gangly legs.

"Maybe we're antsy," he acknowledged. "But ever since that Son of Sam thing, everyone in the Department's been super-alert for repeat homicides. We should have been onto the Son of Sam killings earlier. It took Ballistics to tip us off. Now maybe we're all too eager to put together two unconnected snuffings and yell, 'Mass killer!' But not in this case. These two are identical."

Chief Edward X. Delaney stared at him, but not seeing him. He felt the familiar tingle, the excitement, the challenge. More than that, he felt the anger and the resolve.

"Want to tell me about it?" he asked Boone.

"Do I ever!" Boone said fervently. "Maybe you'll see something we've missed."

"I doubt that very much," Delaney said. "But try me."

Detective Sergeant Abner Boone recited the facts in a

rapid staccato, toneless, as if reporting to a superior officer. It was obvious he had been living with this investigation for many long hours; his recital never faltered.

"First homicide: February fifteenth, this year. Victim: male Caucasian, fifty-four years old, found stabbed to death in Room 914 of the Grand Park Hotel. Naked body discovered by chambermaid at approximately 9:45 A.M. Victim had throat cut open and multiple stab wounds in the genitals. Cause of death according to autopsy: exsanguination. That first throat slash didn't kill him. Weapon: a sharp instrument about three inches long."

"Three inches!" Delaney cried. "My God, that's a pocket knife, a jackknife!"

"Probably," Boone said, nodding. "Maximum width of the blade was about three-quarters of an inch, according to the ME who did the cut-'em-up."

The sergeant picked up his glass from the floor, began to chew on the ice cubes. Now that he was talking, he seemed to relax. His speech slowed, became more discursive.

"So the chambermaid knocks and goes in to clean," he continued. "She's an old dame who doesn't see too good. She's practically alongside the bed, standing in the blood, when she sees him. She lets out a scream and faints, right into the mess. A porter comes running. After him come two hotel guests passing in the corridor. The porter calls the security man, using the room phone of course, and ruining any prints. The security man comes running with his assistant, and he calls the manager who comes running with *his* assistant. Finally someone has enough brains to call 911. By the time the first blues got there, there's like maybe ten people milling about in the room. Instant hysteria. Beautiful. I got there about the same time the Crime Scene Unit men showed up. They were furious, and I don't blame them. You could have galloped the Seventh Cavalry through that room and not done any more damage."

"These things happen," Delaney said sympathetically.

"I suppose so," Boone said, sighing, "but we sure weren't overwhelmed with what you might call clues. The victim was a guy named George T. Puller, from Denver. A wholesale jewelry salesman. His line was handmade silver things set with turquoise and other semiprecious stones. He was in town for a jewelry show being held right there at the Grand Park. It was his second night in New York."

"Forced entry?"

"No sign," Boone said.

He explained that Room 914 was equipped with a split-lock—half spring-latch and half dead-bolt. The door locked automatically when closed, but the dead-bolt could only be engaged by a turn of the key after exiting or by a thumb knob inside.

"When the chambermaid came in," Boone said, "the spring-latch was locked, but not the dead-bolt. That looks like the killer exited and just pulled the door closed."

Delaney agreed.

"No signs of fiddling on the outside of the lock," Boone went on. "And the Crime Scene Unit took that mother apart. No scratches on the tumblers, no oil, no wax. So the chances are good the lock hadn't been picked; George T. Puller invited his killer inside."

"You went through the drill, I suppose," the Chief said. "Friends, business acquaintances? Personal enemies? A feud? Business problems? A jealous partner?"

"And hotel guests," the sergeant said wearily. *"And* hotel staff. *And* bartenders and waiters in the cocktail lounge and dining room on the lobby floor. A lot of 'Well, perhaps . . .' and 'Maybes . . .' But it all added up to zip. With the jewelry show and all, the hotel was crowded that night. The last definite contact was with two other salesmen in the jewelry show hospitality suite. That was about seven P.M. Then the three men split. Puller told the others he was going to wander around, find a place that served a good steak, and turn in early. They never saw him again.

"The CSU found a lot of prints, but mostly partials and smears. They're still working on elimination prints. My God, Chief, in that hotel room you've got to figure all the people who crowded in there after the body was discovered, plus the hotel staff, plus people who stayed in the room before Puller checked in. Hopeless. But we're still working on it."

"You've got no choice," Delaney said stonily.

"Right. One other thing: The Crime Scene Unit took

the bathroom apart. They found blood in the bathtub drain. Not enough for a positive make, but the Lab Services Unit thinks it's the victim's blood. Same type and also, the victim was on Thorazine, and it showed up in the blood taken from the drain."

"Thorazine? What the hell was he taking that for?"

"You're not going to believe this, but he had bad attacks of hiccups. The Thorazine helped. Anyway, it's almost certain it was his blood in the drain, and no one else's. There was no way he was going to get from that bed to the bathroom, take a shower, and then go back to bed to bleed to death. So it had to be the killer—right? Covered with blood. Takes a shower to wash it off. Then makes an exit."

"No hairs in the drain? Hairs that didn't belong to the victim?"

"Nothing," Boone said mournfully. "We should be so lucky!"

"A damp towel?" the Chief asked.

Boone smiled, for the first time.

"You don't miss a thing, do you, sir? No, there was no damp towel. But one of the hotel's bath towels was missing. I figure the killer took it along."

"Probably," Delaney said. "A smart apple."

Sergeant Boone, intent again, serious, leaned forward.

"Chief," he said, "I think I've given you everything I had on the Puller homicide in the first couple of days. If you had caught the squeal, how would you have handled it? The reason I ask is that I'm afraid I blew it. Well, maybe not blew it, but spent too much time charging off in the wrong direction. How would you have figured it?"

Edward X. Delaney was silent a moment. Then he got to his feet, went over to the liquor cabinet. He mixed himself another highball, using the last of the ice in the bucket.

"Another club soda?" he asked Boone. "Coffee? Anything?"

"No, thanks, sir. I'm fine."

"I'm going to have a cigar. How about you?"

"I'll pass, thank you. Stick to these."

Boone shook another cigarette from his pack. The Chief held a light for him, then used the same wooden match for his cigar.

From the living room and hallway, they heard the sounds of departing guests: cries and laughter, the front door slamming. Monica Delaney opened the door to the kitchen and poked her head in.

"They're leaving," she announced, "but it'll take another hour to clean up."

"Need any help?" the Chief asked.

"What if I said, 'Yes'?"

"I'd say, 'No.'"

"Grouch," she said, and withdrew.

Delaney sat down heavily in his swivel chair. He tilted back, puffing his cigar, staring at the ceiling.

"What would I have done?" he asked. "I'd have figured it just as you probably did. Going by percentages. A salesman in New York for a convention or sales meeting or whatever. He goes out on the town by himself. He finds that good steak he was looking for. Has a few drinks. Maybe a bottle of wine. More drinks."

Boone interrupted. "That's what the stomach contents showed."

"He wanders around," Delaney continued. "Visits a few rough joints. Picks up a prostitute, brings her back to his room. Maybe they had a fight about money. Maybe he wanted something kinky, and she wouldn't play. She's got a knife in her purse. Most hookers carry them. He gets ugly, and she offs him. That's the way I would have figured it. Didn't you?"

Abner Boone exhaled a great sigh of relief.

"Exactly," he said. "I figured the same scenario. A short-bladed knife—that's a woman's weapon. And the killer had to be naked when Puller was killed. Otherwise, why the shower and missing towel? So I started the wheels turning. We picked up a zillion hookers, as far west as Eleventh Avenue. We alerted all our whore and pimp snitches. Hit every bar in midtown Manhattan and flashed Puller's photograph. Zilch. Then I began to wonder if we weren't wasting our time. Because of something I haven't told you. Something I didn't find out myself for sure until three days after the body was found."

"What's that?"

"Puller wasn't rolled. He had an unlocked sample case in the room with about twenty G's of silver and turquoise jewelry. Nothing taken. He had a wallet filled with cash and credit cards. All still there. We went back over his movements since he left Denver. His wife and partner knew how much he was carrying. We figured how much he would spend in one day and two nights in New York. It came out right. It was all there. He wasn't rolled."

Edward X. Delaney stared a moment, then shook his massive head from side to side.

"It doesn't listen," he said angrily. "A prostie would have taken him. For *something*. She didn't panic because she was smart enough to shower away his blood before she left. So why didn't she fleece him?"

The sergeant threw his hands in the air.

"Beats the hell out of me," he said bitterly. "It just doesn't figure. And there's another thing that doesn't make sense: there was no sign of a struggle. Absolutely none. Nothing under Puller's fingernails. No hairs other than his on the bed. The guy was fifty-four, sure, but he was heavy and muscular. If he had a fight with a whore, and she comes after him with a shiv, he's going to do *something*—right? Roll out of bed, smack her, throw a lamp—*something*. But there is no evidence he put up any resistance at all. Just lay there happily and let her slit his throat. How do you figure *that?*"

"Wasn't unconscious, was he?"

"The Lab Services Unit did the blood alcohol level and says he was about half-drunk, but unconsciousness would be highly improbable."

Then both men were silent, staring blankly at each other. Finally . . .

"You mentioned his wife," Delaney said. "Children?"

"Three," Boone said.

"Shit."

Boone nodded sadly.

"Anyway, Chief, they gave me more men, and we've really been hacking it. Out-of-town visitor in New York for a sales meeting gets stiffed in a midtown hotel. You can imagine the flak the Commissioner has been getting—from the hotel association and tourist bureau right up through a Deputy Mayor."

"I can imagine," Delaney said.

"All right," the sergeant said, "that was the first killing. Listen, Chief, are you sure I'm not disturbing you? I don't want to bore you silly with my problems."

"No, no, you're not boring me. Besides, our other choice is to go out and help Rebecca and Monica clean up the mess. You want to do that?"

"God forbid!" Boone said. "I'll just keep crying on your shoulder. Well, the second homicide was six days ago."

"How many days between killings?" the Chief said sharply.

"Uh . . . twenty-seven, sir. Is that important?"

"Might be. Same MO?"

"Practically identical. The victim's name was Frederick Wolheim, male Caucasian, fifty-six, stabbed to death in Room 3015 of the Hotel Pierce, that new palace on Sixth Avenue. Naked, throat slit, multiple stab wounds in the genitals. This time the victim died from that first slash. The killer got the carotid and the jugular. Blood? You wouldn't believe! A swimming pool. The—"

"Wait a minute," Delaney interrupted. "Those stab wounds in the genitals—vicious?"

"Very. The ME counted at least twenty in each case, and then gave up and called them 'multiple.' Delivered with force. A few wounds in the lower groin showed bruise marks indicating the killer's knuckles had slammed into the surrounding skin."

"I'm aware of what bruise marks indicate," Edward X. Delaney said.

"Oh," Boone said, abashed. "Sorry, sir. Well, this time everything went off all right. I mean, as far as protecting the murder scene. Wolheim was supposed to deliver a speech at a morning meeting of marketing managers of electrical appliances. It was a convention being held at the Pierce. When he didn't show up on time, the guy who had organized the program came up to his room looking for him. He got the chambermaid to open the door. They took one look, slammed the door, and called hotel security. The security man took one look, slammed the door, and called us. When my crew got there, and the Crime Scene Unit showed up, it was virgin territory, untouched by human hands. The security guy was standing guard outside the door."

"Good man," Delaney said.

"Ex-cop," Boone said, grinning. "But it wasn't all that much help. The Hotel Pierce is new, just opened last

November, so the print problem was a little easier. But the CSU found nothing but Wolheim's prints and the chambermaid's. So the killer must have been very careful or smeared everything. Before he died, the victim had been drinking a brandy. His prints were on the glass and on the bottle on the dresser. There was another glass with a small shot of brandy on a table next to an armchair. Wolheim's prints on that. No one else's."

"The door?" the Chief asked.

"Here's where it gets cute," Boone said. "No keyhole showing on the outside."

He explained how the new electric locks worked. The door was opened by the insertion of a coded magnetic card into an outside slot. When closed, the door locked automatically. It was even necessary to insert the card into an inside slot when exiting from the room.

"A good security system," he told Delaney. "It's cut way down on hotel B-and-E's. They don't care if you don't turn in the card when you leave because the magnetic code for the lock is changed when a guest checks out, and a new card issued. No way for a locksmith to duplicate the code."

"There must be a passcard for all the rooms," the Chief said.

"Oh sure. Held by the Security Section. The chambermaids have cards only for the rooms on the floor they service."

"Well," Delaney said grudgingly, "it sounds good, but sooner or later some wise-ass will figure out how to beat it. But the important thing is that the killer couldn't have left Wolheim's room without putting the card in the slot on the inside of the door. Have I got that right?"

"Right," Boone said, nodding. "The card had apparently been used to open the door, then it was tossed on top of a bureau. It's white plastic that would take nice prints, but it had been wiped clean."

"I told you," the Chief said with some satisfaction. "You're up against a smart apple. Any signs of a fight?"

"None," Boone reported. "The ME says Wolheim must have died almost instantly. Certainly in a second or two after his throat was ripped. Chief, I saw him. It looked like his head was ready to fall off."

Delaney took a deep breath, then a swallow of his

highball. He could imagine how the victim looked; he had seen similar cases. It took awhile before you learned to look and not vomit.

"Anything taken?" he asked.

"Not as far as we could tell. He had a fat wallet. Cash and travelers checks. Credit cards. All there. A gold wristwatch worth at least one big one. A pinkie ring with a diamond as big as the Ritz. Untouched."

"Son of a bitch!" Delaney said angrily. "It doesn't make sense. Anything from routine?"

"Nothing, and we've questioned more than 200 people so far. That Hotel Pierce is a city, a *city!* No one remembers seeing him with anyone. His last contact was with some convention buddies. They had dinner right there in the hotel. Then his pals wanted to go down to the traps in Greenwich Village, but Wolheim split. As far as we've been able to discover, they were the last to see him alive."

"Was he married?"

"Yes. Five children. He was from Akron, Ohio. The cops out there broke the news. Rather them than me."

"I know what you mean." Delaney was silent a moment, brooding. Then: "Any connection between the two men—Puller and Wolheim?"

"We're working on that right now. It doesn't look good. As far as we can tell, they didn't even know each other, weren't related even distantly, never even met, for God's sake! Went to different schools. Served in different branches of the armed forces. If there's a connection, we haven't found it. They had nothing in common."

"Sure they did."

"What's that?"

"They were both men. And in their mid-fifties."

"Well . . . yeah," Boone acknowledged. "But, Chief, if someone is trying to knock off every man in his mid-fifties in Manhattan, we got real trouble."

"Not *every* man," the Chief said. "Out-of-towners in the city for a convention, staying at a midtown hotel."

"How does that help, sir?"

"It doesn't," Delaney said. "But it's interesting. Did the Crime Scene Unit come up with anything?"

"No unidentified prints. But they took the bathroom apart again. This time there were traces of the victim's blood in the trap under the sink, so I guess the killer didn't have to take a shower. Just used the sink."

"Towel missing again?"

"That's right. But the important thing is that they found hairs. Three of them. One on the pillow near the victim's head. Two on the back of the armchair. Black hairs. Wolheim had reddish-gray hair."

"Well, my God, that's *something*. What did the lab men say?"

"Nylon. From a wig. Too long to be from a toupee."

Delaney blew out his breath. He stared at the sergeant. "The plot thickens," he said.

"Thickens?" Boone cried. "It curdles!"

"It could still be a hooker."

"Could be," the sergeant agreed. "Or a gay in drag. Or a transvestite. Anyway, the wig is a whole new ballgame. We've got pretty good relations with the gays these days, and they're cooperating—asking around and trying to turn up something. And of course we have some undercover guys they don't know about. And we're covering the black leather joints. Maybe it was a transvestite, and the victims didn't know it until they were in bed with a man. Some of those guys are so beautiful they could fool their mother."

Edward X. Delaney pondered awhile, frowning down into his empty highball glass.

"Well . . ." he said, "maybe. Was the penis cut off?"

"No."

"In all the homosexual killings I handled, the cock was hacked off."

"I talked to a sergeant in the Sex Crimes Analysis Unit, and that's what he said. But he doesn't rule out a male killer."

"I don't either."

Then the two men were silent, each looking down, busy with his own thoughts. They heard Rebecca Boone laughing in the kitchen. They heard the clash of pots and pans. Comforting domestic noises.

"Chief," Sergeant Boone said finally, "what do you think we've got here?"

Delaney looked up.

"You want me to guess? That's all I can do—guess. I'd guess it's the start of a series of random killings. Motive unknown for the moment. The more I think about it, the more reasonable it seems that your perp is a male. I never heard of a female random killer."

"You think he'll hit again?"

"I'd figure on it," Delaney advised. "If it follows the usual pattern, the periods between killings will become shorter and shorter. Not always. Look at the Yorkshire Ripper. But usually the random killer gets caught up in a frenzy, and hits faster and faster. Going by the percentages, he should kill again in about three weeks. You better cover the midtown hotels."

"How?" Boone said desperately. "With an army? And if we alert all the hotels' security sections, the word is going to get around that New York has a new Son of Sam. There goes the convention business and the tourist trade."

Edward X. Delaney looked at him without expression.

"That's not your worry, sergeant," he said tonelessly. "Your job is to nab a murderer."

"Don't you think I know that?" Boone demanded. "But you've got no idea of the pressure to keep this thing under wraps."

"I've got a very good idea," the Chief said softly. "I lived with it for thirty years."

But the sergeant would not be stopped.

"Just before I came over here," he said angrily, "I got a call from Deputy Commissioner Thorsen, and he . . ." His voice trailed away.

Delaney straightened up, leaned forward.

"Ivar?" he said. "Is he in on this?"

Boone nodded, somewhat shamefacedly.

"Did he tell you to brief me on the homicides?"

"He didn't exactly *tell* me, Chief. He called to let me know about the lieutenant who was taking over. I told him I was beat, and I was taking off. I happened to mention I was coming over here to pick up Rebecca, and he suggested it wouldn't do any harm to fill you in."

Delaney smiled grimly.

"If I did anything wrong, sir, I apologize."

"You didn't do anything wrong, sergeant. No apologies necessary."

"To tell you the truth, I need all the help on this I can get."

"So does Deputy Commissioner Thorsen," Delaney said dryly. "Who's the loot coming in?"

"Slavin. Marty Slavin. You know him?"

Delaney thought a moment.

"A short, skinny man?" he asked. "With a mean, pinched-up face? Looks like a ferret?"

"That's the guy," Boone said.

"Sergeant," the Chief said solemnly, "you have my sympathy."

The door to the living room burst open. Monica Delaney stood there, hands on her hips, challenging.

"All right, you guys," she said. "That's enough shop talk and 'Remember whens . . .' for one night. Coffee and cake in the living room. Right now. Let's go."

They rose smiling and headed out.

At the door, Sergeant Abner Boone paused.

"Chief," he said in a low voice, "any suggestions? Anything at all that I haven't done and should do?"

Edward X. Delaney saw the fatigue and worry in the man's face. With Lieutenant Martin Slavin coming in to take over command, Boone had cause for worry.

"Decoys," the Chief said. "If they won't let you alert the hotels, then put out decoys. Say between the hours of seven P.M. and midnight. Dress them like salesmen from out of town. Guys in their early fifties. Loud, beefy, flashing money. Have them cruise bars and hotel cocktail lounges. Probably a waste of time, but you never can tell."

"I'll do it," the sergeant said promptly. "I'll request the manpower tomorrow."

"Call Thorsen," Delaney advised. "He'll get you what you need. And sergeant, if I were you, I'd get the decoy thing rolling before Slavin shows up. Make sure everyone knows it was your idea."

"Yes. I'll do that. Uh, Chief, if this guy hits again like you figure, and I get the squeal, would you be willing to come over to the scene? You know—just to look around. I keep thinking there might be something we're missing."

Delaney smiled at him. "Sure. Give me a call, and I'll be there. It'll be like old times."

"Thank you, Chief," Boone said gratefully. "You've been a great help."

"I have?" Delaney said, secretly amused, and they went in for coffee and cake.

Chief Edward X. Delaney inspected the living room critically. It had been tidied in satisfactory fashion. Ashtrays had been cleaned, footstools were where they belonged. His favorite club chair was in its original position.

He turned to see his wife regarding him mockingly.

"Does it pass inspection, O lord and master?" she inquired.

"Nice job," he said, nodding. "You can come to work for me anytime."

"I don't do windows," she said.

The oak cocktail table had been set with coffeepot, creamer, sugar, cups, saucers, dessert plates, cutlery. And half a pineapple cheesecake.

"Ab," Rebecca Boone said, "the coffee is decaf, so you won't have any trouble sleeping tonight."

He grunted.

"And the cheesecake is low-cal," Monica said, looking at her husband.

"Liar," he said cheerfully. "I'm going to have a thin slice anyway."

They helped themselves, then settled back with their coffee and cake. Delaney was ensconced in his club chair, Sergeant Boone in a smaller armchair. The two women sat on the sofa.

"Good cake," the Chief said approvingly. "Rich, but light. Where did you get it?"

"Clara Webster made it," Monica said. "She insisted on leaving what was left."

"How did the meeting go?" Boone asked.

"Very well," Monica said firmly. "Interesting and—and instructive. Didn't you think so, Rebecca?"

"Absolutely," Mrs. Boone said loyally. "I really enjoyed the discussion after the lecture."

"What was the lecture about?" Boone said.

Monica Delaney raised her chin, glanced defiantly at her husband.

"The Preorgasmic Woman," Monica said.

"Good God!" the Chief said, and the two women burst out laughing.

"Monica told me you'd say that," Rebecca explained.

"Oh she did, did she?" Delaney said. "Well, I think it's a natural, normal reaction. What, exactly, is a Pre-orgasmic Woman?"

"It's obvious, isn't it?" Monica said. "It's a woman who has never had an orgasm."

"A frigid woman?" Boone said.

"Typical male reaction," his wife scoffed.

"'Frigid' is a pejorative word," Mrs. Delaney said. "A loaded word. Actually, 'frigid' means being averse to sex, applying to both men and women. But the poor men, with their fragile little egos, couldn't stand the thought of there being a sexless male, so they've used the word 'frigid' to describe only women. But our speaker tonight said there is no such irreversible condition in men or women. They're just preorgasmic. Through therapy training, they can achieve orgasmic sexuality."

"And assume their rightful place in society," Chief Delaney added with heavy irony.

Monica refused to rise to the bait. She was aware that he was proud of her activities in the feminist movement. They might have discussions that sometimes degenerated into bitter arguments. But Monica knew that his willingness to debate was better than his saying, "Yes, dear . . . Yes, dear . . . Yes, dear," with his nose stuck in the obituary page of *The New York Times*.

And he *was* proud of her. Following the death of their infant son, she had gone into such a guilt-ridden depression that he had despaired of her sanity and tried to steel himself to the task of urging her to seek professional help.

But she was a strong woman and had pulled herself up. The presence of her two young girls helped, of course; their needs, problems, and demands could not be met if she continued to sit in a darkened room, weeping.

And after they went away to school, she had found an outlet for her physical energy and mental inquisitiveness in the feminist movement. She embarked on a whirlwind of meetings, lectures, symposiums, picketings, petition-signing, letter-writing, and neighborhood betterment.

Edward X. Delaney was delighted. It gave him joy to see her alive, flaming, eager to advance a cause in which she believed. If she brought her "job" home with her, it was no more than he had done when he was on active duty.

He had discussed all his cases with Monica and with Barbara, his first wife. Both had listened patiently, understood, and frequently offered valuable advice.

But admiring Monica's ardor for the feminist cause didn't mean he had to agree with all the tenets she espoused. Some he did; some he did not. And he'd be damned if he'd be reticent about expressing his opinion.

Now, sitting across from his wife as she chatted with the Boones, he acknowledged, not for the first time, how lucky he had been with the women in his life.

Monica Delaney was a heavy-bodied woman, with a good waist between wide shoulders and broad hips. Her bosom was full, her legs tapered to slender ankles. There was a soft sensuality about her, a physical warmth. Her ardor was not totally mental.

Thick black hair, with a sheen, was combed back from a wide, unlined brow and fell almost to her shoulders. She made no effort to pluck her solid eyebrows, and her makeup was minimal. She was a big, definite woman, capable of tenderness and tears.

Watching his wife's animation as she talked to the Boones, Edward X. Delaney felt familiar stirrings and wished his guests gone. Monica turned her head suddenly to look at him. As usual, she caught his mood. She winked.

"Tell me, Chief," Rebecca said in her ingenuous way, "what do you *really* think of the women's movement?"

He kept his eyes resolutely averted from Monica, and addressed his remarks directly to Rebecca.

"What do I *really* think?" he repeated. "Well, I have no quarrel with most of the aims."

"I know," she said, sighing resignedly. "Equal pay for equal work."

"No, no," he said quickly. "Monica has taught me better than that. Equal pay for *comparable* work."

His wife nodded approvingly.

"And what do you object to?" Rebecca asked pertly.

He marshaled his thoughts.

"Not objections," he said slowly. "Two reservations. The first is no fault of the feminist movement. It's a characteristic of all minority or subjugated groups that desire to be treated as individuals, not stereotypes. No argument there. But to achieve that aim, they must organize. Then, to obtain political and economic power, they must project as—as monolithic a front as they can. The blacks, Chicanos, Indians, Italian-Americans, women—whatever. To wield maximum power, they must form a group, association, bloc, and speak with a single, strong voice. Again, no argument.

"But by doing that, they become—or at least this is their public image—less individuals and more stereotypes. They become capitalized Women, Blacks, and so forth. There is a contradiction there, a basic conflict. Frankly, I don't know how it can be resolved—if it can. If the answer is fragmentation, allowing the widest possible expressions of opinion within the bloc, then they sacrifice most of the social, political, and economic power which was the reason for their organizing in the first place."

"Do you think I'm a feminist stereotype?" Monica said hotly.

"No, I do not," he replied calmly. "But only because I know you, am married to you, live with you. But can you deny that since the current women's movement started— when was it, about fifteen years ago?—a stereotype of the feminist has been evolving?"

Monica Delaney slammed her palm down on the top of the cocktail table. Empty coffee cups rattled on their saucers.

"You're infuriating!" she said.

"That's true," he said equably.

"What's the second thing?" Rebecca Boone said hastily, thinking to avert a family squabble. "You said you had two objections to the feminist movement. What's the second?"

"Not objections," he reminded her. "Reservations. The second is this:

"Women in the feminist movement are working to achieve equality of opportunity, equal pay, and the same chances for advancement offered to men in business, government, industry, and so forth. Fine. But have you really thought through what you call 'equality' might entail?

"Look at poor Sergeant Boone there—dead to the world." The sergeant grinned feebly. "I'd guess he's been working eighteen hours a day for the past six weeks. Maybe grabbing a catnap now and then. Greasy food when he can find the time to eat. Under pressures you cannot imagine.

"Rebecca, have you seen him as often as you'd like in the last six weeks? Have you had a decent dinner with him? Gone out to a show? Or just a quiet evening at home? Have you even known where he's been, the dangers he's been facing? My guess would be that you have not.

"You think your husband enjoys living this way? But he's a professional cop, and he does the best he can. Would you like a comparable job with all its demands and stress and strain and risk? I don't believe it.

"What I'm trying to say is that I don't believe that feminists fully realize what they're asking for. You don't knock down a wall until you know what's behind it. There are dangers, drawbacks, and responsibilities you're not aware of."

"We're willing to accept those responsibilities," Rebecca Boone said stoutly.

"Are you?" the Chief said with gentle sarcasm. "Are you really? Are you willing to charge into a dark alley after some coked-up addict armed with a machete? Are you willing to serve in the armed forces in combat and go forward when you know your chances of survival are practically nil?

"On a more prosaic level, are you willing to work the hours that a fast-track business executive does? Willing to meet the demands of bosses and workers, make certain your schedules are met, stay within budget, turn a profit—and risk peptic ulcers, lung cancer, alcoholism, and keeling over from a coronary or cerebral hemorrhage at the age of forty?

"Look, I'm not saying all men's jobs are like that. A lot of men can handle the pressures of a top-level position and go home every night and water the petunias. They die in bed at a ripe old age. But just as many crack up, mentally or physically. The upper echelons of the establishment to which women aspire produce a frightening percentage of broken, impotent, or just burned-out men. Is that the equality you want?"

Rebecca Boone was usually a placid dumpling of a

woman. But now she exhibited an uncharacteristic flash of anger.

"Let *us* be the judge of what makes us happy," she snapped. "That's what the movement is all about."

Just as surprising, Monica Delaney didn't react with scorn and fury to her husband's words.

"Edward," she said, "there's a lot of truth in what you said. It's not *all* true, but there's truth in it."

"So?" he said.

"So," she said, "we recognize that when women achieve their rightful position in the upper levels of the establishment, they will be subject to the same strains, stresses, and pressures that men endure. But does it have to be that way? We don't think so. We believe the system can be changed, or at least modified, so that success doesn't necessarily mean peptic ulcers, coronaries, and cerebral hemorrhages. The system, the highly competitive, dog-eat-dog system, isn't carved on tablets of stone brought down from a mountain. It was created by men. It can be changed by liberated men—and women."

He stared at her.

"And when do you figure this paradise is going to come about?"

"Not in our lifetime," she admitted. "It's a long way down the road. But the first step is to get women into positions of power where they can influence the future of our society."

"Bore from within?" he said.

"Sometimes you're nasty," she said, smiling. "But the idea is right. Yes. Influence the system by becoming an integral part of it. First comes equality. Then liberation. For both women and men."

Sergeant Abner Boone rose shakily to his feet.

"Listen," he said hoarsely, "this is really interesting, and I'd like to stay and hear some more. But I'm so beat, I'm afraid I'll disgrace myself by falling asleep. Rebecca, I think we better take off."

She went over, took his arm, looked at him anxiously.

"Sure, hon," she said, "we'll go. I'll drive."

Chief Delaney went for hats and coats. The women kissed. The men shook hands. Farewells were exchanged, promises to get together again as soon as possible. The Delaneys stood inside their open front door, watched as the Boones got into their car and drove off, waving.

Then the Chief closed the front door, double-locked and chained it. He turned to face his wife.

"Alone at last," he said.

She looked at him.

"You covered yourself with glory tonight, buster," she said.

"Thank you," he said.

She glared, then burst out laughing. She took him into her strong arms. They were close, close. She drew back.

"What would I do without you?" she said. "I'll stack the dishes; you close up."

He made the rounds. He did it every night: barring the castle, flooding the moat, hauling up the drawbridge. He started in the attic and worked his way down to the basement. He checked every lock on every door, every latch on every window. This nightly duty didn't seem silly to him; he had been a New York cop.

When he had finished this chore, he turned off the lights downstairs, leaving on the outside stoop light and a dim lamp in the hallway. Then he climbed the stairs to the second-floor bedroom. Monica was turning down the beds.

He sat down heavily in a fragile, cretonne-covered boudoir chair. He bent over, began to unlace his thick-soled, ankle-high shoes of black kangaroo leather, polished to a high gloss. He didn't know of a single old cop who didn't have trouble with his feet.

"Was it really a good meeting?" he asked his wife.

"So-so," she said, flipping a palm back and forth. "Pretty basic stuff. The lecture, I mean. But everyone seemed interested. And they ate. My God, did they eat! What did you have?"

"A sandwich and a beer."

"Two sandwiches and two beers. I counted. Edward, you've got to stop gorging on sandwiches. You're getting as big as a house."

"More of me to love," he said, rising to his bare feet, beginning to strip off his jacket and vest.

"What does that mean?" she demanded. "That when you weigh 300 pounds I won't be able to contain my passion?"

They both undressed slowly, moving back and forth, to

the closet, their dressers, the bathroom. They exchanged disconnected remarks, yawning.

"Poor Abner," he said. "Did you get a close look at him? He's out on his feet."

"I wish Rebecca wouldn't wear green," she said. "It makes her skin look sallow."

"The cheesecake was good," he offered.

"Rebecca said she's lucky if she sees him three hours a day."

"Remind me to buy more booze; we're getting low."

"You think the cheesecake was as good as mine?"

"No," he lied. "Good, but not as good as yours."

"I'll make you one."

"Make *us* one. Strawberry, please."

He sat on the edge of his bed in his underdrawers. Around his thick neck was a faded ring of blue: a remembrance of the days when New York cops wore the old choker collars. He watched his wife become naked.

"You've lost a few pounds," he said.

"Does it show?" she said, pleased.

"It does indeed. Your waist . . ."

She regarded herself in the full-length mirror on the closet door.

"Well . . ." she said doubtfully, "maybe a pound or two. Edward, we've got to go on a diet."

"Sure."

"No more sandwiches for you."

He sighed.

"You never give up, do you?" he said wonderingly. "You'll never admit defeat. Never admit that you're married to the most stubborn man in the world."

"I'll keep nudging you," she vowed.

"Lots of luck," he said. "Have you heard from Karen Thorsen lately?"

"As a matter of fact, she called yesterday. Didn't I tell you?"

"No."

"Well, she did. Wants to get together with us. I told her I'd talk to you and set a time."

"Uh-huh."

Something in his tone alerted her. She finished pulling the blue cotton nightgown over her head. She smoothed it down, then looked at him.

"What's it about?" she said. "Does Ivar want to see you?"

"I don't know," he said. "All he has to do is pick up the phone."

She guessed. She was so shrewd.

"What did you and Abner talk about—a case?"

"Yes," he said.

"Can you tell me about it?"

"Sure," he said.

"Wait'll I cream my face," she said. "Don't fall asleep first."

"I won't," he promised.

While she was in the bathroom, he got into his flannel pajama pants with a drawstring top. He sat on the edge of his bed, longing for a cigar but lighting one of Monica's low-tar cigarettes. It didn't taste like anything.

He was a rude, blocky man who lumbered when he walked. His iron-gray hair was cut *en brosse*. His deeply lined, melancholy features had the broody look of a man who hoped for the best and expected the worst.

He had the solid, rounded shoulders of a machine-gunner, a torso that still showed old muscle under new fat. His large, yellowed teeth, the weathered face, the body bearing scars of old wounds—all gave the impression of a beast no longer with the swiftness of youth, but with the cunning of years, and vigor enough to kill.

He sat there solidly, smoking his toy cigarette. He watched his wife get into bed, prop her back against the headboard. She pulled sheet and blanket up to her waist.

"All right," she said. "Tell."

But first he went to his bedside table. It held, among other things, his guns, cuffs, a sap, and other odds and ends he had brought home when he had cleaned out his desk at the old headquarters building on Centre Street.

It also contained a bottle of brandy and two cut-glass snifters. He poured Monica and himself healthy shots.

"Splendid idea," she said.

"Better than pills," he said. "We'll sleep like babies."

He sat on the edge of her bed; she drew aside to make room for him. They raised their glasses to each other, took small sips.

"Plasma," he said.

He then recounted to her what Sergeant Boone had told him of the two hotel murders. He tried to keep his report as brief and succinct as possible. When he described the victims' wounds, Monica's face whitened, but she didn't ask him to stop. She just took a hefty belt of her brandy.

"So," he concluded, "that's what Boone's got—which isn't a whole hell of a lot. Now you know why he was so down tonight, and so exhausted. He's been going all out on this for the past month."

"Why haven't I read anything about it in the papers?" Monica asked.

"They're trying to keep a lid on it—which is stupid, but understandable. They don't want a rerun of the Son of Sam hysteria. Also, tourism is big business in this town. Maybe the biggest, for all I know. You can imagine what headlines like HOTEL KILLER ON LOOSE IN MANHATTAN would do to the convention trade."

"Maybe Abner will catch the killer."

"Maybe," he said doubtfully. "With a lucky break. But I don't think he'll do it on the basis of what he's got now. It's just too thin. Also, he's got another problem: they're bringing in Lieutenant Martin Slavin to take command of the investigation. Slavin is a little prick. An ambitious conniver who always covers his ass by going strictly by the book. Boone will have his hands full with him."

"Why are they bringing in someone over Boone? Hasn't Abner been doing a good job?"

"I know the sergeant's work," the Chief said, taking a sip of brandy. "He's a good, thorough detective. I believe that he's done all that could be done. But they've got— what did he tell me?—about twenty-five men working on this thing now, so I guess they feel they need higher rank in command. But I do assure you, Slavin's not going to break this thing. Unless there's another homicide and the killer slips up."

"You think there will be another one, Edward?"

He sighed, looked down at his brandy glass. Then he stood, began to pace back and forth past the foot of her bed. She followed him with her eyes.

"I practically guarantee it," he said. "It has all the earmarks of a psychopathic repeater. The worst, absolutely the worst kind of homicides to solve. Random killings. Apparently without motive. No connection except chance between victim and killer."

"They don't know each other?"

"Right. The coming together is accidental. Up to that time they've been strangers."

Then he explained things to her that he didn't have to explain to Sergeant Boone.

"Monica, when I got my detective's shield, many, many years ago, about seventy-five percent of all homicides in New York were committed by relatives, friends, acquaintances, or associates of the victims.

"The other homicides, called 'stranger murders,' were committed by killers who didn't know their victims. They might have been felony homicides, committed during a burglary or robbery, or snipings, or—worst of all—just random killing for the pleasure of killing. There's a German word for it that I don't remember, but it means death lust, murder for enjoyment.

"Anyway, in those days, when three-quarters of all homicides were committed by killers who knew their victims, we had a high solution rate. We zeroed in first on the husband, wife, lover, whoever would inherit, a partner who wanted the whole pie, and so forth.

"But in the last ten years, the percentage of stranger murders has been increasing and the solution rate has been declining. I've never seen a statistical correlation, but I'd bet the two opposing curves are almost identical, percentage-wise; as stranger murders increase, the solution rate decreases.

"Because stranger murders are bitches to break. You've got nothing to go on, nowhere to start."

"You did," she said somberly. "You found Bernard's killer."

"I didn't say it couldn't be done. I just said it's very difficult. A lot tougher than a crime of passion or a murder that follows a family fight."

"So you think there's a chance they'll catch him—the hotel killer?"

He stopped suddenly, turned to face her.

"Him?" he said. "After what I told you, you think the murderer is a man?"

She nodded.

"Why?" he asked her curiously.

"I don't know," she said. "I just can't conceive of a woman doing things like that."

"A short-bladed knife is a woman's weapon," he told her. "And the victims obviously weren't expecting an attack. And the killer seems to have been naked at the time of the assault."

"But *why?*" she cried. "Why would a woman do a thing like that?"

"Monica, crazies have a logic all their own. It's not our logic. What they do seems perfectly reasonable and justifiable to them. To us, it's monstrous and obscene. But to them, it makes sense. *Their* sense."

He came over to sit on the edge of her bed again. They sipped their brandies. He took up her free hand, clasped it in his big paw.

"I happen to agree with you," he said. "At this point, knowing only what Sergeant Boone told me, I don't think it's a woman either. But you're going by your instinct and prejudices; I'm going by percentages. There have been many cases of random killings: Son of Sam, Speck, Heirens, Jack the Ripper, the Boston Strangler, the Yorkshire Ripper, Black Dahlia, the Hillside Strangler— all male killers. There have been multiple murders by women—Martha Beck in the Lonely Hearts Case, for instance. But the motive for women is almost always greed. What I'm talking about are random killings with no apparent motive. Only by men, as far as I know."

"Could it be a man wearing a long black wig? Dressed like a woman?"

"Could be," he said. "There's so much in this case that has no connection with anything in my experience. It's like someone came down from outer space and offed those salesmen."

"The poor wives," she said sadly. "And children."

"Yes," he said. He finished his brandy. "The whole thing is a puzzle. A can of worms. I know how Boone feels. So many contradictions. So many loose ends. Finish your drink."

Obediently, she drained the last of her brandy, handed him the empty snifter. He took the two glasses into the bathroom, rinsed them, set them in the sink to drain. He turned off the bathroom light. He came back to Monica's bedside to swoop and kiss her cheek.

"Sleep well, dear," he said.

"After *that?*" she said. "Thanks a lot."

"You wanted to hear," he reminded her. "Besides, the brandy will help."

He got into his own bed, turned off the bedside lamp.

"Get a good night's sleep," Monica muttered drowsily. "I love you."

"I love you," he said, and pulled sheet and blanket up to his chin.

He went through all the permutations and combinations in his mind: man, woman, prostitute, homosexual, transvestite. Even, he considered wildly, a transsexual. That would be something new.

He lay awake, wide-eyed, listening. He knew the moment Monica was asleep. She turned onto her side, her breathing slowed, became deeper, each exhalation accompanied by a slight whistle. It didn't annoy him any more than his own grunts and groans disturbed her.

He was awake a long time, going over Boone's account again and again. Not once did he pause to wonder why the investigation interested him, why it obsessed him. He was retired; it was really none of his business.

If his concern had been questioned, he would have replied stolidly: "Well . . . two human beings have been killed. That's not right."

He turned to peer at the bedside clock. Almost 2:30 A.M. But he couldn't let it go till tomorrow; he had to do it *now*.

He slid cautiously out of bed, figuring to get his robe and slippers from the closet. He was halfway across the darkened room when:

"What's wrong?" came Monica's startled voice.

"I'm sorry I woke you up," he said.

"Well, I *am* up," she said crossly. "Where are you going?"

"Uh, I thought I'd go downstairs. There's a call I want to make."

"Abner Boone," she said instantly. "You never give up, do you?"

He said nothing.

"Well, you might as well call from here," she said. "But you'll wake him up, too."

"No, I won't," Delaney said with certainty. "He won't be sleeping."

He sat on the edge of his bed, switched on the lamp. They both blinked in the sudden light. He picked up the phone.

"What's their number?" he asked.

She gave it to him. He dialed.

"Yes?" Boone said, picking up after the first ring. His voice was clogged, throaty.

"Edward X. Delaney here. I hope I didn't wake you, sergeant."

"No, Chief. I thought I'd pass out, but I can't get to sleep. My brain is churning."

"Rebecca?"

"No, sir. She'd sleep through an earthquake."

"Sergeant, did you check into the backgrounds of the victims? The personal stuff?"

"Yes, sir. Sent a man out to Denver and Akron. If you're wondering about their homosexual records, it's nil. For both of them. No sheets, no hints, no gossip. Apparently both men were straight."

"Yes," Delaney said, "I should have known you'd look into that. One more thing . . ."

Boone waited.

"You said that after the second homicide, the Crime Scene Unit found two black hairs on the back of an armchair?"

"That's correct, sir. And one on the pillow. All three were black nylon."

"It's the two they found on the armchair that interest me. Did they take photographs?"

"Oh, hell yes. Hundreds of them. And made sketches. To help the cartographer."

"Did they photograph those two hairs on the armchair before they picked them up?"

"I'm sure they did, Chief. With a ruler alongside to show size and position."

"Good," Delaney said. "Now what you do is this: Get that photograph of the exact position of the two hairs on the armchair. Take a man with you from the Lab Services Unit or the Medical Examiner's office. Go back to the murder scene and find that armchair. Measure carefully from the point where the hairs were found to the seat of the chair. Got that? Assuming the hairs came from the killer, you'll get a measurement from the back of his head to the base of his spine. From that, the technicians should be able to give you the approximate height of the killer. It won't be exact, of course; it'll be a rough approximation. But it'll be *something.*"

There was silence a moment. Then:

"Goddamn it!" Boone exploded. "Why didn't I think of that?"

"You can't think of everything," Delaney said.

"I'm supposed to," Boone said bitterly. "That's what they're paying me for. Thank you, sir."

"Good luck, sergeant."

When he hung up, he saw Monica looking at him with wonderment.

"You're something, you are," she said.

"I just wanted to help him out."

"Oh sure."

"I really am sorry I woke you up," he said.

"Well," she said, "so it shouldn't be a total loss . . ."

She reached for him.

3

Zoe Kohler had read the autobiography of a playwright who had suffered from mental illness. He had been confined for several years.

He said it was not true that the insane thought themselves sane. He said that frequently the mad knew themselves to be mad. Either they were unable to fight their affliction, or had no desire to. Because, he wrote, there were pleasures and beauties in madness.

The phrase "pleasures and beauties" stuck in her mind; she thought of it often. The pleasures of madness. The beauties of madness.

On the afternoon after her second adventure (that was what Zoe Kohler called them: "adventures"), Everett Pinckney came into her office at the Hotel Granger. He parked his lank form on the edge of her desk. He leaned toward her; she smelled the whiskey.

"There's been another one," he said in a low voice.

She looked at him, then shook her head.

"I don't understand, Mr. Pinckney."

"Another murder. A stabbing. This one at the Pierce. Just like that one at the Grand Park last month. You read about that?"

She nodded.

"This one was practically identical," he said. "Same killer."

"How awful," she said, her face twisting with distaste.

"It looks like another Son of Sam," he said with some relish.

She sighed. "I suppose the newspapers will have a field day."

"They're trying to keep the connection out of the papers. For the time being. Not good news for the hotel business. But it's got to come out, sooner or later."

"I suppose so," she said.

"They'll catch him," he said, getting off her desk. "It's just a question of time. How are you feeling today?"

"Much better, thank you."

"Glad to hear it."

She watched him shamble from her office.

"Him," he had said. "They'll catch *him*." They thought it was a man; that was comforting. But what Pinckney had said about the newspapers—that was exciting.

She looked up the telephone number of *The New York Times*. It was an easy number to remember. She stopped at the first working phone booth she could find on her way home that night.

She tried to speak in a deep, masculine voice, and told the *Times* operator that she wanted to talk to someone about the murder at the Hotel Pierce. There was a clicking as her call was transferred. She waited patiently.

"City desk," a man said. "Gardner."

"This is about that murder last night at the Hotel Pierce," she said, trying to growl it out.

"Yes?"

"It's exactly like the one last month at the Grand Park Hotel. The same person did both of them."

There was silence for a second or two. Then:

"Could you give me your name and—"

She hung up, smiling.

She recalled, as precisely as she could, her actions of the previous night after she had waved goodbye to Ernest Mittle outside her apartment house door. She concentrated on the areas of risk.

When she had exited again, the doorman had hardly given her a glance. He would not remember the black-seamed hose, the high-heeled shoes. The cabdriver would never remember the woman he had driven to 72nd Street and Central Park West. And even if he did, what had that to do with a midnight murder at the Hotel Pierce?

No one in the ladies' room of the Filmore had seen her don wig and apply makeup. She had left from the hotel exit; the bartender could not have noted the transformation. The driver of the taxi that had taken her to a corner

three blocks from the Pierce had hardly looked at her.
They had exchanged no conversation.

The cocktail lounge, El Khatar, had been thronged,
and there had been women more flamboyantly dressed
than she. There had been another couple in the crowded
elevator who had gotten off on the 30th floor. But they
had turned away in the opposite direction, talking and
laughing. Zoe Kohler didn't think she and Fred had been
noticed.

Within the room, she had been careful about what she
touched. After he was gone (she did not use the word
"dead"; he was just gone), she was surprised to see that
she was blood-splattered only from the elbows down.

She had stared at the blood a long time. Her hands and
forearms dripping the bright, viscid fluid. She sniffed it. It
had an odor. Not hers, but it did smell.

Then she had gone into the bathroom to wash the
crimson stains away. Rinsing and rinsing with water as hot
as she could endure. And then letting the hot water run
steadily to cleanse the sink and drain while she dried her
arms and hands. She went back to the bedroom to dress,
not glancing at what lay on the bed.

Then, returning to the bathroom, she had turned off
the water and used the damp towel to wipe the faucet
handles, the inside doorknob and later, the white plastic
card Fred had tossed atop the bureau near the outside
door.

Before she left, she had removed her wig and makeup,
scrubbing her face with the towel. Wig and towel went
into her shoulder bag. She took a final look around and
decided there was nothing she should have done that she
had not.

The descending elevator was crowded and no one had
looked at her: a pale-faced, mousy-haired woman wearing
a loose-fitting trenchcoat buttoned up to the chin. Of
course no one looked at her; she was Zoe Kohler again,
the invisible woman.

She had walked over to Fifth Avenue and taken a cab
downtown to 38th Street and Fifth. She walked from that
corner to her apartment house. She felt no fear alone on
the street. Her life could have ended at that moment and
it would have been worthwhile. That was how she felt.

Locked and chained inside her own apartment, she had

showered (the third time that day). She replaced all her secret things in their secret places. She pushed the damp towel deep into the plastic bag in her garbage can, to be thrown into the incinerator in the morning.

She hadn't been aware of her menstrual cramps for hours and hours. But now she began to feel the familiar pains, gripping with increasing intensity. She inserted a tampon and swallowed a Midol, two Anacin, a vitamin B-complex capsule, a vitamin C tablet, and ate half a container of blueberry yogurt.

Just before she got into bed, she shook a Pulvule 304 from her jar of prescription Tuinal and gulped it down.

She slept like a baby.

During the month that followed, Zoe Kohler had the sense of her ordered life whirling apart. She was conscious of an accelerated passage of time. Days flashed, and even weeks seemed condensed, so that Fridays succeeded Mondays, and it was an effort to recall what had happened between.

Increasingly, the past intruded on the present. She found herself thinking more and more of her marriage, her husband, mother, father, her girlhood. She spent one evening trying to remember the names of friends who had attended her 13th birthday party, and writing them down.

The party had been a disaster. Partly because several invited guests had not shown up, nor bothered to phone apologies. And partly because her periods had started on that day. She had begun to bleed, and was terrified. She thought it would never stop, and saw herself as an emptied sack of wrinkled white skin.

Ernest Mittle phoned her at home a week after their meeting. She hadn't expected him to call, as he had promised—men never did—and it took her a moment to bring him to mind.

"I hope I'm not disturbing you," he said.

"Oh no," she said. "No."

"How are you, Zoe?"

"Very well, thank you. And you?"

"Just fine," he said in his light, boyish voice. "I was hoping that if you didn't have any plans for tomorrow night, we might have dinner and see a movie, or something."

"I'm sorry," she said quickly. "I do have plans."

He said he was disappointed and would try again. They chatted awkwardly for a few minutes and then hung up. She stared at the dead, black phone.

"Don't be too eager, Zoe," her mother had instructed firmly. "Don't let men get the idea that you're anxious or *easy.*"

She didn't know if it was her mother's teaching or her own lack of inclination, but she wasn't certain she wanted to see Ernest Mittle again. If she did, it would just be something to do.

He did call again, and this time she accepted his invitation. It was for Saturday night, which she took as a good omen. New York men dated second or third choices during the week. Saturday night was for favorites: an occasion.

Ernest Mittle insisted on meeting her in the lobby of her apartment house. From there, they took a cab to a French restaurant on East 60th Street where he had made a reservation. The dining room was warm, cheerfully decorated, crowded.

Relaxing there, smoking a cigarette, sipping her white wine, listening to the chatter of other diners, Zoe Kohler felt for a moment that she was visible and belonged in the world.

After dinner, they walked over to 60th Street and Third Avenue. But there was a long line before the theater showing the movie he wanted to see. He looked at her, dismayed.

"I don't want to wait," he said. "Do you?"

"Not really," she said. And then, without considering it, she added: "Why don't we go back to my apartment and watch TV, or just talk?"

Something happened to his face: a quick twist. But then he was the eager spaniel again, anxious to please, his smile hopeful. He seemed constantly prepared to apologize.

"That sounds just fine," he said.

"I'm afraid I have nothing to drink," she said.

"We'll stop and pick up a couple of bottles of white wine," he said. "All right?"

"One will be plenty," she assured him.

They had exhausted remembrances of their youth in

Minnesota and Wisconsin. They had no more recollections to exchange. Now, tentatively, almost fearfully, their conversation became more personal. They explored a new relationship, feinting, pulling back, trying each other, ready to escape. Both stiff with shyness and embarrassment.

In her apartment, she served the white wine with ice cubes. He sat in an armchair, his short legs thrust out. He was wearing a vested tweed suit, a tattersall shirt with a knitted tie. He seemed laden and bowed with the weight of his clothing, made smaller and frail. He had tiny feet.

She sat curled into a corner of the living room couch, her shoes off, legs pulled up under her gray flannel jumper. She felt remarkably at ease. No tension. He did not frighten her. If she had said, "Go," he would have gone, she was certain.

"Why haven't you married?" she asked him suddenly, thinking he might be gay.

"Who'd have me?" he said, showing his small white teeth. "Besides, Zoe, there isn't the pressure to marry anymore. There are all kinds of different lifestyles. More and more single-person households every year."

"I suppose," she said vaguely.

"Are you into the women's movement?"

"Not really," she said. "I don't know much about it."

"I don't either," he said. "But what I've read seems logical and reasonable."

"Some of those women are so—so loud and crude," she burst out.

"Oh my, yes," he said hurriedly. "That's true."

"They just—just *push* so," she went on. "They call themselves feminists, but I don't think they're very feminine."

"You're so right," he said.

"I think that, first and foremost, women should be ladies. Don't you? I mean, refined and gentle. Low-voiced and modest in her appearance. That's what I was always taught. Clean and well-groomed. Generous and sympathetic."

"I was brought up to respect women," he said.

"That's what my mother told me—that men will always respect you if you act like a lady."

"Is your mother still alive?" he asked.

"Oh yes."

"She sounds like a wonderful woman."

"She is," Zoe said fervently, "she really is. She's over sixty now, but she's very active in her bridge club and her garden club and her book club. She reads all the best-sellers. And she's in charge of the rummage sales at the church. She certainly does keep busy.

"What I mean is that she doesn't just sit at home and do housecleaning and cook. She has a life of her own. That doesn't mean she doesn't take care of Father; she does. But goodness, he's not her *entire* life. She's a very independent woman."

"That's marvelous," Ernest said, "that she finds so much of interest to do."

"You should see her," Zoe said. "She looks much younger than her age. She has her hair done every week, a blue rinse, and she dresses just so. She's got wonderful taste in clothes. She's immaculate. Not a hair out of place. She's a little overweight now, but she stands just as straight as ever."

"Sounds like a real lady," he said.

"Oh, she is. A real lady."

Then Ernest Mittle began to talk about *his* mother, who seemed to be a woman much like Zoe had described. After a while she heard his voice as a kind of drone. She was conscious of what he was saying. She kept her eyes fixed on his face with polite interest. But her thoughts were free and floating, the past intruding.

She had lived in New York for about a year. Then, shriveled with loneliness, had ventured out to a highly publicized bar on Second Avenue that advertised: "For discriminating, sophisticated singles who want to get it on and get it off!" It was called The Meet Market.

She had given a great deal of thought to how she would dress and how she would comport herself. She would be attractive, but not in a brazen, obvious way. She would be alert, sparkling, and would listen closely to what men said, and speak little. Friendly but not forward. She would not express an opinion unless asked.

She had worn a black turtleneck sweater cinched with a wide, crushed leather belt. Her long wool skirt fitted snugly but not immodestly. Her pantyhose were sheer, and she wore pumps with heels that added an inch to her 5′ 6″ height.

She tried a light dusting of powder, a faint blush of rouge and lipstick. Observing the effect, she added more. Her first experiment with false eyelashes was not a success; she got them on crooked, giving her a depraved, Oriental look. Finally, she stripped them away and darkened her own wispy lashes.

The Meet Market had been a shock. It was smaller than she had envisaged, and so crowded that patrons were standing outside on the sidewalk. They were drinking beers and shouting at each other to be heard above the din of the jukebox just inside the door.

She edged herself nervously inside and was dismayed to see that most of the women there, the singles and those with escorts, were younger than she. Most were in their late teens and early twenties, and were dressed in a variety of outlandish costumes, brightly colored, that made her look like a frump.

It took her fifteen minutes to work her way to the bar, and another five minutes to order a glass of beer from one of the busy, insolent bartenders. She was bumped continually, shouldered, jostled back and forth. No one spoke to her.

She stood there with a fixed smile, not looking about. Life surged around her: shouts of laughter, screamed conversation, blare of jukebox, obscene jesting. The women as lewd as the men. Still she stood, smiling determinedly, and ordered another glass of beer.

"Sorry, doll," a man said, knocking her shoulder as he reached across to take drinks from the bartender.

She turned to look. A husky young man, dark, with a helmet of greasy ringlets, a profile from a Roman coin. He wore an embroidered shirt unbuttoned to the waist. About his muscled neck were three gold chains. Ornate medallions swung against the thick mat of hair on his chest.

He had a musky scent of something so cloying that she almost gagged. His teeth were chipped, and he needed a shave. There were wet stains on the shirt beneath his armpits.

He doesn't care, she had thought suddenly. He just doesn't care.

She admired him for not caring.

She stayed at the bar, drinking the watery beer, and watched the strange world swirl about her. She felt that she had strayed into a circus. Everyone was a performer except her.

She had seen that most of the women were not only younger than she, but prettier. With ripe, bursting bodies they flaunted without modesty.

Zoe saw blouses zipped down to reveal cleavage. Tanktops so tight that hard nipples poked out. Sheer shirts that revealed naked torsos. Jeans so snug that buttocks were clearly delineated, some bearing suggestive patches: SMART ASS. BOTTOMS UP. SEX POT.

She had arrived at The Meet Market shortly after 11:30 P.M. The noise and crush were at their worst an hour later. Then, slowly, the place began to empty out. Contacts were made; couples disappeared. Still Zoe Kohler stood at the bar, drinking her flat beer, her face aching with her smile.

"Wassamatta, doll?" the dark young man said, at her elbow again. "Get stood up?"

He roared with laughter, putting his head back, his mouth wide. She saw his bad teeth, a coated tongue, a red tunnel.

He took another drink from the bartender, gulped down half of it without stopping. A rivulet of beer ran down his chin. He wiped it away with the back of his hand. He looked around at the emptying room.

"I missed the boat," he said to Zoe. "Always looking for something better. Know what I mean? Then I end up with Mother Five-fingers."

He laughed again, in her face. His breath smelled sour: beer, and something else. He clapped her on the shoulder.

"Where you from, doll?" he said.

"Manhattan," she said.

"Well, that's *something*," he said. "Last night I connected with a *real* doll, and she's from Queens and wants to go to her place. My luck—right? No way am I going to Queens. North of Thirty-fourth and south of Ninety-sixth:

that's my motto. I live practically around the corner."

"So?" she said archly.

"So let's go," he said. "Beggars can't be choosers."

She had never decided if he meant her or himself.

He lived in a dreadful one-room apartment in a tenement on 85th Street, off Second Avenue. The moment they were inside, he said, "Gotta piss," and dashed for the bathroom.

He left the door open. She heard the sound of his stream splashing into the bowl. She put her palms over her ears and wondered dully why she did not run.

He came out, stripping off his shirt, and then stepping out of his jeans. He was wearing a stained bikini no larger than a jockstrap. She could not take her eyes from the bulge.

"I got half a joint," he said, then saw where she was looking. He laughed. "Not here," he said, pointing. "I mean good grass. Wanna share?"

"No, thank you," she said primly. "But you go right ahead."

He found the butt in a dresser drawer, lighted up, inhaled deeply. His eyelids lowered.

"Manna from Heaven," he said slowly. "You know what manna is, doll?"

"A food," she said. "From the Bible."

"Right on," he said lazily. "But they didn't call it womanna, did they? Manna. You give good head, doll?"

"I don't know," she said truthfully, not understanding.

"Sure you do," he said. "All you old, hungry dames do. And if you don't know how, I'll teach you. But that comes later. Let's get with it. Off with the uniform, doll."

It was more of a cot than a bed, the thin mattress lumpy, sheet torn and blotched. He would not let her turn off the light. So she saw him, saw herself, could only block out what was happening by closing her eyes. But that was not enough.

He smelled of sweat and the awful, musky scent he was wearing. And he was so hairy, so hairy. He wore a singlet of black wire wool that covered chest, shoulders, arms, back, legs. His groin was a tangle. But his buttocks were satiny.

"Oh," she had cried out. "Oh, oh, oh."

"Good, huh?" he said, grunting with his effort. "You

like this . . . and this . . . and this? Oh God!"

Moaning, just as Maddie Kurnitz had advised. And Remedial Moaning. Zoe Kohler did as she had been told. Going through the motions. Threshing about. Digging nails into his meaty shoulders. Pulling his hair.

"So good!" she kept crying. "So *good!*" Wondering if she had remembered to turn off the gas range before she left her apartment.

Then, as he kept pumping, and she heaved up to meet him, she recalled her ex-husband Kenneth and his fury at her mechanical response.

"You're just not *there!*" he had complained.

Finally, finally, the hairy thing lying atop her and punishing her with its weight, finished with a sob, and almost immediately rolled away.

He lighted the toke again, a roach now that he impaled on a thin wire.

"That was something," he said. "Wasn't that something?"

"The best I've ever had," she recited.

"You made it?"

"Of course," she lied. "Twice."

"What else?" he said, smiling complacently. "Haven't had any complaints yet."

"I've got to go," she said, sitting up.

"Oh no," he said, pushing her back down. "Not yet. We've got some unfinished business."

Something in his tone frightened her. Not menace; he was not threatening her. It was the brute confidence.

Kenneth had suggested it once, but she had refused. Now she could not refuse. He clamped her head between his strong hands and guided her mouth.

"Now you're getting it," he instructed her. "Up. Down. That's it. Around. Right there. The tongue. It's all in knowing how, doll. Take it easy with the teeth."

Later, on her way home in a cab, she had realized that she didn't even know his name and he didn't know hers. That was some comfort.

"More wine?" she asked Ernest Mittle. "Your glass is empty."

"Sure," he said, smiling. "Thank you. We might as well finish the bottle. I'm really enjoying this."

She rose, staggered just briefly, giddy from the memory, not the wine. She brought more ice cubes from the kitchen.

They sat at their ease. Remarkably alike. Mirror images. With their watery coloring, pinched frames, their soft, wistful vulnerability, they could have been brother and sister.

"This is better than standing on line to see a movie," he said. "It was probably no good anyway."

"Or going to some crowded party," she said. "Everyone getting drunk as fast as they can—like at Maddie's."

"I suppose you go out a lot?"

"I really do prefer a quiet evening at home," she said. "Like this."

"Oh yes," he agreed eagerly. "One gets tired of running around. I know I do."

They stared at each other, blank-eyed liars. He broke first.

"Actually," he said in a very low voice, "I don't go out all that much. Very rarely, in fact."

"To tell you the truth," she said, not looking at him, "I don't either. I'm alone most of the time."

He looked up, intent. He hunched forward.

"That's why I enjoy seeing you, Zoe," he said. "I can talk to you. When I do go to a party or bar, everyone seems to shout. People don't talk to each other anymore. I mean about important things."

"That's very true," she said. "Everyone seems to shout. And no one has good manners either. No common courtesy."

"Yes!" he said excitedly. "Right! Exactly the way I feel. If you try to be gentle, everyone thinks you're dumb. It's all push, rush, shove, walk over anyone who gets in your way. I, for one, think it's disgusting."

She looked at him with admiration.

"Yes," she said, "I feel the same way. I may be old-fashioned, but—"

"No, no!" he protested.

"But I'd rather sit home by myself," she went on, "with a good book or something tasteful on educational TV— I'd rather do that than get caught up in the rat race."

"I couldn't agree more," he said warmly. "Except . . ."

"Except what?" she asked.

"Well, look, you and I work in the most frantic city in the world. And I wonder—I've been thinking a lot about this lately—that in spite of the way I feel, if it isn't getting to me. I mean, the noise, the anger, the frustration, the dirt, the violence. Zoe, they've got to be having *some* effect."

"I suppose," she said slowly.

"What I mean," he said desperately, "is that sometimes I feel I can't cope, that I'm a victim of things I can't control. It's all changing so fast. Nothing is the same. But what's the answer? To drop out and go live in the wilderness? Who can afford that? Or to try to change things? I don't believe an individual can do anything. It's just—just forces."

He drew a deep breath, drained off his wine. He laughed shakily.

"I'm probably boring you," he said. "I'm sorry."

"You're not boring me, Ernest."

"Ernie."

"You're not boring me, Ernie. What you said is very interesting. You really think we can be influenced by our environment? Even if we recognize how awful it is and try to—to rebel against it?"

"Oh yes," he said. "Definitely. Did you take any psychology courses?"

"Two years."

"Well, then you know you can put rats in a stress situation—loud noise, overcrowding, bad food, flashing lights, and so forth—and drive them right up the wall. All right, admittedly human beings have more intelligence than rats. We have the ability to know when we *are* in a stress situation, and can make a conscious effort to endure it, or escape it. But I still say that what is going on about us today, in the modern world, is probably affecting us in ways we're not even aware of."

"Physically, you mean? Affecting us physically?"

"That, of course. Polluted air, radiation, bad water, junk food. But what's worse is what's happening to *us,* the kind of people we are. We're changing, Zoe. I know we are."

"How are we changing?"

"Getting harder, less gentle. Our attention span is shortening. We can't concentrate. Sex has lost its significance. Love is a joke. Violence is a way of life. No respect for the law. Crime *does* pay. Religion is just another cult. And so forth and so on. Oh God, I must sound like a prophet of doom!"

She went back to what fascinated her most.

"And feeling this way," she said, "knowing all this, you still feel that *you* are being changed?"

He nodded miserably.

"The other night," he said, "I was eating my dinner in front of the TV set. Franks and beans. With a can of beer. I was watching the evening news. They had films from the refugee camps in Thailand. The Cambodians.

"I sat there eating and drinking, and saw kids, babies, with pipe-stem arms and legs, and swollen bellies, flies on their eyes. I sat there eating my franks and beans, drinking my beer, and watched people dying. And after a while I discovered I was crying."

"I know," she said sympathetically. "It was terrible."

"No, no," he said in anguish. "That wasn't why I was crying—because it was so terrible. I was crying because I wasn't feeling anything. I was watching those pictures, and I knew they were true, and those people really were dying, and I didn't feel a thing. I just ate my franks and beans, drank my beer, and watched a TV show. But I didn't *feel* anything, Zoe. I swear, I didn't feel *anything*. That's what I mean about this world changing us in ways we don't want to be changed."

Suddenly, without warning, his eyes brimmed over, and he began to weep. She watched him helplessly for a moment, then held her arms out to him.

He stumbled over to collapse next to her on the couch. She put an arm about his thin shoulders, drew him close. With her other hand she smoothed the fine flaxen hair back from his temples.

"There," she said in a soft, crooning voice. "There, Ernie. There. There."

In the days following Zoe Kohler's phoned tip to *The New York Times,* she searched the newspaper with avid interest. But nothing appeared other than a few brief follow-ups on the slaying of Frederick Wolheim at the Hotel Pierce.

Soon, even this case disappeared from the paper. Zoe

was convinced a cover-up was in effect. As Everett Pinckney had said, it wasn't good for the hotel business. Hotels advertised in newspapers. The economy of the city was based to a large extent on tourism. So the newspapers were silent.

But on March 24th, a two-column article appeared in the *Times'* Metropolitan Report. Headlined: KILLER SOUGHT IN TWO HOMICIDES, it reviewed the murders of George T. Puller and Frederick Wolheim, pointing out the similarities, and said the police were working on the theory that both killings were committed by the same person. The motive was unknown.

The *Times'* article reported that the investigation was under the command of Detective Lieutenant Martin Slavin. He had stated: "We are exploring several promising leads, and an arrest is expected shortly." A special phone number had been set up for anyone with information on the crimes.

The *Times* did not mention the Son of Sam killings, but the afternoon *Post* and the evening's *Daily News* were not so restrained. The *Post* headline was: ANOTHER SON OF SAM? The *News* bannered their page 4 report with: COPS CALL 'DAUGHTER OF SAM' A POSSIBILITY.

Both papers suggested the police were afraid that the Puller and Wolheim murders might be just the first of a series of psychopathic, motiveless slayings. Both papers repeated Lieutenant Slavin's statement: "We are exploring several promising leads, and an arrest is expected shortly."

After a brief initial shock, Zoe Kohler decided she had nothing to fear from Slavin's optimistic prediction; it was intended to reassure New Yorkers that everything that could be done was being done, and this menace to the public safety would soon be eliminated.

More worrisome was the *Daily News'* reference to "Daughter of Sam." But a careful reading of the story indicated that the police were merely investigating the possibility that a prostitute had been responsible for both murders. Midtown whores and their pimps were being rousted and questioned in record numbers.

So, Zoe Kohler felt, nothing had been discovered that really threatened her. It was, she admitted, becoming increasingly exciting. All those policemen running around. Millions of newspaper readers titillated and frightened. She was becoming someone.

Her exhilaration was dampened two days later when Everett Pinckney came into her office with a notice that had been hand-delivered by the police to the chiefs of security in every hotel in midtown Manhattan.

It was, in effect, a WANTED poster, asking the security officers to aid in apprehending the killer of George T. Puller and Frederick Wolheim. It was believed the murderer made contact with the victims in the bars, cocktail lounges, or dining rooms of hotels, especially those hosting conventions, sales meetings, or large gatherings of any type.

The description of the person "wanted for questioning" was sparse. It said only that the suspect could be male or female, approximately 5′ 5″ to 5′ 7″ tall, wearing a wig of black nylon.

"Not much to go on," Pinckney said. "If we grabbed every man and woman wearing a black nylon wig, we'd really be in the soup. Can you imagine the lawsuits for false arrest?"

"Yes," Zoe said.

"Well," Mr. Pinckney said, studying the notice, "the two murders happened around midnight. I'll make sure Joe Levine sees this when he comes on at five tonight. Then I'll leave it on my desk. If I miss Barney McMillan in the morning, will you make sure he sees it?"

"Yes, sir," she said.

When he was gone, she sat upright at her desk, spine rigid, her back not touching her chair. She clasped her hands on the desktop. Knuckles whitened.

The black nylon wig didn't bother her. That was a detail that could be remedied. But how had they come up with the correct height?

She went over and over her actions during her two adventures. She could recall nothing that would give the police an accurate estimation of her height. She had a shivery feeling that there was an intelligence at work of which she knew nothing. Something or someone secret who *knew*.

She wondered if it might be a medium or someone versed in ESP, called in by the police to assist in their investigation. "I see a man or woman with—yes, it's black hair. No, not hair—it's a wig, a black nylon wig. And this person is of average height. Yes, I see that clearly. About five-five to five-seven. Around there."

That might have been how it was done. Zoe Kohler nodded, convinced; that was how.

On Thursday night, she went down to Wigarama on 34th Street. She tried on a nylon, strawberry blond wig, styled just like her black one. She looked in the mirror, pulling, tugging, poking it with her fingers.

"It'll make you a new woman, dearie," the salesclerk said.

"I'm sure it will," Zoe Kohler said, and bought it.

Madeline Kurnitz called and insisted they meet for lunch. Zoe was wary; a lunch with Maddie could last more than two hours.

"I really shouldn't," she said. "I'm a working woman, you know. I usually eat at my desk."

"Come on, kiddo," Maddie said impatiently. "You're not chained to the goddamned desk, are you? Live a little!"

"How about right here?" Zoe suggested. "In the hotel dining room?"

"How tacky can you get?" Maddie said disgustedly.

When she showed up, twenty minutes late, she was wearing her ranch mink, so black it was almost blue, over a tight sheath of brocaded satin. The dress had a stain in front; a side seam gapped. She couldn't have cared less.

She led the way grandly into the Hotel Granger dining room.

A wan maitre d' approached, gave them a sad smile.

"Two, ladies?" he said in sepulchral tones. "This way, please."

He escorted them to a tiny table neatly tucked behind an enormous plaster pillar.

Maddie Kurnitz opened her coat and put a soft hand on his arm.

"You sweet man," she said, "couldn't we have a table just a *wee* bit more comfortable?"

His eyes flicked to her unholstered breasts. He came alive.

"But of course!" he said.

He conducted them to a table for four in the center of the dining room.

"Marvelous," Maddie caroled. She gave the maitre d' a warm smile. "You're a perfect dear," she said.

"My pleasure!" he said, glowing. "Enjoy your luncheon, ladies."

He helped Maddie remove her mink coat, touching her tenderly. Then he moved away regretfully.

"I made his day," Maddie said.

"How do you do it?" Zoe said. She shook her head. "I'd never have the nerve."

"Balls, luv," Maddie advised. "All it takes is balls."

As usual, her hair seemed a snarl, her makeup a blotch of primary colors. Her feral teeth shone. Diamonds glittered. She dug into an enormous snakeskin shoulder bag and came out with a crumpled pack of brown cigarillos. She offered it to Zoe.

"No, thank you, Maddie. I'll have one of my own."

"Suit yourself."

Maddie twirled a cigarillo between her lips. Instantly, a handsome young waiter was hovering over her, snapping his lighter. She grasped his hand to steady the flame.

"Thank you, you beautiful man," she said, smiling up at him. "May we have a drink now?"

"But of course, madam. What is your pleasure?"

"I'd tell you," she said, "but it would make you blush. For a drink, I'll have a very dry Tanqueray martini, straight up, with two olives. Zoe?"

"A glass of white wine, please."

The waiter scurried off with their order. Maddie looked around the crowded room.

"Never in my life have I seen so many women with blue hair," she said. "What's the attraction here—free Geritol?"

"The food is very good," Zoe said defensively.

"Let me be the judge of that, kiddo." She regarded Zoe critically. "You don't look so bad. Not so good, but not so bad. Feeling okay?"

"Of course. I'm fine."

"Uh-huh. Have a good time at our bash the other night?"

"Oh yes. I meant to thank you before I left, but I couldn't find you. Or Harry."

"Never did meet David something, did you? The guy I told you about?"

"No," Zoe said, "I never met him."

"You're lucky," Maddie said, laughing. "He was picked up later that night with a stash of coke on him. The moron! But you didn't leave alone, did you?"

Zoe Kohler hung her head.

The waiter came bustling up with their drinks and left menus alongside their plates.

"Whenever you're ready, ladies," he said.

"I'm always ready," Maddie said, "but we'll order in a few minutes."

They waited until he moved away.

"How did you know?" Zoe asked.

"My spies are everywhere," Maddie said. "What's his name?"

"Ernest Mittle. He works for your husband."

Madeline Kurnitz spluttered into her martini.

"Mister Meek?" she said. "That nice little man?"

"He's not so little."

"I know, sweetie. He just *looks* little. Didn't try to get into your pants, did he?"

"Oh Maddie," she said, embarrassed. "Of course not. He's not like that at all."

"Didn't think so," Maddie said. "Poor little mouse."

"Could we order, Maddie? I really have to get back to work."

Zoe ordered a fresh fruit salad.

Maddie would have the fresh oysters. Bluepoints weren't her favorite, but they were the only kind available. On each oyster she wanted a spoonful of caviar topped with a sprinkling of freshly ground ginger.

Then she would have thin strips of veal sautéed in unsalted butter and Marsala wine, with a little lemon and garlic. Cauliflower with bacon bits would be nice with that, she decided. And a small salad of arrugola with sour cream and chives.

The ordering of her luncheon took fifteen minutes and required a conference of maitre d', headwaiter, and two waiters, with a busboy hovering in the background. All clustered about Maddie, peered down her neckline, and conversed volubly in rapid Italian. Other diners observed this drama with bemusement. Zoe Kohler wished she were elsewhere.

Finally their meals were served. Maddie sampled one of her oysters. The waiters watched anxiously.

"Magnifico!" she cried, kissing the tips of her fingers.

They relaxed with grins, bowed, clapped each other on the shoulder.

"So-so," Maddie said to Zoe Kohler in a low voice. "The oysters are a bit mealy, but those dolts were so sweet, I didn't have the heart . . . Want to try one?"

"Oh no! Thank you."

"Still popping the pills, kiddo?"

"I take vitamins," Zoe said stiffly. "Food supplements."

Maddie finished the oysters, sat back beaming.

"Not bad," she admitted. "Not the greatest, but not bad. By the way," she added, "this is on me. I should have told you; maybe you'd have ordered a steak."

"We'll go Dutch," Zoe said.

"Screw that. I have a credit card from Harry's company. This is a business lunch in case anyone should ask." She laughed.

She had another martini while waiting for her veal. Zoe had another glass of white wine. Then their entrees were served.

"Beautiful," Maddie said, looking down at her plate. "You've got to order for color as well as taste. Isn't that a symphony?"

"It looks nice."

Maddie dug in, sampled a slice of veal. She closed her eyes.

"I'm coming," she said. "God, that's almost as good as a high colonic." She attacked her lunch with vigor. "Sweetie," she said, while masticating, "I never asked you about your divorce. Never. Did I?"

"No, you never did."

"If you don't want to talk about it, just tell me to shut my yap. But I'm curious. Why the hell did you and what's-his-name break up?"

"Kenneth."

"Whatever. I thought you two had the greatest love affair since Hitler and Eva Braun. That's the way your letters sounded. What happened?"

"Well . . . ah . . ." Zoe Kohler said, picking at her salad, "we just drifted apart."

"Bullshit," Madeline Kurnitz said, forking veal into her mouth. "Can I guess?"

"Can I stop you?" Zoe said.

"No way. My guess is that it was the sex thing. Am I right?"

"Well . . . maybe," Zoe said in a low voice.

Maddie stopped eating. She sat there, fork poised, staring at the other woman.

"He wanted you to gobble ze goo?" she asked.

"What?"

"Chew on his schlong," Maddie said impatiently.

Zoe looked about nervously, fearing nearby diners were tuned in to this discomfiting conversation. No one appeared to be listening.

"That was one of the things," she said quietly. "There were other things."

Maddie resumed eating, apparently sobered and solemn. She kept her eyes on her food.

"Sweetie," she said, "were you cherry when you got married?"

"Yes."

"After all I told you at school?" Maddie said, looking up angrily. "I tried to educate you, for God's sake. Stupid, stupid, stupid! Well, how was it?"

"How was what?"

"The wedding night, you idiot. The first bang. How was it?"

"It wasn't the greatest adventure I've ever had," Zoe Kohler said dryly.

"Did you make it?"

"He did. I didn't, no."

Maddie stared long and thoughtfully at her.

"Have you ever made it?"

"No. I haven't."

"What? Speak up. I didn't hear that."

"No, I haven't," Zoe repeated.

They finished their food in silence. Maddie pushed her plate away, belched, relighted the butt of her cigarillo. She looked at Zoe with narrowed eyes through a plume of smoke.

"Poor little scut," she said. "Sweetie, I know this

wonderful woman who treats women like—"

"There's nothing wrong with me," Zoe Kohler said hotly.

"Of course there isn't, luv," Maddie said soothingly. "But it's just a shame that you're missing out on one of the greatest pleasures of this miserable life. This woman I know holds classes. Small classes. Five or six women like you. She explains things. You have discussions about what's holding you back. She gives you exercises and things to do by yourself at home. She's got a good track record for helping women like you."

"It's not me," Zoe Kohler burst out. "It's the men."

"Uh-huh," Maddie said, squashing the cigarillo butt in an ashtray. "Let me give you this woman's name."

"No," Zoe said.

Maddie Kurnitz shrugged. "Then let's have some coffee," she suggested. "And some rich, thick, fattening dessert."

She was conscious of other things happening to her. Not only the acceleration of time, and the increasing intrusion of the past into the present so that memories of ten or twenty years ago had the sharp vividness of the *now*. She was also beginning to see reality in magnified close-ups, intimate and revealing.

She had seen the pores in Maddie's nose, the nubby twist of Mr. Pinckney's tweed suit, the fine grain of the paper money in her purse. But not only the visual images. All her senses seemed more alert, tender and receptive. She heard new sounds, smelled new odors, felt textures that were strange and wonderful.

All of her was becoming more perceptive, open and responsive to stimuli. It seemed to her that she could hear the sounds of colors and taste the flavor of a scent. She twanged with this new sensitivity. She saw herself as raw, touched by life in marvelous and sometimes frightening ways.

She wondered that if this growing awareness increased, she might not develop X-ray vision and the ability to communicate with the dead. A universe was opening up to her, unfolding and spreading like a bloom. It had never happened to anyone before, she knew. She was unique.

It had all started with her first adventure, a night of

fear, anguish and resolve. Then, when it was over, she was flooded with a warm peace, an almost drunken exaltation. When she had returned home, she had stared at herself in a mirror and was pleased with what she saw.

It seemed to her that, for self-preservation, she could not, should not stop. She was rational enough to recognize the dangers, to plan coldly and logically. But logic was limited. It was not an end in itself, a way of life. It was a means to an end, to a transfigured life.

The gratification was not sexual. Oh no, it was not that, although she loved those men for what they had given her. But she did not experience an orgasm or even a thrill when she—when those men went. But she felt a thawing of her hurts. The adventures were a sweet justification. Of what, she could not have said.

"It's God's will," her mother was fond of remarking.

If a friend sickened, a coffee cup was broken, or a million foreigners died in a famine—"It's God's will," her mother said.

Zoe Kohler felt much the same way about what she was doing. It was God's will, and her newfound sensibility was her reward. She was being allowed to enter a fresh world, reborn.

Dr. Oscar Stark, an internist, had his offices on the first floor of his home, a converted brownstone on 35th Street just east of Park Avenue. It was a handsome five-story structure with bow windows and a fanlight over the front door said to have been designed by Louis Tiffany.

The suite of offices consisted of a reception room, the doctor's office, two examination rooms, a clinic, lavatories, storage cubicles, and a "resting room."

All these chambers had the high, ornate ceilings, wood paneling, and parquet floors installed when the home was built in 1909. The waiting room and the doctor's office were equipped with elaborate, marble-manteled fireplaces. There were window seats, wall niches, and sliding oak doors.

Dr. Stark and his wife of forty-three years had found it impossible to reconcile this Edwardian splendor with the needs of a physician's office: white enameled furniture, stainless steel equipment, glass cabinets, and plastic plants. Regretfully, they had surrendered to the demands of his profession and moved their heavy antiques and gloomy paintings upstairs to the living quarters.

Dr. Stark employed a receptionist and two nurses, both RNs. His waiting room was invariably occupied, and usually crowded, from 9:00 A.M. to 7:00 P.M. These hours were not strictly adhered to; the doctor sometimes saw patients early in the morning, late in the evening, and on weekends.

Zoe Kohler had a standing appointment for 6:00 P.M. on the first Tuesday of every month. Dr. Stark had tried to convince her that these monthly visits were not necessary.

"Your illness doesn't require it," he had explained with his gentle smile. "As long as you keep on the medication faithfully, every day. Otherwise, you're in excellent health. I'd like to see you twice a year."

"I'd really prefer to get a checkup every month," she said. "You never can tell."

He shrugged his meaty shoulders, brushed cigar ashes from the lapels of his white cotton jacket.

"If it makes you feel better," he said. "What is it, exactly, you'd like me to do for you every month?"

"Oh . . ." she said, "the usual."

"And what do you consider the usual?"

"Weight and blood pressure. The lungs. Urine and blood tests. Breast examination. A pelvic exam. A Pap test."

"A Pap smear every month?" he cried. "Zoe, in your case it's absolutely unnecessary. Once or twice a year is sufficient, I assure you."

"I want it," she said stubbornly, and he had yielded.

He was a short, blunt teddy bear of a man in his middle sixties. An enormous shock of white hair crowned his bullet head like a raggedy halo. And below, ruddy, pendulous features hung in bags, dewlaps, jowls, and wattles. All of his thick face sagged. It waggled when he moved.

His hands were wide and strong, fingers fuzzed with black hair. He wore carpet slippers with white cotton socks. Unless a patient objected, he chain-smoked cigars. More than once his nurse had plucked a lighted cigar from his fingers as he was about to start a rectal examination.

He was, Zoe Kohler thought, a sweet old man with eyes

of Dresden blue. He did not frighten her or intimidate her. She thought she might tell him anything, *anything*, and he would not be shocked, angered, or disgusted.

On the first Tuesday of that April, the first day of the month, Zoe Kohler arrived at Dr. Stark's office a few minutes early for her 6:00 P.M. appointment. Mercifully, there were only two other patients in the waiting room. She checked in with the receptionist, then settled down with a year-old copy of *Architectural Digest*. It was 6:50 before Gladys, the chief nurse, came into the reception room and gave Zoe as pleasant a smile as she could manage.

"Doctor will see you now," she said.

Gladys was a gorgon, broad-shouldered and wide-hipped, with a faint but discernible mustache. Zoe had once seen her pick up a steel cabinet and reposition it as easily as if it had been a paper carton. Dr. Stark had told her that Gladys was divorced and had a twelve-year-old son in a military academy in Virginia. She lived alone with four cats.

A few moments later Zoe Kohler was seated in Dr. Stark's office, watching him light a fresh cigar and wave the cloud of smoke away with backhand paddle motions.

He peered at her genially over the tops of his half-glasses.

"So?" he said. "Feeling all right?"

"Fine," she said.

"Regular bowel movements?"

She nodded, lowering her eyes.

"What about your food?"

"I eat well," she said.

He looked down at the opened file Gladys had placed on his desk.

"You take vitamins," he noted. "Which ones?"

"Most of them," she said. "A, B-complex, C, E, and some minerals."

"Which minerals?"

"Iron, zinc, magnesium."

"And? What other pills?"

"My birth control pill," she said. "The blood medicine. Choline. Alfalfa. Lecithin and kelp."

"And?"

"Sometimes a Librium. Midol. Anacin. Occasionally a

Darvon for my cramps. A Tuinal when I can't sleep."

He looked at her and sighed.

"Oy gevalt," he said. "What a stew. Believe me, Zoe, if you're eating a balanced diet the vitamins and minerals and that seaweed just aren't needed."

"Who eats a balanced diet?" she challenged.

"What about the choline? Why choline?"

"I read somewhere that it prevents premature senility."

He leaned back and laughed, showing strong, yellowed teeth.

"A young woman like you," he chided, "worrying about senility. Me, *I* should be worrying. Try to cut down on the pills. All right?"

"All right," she said.

"You promise?"

She nodded.

"Good," he said, pushing a buzzer on his desk. "Now go with Gladys. I'll be along in a minute."

In the examination room, she took off all her clothes and put them on plastic hangers suspended from the top edge of a three-paneled metal screen. She draped a sheet about herself. Gladys came in with an examination form fastened to a clipboard.

Zoe stepped onto the scale. Gladys moved the weights back and forth.

"One twenty-three," she announced. "How do you do it? One of my legs weighs one twenty-three. Better put on your shoes, dear; the floor is chilly."

She handed Zoe a wide-mouthed plastic cup.

"The usual contribution, please," she said, motioning toward the lavatory door.

Zoe went in there and tried. Nothing. In a few moments Gladys opened the door a few inches.

"Having trouble?" she asked. "Run some warm water on your hands and wrists."

Zoe did as directed, and it worked. She came back into the examination room bearing half a cup of warm urine. She had filled the cup but, embarrassed, had poured half of it down the sink. She handed the cup to Gladys without looking at her.

Dr. Stark came in a few moments later. He set his cigar carefully aside. Zoe sat in an armless swivel chair of white-enameled steel. The doctor sat on a swivel stool facing her. His bulk overflowed the tiny seat.

"All right," he said, "let's get this critical operation going."

The nurse handed a stethoscope to Stark. He motioned Zoe to drop the sheet. She slid it from her shoulders, held it gathered about her waist.

He warmed the stethoscope on his hairy forearm for a moment, then applied the metal disk to Zoe's chest, sternum, ribcage.

"Deep breath," he said. "Another. Another."

She did as he commanded.

"Fine, fine, fine," he said. He spun her chair around and moved the plate over her shoulders, back. He rapped a few times with his knuckles. "All the machinery is in tiptop condition," he reported.

He hung the stethoscope around his neck and reached to Gladys without looking. The nurse had the sphygmomanometer ready and waiting. Stark wrapped the cuff about Zoe's upper arm and pumped the bulb. Gladys leaned down to take the readings.

"A little high," the doctor noted. "Just a tiny bit. Nothing to worry about. Now let's do the Dracula bit."

Gladys handed him the syringe and needle. She swabbed the inside of Zoe's forearm. Zoe looked away. She felt Dr. Stark's strong fingers feeling deftly along her arm. He found a vein; the needle went in unerringly. He had a light, butterfly touch. Still she felt the needle pierce, her body penetrated. Her tainted blood drained away.

In a few moments, the doctor pressed her arm, withdrew the needle and full syringe. He handed it to Gladys. The nurse set it aside, applied a small, round adhesive patch to the puncture in Zoe's arm.

"Now for the fun part," Dr. Oscar Stark said.

He hitched his wheeled stool closer and stared critically at Zoe Kohler's naked bosom through his half-glasses. He began to palpate her breasts. She hung her head. Through half-closed eyes she watched his furred fingers moving over her flesh. Like black caterpillars.

He used the flats of his wide fingertips, moving his hand in a small circle to feel the tissue under the skin. He examined each breast thoroughly, probing to the middle of her chest and under her arms. He finished by squeezing each nipple gently to detect exudation. By that time, Zoe Kohler had her eyes tightly shut.

"A-Okay," Stark said. "You can wake up now. Do you examine your breasts yourself, Zoe?"

"Uh . . . no, I don't."

"Why not? I showed you how."

"I, ah, rather have it done by a doctor. A professional."

"Uh-huh. Do you jog?"

"No."

"Good. You'd be surprised at how many women I'm getting with their boobs down to their knees. If you start to jog, make sure you wear a firm bra. All right, let's ride the iron pony."

Gladys assisted her onto the padded examination table, adjusted the pillow under her head. She placed Zoe's heels in the stirrups, smoothed the sheet to cover her body down to the waist. Dr. Stark, propelling himself with his feet, wheeled over to place himself between Zoe's legs. The nurse helped him into rubber gloves.

He leaned close, peering. He examined the vulva, using one hand to open the entrance to the vagina. He pushed back the clitoral hood. Then he reached sideways, and the nurse smacked a plastic speculum into his palm.

"Tell me if it hurts," the doctor said. "It shouldn't; it's your size."

He inserted the speculum slowly and gently, pressing with one finger on the bottom wall of her vagina to guide the instrument. Once inserted, the handle was turned to spread and lock the blades. They locked with an audible click. Zoe was expecting the sound, but couldn't resist twitching when she heard the crack.

"All right?" Dr. Stark asked.

"Fine," she said faintly.

She stared at the ceiling, biting on her lower lip. She felt no pain. Only the humiliation.

"Relax," he said. "It'll help if you try to relax. You're all rigid. Take deep breaths."

She tried to relax. She thought of blue skies, fair fields, calm waters. She breathed deeply.

"Spatula," the doctor said in a low voice.

She felt nothing, but knew he was getting the Pap

smear, the plastic spatula scraping cells from her cervix. Part of Zoe Kohler ravaged and removed from her.

Stark and the nurse worked swiftly, efficiently. In a moment, the spatula was withdrawn, the speculum closed. She understood it was being withdrawn. Something, a stretched fullness, was subsiding.

Then Dr. Oscar, that sweet, sweet teddy bear of a man, was standing between her legs.

"Don't tense up," he cautioned.

He inserted two gloved fingers into her vagina slowly, pressing the walls apart as he went. He placed his other hand flat on her groin. Fingers pressed gently upward, palm downward.

"Pain?" he asked.

"No," she gasped.

"Tenderness?"

"No."

He began to probe her abdomen, feeling both sides, the center, down toward the junction of her thighs.

"Pain here?"

"No."

"Anything here?"

"No."

"Here?"

"No."

"Just another minute now."

She waited, knowing what was coming.

Slowly, easily, he inserted one gloved finger, coated with a jelly, into her rectum. Between that finger and the one still within her vagina, he felt the muscular wall separating the two passages as the fingertips of his other hand pressed deep into her groin.

She had been staring wide-eyed at the ceiling. She was determined not to cry. It was not the pain; she felt no pain. A twinge now and then, a sensation of being stretched, opened to the foreign world, but no pain. So why did she have to fight to hold back her tears? She did not know.

Slowly, easily, gently, fingers and hands were withdrawn. Dr. Stark stripped off his gloves. He slapped her bare knee lightly.

"Beautiful," he said. "Not a thing wrong. You're in great shape. Get dressed and stop by my office."

He reclaimed his cigar and lumbered out.

Gladys helped her off the table. Her legs were trembling. The big nurse held her until her knees steadied.

"Okay?" she asked.

"Fine. Thank you, Gladys."

"There are tissues in the bathroom if you have any jelly on you. You can go right into the doctor's when you're dressed."

She put on her clothes slowly. Drew a comb through her hair. She felt drained and, somehow, satisfied and content.

Dr. Stark was slumped behind his desk, his glasses pushed up atop that cloud of snowy hair. He rubbed his lined forehead wearily.

"Everything looks normal," he reported to Zoe. "We'll have the reports of the lab tests in three days. I don't anticipate anything unusual. If there is, I'll call. If not, I won't."

"Can I call?" she asked anxiously. "If I don't hear from you? In three or four days?"

"Sure," he said equably. "Why not?"

He put the short stub of his cigar aside. He yawned, showing those big, stained teeth. Then he laced his fingers comfortably across his thick middle. He regarded her kindly.

"Regular periods, Zoe?"

"Oh yes," she said. "Twenty-six or -seven or -eight days. Around there."

"Good," he said. "When's the next?"

"April tenth," she said promptly.

"Still have the cramps?"

"Yes."

"When do they start?"

"A day or two before."

"Severe?"

"They get worse. They don't stop until I begin to bleed."

He made an expression, a wince, then shook his head.

"I told you, Zoe, I can't find any physical cause. I wish you'd take my advice and see, uh, a counselor."

"Everyone wants me to see a shrink!" she burst out.

He looked up sharply. "Everyone?"

She wouldn't look at him. "A friend."

"And what did you say?"

"No."

He sighed. "Well, it's your body and your life. But you shouldn't have to suffer that. The cramps, I mean."

"They're not so bad," she said.

But they were.

At about 8:30 that evening, Dr. Oscar Stark pushed a button fixed to the doorjamb of his office. It rang a buzzer upstairs in the kitchen and alerted his wife that he'd be up in ten or fifteen minutes, ready for dinner.

He had already said goodnight to his receptionist and nurses. He took off his white cotton jacket. He washed up in one of the lavatories. He donned a worn velvet smoking jacket, so old that the elbows shone. He wandered tiredly through the first floor offices, turning off lights, making certain the drug cabinet was locked, trying doors and windows.

He climbed the broad staircase slowly, pulling himself along with the banister. Once again he vowed that he would retire in two years. Sell the practice and the building. Spend a year breaking in the new man.

Then he and Berthe would leave New York. Buy a condominium in Florida. Most of their friends had already gone. The children had married and left. He and Berthe deserved some rest. At peace. In the sun.

He knew it would never happen.

That night Berthe had prepared mushroom-and-barley soup, his favorite, and a pot roast made with first-cut brisket. His spirits soared. He had a Scotch highball and lighted a cigar.

"It was a hard day?" his wife asked.

"No better or worse than usual," he said.

She looked at him narrowly.

"That Zoe Kohler woman?" she said.

He was astonished. "You know about her?"

"Of course. You told me."

"I did?"

"Twice," she said, nodding. "The first Tuesday of every month."

"Oh-ho," he said, looking at her lovingly. "Now I understand the mushroom-and-barley soup."

"The first Tuesday of every month," Berthe said, smiling. "To revive you. Oscar, you think she . . . Well, you know, some women enjoy . . . You told me so."

"Yes," he said seriously, "that's so. But not her. For her it's painful."

"Painful? It hurts? You hurt her?"

"Oh no, Berthe. No, no, no. You know me better than that. But I think it's a kind of punishment for her. That's how she sees it."

"Punishment for what? Has she done something?"

"Such a question. How would I know?"

"Come, let's eat."

They went into the dining room. It was full of shadows.

"I don't think she's done something," he tried to explain. "I mean, she doesn't want punishment because she feels guilty. I think she feels unworthy."

"My husband the psychologist."

"Well, that's what I think it is," he repeated stubbornly. "She comes every month for an examination she doesn't need and that she hates. It's punishment for her unworthiness. That's how she gets her gratification."

"Sha," his wife said. "Put your cigar down and eat your soup."

The cramps were bad. None of her pills helped. The pain came from deep within her, in waves. It wrenched her gut, twisted her inside. It was a giant hand, clawing, yanking this way and that, turning her over. She wanted to scream.

She left work early on Wednesday night, April 9th. Mr. Pinckney was sympathetic when she told him the cause.

"Take tomorrow off," he said. "We'll manage."

"Oh no," she said. "I'll be all right tomorrow."

She went directly home and drew a bath as hot as she could endure. She soaked for an hour, running in more hot water as the tub cooled. She searched for telltale stains, but the water remained clear; her menses had not yet started.

She swallowed an assortment of vitamins and minerals before she dressed. She didn't care what Dr. Stark said; she was convinced they were helping her survive. And she sipped a glass of white wine while she dressed. The cramps had diminished to a dull, persistent throbbing.

She regretted the necessity of going up to the Filmore

on West 72nd Street to put on makeup and don her new strawberry blond wig. But she didn't want to risk the danger of having her neighbors and doorman see her transformed.

Also, there was a risk of going directly from her apartment house to the Hotel Coolidge. The cabdriver might remember. A circuitous route was safer.

She had selected the Coolidge because the hotel trade magazine, in its directory of conventions and sales meetings, had listed the Coolidge as hosting two conventions and a political gathering on the night of April 9th. It was an 840-room hotel on Seventh Avenue and 50th Street. Close enough to Times Square to get a lot of walk-in business in its cocktail lounges and dining rooms.

She wore fire-engine-red nylon lingerie embroidered with small hearts, sheer pantyhose with a reddish tint, her evening sandals with their "hookers' heels." The dress, tightly fitted, was a bottle-green silk so dark it was almost black. It shimmered, and was skimpy as a slip, suspended from her smooth shoulders by spaghetti straps.

Two hours later she was seated alone at a small banquette in the New Orleans Room of the Hotel Coolidge. Her trenchcoat was folded on the seat beside her. She was smoking a cigarette and sipping a glass of white wine. She did not turn her head, but her eyes were never still.

It was a small, dimly lighted room, half-filled. A three-piece band played desultory jazz from a raised platform in one corner. It was all relatively quiet, relaxed. Zoe Kohler wondered if she might do better in the Gold Coast Room.

Most of the men who entered were in twos and threes, hatless and coatless, but bearing badges on the lapels of their suit jackets. They invariably headed directly for the bar. There were a few couples at the small tables, but not many.

Shortly after 11:00 P.M., a single man came to the entrance of the New Orleans Room. He stood a moment, looking about.

Come to me, Zoe Kohler willed. *Come to me.*

He glanced in her direction, hesitated, then moved casually toward the wall of banquettes.

Lover, she thought, not looking at him.

He slid behind the table next to hers. She pulled her shoulder bag and trenchcoat closer. The cocktail waitress came over and he ordered a bourbon and water. His voice was a deep, resonant baritone.

He was tall, more than six feet, hunched, and almost totally bald. He wore rimless spectacles. His features were pleasant enough, his cheeks somewhat pitted. The backs of his hands were badly scarred. He wore the ubiquitous name-badge on his breast pocket. Zoe caught a look at it. HELLO! CALL ME JERRY.

They sat at their adjoining tables. She ordered another glass of wine, he another bourbon. They did not speak nor look in each other's direction. Finally . . .

"I beg your pardon," he said, leaning toward her.

She turned to look coldly at him. He blushed, up into his bald head. He seemed about to withdraw.

"Uh, I, ah, uh, wondered if I could ask you a personal question?"

"You may ask," she said severely. "I may or may not answer."

"Uh," he said, gulping, "that dress you're wearing . . . It's so beautiful. I want to bring my wife a present from New York, and she'd look great in that." He added hastily, "Not as good as you do, of course, but I wondered where you bought it, and if . . ." His voice trailed away.

She smiled at him.

"Thank you—" She peered closer at his badge as if seeing it for the first time. "Thank you, Jerry, but I'm sorry to tell you that the shop where I bought it has gone out of business."

"Oh," he said, "that's too bad. But listen, maybe you can suggest a store where I can buy something nice."

Now they had turned to face each other. He kept lifting his eyes from her shoulders and cleavage, and then his eyes would slide down again.

They talked awhile, exploring. He was from Little Rock, Arkansas, and was regional manager for a chain of fast-food restaurants that sold chicken-fried steaks and was about to go the franchise route.

She touched the scars on the backs of his hands.

"What happened?" she asked. "A war wound?"

"Oh no," he said, laughing for the first time. He had a

nice, sheepish laugh. "A stove caught fire. They'll heal. Eventually."

"My name's Irene," she said softly.

He bought them two more rounds of drinks. By that time, she had moved her coat and shoulder bag to her other side, and he was sitting beside her, at her table. She pressed her thigh against his. He drew his leg hastily away. Then it came back.

The New Orleans Room had filled up, every table taken. Patrons were standing two and three deep at the bar. The jazz trio was playing with more verve, music blasting. The distracted waitresses were scurrying about. Zoe Kohler was reassured; no one would remember her.

"Noisy in here," Jerry said, looking about fretfully. "We can't rightly talk."

"Where are you staying, Jerry?" she asked.

"What?" he said. "Snow again; I don't get your drift."

She put her lips close to his ear. Close enough to touch. She repeated her question.

"Why, uh, right here in the hotel," he said, shaken. "The fourteenth floor."

"Have anything to drink in your room?"

"I got most of a pint of sippin' whiskey," he said, staring at her. "Bourbon."

She put her lips to his ear again.

"Couldn't we have a party?" she whispered. Her tongue darted.

"I've never done anything like this before," he said hoarsely. "I swear, I never have."

There was one other couple in the automatic elevator, but they got off on the ninth floor. Jerry and Irene rode the rest of the way alone.

"Notice they got no thirteenth floor?" he said nervously. "It goes from twelve to fourteen. I guess they figure no one would want a room on the thirteenth. Bad luck. But I'm on the fourteenth which is really the thirteenth. Makes no never-mind to me."

She put a hand on his arm.

"You're sweet," she said.

"No kidding?" he said, pleased.

Inside his room, the door locked, he insisted on showing her wallet photographs of his wife, his home, his

Labrador retriever, named Boots. Zoe looked at what she thought were a dumpy blonde, a naked development house with no landscaping, and a beautiful dog.

"Jerry, you're a very lucky man," she said, handling the photos by the edges.

"Don't I know it!"

"Children?"

"No," he said shortly. "No children. Not yet."

She thought he was in his late thirties, maybe forty. No children. That was too bad. But his widow would remarry. Zoe was sure of it; she had that look.

He rummaged in his open suitcase and came up with an almost full pint bottle of bourbon.

"Voilà!" he said, pronouncing it, "Viola." Zoe didn't know if he was making a joke or not.

"I think I'll skip," she said. "All that white wine has got me a tiny bit tipsy. But you go right ahead."

"You're sure?"

"I'm sure."

He poured a small shot into a water glass. His hand was trembling; the bottle neck rattled against the rim of the glass.

"Listen," he said, not looking at her, "I told you I've never done anything like this before, and that's God's own truth. I got to be honest with you; I don't know whether you . . ."

He looked at her helplessly.

She went over to him, held him by the arms, smiled up at him.

"I know what you're wondering," she said. "You're wondering if I want money and if you should pay me before or after. Isn't that so?"

He nodded dumbly.

"Jerry," she said gently, "I'm not a professional, if that's what you think. I just enjoy being here with you. If a man wants to give me a little gift later because he's had such a good time . . ."

"Oh sure, Irene," he said swallowing. "I understand."

"You've got a radio?" she said briskly. "Turn on the radio. Let's get this show on the road."

He turned on the bedside radio. The station was playing disco.

"Wow," she said, snapping her fingers, "that's great. Do you like to dance?"

He took a gulp of bourbon.

"I'm not very good at it," he said.

"Then I'll dance by myself," she said.

She began to move about the room, dipping, swaying, her hips moving. Her arms were extended overhead, fingers still snapping. She bowed, writhed, twisted, twirled. Her heels caught in the heavy shag rug. A shoulder strap slipped off and hung loose.

He sat on the edge of the bed, touching the bourbon to his lips, and watched her with wondering eyes.

"Too many clothes," she said. In time to the music, she sashayed over to him, turned her back, and motioned. "Open me up," she commanded.

Obediently, he drew her back zipper down. It hissed. She slid off the remaining strap, let her dress fall, stepped out. She tossed it onto a chair.

She stood there a moment, facing him, in her heart-flecked lingerie, reddish pantyhose, high heels. They stared at each other. Then the music changed to a tango. She began to swoop and glide about the room.

"I swear to God," he said, his voice a croak, "this is the damndest thing that ever happened to me. Irene, you are one beautiful lady. I just can't believe it."

"You better believe it," she said, laughing. "It's true."

She continued dancing for him until the music ended. An announcer came on, talking about motor oil. Zoe Kohler took off her sandals, wiggled out of her pantyhose. Jerry was staring at the floor.

"Jerry," she said.

He raised his head, looked at her.

"You like?" she said, posing with hands on her waist, weight on one leg. She cocked her head quizzically.

He nodded. He looked frightened and miserable. She went over to him, stood close, between his legs. She pressed his head between her palms, pulled his face into her soft, scented belly.

"You get out of all those clothes, honey," she said throatily. "I have to go make wee-wee. Be back in a minute."

She took her shoulder bag and headed for the bathroom. She glanced back, but he wasn't looking at her. He was staring at the floor again.

She made her usual preparations, thinking that he was a difficult one. He didn't come on. He was troubled. He had no confidence. That wasn't fair.

She came out of the bathroom naked, towel draped over her right forearm and hand. "Here I am!" she said gaily.

He wasn't lying naked under the sheet. He had taken off only his jacket and vest, had loosened his tie and opened his collar. He was still sitting on the edge of the bed, hunched over, elbows on knees. He was turning his glass around and around in his scarred hands. Now it was filled with whiskey, almost to the brim.

When he heard her voice, he turned to look over his shoulder.

"Good lord a'mighty," he said with awe.

She came over to the bed, on the other side. She kneeled behind him. With her left hand, she pulled him gently back until he was leaning against her, pressing her breasts, stomach, thighs.

"Jerry," she said, "what's wrong?"

He groaned. "Irene, this is no good. I just can't do it. I'm sorry, but I can't. Listen, I'll give you money. I hate wasting your time like this. But when I think of my little girl waiting at home for me, I just can't . . ."

"Shh, shh," she said soothingly. She put the soft palm of her left hand on his brow and drew his head back toward her, between her breasts. "Don't think about that. Don't think about a thing."

She let the towel fall free. She plunged the point of the knife blade below his left ear and pulled it savagely to the right, tugging when it caught.

His body leaped convulsively off the bed. Glass fell. Drink spilled. He went flopping to the floor, limbs flailing.

That wasn't what surprised her. The shock was the fountain of blood, the giant spurt, the wild gush. It had gone out so far that gobbets had hit the wall and were beginning to drip downward.

She watched those trickles for a brief moment, fascinated. Then she scrambled across the bed and stood astride him, bent over. He was still threshing, limbs twitching, eyelids fluttering.

He was clothed, but it made no difference. She didn't want to see that knobbed thing, that club. She drove the blade through his clothing into his testicles, with the incantation, "There. There. There."

After a while she straightened up, looked about dully. Nothing had changed. She heard, dimly, traffic sounds from Seventh Avenue. An airliner droned overhead. Someone passed in the outside corridor; a man laughed. Next door, a toilet flushed.

She looked down at Jerry. He was gone, his life soaked into the carpet. The bedside radio was still playing. Disco again. She went into the bathroom for sheets of toilet paper before she handled the radio knob, stopping the music.

She was so careful.

4

Edward X. Delaney found himself obsessed with the puzzle of the two hotel deaths. He tried to turn his mind to other concerns, to keep himself busy. Inevitably, his thoughts returned to the murder of the two men: how it was done, why it was done, who might have done it.

Sighing, he surrendered to the challenge of the mystery, put his feet on his desk, smoked a cigar, and stared at the far wall.

Everything in his cop's instinct and experience told him it was the work of a criminal psychopath, a crazy, a nut. It was almost hopeless to try to imagine a motive. But it didn't seem to be greed; nothing had been stolen.

On impulse, he searched through the pages of an annual diary and appointment book, looking for the section that listed phases of the moon. There was no connection between the full moon and the dates of the slayings. He slammed the desk drawer in disgust.

The problem was, there was no brilliantly deductive way to approach a case in which a random killer selected victims by chance and murdered for apparently no reason. There was no handle, nowhere to start.

Because, Delaney told himself, he had nothing better to do, he wrote out dossiers of the two victims, trying to recall everything Sergeant Abner Boone had told him. Then he headed a third sheet: Perpetrator.

He pored over the known facts about the two victims, trying to find a link, a connection. He found nothing other than what he had mentioned to Boone: they were both middle-aged men, visitors to New York, staying at midtown hotels. That, he knew, meant next to nothing. But in his meticulous way, he made a careful note of it.

The sheet of paper devoted to the killer had few notations:

1. Could be male or female.
2. Wears black nylon wig.
3. Clever; careful; crafty if not intelligent.

Just writing all this down gave him a certain satisfaction. It brought a solution no closer, he knew, but it was a start in bringing order and form to a chaotic enigma. It was the only way he knew to apply logic to solving a crime born of abnormal motives and an irrational mentality.

He was back in his study again, on the morning of March 21st, ruminating about the case.

He was playing with the idea that perhaps the two victims, George T. Puller and Frederick Wolheim, had, at some time in their business careers, employed the same man, and had fired this man, for whatever reasons.

Then, years later, the discharged employee, his resentment turned to homicidal fury, had sought out his two former employers and slashed them to death. A fanciful notion, the Chief acknowledged, but not impossible. In fact, not farfetched at all.

He was still considering this possibility and how it might be checked out when his phone rang. He reached for it absently.

"Edward X. Delaney here," he said.

"Chief, this is Boone," the sergeant said. "I thought you'd like to know . . . I did what you said: took a Crime Scene Unit man back to the room at the Hotel Pierce where Wolheim was chilled. We took measurements on that armchair where the two black nylon hairs were found."

"And?"

"Chief, it was approximate. I mean, when you sit in that chair, it has a soft seat cushion that depresses. You understand? So it was tough getting an exact measurement from the back of the head to the tailbone."

"Of course."

"Anyway," Boone went on, "we did what we could. Then there was no one in the Lab Services Unit or ME's office who could help. But one of the assistant ME's suggested we call a guy up at the American Museum of

Natural History. He's an anthropologist, supposed to be a
hotshot on reconstructing skeletons from bone frag-
ments."

"Good," Delaney said, pleased with Boone's thorough-
ness. "What did he say?"

"I gave him the measurement and he called back within
an hour. He said his estimate—and he insisted it was only
a guess—was that the person who sat in that chair was
about five feet five to five feet seven."

There was silence.

"Chief?" Boone said. "You still there?"

"Yes, sergeant," Delaney said slowly, "I'm still here.
Five-five to five-seven? That could be a smallish man or a
tallish woman."

"Right," the sergeant said. "But it's *something*, isn't it,
Chief? I mean, it's more than we had before."

"Of course," Edward X. Delaney said, as heartily as he
could. He didn't want to say how frail that clue was; the
sergeant would know that. "How are you getting along
with Slavin?"

"Okay," Boone said, lowering his voice. "So far. He's
been making us recheck everything we did before he came
aboard. I guess I can understand that; he doesn't want to
be responsible for anything that happened before he took
command."

"Uh-huh," Delaney said, thinking that Slavin was a
fool to waste his men's time in that fashion and to imply
doubt of their professional competence.

"Chief, I'd like to ask you a favor . . ."

"Of course. Anything."

"Could I call you about the investigation?" the sergeant
asked, still speaking in a muffled voice. "Every once in a
while? To keep you up on what's going on and ask your
help on things?"

That would be Deputy Commissioner Ivar Thorsen's
suggestion, the Chief knew. "Sergeant, why don't you call
Delaney every day or so? You're friends, aren't you?
Keep him up on the progress of the investigation. See if
he has any ideas."

Which meant that Thorsen didn't entirely trust the
expertise of Lieutenant Martin Slavin.

"Call me any time you like, sergeant," Edward X.
Delaney said. "I'll be here."

"Thank you, sir," Boone said gratefully.

Delaney hung up. On the dossier headed Perpetrator, he added:

4. Approx. 5-5 to 5-7.

Then he went into the kitchen and made a sandwich of sliced kielbasa and Jewish coleslaw, on sour rye. Since it was a "wet" sandwich, he ate it standing over the sink.

There was one person Edward X. Delaney was eager to talk to—but he wasn't sure the old man was still alive. He had been Detective Sergeant Albert Braun, assigned to the office of the District Attorney of New York County. But he had retired about fifteen years ago and Delaney lost track of him.

Braun had joined the New York Police Department with a law degree at a time when the force was having trouble recruiting qualified high school graduates. During his first five years, he served as a foot patrolman and continued his education with special studies at local universities in criminal law, forensic science and, his particular interest, the psychology of criminal behavior.

During his early years in the Department, he had won the reputation of being a dependable, if unspectacular, street cop. His nickname during this period of service was "Arf," from Little Orphan Annie's dog. That hound wasn't a bulldog, but Albert Braun was—and that's how he got the canine monicker.

Delaney remembered that it was said of Braun that if he was assigned to a stakeout in front of a house, and told, "Watch for a male Caucasian, 5-11, 185 pounds, about fifty-five, grayish hair, wearing a plaid sport jacket," you could come back two years later and Arf would look up and say, "He hasn't shown up yet."

Finally, Albert Braun's background, erudition, and intelligence were recognized. He earned the gold shield of a detective, received rapid promotions, and ended up a sergeant in the Manhattan DA's office where he remained until his retirement.

Long before that, he was recognized as the Department's top expert in the history of crime. He possessed a library of more than 2,000 volumes on criminology, and his knowledge of old cases, weapons, and criminal methodology was encyclopedic.

He had been consulted many times by police departments outside New York City and even by foreign police bureaus and Interpol. In addition, he taught a popular course on investigative techniques to detectives of the NYPD and was a frequent guest lecturer at John Jay College of Criminal Justice.

Delaney remembered that Braun had never married, and lived somewhere in Elmhurst, in Queens. The Chief consulted his personal telephone directory, a small, battered black book that contained numbers so ancient that instead of a three-digit prefix some bore designations such as Murray Hill-3, Beekman-5, and Butterfield-8.

He found Albert Braun's number and dialed. He waited while the phone rang seven times. He was about to hang up when a woman came on the line with a breathless "Yes?"

"Is this the Albert Braun residence?" Delaney asked.

"Yes, it is."

He didn't want to ask anything as crude as, "Is the old man still alive?" He tried, "Is Mr. Braun available?"

"Not at the moment," the woman said. "Who's calling, please?"

"My name is Edward X. Delaney. I'm an old friend of Mr. Braun. I haven't seen or spoken to him in years. I hope he's in good health?"

"Not very," the woman said, her voice lowering. "He fell and broke his hip about three years ago and developed pneumonia from that. Then last year he had a stroke. He's recovering from that, somewhat, but he spends most of his time in bed."

"I'm sorry to hear it."

"Well, he's doing as well as can be expected. A man of his age."

"Yes," Delaney said, wanting to ask who she was and what she was doing there. She answered his unspoken question.

"My name is Martha Kaslove. *Mrs.* Martha Kaslove," she added firmly. "I've been Mr. Braun's housekeeper since he fell."

"Well, I'm glad he's not alone," the Chief said. "I had hoped to talk to him, but under the circumstances I won't bother him. I'd appreciate it if you'd tell him I called. The name is Edward X.—"

"Wait a minute," she said. "You knew him when he was a policeman? Before he retired?"

"Yes, I knew him well."

"Mr. Braun doesn't have many visitors," she said sadly. "None, in fact. He doesn't have any family. Oh, neighbors stop by occasionally, but it's really to visit with me, not him. I think a visit from an old friend would do him the world of good. Would you be willing to . . . ?"

"Of course," Delaney said promptly. "I'll be glad to. I'm in Manhattan. I could be there in half an hour or so."

"Good," she said happily. "Let me ask him, Mr. Laney."

"*De*laney," he said. "Edward X. Delaney."

"Hang on just a minute, please," she said.

He hung on for several minutes. Then Mrs. Kaslove came back on the phone.

"He wants to see you," she reported. "He's all excited. He's even putting clothes on and he wants me to shave him."

"Wonderful," the Chief said, smiling at the phone. "Tell him I'm on my way."

He made sure he had his reading glasses, notebook, two ballpoint pens, and a sharpened pencil. He pulled on his heavy, navy-blue melton overcoat, double-breasted. He set his hard black homburg squarely atop his big head. Then he went lumbering over to a liquor store on Second Avenue where he bought a bottle of Glenlivet Scotch. He had it gift-wrapped and put in a brown paper bag.

He stopped an empty northbound cab, got in, closed the door. He gave Albert Braun's address in Elmhurst.

The driver turned around to stare at him. "I don't go to Queens," he said.

"Sure you do," Edward X. Delaney said genially. "Or we can go to the Two-five-one Precinct House, just a block away. Or, if you prefer, you can take me downtown to the Hack Bureau and I'll swear out a complaint there."

"Jesus Christ!" the driver said disgustedly and slammed the cab into gear.

They made the trip in silence, which was all right with Delaney. He was rehearsing in his mind the questions he wanted to ask Albert Braun.

It was a pleasant house on a street of lawns and trees. In spring and summer, Delaney thought, it would look like a residential street in a small town, with people mowing the grass, trimming hedges, poking at flower borders. He had almost forgotten there were streets like that in New York.

She must have been watching for him through the front window, for the door opened as he came up the stoop. She filled the doorway: a big, motherly woman with twinkling eyes and a flawless complexion.

"Mr. Delaney?" she said in a warm, pleasing voice.

"Yes. You must be Mrs. Kaslove. Happy to meet you."

He took off his homburg. They shook hands. She ushered him into a small entrance hall, took his hat and coat, hung them away in a closet.

"I can't tell you how he's looking forward to your visit," she said. "I haven't seen him so alive and chirpy in months."

"If I had known . . ."

"Now you must realize he's been a very sick man," she rattled on, "and not be shocked at the way he looks. He's not bedridden, but when he gets up, he uses a wheelchair. He's lost a lot of weight and the left side of his face—you know—from the stroke . . ."

Delaney nodded.

"An hour," she said definitely. "The doctor said he can sit up an hour at a time. And try not to upset him."

"I won't upset him," the Chief said. He held up his brown paper bag. "Can he have a drink?"

"One weak highball a day," she said firmly. "You'll find glasses in his bathroom. Now I'm going to run out and do some shopping. But I'll be back long before your hour is up."

"Take your time," Delaney said, smiling. "I won't leave until you get back."

"His bedroom is at the head of the stairs," she said, pointing. "On your right. He's waiting for you."

The Chief took a deep breath and climbed the stairs slowly, looking about. It was a cheerful, informal home. Patterned wallpaper. Lots of chintz. Bright curtains. Some good rugs. Everything looked clean and shining.

The man in the bedroom was a bleached skeleton propped up in a motorized wheelchair parked in the middle of the floor. A crocheted Afghan covered his lap and legs and was tucked in at the sides. A fringed paisley shawl was draped about his bony shoulders. He wore a starched white shirt, open at the neck to reveal slack, crepey skin.

His twisted face wrenched in a grimace. Delaney realized that Albert Braun was trying to grin at him. He stepped forward and picked up the man's frail white hand and pressed it gently. It felt like a bunch of grapes, as soft and tender.

"How are you?" he asked, smiling.

"Getting along," Braun said in a wispy voice. "Getting along. How are *you*, Captain? I thought you'd be in uniform. How are things at the precinct? The usual hysteria, eh?"

Delaney hesitated just a brief instant, then said, "You're right. The usual hysteria. It's good to see you again, Professor."

"Professor," Braun repeated, his face wrenching again. "You're the only cop I ever knew who called me 'Professor.'"

"You *are* a professor," Delaney said.

"I was," Braun said, "I was. But not really. It was just a courtesy, an honorary title. It meant nothing. Detective Sergeant Albert Braun. That's who I was. That meant something."

The Chief nodded understandingly. He held out the brown paper bag. "A little something to keep you warm."

Braun made a feeble gesture. "You didn't have to do that," he protested. "You better open it for me, Captain. I don't have much strength in my hands these days."

Delaney tore the wrappings away and held the bottle close to the man in the wheelchair.

"Scotch," Braun said, touching the bottle with trembling fingers. "What makes the heart grow fonder. Let's have one now for old times' sake."

"I thought you'd never ask," Delaney said, and left the old man cackling while he went into the bathroom to mix drinks. He poured himself a heavy shot, tossed it down, and stood there, gripping the sink as he felt it hit. He thought he had been prepared, but the sight of Albert Braun had been a shock.

Then he mixed two Scotch highballs in water tumblers, a weak one for the Professor, a dark one for himself. He brought the drinks back into the bedroom. He made certain Braun's thin fingers encircled the glass before he released it.

"Sit down, Captain, sit down," the old man said. "Take that armchair there. I've got the cushions all broke in for you."

Edward X. Delaney sat down gingerly in what seemed to him to be a fragile piece of furniture. He hoisted his glass.

"Good health and a long life," he toasted.

"I'll drink to good health," Braun said, "but a long life is for the birds. All your friends die off. I feel like the Last of the Mohicans. Say, whatever happened to Ernie Silverman? Remember him? He was with the . . ."

Then they were off and running—twenty minutes of reminiscences, mostly gossip about old friends and old enemies. Braun did most of the talking, becoming more garrulous as he touched the watery highball to his pale lips. Delaney didn't see him swallowing, but noted the level of liquid was going down.

Then the old man's glass was empty. He held it out in a hand that had steadied.

"That was just flavored water," he said. "Let's have another with more kick to it."

Delaney hesitated. Braun stared at him, face mangled into a gargoyle's mask.

All his bones seemed to be knobby, pressing out through parchment skin. Feathers of grayish hair skirted his waxen skull. Even his eyes were filmed and distant, gaze dulled and turned inward. Black veins popped in his sunken temples.

"I know what Martha told you," Braun said. "One weak drink a day. Right?"

"Right," Delaney said. Still he hesitated.

"She keeps the booze downstairs," the skeleton complained. "I can't get at it. I'm eighty-four," he added in a querulous tone. "The game is up. You think I should be denied?"

Edward X. Delaney made up his mind. He didn't care to analyze his motives.

"No," he said, "I don't think you should be denied."

He took Braun's glass, went back to the bathroom. He mixed two more Scotch-and-waters, middling strong. He brought them into the bedroom, and Braun's starfish hand plucked the glass from his hand. The old man sampled it.

"That's more like it," he said, leaning back in his wheelchair. He observed Delaney closely. The cast over his eyes had faded. He had the shrewd, calculating look of a smart lawyer.

"You didn't come all the way out here to hold a dying man's hand," he said.

"No. I didn't."

"Old 'Iron Balls,'" Braun said affectionately. "You always did have the rep of using anyone you could to break a case."

"That's right," Delaney agreed. "Anyone, anytime. There *is* something I wanted to ask you about. A case. It's not mine; a friend's ass is on the line and I promised I'd talk to you."

"What's his name?"

"Abner Boone. Detective Sergeant. You know him?"

"Boone? Boone? I think I had him in one of my classes. Was his father a street cop? Shot down?"

"That's the man."

"Sure, I remember. Nice boy. What's his problem?"

"It looks like a repeat killer. Two so far. Same MO, but no connection between the victims. Stranger homicides. No leads."

"Another Son of Sam?" Braun said excitedly, leaning forward. "What a case that was! Did you work that one, Captain?"

"No," Delaney said shortly, "I never did."

"I was retired then, of course, but I followed it in the papers and on TV every day. Made notes. Collected clippings. I had a crazy idea of writing a book on it some day."

"Not so crazy," Delaney said. "Now this thing that Boone caught is—"

"Fascinating case," Albert Braun said slowly. His head was beginning to droop forward on the skinny stem of his neck. "Fascinating. I remember the last lecture I gave at John Jay was on that case. Multiple random homicides. The motives . . ." His loose dentures clacked.

"Yes, yes," Delaney said hurriedly, wondering if he was losing the man. "That's what I wanted to talk to you about—the motives. And also, has there ever been a female killer like Son of Sam? A woman who commits several random homicides?"

"A woman?" the old man said, raising his head with an effort. "It's all in my lecture."

"Yes," Delaney said, "but could you tell me now? Do you remember if there was ever a case like Son of Sam when a woman was the perp?"

"Martha Beck," Braun said, trying to recall. "A woman in Pennsylvania—what was her name? I forget. But she was a baby-sitter and knew the victims. All kids. A woman at a Chicago fair, around the turn of the century, I think. I'd have to look it up. She ran a boardinghouse. Killed her boarders. Greed, again." His face tried to make a grin. "Ground them into sausages."

"But *stranger* homicides," Delaney insisted. "Any woman involved in a series of killings of *strangers?*"

"It's all in my last lecture," Albert Braun said sadly. "Two days later I fell. The steps weren't even slippery. I just tripped. That's how it ends, Captain; you trip."

He held out his empty glass. Delaney took it to the bathroom, mixed fresh highballs. When he brought the drinks back to the bedroom, he heard the outside door slam downstairs.

Braun's head had fallen forward, sharp chin on shrunken chest.

"Professor?" the Chief said.

The head came up slowly.

"Yes?"

"Here's your drink."

The coiled fingers clamped around.

"That lecture of yours," Delaney said. "Your last lecture. Was it written out? Typed?"

The head bobbed.

"Would you have a copy of it? I'd like to read it."

Albert Braun roused, looking at the Chief with eyes that had a spark, burning.

"Lots of copies," he said. "In the study. Watch this . . ."

He pushed the controls in a metal box fixed to the arm of his wheelchair. He began to move slowly toward the doorway. Delaney stood hastily, hovered close. But

Braun maneuvered his chair skillfully through the doorway, turned down the hallway. The Chief moved nearby, ready to grab the old man if he toppled.

But he didn't. He steered expertly into the doorway of a darkened room and stopped his chair.

"Switch on your right," he said in a faint voice.

Delaney fumbled, found the wall plate. Light blazed. It was a long cavern of a room, a study-den-library. Rough, unpainted pine bookshelves rose to the ceiling. Bound volumes, some in ancient leather covers. Paperbacks. Magazines. Stapled and photocopied academic papers. One shelf of photographs in folders.

There was a ramshackle desk, swivel chair, file cabinet, typewriter on a separate table. A desk lamp. A wilted philodendron.

The room had been dusted; it was not squalid. But it had the deserted look of a chamber long unused. The desktop was blank; the air had a stale odor. It was a deserted room, dying.

Albert Braun looked around.

"I'm leaving all my books and files to the John Jay library," he said. "It's in my will."

"Good," Delaney said.

"The lectures are over there in the lefthand corner. Third shelf up. In manila folders."

Delaney went searching. He found the most recent folder, opened it. At least a dozen copies of a lecture entitled: "Multiple Random Homicides; History and Motives."

"May I take a copy?" he asked.

No answer.

"Professor," he said sharply.

Braun's spurt of energy seemed to have depleted him. He raised his head with difficulty.

"May I take a copy?" Delaney repeated.

"Take all you want," Braun said in a peevish voice. "Take everything. What difference does it make?"

The Chief took one copy of Detective Sergeant Albert Braun's last lecture. He folded it lengthwise, tucked it into his inside jacket pocket.

"We'll get you back to your bedroom now," he said.

But there in the doorway, looming, was big, motherly Mrs. Martha Kaslove. She looked down with horror at the lolling Albert Braun and snatched the glass from his nerveless fingers. Then she looked furiously at Edward X. Delaney.

"What did you do to him?" she demanded.

He said nothing.

"You got him drunk," she accused. "You may have killed him! You get out of here and never, never come back. Don't try to call; I'll hang up on you. And if I see you lurking around, I'll call the cops and have you put away, you disgusting man."

He waited until she had wheeled Albert Braun back to his bedroom. Then Delaney turned off the lights in the study, went downstairs, and found his hat and coat. He called a taxi from the living room phone.

He went outside and stood on the sidewalk, waiting for the cab. He looked around at the pleasant, peaceful street, so free of traffic that kids were skateboarding down the middle of the pavement. Nice homes. Private lives.

He was back in Manhattan shortly after 3:30 P.M. In the kitchen, taped to the refrigerator door—she knew how to communicate with him—was a note from Monica. She had gone to a symposium and would return no later than 5:30. He was to put the chicken and potatoes in the oven at precisely 4:00.

He welcomed the chore. He didn't want to think of what he had done. He was not ashamed of how he had used a dying man, but he didn't want to dwell on it.

There were six chicken legs. He cut them into pieces, drumsticks and thighs, rinsed and dried them. Then he rubbed them with olive oil, sprinkled on toasted onion flakes, and dusted them with garlic and parsley salt. He put the twelve pieces (the thighs skin side down) in a disposable aluminum foil baking pan.

He washed and dried the four Idaho potatoes. He rubbed them with vegetable oil and wrapped them in aluminum foil. Monica and he could never eat four baked potatoes, but the two left over would be kept refrigerated, sliced another day, and fried with butter, chopped onions, and lots of paprika. Good homefries.

He set the oven for 350° and put in chicken and potatoes. He searched in the fridge for salad stuff and found a nice head of romaine. He snapped it into single long leaves, washed them, wrapped them in a paper towel. Then he put them back into the refrigerator to chill. He and Monica liked to eat romaine leaf by leaf, dipped into a spicy sauce.

He made the sauce, a tingly mixture of mayonnaise, ketchup, mustard, Tabasco, salt, pepper, garlic powder, and parsley flakes. He whipped up a bowl of the stuff and left it to meld.

He was not a good cook; he knew that. He smoked too much and drank too much; his palate was dulled. That was why he overspiced everything. Monica complained that when he cooked, sweat broke out on her scalp.

He had accomplished all his tasks in his heavy, vested sharkskin suit, a canvas kitchen apron knotted about his waist. Finished, he untied the apron, took an opened can of Ballantine ale, and went into his study.

He settled down, took a sip of the ale, donned his reading glasses. He began to read Detective Sergeant Albert Braun's last lecture. He read it twice. Between readings, he went into the kitchen to turn the chicken, sprinkling on more toasted onion flakes and garlic and parsley salt. And he opened another ale.

Multiple Random Homicides
History and Motives
by Albert Braun, Det. Sgt., NYPD, Ret.

"Good evening, ladies and gentlemen . . .

"The homicide detective, in establishing the guilt or innocence of a suspect must concern himself—as we have previously discussed—with means, opportunity, and motive. The criminal may choose his weapon and select his opportunity. His motive cannot be manipulated; he is its creature. And it is usually motive by which his crime succeeds or fails.

"What are we to make of the motive of New York's current multiple murderer—an individual described in headlines as 'The .44 Caliber Killer' or 'Son of Sam'? The former title refers to the handgun used to kill six and wound seven—to date. The latter is a self-awarded nickname used by the killer in taunting notes to the police and press and, by extension, to all of us.

"The detective's mind at work: He calls himself 'Son of Sam.' Invert to Samson, who lost his potency when his

long hair was shorn. Then we learn the victims had long
hair. A connection here? A clue? No, I do not believe so.
Too tenuous. But it illustrates how every possibility, no
matter how farfetched, must be explored in attempting to
establish the criminal's motive or plural motives.

"In researching the murky drives of the wholesale
killer, the detective goes to the past history of similar
crimes, and finds literature on the topic disturbingly scant.
Rape, robbery, even art forgery have been thoroughly
studied, analyzed, charted, computerized, dissected,
skinned, and hung up to dry.

"But where are the psychologists, criminologists, sociologists, and amateur aficionados of murder most foul
when it comes to resolving the motives of those who kill,
and kill again, and again, and again. . . ?

"Good reason for this, I think. Cases of mass homicide
are too uncommon to reveal a sure pattern. Each massacre is different, each slaughter unique. Where is the link
between Jack the Ripper, Charles Manson, Unruh, the
Black Dahlia, Speck, the Boston Strangler, Panzram,
William Heirens ('Stop me before I kill again!'), Zodiac
(never caught, that one), the rifleman in the Texas tower,
the Los Angeles 'Trash Bag' butchers, the homosexual
killers in Houston, the executioner of the California
itinerant workers? What do all these monsters have in
common?

"'They were all quite mad,' you say. An observation of
blinding brilliance rivaled only by John F. Kennedy's,
'Life is unfair.'

"No, the puzzling denominator is that they are all male.
Where are the ladies in this pantheon of horror? Victims
frequently, killers never. Oh, there was Martha Beck,
true, but she 'worked' with a male paramour and slaughtered from corruptive greed. Shoddy stuff.

"We are not here concerned with greed as a motive for
multiple homicide. Nor shall we muse on familial tensions
which erupt in the butchery of an entire Nebraska family
or Kentucky clan, including in-laws and, oddly enough,
usually the family dog.

"What concerns us this evening is a series of isolated
murders, frequently over a lengthy period of time, the
victims unrelated and strangers to the slayer. Let us also
eliminate political and military terrorism. What remains

of motive? It is not enough to intone, 'Paranoiac schizophrenic,' and let it go at that. It may satisfy a psychologist, but should not satisfy the homicide detective since labels are of no use to him in solving the case.

"What, then, should the detective look for? What possible motives for random slayings may exist that will help him apprehend the perpetrator?

"Pay attention here; watch your footing. We are in a steamy place of reaching vines, barbed creepers, roots beneath and swamp around. Beasts howl. Motives intertwine and interact. Words fail, and the sun is blocked. Poor psychologists. Poor sociologists. No patterns, no paths. But shivery shadows—plenty of those.

"First, *maniacal lust*. Oh yes. This staple of penny dreadfuls did exist, does exist and, if current statistics on rape are correct, seems likely to increase tomorrow. It might—and that was the first of many 'mights' you will hear from me tonight—it might account for the barbarities of Jack the Ripper, the Boston Strangler, the Black Dahlia, Heirens, Speck, and others whose names, fortunately, escape me. I have a good memory for old lags, con men, outlaws and safecrackers. When it comes to recalling mass killers, my mind fuzzes over. It is, I think, an unconscious protective mechanism. The horror is too bright; it shines a light in corners better left in gloom.

"Sexual frenzy: passion becomes violence through hatred, impotence, a groaning realization of the emptiness of sex without love. Water results; blood is wanted. Then blood is needed, and the throat-choked slayer seeks the ultimate orgasm. And aware—oh yes, aware!—and weeping for himself—never for his victim; his own anguish fills him—he scrawls in lipstick on the bathroom mirror, 'Stop me before I kill again!' As if anyone could rein his demented desire or want to. Leave that to the hangman's noose. It is stated that capital punishment does not deter. It will deter *him*.

"Second, *revenge*. It might serve for Jack the Ripper, the Boston Strangler, Unruh, the killer of those California farmhands, the homosexual executioner in Houston—ah, it might serve for the whole scurvy lot, including the latest addition, Son of Sam.

"Revenge, as a motive, I interpret as hatred of a type of individual or a class of individuals who, in the killer's sick mind, are deserving of death. All women, all blacks, all homosexuals, the poor, the mighty, or attractive young girls with long brown hair.

"When the New York Police Department compared ballistics reports and came to the stunned conclusion that it was up against a repeat killer, one of the first theories advanced involved the long hair of the victims. It was suggested that the murderer, having been spurned or humiliated by a girl with flowing tresses, vowed vengeance and is intent on killing her over and over again.

"More recent reports demolish this hypothesis. Males have been shot (one was killed), and not all the female victims had brown, shoulder-length hair. One was blonde; others had short coiffures.

"But still, revenge as a motive has validity. It has been proposed that Jack the Ripper executed and mutilated prostitutes because one had infected him with a venereal disease. A neat theory. Just as elegant, I believe, is my own belief: that he was the type of man who compulsively sought the company of whores (there are such men) and killed to eradicate his own weakness, eliminate his shame.

"I told you we are in a jungle here, and nowhere does the sun shine through. We are poking around the dark, secret niches of the human heart, and our medical chart resembles antique maps with the dread legends: 'Terra incognita' and 'Here be dragons.'

"Third, *rejection*. Closely allied to revenge, but rejection not by individual or class but by society, the world, life itself. 'I didn't ask to be born,' the killer whines, and the only answer can be, 'Who did?' Is Son of Sam of this rejected brotherhood?

"There was once a mass killer named Panzram. He was an intelligent man, a thinking man, but a bum, a drifter, scorned, abused, and betrayed. He rejected, scorned, and abused in turn. And he slew, so many that it seemed he wanted to kill not people but life itself. Wipe out all humanity, then all things that pulse, and leave only a cinder whirling dead through freezing space.

"*That* was total rejection: rejection of the killer by society, and of society by the killer. Has no one ever turned his back on you, or you to him? We are dealing here not with another planet's language that no one speaks on ours. The vocabulary is in us all, but we dast not give it tongue.

"The flip side of rejection, real or fancied, is the need to assert: 'I *do* exist. I am I. A person of consequence. You must pay attention. And to make certain you do, I shall kill a baker's dozen of those lumps who look through me on the street. Then you will recognize who I am.' Is that what Unruh was thinking as he strolled along the New Jersey street, shooting passersby, drivers of cars, pausing to reload, stopping in stores to pot a few more?

"'I am I. World, take notice!' First, rejection; then, need to prove existence. Murder becomes a mirror.

"Finally, *punk rock, punk fashion, punk souls*. Not 'Small is better than big,' but 'Nothing is better than something.' So, what's new? Surely there were a few wild-eyed Neanderthals rushing about the caves, screaming, 'Down with up!'

"We can afford a low-kilowatt smile at combat boots worn with gold lamé bikinis, at the splintered dissonance of punk rock, at the touching fervor with which punkists assault the establishment. We can smile, oh yes, knowing how quickly their music, fashions, language, and personal habits will be preempted, smoothed, glossed, gussied-up, and sold tomorrow via 30-second commercials at highly inflated prices.

"But there are a few punk souls whose nihilism is so intense, who are so etched by negativism and riddled by despair, that they will never be preempted. Never! Anarchy was not invented yesterday; the demons of Dostoevski have been with us always. To the man who believes 'Nothing is evil,' it is but one midget step to 'Everything is good.'

"The nihilist may murder to prove himself superior to the tribal taboo (the human tribe): 'Thou shalt not kill.' Or he may slay to prove to his victims the fallacy and ephemerality of their faith. In either case, the killer is acting as an evangelist of anarchy. It is not enough that *he* not believe; he must convert—at the muzzle of a revolver or the point of a knife.

"Because the hell of punk souls is this: if *one* other person in the world believes, he is doomed. And so the spiritual anarchist will kill before he will acknowledge that he has spent his life in thin sneers while other, more ignorant and less cynical men have affirmed, and accepted the attendant pain with stoicism and resolve.

"The acrid stink of nihilism followed Charles Manson and his merry band on all their creepy-crawlies. And a charred whiff of spiritual anarchy rises from the notes and deeds of Son of Sam. But I do not believe this his sole goad. Two or more motives are interacting here.

"And that is the thought I wish to leave with you tonight. The motives of mass killers are rarely simple and rarely single. We are not earthworms. We are infinitely complex, infinitely chimerical organisms. In the case of multiple random killings, it is the task of the homicide detective to pick his way through this maze of motives and isolate those strands that will, hopefully, enable him to apprehend the murderer.

"Any questions?"

There was nothing wrong with the dinner. The chicken was crisp and tasty. The baked potatoes, with dabs of sweet butter and a bit of freshly ground pepper, were light and fluffy. The sauce for the romaine leaves was not too spicy. And there was a chilled jug of California chablis on the table.

But the meal was spoiled by Monica's mood. She was silent, morose. She picked at her food or sat motionless for long moments, fork poised over her food.

"What's wrong?" Delaney asked.

"Nothing," she said.

They cleaned the table, sat silently over coffee and small anise biscuits.

"What's wrong?" he asked again.

"Nothing," she said, but he saw tears welling in her eyes. He groaned, rose, bent over her. He put a meaty arm about her shoulders.

"Monica, what *is* it?"

"This afternoon," she sniffled. "It was a symposium on child abuse."

"Jesus Christ!" he said. He pulled his chair around next to hers. He sat holding her hand.

"Edward, it was so *awful*," she said. "I thought I was prepared, but I wasn't."

"I know."

"They had a color film of what had been done to those kids. I wanted to die."

"I know, I know."

She looked at him through brimming eyes.

"I don't know how you could have endured seeing things like that for thirty years."

"I never got used to it," he said. "Never. Why do you think Abner Boone cracked up and started drinking?"

She was shocked. "Was that it?"

"Part of it. Most of it. Seeing what people are capable of. What they do to other people—and to children."

"Do you suppose he told Rebecca? Why he started drinking?"

"I don't know. Probably not. He's ashamed of it."

"Ashamed!" she burst out. "Of feeling horror and revulsion and sympathy for the victims?"

"Cops aren't supposed to feel those things," he said grimly. "Not if it interferes with doing your job."

"I think I need a brandy," she said.

After the brandy, and after they had cleaned up the kitchen, they both went into the study. Monica sat behind the desk. The lefthand stack of drawers was hers, where she kept her stationery, correspondence, notepaper, appointment books, etc. She began to write letters to the children: Eddie, Jr., Liza, Mary, and Sylvia.

When she was finished, Delaney would append short notes in his hand. Usually things like: "Hope you are well. Weather here cold but clear. How is it there?" The children called these notes "Father's weather reports." It was a family joke.

While Monica wrote out her long, discursive letters at the desk, Edward X. Delaney sat opposite her in the old club chair. He slowly sipped another brandy and read, for the third time, the last lecture of Albert Braun, Det. Sgt., NYPD, Ret.

What Braun had to say about motives came as no surprise. During thirty years in the Department, most of them as a detective, Delaney had worked cases in which all those motives were involved, singly or coexistent.

The problem, he decided, was one that Braun had recognized when he had made a brief reference to labels satisfying the criminologist or psychologist, but being of little value to the investigating detective.

An analogy might be made to a man confronting a wild beast in the woods. An animal that threatens him with bared fangs and raised claws.

In his laboratory, the biologist, the *scientist*, would be interested only in classifying the beast: family, genus, species. Its external appearance, bone structure, internal organs. Feeding and mating habits. From what previous animal forms it had evolved.

To the man in the forest, menaced, all this would be extraneous if not meaningless. All he knew was the fear, the danger, the threat.

The homicide detective was the man in the woods. The criminologist, psychologist, or sociologist was the man in the laboratory. The lab man was interested in causes. The man in the arena was interested in events.

That was one point Delaney found not sufficiently emphasized in Braun's lecture. The other disappointment was lack of any speculation on *why* women were conspicuously missing from the rolls of multiple killers.

Braun had made a passing reference to Martha Beck and other females who had killed many from greed. But a deep analysis of why random murderers were invariably male was missing. And since Braun's lecture had been delivered, the additional cases of the Yorkshire Ripper and the Chicago homosexual butcher had claimed headlines. Both murderers were men.

Delaney let the pages of the lecture fall into his lap. He took off his reading glasses, massaged the bridge of his nose. He rubbed his eyes wearily.

"Another brandy?" he asked his wife.

She shook her head, without looking up. He regarded her intently. In the soft light of the desk lamp, she seemed tender and womanly. Her smooth skin glowed. The light burnished her hair; there was a radiance, almost a halo.

She wrote busily, tongue poking out one cheek. She smiled as she wrote; something humorous had occurred to her, or perhaps she was just thinking of the children. She seemed to Edward X. Delaney, at that moment, to be a perfect portrait of the female presence as he conceived it.

"Monica," he said.

She looked up inquiringly.

"May I ask you a question about that child abuse symposium? I won't if it bothers you."

"No," she said, "I'm all right now. What do you want to know?"

"Did they give you any statistics, national statistics, on the incidence of child abuse cases and whether they've been increasing or decreasing?"

"They had all the numbers," she said, nodding. "It's been increasing in the last ten years, but the speaker said that's probably because more doctors and hospitals are becoming aware of the problem and are reporting cases to the authorities. Before, they took the parents' word that the child had been injured in an accident."

"That's probably true," he agreed. "Did they have any statistics that analyzed the abusers by sex? Did more men than women abuse children, or was it the other way around?"

She thought a moment.

"I don't recall any statistics about that," she said. "There were a lot of cases where both parents were involved. Even when only one of them was the, uh, active aggressor, the other usually condoned it or just kept silent."

"Uh-huh," he said. "But when just one parent or relative was the aggressor, would it more likely be a man or a woman?"

She looked at him, trying to puzzle out what he was getting at.

"Edward, I told you, there were no statistics on that."

"But if you had to guess, what would you guess?"

She was troubled.

"Probably women," she admitted finally. Then she added hastily, "But only because women have more pressures and more frustrations. I mean, they're locked up all day with a bunch of squalling kids, a house to clean, meals to prepare. While the husband has escaped all that in his office or factory. Or maybe he's just sitting in the neighborhood tavern, swilling beer."

"Sure," Delaney said. "But it's your guess that at least half of all child abusers are women—and possibly a larger proportion than half?"

She stared at him, suddenly wary.

"Why are you asking these questions?" she demanded.

"Just curious," he said.

• • • •

On the morning of March 24th, Delaney walked out to buy his copy of *The New York Times* and pick up some fresh croissants at a French bakery on Second Avenue. By the time he got back, Monica had the kitchen table set with glasses of chilled grapefruit juice, a jar of honey, a big pot of black coffee.

They made their breakfasts, settled back. He gave her the Business Day section, began leafing through the Metropolitan Report.

"Damn it," she said.

He looked up. "What's wrong?"

"Bonds are down again. Maybe we should do a swap."

"What's a swap?"

"The paper-value of our tax-exempts are down. We sell them and take the capital tax loss. We put the money back into tax-exempts with higher yields. We can write the loss off against gains in our equities. If we do it right, our annual income from the new tax-exempts should be about equal to what we're getting now. Maybe even more."

He was bewildered. "Whatever you say," he told her. "Oh God, look at this . . ."

He showed her the article headlined: KILLER SOUGHT IN TWO HOMICIDES.

"That's Abner's case," he said. "The hotel killings. The newspapers will be all over it now. The hysteria begins."

"It had to happen sooner or later," she said. "Didn't it? It was only a question of time."

"I suppose," he said.

But when he took the newspaper and a second cup of coffee into the study, the first thing he did was look up the phone number of Thomas Handry in his private telephone directory. Handry was a reporter who had provided valuable assistance to Delaney during Operation Lombard.

The phone was picked up after the first ring. The voice was terse, harried . . .

"Handry."

"Edward X. Delaney here."

A pause, then: "Chief! How the hell are you?"

"Very well, thank you. And you?"

They chatted a few minutes, then Delaney asked:

"Still writing poetry?"

"My God," the reporter said, "you never forget a thing, do you?"

"Nothing important."

"No, I've given up on the poetry. I was lousy and I knew it. Now I want to be a foreign correspondent. Who knows, next week I may want to be a fireman or a cop or an astronaut."

Delaney laughed. "I don't think so."

"Chief, it's nice talking to you after all these years, but I've got the strangest feeling that you didn't call just to say hello. You want something?"

"Yes," Delaney said. "There was an article on page three of the Metropolitan Report this morning. About two hotel murders."

"And?"

"No byline. I just wondered who wrote it."

"Uh-huh. In this case three guys provided information for the story, including me. Three bylines would have been too much of a good thing for a short piece like that. So they just left it off. That's all you wanted to know?"

"Not exactly."

"I didn't think so. What else?"

"Who made the connection? Between the two killings? They were a month apart, and there are four or five homicides every day in New York."

"Chief, you're not the only detective. Give us credit for a little intelligence. We studied the crimes and noted the similarities in the MOs."

"Bullshit," Delaney said. "You got a tip."

Handry laughed. "Remember," he said, "you told me, I didn't tell you."

"Phone or mail?" Delaney asked.

"Hey, wait a minute," the reporter said. "This is more than idle curiosity. What's your interest in this?"

Delaney hesitated. Then: "A friend of mine is on the case. He needs all the help he can get."

"So why isn't he calling?"

"Fuck it," Delaney said angrily. "If you won't—"

"Hey, hold it," Handry said. "I didn't say I wouldn't. But what do I get out of it?"

"An inside track," Delaney said, "that you didn't have

before. It may be something and it may add up to zilch."

Silence a moment.

"All right," the reporter said, "I'll gamble. Harvey Gardner took the call. About a week ago. We've been checking it out ever since."

"Did you talk to Gardner about it?"

"Of course. The call came in about five-thirty in the evening. Very short. The caller wouldn't give any name or address."

"Man or woman?"

"Hard to tell. Gardner said it sounded like someone trying to disguise their voice, speaking in a low growl."

"So it could be a man or a woman?"

"Could be. Another thing . . . Gardner says the caller said, 'The same person did both of them.' Not, 'It's the same killer' or 'The same guy did both of them,' but 'The same *person* did both of them.' What do you think?"

"I think maybe you wouldn't make a bad cop after all. Thanks, Handry."

"I expect a little quid pro quo on this, Chief."

"You'll get it," Delaney promised. "Oh, one more thing . . ."

"There had to be," Handry said, sighing.

"I may need some research done. I'll pay, of course. Do you know a good researcher?"

"Sure," Thomas Handry said. "Me."

"You? Nah. This is dull, statistical stuff."

"I'll bet," the reporter said. "Listen, I've got the best sources in the world right here. Just give me a chance. You won't have to pay."

"I'll think about it," Delaney said. "Nice talking to you."

"Keep in touch," Handry said.

The Chief hung up and sat a moment, staring at the phone. "The same person did both of them." The reporter was right; there was a false note there in the use of the word "person."

It would have to be the killer who called in the tip, or a close confederate of the killer. It seemed odd that either would say, "The same person . . ." That was a prissy way of putting it. Why didn't they say "guy" or "man" or "killer"?

He sighed, wondering why he had called Handry, why

he was becoming so involved in this thing. He was a private citizen now; it wasn't his responsibility. Still . . .

There were a lot of motives involved, he decided. He wanted to help Abner Boone. His retirement was increasingly boring; he needed a little excitement in his life. There was the challenge of a killer on the loose. And even a private citizen owed an obligation to society, and especially to his community.

There was one other factor, Delaney acknowledged. He was getting long in the tooth. Why deny it? When he died, thirty years of professional experience would die with him. Albert Braun would leave his books and lectures to instruct detectives in the future. Edward X. Delaney would leave nothing.

So it seemed logical and sensible to put that experience to good use while he was still around. A sort of legacy while he was alive. A living will.

Detective Sergeant Abner Boone called on the morning of March 26th. He asked if he could stop by for a few moments, and Delaney said sure, come ahead; Monica was at a feminist meeting where she was serving as chairperson for a general discussion of government-financed day-care centers.

The two men had talked almost every day on the phone. Boone had nothing new to report on the killer who was now being called the "Hotel Ripper" in newspapers and on TV.

Boone did say that Lieutenant Martin Slavin was convinced that the murderer was not a prostitute, since nothing had been stolen. Most of the efforts of the cops under his command were directed to rousting homosexuals, the S&M joints in the Village, and known transvestites.

"Well," Delaney said, sighing, "he's going by the percentages. I can't fault him for that. Almost every random killer of strangers has been male."

"Sure," Boone said, "I know that. But now the Mayor's office has the gays yelling, plus the hotel associations, plus the tourist people. It's heating up."

But when Sergeant Abner Boone appeared on the morning of March 26th, he was the one who was heated up.

"Look at this," he said, furiously, scaling a flyer onto Delaney's desk. "Slavin insisted on sending one of these to the head of security in every midtown hotel."

Delaney donned his glasses, read the notice slowly. Then he looked up at Boone.

"The stupid son of a bitch," he said softly.

"Right!" the sergeant said, stalking back and forth. "I pleaded with him. Leave out that business about the black nylon wig, I said. There's no way, *no* way, we'll be able to keep that out of the papers if every hotel in midtown Manhattan knows about it. So it gets in the papers, and the killer changes his wig—am I right? Blond or red or whatever. Meanwhile, all our guys are looking for someone in a black wig. It just makes me sick!"

"Take it easy, sergeant," Delaney said. "The damage has been done; nothing you can do about it. Did you make your objections to Slavin in the presence of witnesses?"

"I sure did," Boone said wrathfully. "I made certain of that."

"Good," Delaney said. "Then it's his ass, not yours. Getting many false confessions?"

"Plenty," the sergeant said. "Every whacko in the city. Another reason I wanted to keep that black nylon wig a secret. It made it easy to knock down the fake confessions. Now we've got nothing up our sleeve. What an asshole thing for Slavin to do!"

"Forget it," Delaney advised. "Let him hang himself. You're clean."

"I guess so," Boone said, sighing. "I don't know what to tell our decoys now. Look for *anyone* in *any* color wig, five-five to five-seven. That's not much to go on."

"No," Delaney said, "it's not."

"We checked out that suggestion you gave me. You know—both victims employing the same disgruntled guy and firing him. We're still working on it, but it doesn't look good."

"It's got to be done," Delaney said stubbornly.

"Sure. I know. And I appreciate the lead. We're grabbing at anything. *Anything*. Also, I remembered what you said about the time between killings becoming shorter and shorter. So I—"

"Usually," Delaney reminded him. "I said *usually*."

"Right. Well, it was about a month between the Puller and Wolheim murders. If there's a third, God forbid, I figure that going by what you say—what you *suggest,* it may be around April third. That would be three weeks after the Wolheim kill. So I'm alerting everyone for that week."

"Won't do any harm," Edward X. Delaney said.

"If there is another one," Boone said, "I'll give you a call. You promised to come over—remember?"

"I remember."

But April 3rd came and went, with no report of another hotel homicide. Delaney was troubled. Not because events had proved him wrong; that had happened before. But he was nagged that this case wasn't following any known pattern. There was no handle on it. It was totally different.

But wasn't that exactly what Albert Braun had said in his last lecture? "Cases of mass homicide are too uncommon to reveal a sure pattern. Each massacre different, each slaughter unique."

Early on the morning of April 10th, about 7:30, Delaney was awake but still abed, loath to crawl out of his warm cocoon of blankets. The phone shrilled. Monica awoke, turned suddenly in bed to stare at him.

"Edward X. Delaney here," he said.

"Chief, it's Boone. There's been another. Hotel Coolidge. Can you come over?"

"Yes," Delaney said.

He got out of bed, began to strip off his pajamas.

"Who was that?" Monica asked.

"Boone. There's been another one."

"Oh God," she said.

Delaney came off the elevator on the 14th floor and looked to the left. Nothing. He looked to the right. A uniformed black cop was planted in the middle of the corridor. He was swinging a nightstick from its leather thong. Beyond him, far down the long hallway, Abner Boone and a few other men were clustered about a doorway.

"I'd like to see Sergeant Boone," Delaney told the cop. "He's expecting me."

"Yeah?" the officer said, giving Delaney the once-over.

He turned and yelled down the corridor, "Hey, sarge!"
When Boone turned to look, the cop hooked a thumb at
Delaney. The sergeant nodded and made a beckoning
motion. The cop moved aside. "Be my guest," he said.

Delaney looked at him. The man had a modified Afro,
a neat black mustache. His uniform fit like it had been
custom-made by an Italian tailor.

"Do you know Jason T. Jason?" he asked.

"Jason Two?" the officer said, with a splay of white
teeth. "Sure, I know that big mother. He a friend of
yours?"

Delaney nodded. "If you happen to see him, I'd
appreciate it if you'd give him my best. The name is
Delaney. Edward X. Delaney."

"I'll remember," the cop said, staring at him curiously.

The Chief walked down the hallway. Boone came
forward to meet him.

"Sorry I'm late," Delaney said. "I couldn't get a cab."

"I'm glad you're late," the sergeant said. "You missed
a mob scene. Reporters, TV crews, a guy from the
Mayor's office, the DA's sergeant, Deputy Commissioner
Thorsen, Chief Bradley, Inspector Jack Turrell—you
know him?—Lieutenant Slavin, and so on and so on. We
had everyone here but the Secretary of State."

"You didn't let them inside?"

"You kidding? Of course not. Besides, none of them
wanted to look at a stiff so early in the morning. Spoil
their breakfast. They just wanted to get their pictures
taken at the scene of the crime and make a statement that
might get on the evening news."

"Did you tell Slavin I was coming over?"

"No, sir, but I mentioned it to Thorsen. He said,
'Good.' So if Slavin comes back and gives us any flak, I'll
tell him to take it up with Thorsen. We'll pull rank on
him."

"Fine," Delaney said, smiling.

He looked around the corridor. There were two ambulance men with a folding, wheeled stretcher and body
bag, waiting to take the corpse away. There were two
newspaper photographers, laden with equipment. The
four men were sitting on the hallway floor, playing cards.

The Chief looked inside the opened door. The usual
hotel room. There were two men in there. One was

vacuuming the rug. The other was dusting the bedside radio for prints.

"The Crime Scene Unit," Boone explained. "They'll be finished soon. The guy with the vacuum cleaner is Lou Gorki. The tall guy with glasses is Tommy Callahan. The same team that worked the Puller and Wolheim kills. They're sore."

"Sore?"

"Their professional pride is hurt because they haven't come up with anything solid. They want this guy so bad they can taste it. This time they rigged up that little canister vacuum cleaner with clear plastic bags. They vacuumed the bathroom, took the bag out and labeled it. Did the same thing to the bed. Then the furniture. Now Lou's doing the rug."

"Good idea," Delaney said. "What have you got on the victim?"

Sergeant Abner Boone took out his notebook, began to flip pages . . .

"Like Puller and Wolheim," he said. "With some differences. The clunk is Jerome Ashley, male Caucasian, thirty-nine, and—"

"Wait a minute," Delaney said. "He's thirty-nine? You're sure?"

Boone nodded. "Got it off his driver's license. Why?"

"I was hoping there might be a pattern—overweight men in their late fifties."

"Not this guy. He's thirty-nine, skinny as a rail, and tops six-one, at least. He's from Little Rock, Arkansas, and works for a fast-food chain. He came to town for a national sales meeting."

"Held where?"

"Right here at the Coolidge. He had an early breakfast date with a couple of pals. When he didn't show up and they got no answer on the phone, they came looking. They had a porter open the door and found him."

"No sign of forced entry?"

"None. Look for yourself."

"Sergeant, if you say there's no sign, then there's no sign. A struggle?"

"Doesn't look like it. But some things are different from Puller and Wolheim. He wasn't naked in bed. He had taken off his suit jacket, but that's all. He's on the floor, alongside the bed. His glasses fell off. His drink spilled. The way I figure it, he was sitting on the edge of the bed, relaxed, having a drink. The killer comes up behind him, maybe pulls his head back, slices his throat. He falls forward onto the floor. That's what it looks like. There's blood on the wall near the bed."

"Stab wounds in the genitals?"

"Plenty of those. Right through his pants. The guy's a mess."

The Crime Scene Unit men moved toward the door carrying their kit bags, cameras, the vacuum cleaner.

"He's all yours," Callahan said to Boone. "Lots of luck."

"Lou Gorki, Tommy Callahan," the sergeant said, introducing them. "This is Edward X. Delaney."

"Chief!" Gorki said, thrusting out his hand. "This is great! I was with you on Operation Lombard, with Lieutenant Jeri Fernandez."

Delaney looked at him closely, shaking his hand.

"Sure you were," he said. "You were in that Con Ed van, digging the street hole."

"Oh, that fucking hole!" Gorki said, laughing, happy that Delaney remembered him. "I thought we'd be down to China before that perp broke."

"See anything of Fernandez lately?" Delaney asked.

"He fell into something sweet," Gorki said. "He's up in Spanish Harlem, doing community relations."

"Who did he pay?" Delaney said, and they all laughed. The Chief turned to Callahan. "What have we got here?" he asked.

The two CSU men knew better than to question why he was present. He was Boone's responsibility.

"Bupkes is what we've got," Callahan said. "Nothing really hot. The usual collections of latents and smears. We even dusted the stiff for prints. It's a new, very iffy technique. Might work on a strangulation. We came up with nil."

"Any black nylon hairs?" Boone said. "Or any other color?"

"Didn't see any," Callahan said. "But they may turn up in the vacuum bags."

"One interesting thing," Gorki said. "Not earth-shaking, but interesting. Want to take a look?"

The two technicians led the way to the corpse alongside the bed. It was uncovered, lying on its side. But the upper torso was twisted, face turned upward. The throat slash gaped like a giant mouth, toothed with dangling veins, arteries, ganglia, muscle, stuff. Unbroken spectacles and water tumbler lay nearby.

To the Chief, the tableau had the frozen, murky look of a 19th century still life in an ornate frame. One of those dark, heavily varnished paintings that showed dead ducks and hares, bloody and limp, fruit on the table, and a bottle and half-filled glass of wine. A brass title plate affixed to the frame: AFTER THE HUNT.

He surveyed the scene. It appeared to him that the murder had happened the way Boone had described it: the killer had come up behind the victim and slashed. A dead man had then fallen from the edge of the bed.

He bent to examine darkened stains in the rug.

"You don't have to be careful," Callahan said. "We got samples of blood from the stiff, the rug, the wall."

"Chances are it's all his," Gorki said disgustedly.

"What's this stain?" Delaney asked. He got down on his hands and knees, sniffed at a brownish crust on the shag rug.

"Whiskey," he said. "Smells like bourbon."

"Right," Gorki said admiringly. "That's what we thought. Where his drink spilled . . ."

Delaney looked up at Boone.

"I've got thirty men going through the hotel right now," the sergeant said. "It's brutal. People are checking in and out. Mostly out. Nobody knows a thing. The bartenders and waitresses in the cocktail lounges don't come on till five tonight. Then we'll ask them about bourbon drinkers."

"Here's what we wanted to show you," Gorki said. "You'll have to get down close to see it. This lousy shag rug fucked us up, but we got shots of everything that shows."

The other three men got down on their hands and knees. The four of them clustered around a spot on the rug where Gorki was pointing.

"See that?" he said. "A footprint. Not distinct, but good enough. The shag breaks it up. Tommy and I figure the perp stood over the stiff to shove the knife in his balls.

He stepped in the guy's blood and didn't realize it. Then he went toward the bathroom. The footprints get fainter as he moved, more blood coming off his feet onto the rug."

On their hands and knees, the four of them moved awkwardly toward the bathroom, bending far over, faces close to the rug. They followed the spoor.

"See how the prints are getting fainter?" Callahan said. "But still, enough to get a rough measurement. The foot is about eight-and-a-half to nine inches long."

"Shit," Delaney said. "That could be a man or a woman."

They looked at him in surprise.

"Well . . . yeah," Gorki said. "But we're looking for a guy—right?"

Delaney didn't answer. He bent low again over the stained rug. He could just barely make out the imprint of a heel, the outside of the foot, a cluster of toes. A bare foot.

"The size of the footprint isn't so important," Callahan said. "It's the distance between prints. The stride. Get it? We measured the distance between footprints. That gives us the length of the killer's step. The Lab Services guys have a chart that shows average height based on length of stride. So we'll be able to double-check that professor up at the museum to see if the perp really is five-five to five-seven."

"Nice," Delaney said. "Very nice. Any stains on the tiles in the bathroom?"

"Nothing usable," Gorki said, "but we took some shots just in case. Nothing in the sink, tub, or toilet drains."

The four men were still kneeling on the rug, their heads raised to talk to each other, when they became conscious of someone looming over them.

"What the fuck's going on here?" an angry voice demanded.

The four men lumbered to their feet. They brushed off their knees. The Chief stared at the man glowering at him. Lieutenant Martin Slavin looked like a bookkeeper who had flunked the CPA exam.

"Delaney!" he said explosively. "What the hell are you doing here? You got no right to be here."

"That's right," Delaney said levelly. He started for the door. "So I'll be on my way."

"Wait a sec," Slavin said, putting out a hand. His voice was high-pitched, strained, almost whiny. "Wait just one goddamned sec. Now that you're here . . . What did you find out?"

Delaney stared at him.

Slavin was a cramped little man with nervous eyes and a profile as sharp as a hatchet. Bony shoulders pushed out his ill-fitting uniform jacket. His cap was too big for his narrow skull; it practically rested on his ears.

Appearances are deceiving? Bullshit, Edward X. Delaney thought. In Slavin's case, appearances were an accurate tipoff to the man's character and personality.

"I didn't find out anything," Delaney said. "Nothing these men can't tell you."

"You'll have our report tomorrow, lieutenant," Lou Gorki said sweetly.

"Maybe later than that," Tommy Callahan put in. "Lab Services have a lot of tests to run."

Slavin glared at them, back and forth. Then he turned his wrath on Delaney again.

"You got no right to be here," he repeated furiously. "This is my case. You're no better than a fucking civilian."

"Deputy Commissioner Thorsen gave his okay," Sergeant Boone said quietly.

The four men looked at the lieutenant with expressionless eyes.

"We'll see about that!" Slavin almost screamed. "We'll goddamned well see about that!"

He turned, rushed from the room.

"He'll never have hemorrhoids," Lou Gorki remarked. "He's such a perfect asshole."

Sergeant Boone walked Delaney slowly back to the elevators.

"I'll let you know what the lab men come up with," he said. "If you think of anything we've missed, please let me know. I'd appreciate it."

"Of course," Delaney said, wondering if he should tell Boone about the phoned tip to the *Times* and deciding against it. Handry had admitted that in confidence.

"Sergeant, I hope I didn't get you in any trouble with Slavin."

"With a rabbi like Thorsen?" Boone said, grinning. "I'll survive."

"Sure you will," Edward X. Delaney said.

He decided to walk home. Over to Sixth Avenue, through Central Park, out at 72nd Street, and up Fifth Avenue. A nice stroll. He stopped in the hotel lobby to buy a Montecristo.

A soft morning in early April. A warming sun burning through a pearly haze. In the park, a few patches of dirty snow melting in the shadows. The smell of green earth thawing, ready to burst. Everything was coming alive.

He strode along sturdily, topcoat open and flapping against his legs. Hard homburg set squarely. Cigar clenched in his teeth. Joggers passed him. Cyclists whizzed by. Traffic whirled around the winding roads. He savored it all—and thought of Jerome Ashley and his giant mouth.

It was smart, Delaney figured, for a detective to go by the percentages. Every cop in the world did it, whether he was aware of it or not. If you had three suspects in a burglary, and one of them was an ex-con, you leaned on the lag, even if you knew shit-all about recidivist percentages.

"It just makes common fucking sense," an old cop had remarked to Delaney.

So it did, so it did. But the percentages, the numbers, the patterns, experience—all were useful up to a point. Then you caught something new, something different, and you were flying blind; no instruments to guide you. What was it the early pilots had said? You fly by the seat of your pants.

Edward X. Delaney wasn't ready yet to jettison percentages. If he was handling the Hotel Ripper case, he'd probably be doing exactly what Slavin was doing right now: looking for a male killer and rounding up every homosexual with a rap sheet.

But there were things that didn't fit and couldn't be ignored just because they belonged to no known pattern.

Delaney stopped at a Third Avenue deli, bought a few things, carried his purchases home. Monica was absent at one of her meetings or lectures or symposiums or colloquies. He was happy she was active in something that interested her. He was just as happy he had the house to himself.

He had bought black bread, the square kind from the frozen food section. A quarter-pound of smoked sable, because sturgeon was too expensive. A bunch of scallions. He made two sandwiches carefully: sable plus scallion greens plus a few drops of fresh lemon juice.

He carried the sandwiches and a cold bottle of Heineken into the study. He sat down behind his desk, put on his reading glasses. As he ate and drank, he made out a dossier on the third victim, Jerome Ashley, trying to remember everything Sergeant Boone had told him and everything he himself had observed.

Finished with sandwiches and beer, he read over the completed dossier, checking to see if he had omitted anything. Then he looked up the number of the Hotel Coolidge and called.

He told the operator that he was trying to locate Sergeant Abner Boone, who was in the hotel investigating the crime on the 14th floor. He asked her to try to find Boone and have him call back. He left his name and number.

He started comparing the dossiers of the three victims, still hoping to spot a common denominator, a connection. They were men from out of town, staying in Manhattan hotels: that was all he could find.

The phone rang about fifteen minutes later.

"Chief, it's Boone. You called me?"

"On the backs of the stiff's hands," Delaney said. "Scars."

"I saw them, Chief. The assistant ME said they looked like burn scars. Maybe a month or so old. Mean anything?"

"Probably not, but you can never tell. Was he married?"

"Yes. No children."

"His wife should know how he got those scars. Can you check it out?"

"Will do."

After Boone hung up, Edward X. Delaney started a fresh sheet of paper, listing the things that bothered him, that just didn't fit:

1. A short-bladed knife, probably a jackknife.
2. No signs of struggles.
3. Two victims with no records of homosexuality found naked in bed.
4. Hairs from a wig.
5. Estimated height from five-five to five-seven.
6. Phoned tip that could have been made by a man or woman.

He reread this list again and again, making up his mind. He thought he was probably wrong. He hoped he was wrong. He called Thomas Handry at the *Times*.

"Edward X. Delaney here."

"There's been another one, Chief."

"So I heard. When I spoke to you a few weeks ago, you said you'd be interested in doing some research for me. Still feel that way?"

Handry was silent a moment. Then . . .

"Has this got anything to do with the Hotel Ripper?" he asked.

"Sort of," Delaney said.

"Okay," Handry said. "I'm your man."

5

Zoe Kohler returned home after her adventure with Jerry. She slid gratefully into a hot tub, putting her head back. She thought she could feel her entrails warm, unkink, become lax and flaccid. All of her thawed; she floated defenseless in amniotic fluid.

When the tub cooled, she sat up, prepared to lather herself with her imported soap. She saw with shock that the water about her knees and ankles was stained, tinged a light pink. Thinking her period had started, she touched herself tenderly, examined her fingers. There was no soil.

She lifted one ankle to the other knee, bent forward to inspect her foot. Between her toes she found clots of dried blood, now dissolving away. There were spots of blood beneath the toes of the other foot as well.

She sat motionless, trying to understand. Her feet were not wounded, nor her ankles cut. Then she knew. It was Jerry's blood. She had stepped into it after he—after he was gone. The blood between her toes was his stigmata, the taint of his guilt.

She scrubbed furiously with brush and washcloth. Then she rinsed again and again under the shower, making certain no stain remained on her skin. Later, she sat on the toilet lid and sprayed cologne on her ankles, feet, between her toes. "Out, damned spot!" She remembered that.

She dried, powdered, inserted a tampon, clenching her teeth. Not against the pain; there was no pain. But the act itself was abhorrent to her: a vile penetration that

145

destroyed her dignity. That little string hanging outside: the fuse of a bomb.

All her life, as long as she could remember, she had been daunted by the thought of blood. As a child, with a cut finger or skinned knee, it had been incomprehensible that her body was a bag, a sack, filled with a crimson viscid fluid that leaked, poured, or spurted when the bag was punctured.

Later, at that dreadful birthday party when her menses began, she was convinced she was going to die.

"Nonsense," her mother had said irritably. "It just means you're not a girl anymore; you're a woman. And you must bear the cross of being a woman."

"The cross." That called up images of the crucified Christ, bleeding from hands and feet. To Him, loss of blood meant loss of life. For her, loss of blood meant loss of innocence, punishment for being a woman.

The cramps began with her early periods and increased in severity as she grew older. In a strange way, she welcomed the pain. It was expiation for her guilt. That dark, greasy monthly flow was her atonement.

She donned her flannel nightgown, went into the kitchen for her vitamins and minerals, capsules and pills. She took a Tuinal and went to bed. An hour later, she was still wide-eyed. She rose, took another sleeping pill, and tried again.

This time she slept.

Harry Kurnitz was having a cocktail party and dinner for employees of his textile company. Maddie called to invite Zoe.

"Harry does this once a year," she said. "He claims it's cheaper than giving raises. Anyway, it's always a big, noisy bash, lots to eat, and people falling-down drunk. All the executives make passes at their secretaries. That's why Harry has it on a Friday night. So everyone can forget what asses they made of themselves by Monday morning. Ernest Mittle will be there, so I thought you'd like to come."

"Thank you, Maddie," Zoe Kohler said.

Ernest had been calling twice a week, on Wednesday and Saturday nights at 9:00 P.M. They talked a long time, sometimes for a half-hour. They nattered about their health, what they had been doing, odd items in the news, movie reviews . . .

Nothing important, but the calls had assumed a growing significance for Zoe. She looked forward to them. They were a lifeline. Someone was out there. Someone who cared.

Once he said:

"Isn't it awful about the Hotel Ripper?"

"Yes," she said. "Awful."

Zoe went to the party directly from work. Harry Kurnitz had taken over the entire second floor of the Chez Ronald on East 48th Street, and Zoe walked, fearing she would be too early.

But when she arrived, the big room was already crowded with a noisy throng. Most of them were clustered about the two bars, but several were already seated at the tables. At the far end of the room, a trio was playing disco, but there was no one on the minuscule dance floor.

Madeline and Harry Kurnitz stood at the doorway, greeting arriving guests. They both embraced Zoe and kissed her cheek.

"Jesus Christ, kiddo," Maddie said, inspecting her, "you dress like a matron at the House of Detention."

"Come on, Maddie," her husband protested. "She looks fine."

"I didn't have time to go home and change," Zoe said faintly.

"That's just the point," Maddie said. "You go to work looking like *that?* You and I have to go shopping together; I'll tart you up. I told Mister Meek you'd be here tonight. He lit up like a Christmas tree." She gave Zoe a gentle shove. "Now go find him, luv."

But Ernest Mittle found her. He must have been waiting, for he came forward carrying two glasses of white wine.

"Good evening, Zoe," he said, beaming. "Mrs. Kurnitz told me you'd be here. She said, 'Your love goddess is coming.'"

"Yes," Zoe said, smiling briefly, "that sounds like Maddie. How are you, Ernie?"

"I've got the sniffles," he said. "Nothing serious, but it's annoying. Would you like to move around and meet people, or should we grab a table?"

"Let's sit down," she said. "I'm not very good at meeting people."

They took a table for four near the wall. Ernest seated her where she could observe the noisy activity at the bars. He took the chair next to her.

"I don't want to get too close," he said. "I don't want you catching my cold. It was really bad for a couple of days, but it's better now."

"You should take care of yourself," she chided. "Do you take vitamin pills?"

"No, I don't."

"I'm going to make out a list for you," she said, "and I want you to buy them and take them regularly."

"All right," he said happily, "I will. Well . . . here's to us."

They hoisted their glasses, sipped their wine.

"I thought it was going to be the flu," he said. "But it was just a bad cold. That's why I haven't asked you out. But I'm getting better now. Maybe we can have dinner next week."

"I'd like that."

"Listen," he said, "would you like to come to my place for dinner? I'm not the world's greatest cook, but we can have, say, hamburgers and a baked potato. Something like that."

"That would be nice," she said, nodding. "I'll bring the wine."

"Oh no," he said. "I'm inviting you; I'll have wine."

"Then I'll bring dessert," she said. "Please, Ernie, let me."

"All right," he said, with his little boy's smile, "you bring the dessert. A small one."

"A small one," she agreed. She looked around. "Who are all these people?"

He began to point out and name some of the men and women moving about the room. It was soon apparent that he had a taste for gossip and the wit to relate scandalous stories in an amusing manner. Once he used the word "screwing," stopped abruptly, looked at her anxiously.

"I hope you're not offended, Zoe?"

"No, I'm not offended."

Ernest told her about office affairs, the personal peccadilloes of some of his co-workers, rumors about others. He pointed out the office lothario and the office seductress—quite ordinary looking people. Then he hitched his chair a little closer, leaned toward Zoe.

"I'll tell you something," he said in a low voice, "but you must promise not to repeat it to a soul. Promise?"

She nodded.

"See that tall man at the end of the bar in front of us? At the right end?"

She searched. "Wearing glasses? In the gray suit?"

"That's the one. He's Vince Delgado, Mr. Kurnitz's assistant. Can you see the woman he's talking to? She's blond, wearing a blue sweater."

Zoe craned her neck to get a better look.

"She's sort of, uh, flashy, isn't she?" she said. "And very young."

"Not so young," he said. "Her name is Susan Weiner. Everyone calls her Suzy. She's a secretary on the third floor. That's our Sales Department."

Zoe watched Vince Delgado put his arm about Susan Weiner's waist and pull her close. They were both laughing.

"Are they having an affair?" she asked Ernest Mittle.

"She is," he said, eyes bright with malice, "but not with Vince. Mr. Kurnitz."

She looked at him. "You're joking?"

He held up a hand, palm outward.

"I swear. But Zoe," he added nervously, "you've got to promise not to repeat this. Especially to Mrs. Kurnitz. Please. It could mean my job."

"I won't say a word." She turned again to stare at the blonde in the blue sweater. "Ernie, are you sure?"

"It's all over the office," he said, nodding. "They think no one knows. Everyone knows."

Zoe finished her wine. Mittle rose immediately, took their glasses, headed for the bar.

"Refill time," he said gaily.

While he was gone, Zoe watched the woman at the bar. She seemed very intimate with Vince Delgado, putting a hand on his arm, smiling at something he said, touching his face lightly, affectionately. They acted like lovers.

Zoe saw them take their drinks, walk over to one of the

vacant tables. Susan Weiner was short but full-bodied. Almost chubby. She had a heavy bosom for a woman of her size. Her hair was worn in frizzy curls. Zoe Kohler thought she looked cheap. She looked available. Soft and complaisant.

Ernest came back with two more glasses of wine.

"I still can't believe it," Zoe said. "She looks so involved with the man she's with."

"Vince?" he said. "He's the 'beard.' That's what they call the other man who pretends to be the lover. He and Suzy and Mr. Kurnitz go out to lunch together, or dinner, or work late. If they're seen, everyone's supposed to think she's with Vince. She's not married, and he's divorced. But she's really with Mr. Kurnitz. Everyone in the office knows it."

"That's so—so sordid," she burst out.

He shrugged.

"What does he see in her?" she demanded.

"Suzy? She's really a very nice person. Pleasant and cheerful. Always ready to do someone a favor."

"Apparently."

"No, you know what I mean. I think if you met her, you'd like her. Zoe, I hope you won't breathe a word of this to Mrs. Kurnitz."

"I won't say anything. I wouldn't hurt her like that. But she'll probably find out, eventually."

"Probably. He just doesn't seem to care. Mr. Kurnitz, that is."

"Ernie, why do men do things like that?"

"Oh, I don't know . . . Mrs. Kurnitz comes on strong; you know that. She's loud and brassy and sort of throws herself around. I know she's a lot of fun, but that can be wearing all the time. Maybe Mr. Kurnitz wants someone a little quieter and more submissive."

"And she's younger than Maddie."

"Yes. That, too."

"It's just not fair," Zoe Kohler said.

"Well . . ." he said, sighing, "I guess not. But that's the way things are."

"I know," she said dully. "That's why I'm divorced."

He put a hand over hers.

"I hope I haven't upset you, Zoe. I guess I shouldn't

have told you."

"That's all right," she said. "It just makes me feel so sad and old-fashioned. When I got married, I thought it would be forever. I never even thought of divorce. I mean, I didn't think, Well, if this doesn't work out, we can always split up. I really thought it would be till death do us part. I was such a simp."

"These things happen," he said, but she would not be comforted.

"It's just so awful," she said. "I can't tell you how ugly it is. People get married and, uh, sleep together for a year or two. Then they wave goodbye and go somewhere else and sleep with someone else. Like animals."

"It doesn't have to be that way," he said in a low voice, looking down at their clasped hands. "Really it doesn't, Zoe."

Dinner was served at seven o'clock: roasted Rock Cornish hens with wild rice, baby carrots, and a salad of escarole and Bibb lettuce. Baked Alaska for dessert. Bottles of wine on every table and, with coffee, a selection of brandies and liqueurs.

Harry Kurnitz made a short, funny speech, and his employees applauded mightily. Then the trio started playing disco again; several couples got up to dance. Guests who lived in the suburbs thanked host and hostess and departed.

"Would you care to dance, Zoe?" Ernest Mittle asked politely. "I'm not very good with that kind of music, but . . ."

"Oh no," she said. "Thank you, but I can't dance to that at all. I'd like to, but I don't know how. Would you be angry if I left early? I ate so much, I'd really like to get home and just relax."

"Me, too," he said. "I think my cold is coming back; I'm all stuffed up. I have an inhaler at home; maybe that will help."

"Take some Anacin or aspirin," Zoe advised, "and get into bed."

"I will."

"Be sure to cover up and keep warm. Will you call me tomorrow?"

"Of course."

"I'll have a list of vitamins all made out and what strength to buy. I'll give it to you over the phone. You must promise to take them faithfully, every day."

"I will. Really I will."

They thanked Madeline and Harry Kurnitz for a pleasant evening and slipped away. They reclaimed their coats and hats downstairs. Ernest wanted to tip the hatcheck girl, but she told him that Mr. Kurnitz had taken care of everything.

Mittle said he wasn't feeling so great, and he was going to take a cab home. He would drop Zoe at her apartment house on his way downtown. Would that be all right? She said it would be fine.

The cab was unheated and Zoe saw he was shivering. She pulled his plaid muffler snugly about his throat and turned up the collar of his overcoat. She made him promise to drink a cup of hot tea the moment he got home.

He held the cab until he saw her safely inside her apartment house lobby. She turned to wave. She hoped he would take the hot tea and aspirin, and get into bed and stay covered up. She worried about him.

There were three letters in her mailbox: bills from Con Edison and New York Telephone, and a squarish, cream-colored envelope with her name and address written in a graceful script. Postmarked Seattle. She didn't know anyone in Seattle.

Inside her apartment, door bolted and chained, she turned on the living room lamp, hung away her coat and knitted hat. She glanced out the bedroom window before she lowered the venetian blind and switched on the bedside lamp. She thought she glimpsed movement in the apartment across the street. That man was watching her windows again.

She let the blind fall with a clatter and pulled the drape across. She sat on the edge of the bed and looked at the squarish, cream-colored envelope. She sniffed at it, but it was not scented. The cursive script read simply: "Zoe Kohler." No Miss, or Mrs., or Ms.

She opened the envelope flap slowly, picking it loose. It seemed a shame to tear such thick, rich-looking stationery. Within the envelope was a smaller envelope. Then she knew what it was. A wedding announcement.

Mr. and Mrs. Arnold Foster Clark
request the pleasure of your company
at the marriage of their daughter
Evelyn Jane to Mr. Kenneth Garvin Kohler,
Saturday, the tenth of May, at eleven o'clock,
St. Anthony's Church,
Pine Crest Drive, Rockville, Washington.
Reception immediately following the ceremony.
R.S.V.P. 20190 Locust Court, Rockville, Washington.

Zoe Kohler read this joyous message several times. Her fingertips drifted lightly over the raised type. She folded the small piece of tissue paper that protected the printed copy, folded it and folded it until it was a tiny square, so minute that she could have swallowed it.

The last she had heard of Kenneth, he was living in San Francisco. That's where his alimony checks were postmarked. Now here he was marrying Evelyn Jane Clark in Rockville, Washington.

She read the invitation again. St. Anthony's Church. Did that mean the bride was a Catholic? Marrying a divorced man? Had Kenneth taken instruction or agreed to raise the children in the Catholic faith? Would Evelyn Jane go to San Francisco to live or would the newly married couple make their home in Rockville? Or Seattle?

Pondering these absurd questions kept her mind busy for a few moments. But soon, soon, she had to let herself recognize the enormity of what he had done. Mailing his wedding invitation to her was a malicious gloat. "I have found the woman you could never be. Now I shall be happy."

It would have been simple, kind, *human* to tell her nothing of his marriage. He was legally free; he could do as he pleased; it was no concern of hers. Sending her an announcement was an act of viciousness, of hatred.

Suddenly she was weary. Physically exhausted, her joints watery. And mentally wrung-out and depleted. Energy gone, resolve vanished. She sat hunched over on the edge of the bed, feeling worn-out and empty. The wedding invitation slipped from her fingers, fluttered to the floor.

Her depression had started when Ernest told her about

Harry Kurnitz and that secretary. Zoe did not know why that saddened her. Maddie had been married previously, and so had Harry. A divorce would not be cataclysmic. Just another failure.

And now here was a message artfully printed on rich stationery to remind her of yet another failure: her own. She searched her memory frantically for a success in her life, but could find none.

"*Must* you empty the ashtray every time I put out a cigarette?" Kenneth had complained. "I'll be smoking all night. Can't you wait to clean the goddamned ashtray until we go to bed?"

And . . .

"Jesus, Zoe, do you have to wear that dull sweater again? It's like a uniform. All the other women at the party will be wearing dresses. You're the youngest frump I've ever seen."

And . . .

"You're not falling asleep, are you? I'd hate to come, and hear you snoring. Pardon me all to hell if I'm keeping you awake."

Always complaining, always criticizing. And she never condemned him or blamed him for anything. *Never!* Though there was plenty she could have said:

"*Must* you leave your dirty socks and underwear on the bathroom floor? Someone has to pick it up, and that someone is me."

And . . .

"Did you have to put your hands on every woman at the party? Do you think I didn't notice? Do you know the kind of reputation you're getting?"

And . . .

"Why do you persist when you know I don't enjoy it? I just go through the motions and hope you'll get it done quickly."

But she had never said those things. Because she had been brought up to believe that a good wife must endure and work hard to make her marriage a success, to keep a clean, comfortable home for her husband. Prepare his meals. Listen to his problems sympathetically. Bear his children. And all that . . .

Until one day, ignoring all her efforts, rejecting her martyrdom, he had shouted in fury and frustration,

"You're not definite! You're just not *there!*" And had stormed out. And was now marrying Evelyn Jane Clark.

Zoe Kohler understood that men were different from women in many ways. Their physical strength frightened her. They swaggered through life, demanding. Violence excited them. Secretly, they were all war lovers. They preferred the company of other males. Gentleness was weakness.

Their physical habits appalled her. Even after bathing they had a strong masculine odor, something deep and musky. They chewed cigars, sniggered over dirty pictures, smacked their lips when they ate, drank, or fucked something pleasurable. They broke wind and laughed. Her father had.

She did not hate men. Oh no. But she saw clearly what they were and what they wanted. Every man she had ever known had acted as if he would live forever. They were without humility. They were so sure, so *sure*. Their confidence stifled her.

Worst of all was their hearty bluffness: voice too loud, smile too broad, manner too open. Even the sly, devious ones adopted this guise to prove their masculinity. Maleness was a role, and the most successful men were the most accomplished players.

She picked the wedding invitation from the floor and set it aside. She might send a gift and she might not. She would think about it. Would a gift shame Kenneth, make him realize the spitefulness of what he had done? Or would a gift confirm what he undoubtedly believed, that she was a silly, brainless, shallow woman who still loved him?

She undressed slowly. She showered, not looking at herself in the medicine cabinet mirror. She pulled on her old flannel robe, slipped her feet into tattered mules.

It was still early, barely ten o'clock, and there were things she could do: write checks for her bills, listen to WQXR or watch Channel 13, read a book.

She did none of these things. She took the Swiss Army knife from her purse. She had already washed it in hot water, dried it carefully. She had inspected it, then oiled the blades lightly.

Now she took the knife into the kitchen. She opened the largest blade. Her electric can opener had a knife sharpening attachment. She put a razor edge on the big blade, touching it to the whirling stone lightly, taking care to sharpen both sides of the steel.

To test its keenness, she took the knife into the bedroom, and with short, violent slashes, cut the wedding announcement of Evelyn Jane Clark and Kenneth Garvin Kohler into thin slivers.

On Saturday, April 26th, at about 6:00 P.M., Zoe Kohler left her apartment house and walked east to Second Avenue. She was carrying a bakery box containing four tarts, two strawberry and two apple, she had purchased that afternoon and kept fresh in her refrigerator.

It was a balmy spring evening, sky clear, the air a kiss. Her depression of the previous week had drifted away with a breeze flowing from the south, bringing a scent of growing things and a resurgence of hope. The setting sun cast a warm and mellow light, softening the harsh angles of the city.

She took a downtown bus, got off at 23rd Street, and walked down to Ernest Mittle's apartment on East 20th Street. As always, she was bemused by the infinite variety of New York, the unexpected appearance of a Gothic church, Victorian townhouse, or a steel-and-glass skyscraper.

He lived in a five-story converted brownstone. It seemed to be a well-maintained building, the little front yard planted with ivy, the cast-iron fence freshly painted. Most of the windowsills displayed boxes of red geraniums. The brass mailboxes and bell register in the tiny vestibule were highly polished.

Mittle was listed in Apartment 3-B, and he buzzed the lock a few seconds after Zoe rang his bell. She climbed stairs padded with earth-colored carpeting. The walls were covered with flowered paper in a rather garish pattern. But they were cheerful and unmarked by graffiti.

Ernest was standing outside his open door, grinning a welcome. He leaned forward eagerly to kiss her cheek and ushered her proudly into his apartment. The first thing she saw was a vase of fresh gladiolus. She thought he had bought the flowers because of her, to mark her visit as an occasion. She was touched.

They looked at each other and burst out laughing. They had agreed on the phone not to dress up for this dinner. Zoe was wearing a gray flannel skirt, dark brown turtleneck sweater, and moccasins. Ernest was wearing gray flannel slacks, a dark brown turtleneck sweater, and moccasins.

"His-and-hers!" she said.

"Unisex!" he said.

"Here's our dessert," she said, proffering the bakery box. "Guaranteed no-cal."

"I'll bet," he scoffed. "Zoe, come sit over here. It's the most comfortable chair in the place—which isn't saying much. I thought that, for a change, we might have a daiquiri to start. Is that all right?"

"Marvelous," she said. "I haven't had one in years. I wish I knew how to make them."

"So do I," he said, laughing. "I bought these ready-mixed. But I tried a sip while I was cooking, and I thought it was good. You tell me what you think."

While he busied himself in the tiny kitchenette, Zoe lighted a cigarette and looked around the studio apartment. It was a single rectangular room, but large and of good proportions, with a high ceiling. It was a front apartment with two tall windows overlooking 20th Street.

The bathroom was next to the kitchenette, which was really no more than an alcove with small stove, refrigerator, sink, and a few cabinets. A wooden kitchen table was in the main room. It bore two plastic placemats and settings of melamine plates and stainless steel cutlery.

There were two armchairs, a convertible sofa, cocktail table. There was no overhead lighting fixture, just two floor lamps and two table lamps, one on a small maple desk. Television set. Radio. A filled bookcase.

Ceiling and walls were painted a flat white. There were two framed reproductions: Van Gogh's *Bedroom at Arles* and Winslow Homer's *Gulf Stream*. On the desk were several framed photographs. The sofa and armchairs were covered with a brown batik print and the same fabric was used for the drapes.

What Zoe Kohler liked best about this little apartment was its clean tidiness. She did not think Ernest had rushed about, transforming it for her visit. It would always look like this: books neatly aligned on their shelves, sofa cover pulled taut, desk and lamps dusted—everything orderly. Almost precise.

Ernest brought the daiquiris in on-the-rocks glasses. He sat in the other armchair, pulling it around so that he faced her. He waited anxiously as she sipped her drink.

"Okay?" he asked.

"Mmm," she said. "Just right. Ernie, have you been taking your vitamins?"

"Oh yes. Regularly. I don't know whether it's the placebo effect or what, but I really do feel better."

She nodded, and they sat a moment in silence, looking at each other. Finally:

"I didn't get any nibbles or anything like that," he said nervously. "I was going to have hamburgers and baked potatoes—remember?—but I decided on a meal my mother used to make that I loved: meatloaf with mashed potatoes and peas. And I bought a jar of spaghetti sauce you put on the meat and potatoes. It's really very good—if everything turns out right. Anyway, that's why I didn't get any nibbles; I figured we'd have enough food, and cheese and olives and things like that would spoil our appetites. My God," he said, trying to laugh, "I'm chattering along like a maniac. I just want everything to be all right."

"It will be," she assured him. "I love meatloaf. Does it have chopped onions in it?"

"Yes, and garlic-flavored bread crumbs."

"That's the way my mother used to make it. Ernie, can I help with anything?"

"Oh no," he said. "You just sit there and enjoy your drink. I figure we'll eat in about half-an-hour. That'll give us time for another daiquiri."

He went back to his cooking. Zoe rose and, carrying her drink, wandered about the apartment. She looked at the framed reproductions on the walls, inspected his books—mostly paperback biographies and histories—and examined the framed photographs on the desk.

"Your family?" she called.

"What?" he said, leaning out of the kitchenette. "Oh yes. My mother and father and three brothers and two sisters and some of their children."

"A big family."

"Sure is. My father died two years ago, but Mother is

still living. All my brothers and sisters are living and married. I now have five nephews and three nieces. How about that!"

She went over to the kitchenette and leaned against the wall, watching him work. He did things with brief, nimble movements: stirring the sauce, swirling the peas, opening the oven door to peer at the meatloaf. He seemed at home in the kitchen. Kenneth, she recalled, couldn't even boil water—or boasted he couldn't.

"One more," Ernest said, pouring a fresh daiquiri into her glass and adding to his. "Then we'll be about ready to eat. I have a bottle of burgundy, but I'm chilling it. I don't like warm wine, do you?"

"I like it chilled," she said.

"Do you have any brothers or sisters, Zoe?" he asked casually.

"No," she said, "I'm an only child."

She watched him mash and then whisk the potatoes with butter and a little milk, salt, pepper.

"You said you can't cook," she commented. "I think you're a very good cook."

"Well . . . I get by. I've lived alone a long time now, and I had to learn if I didn't want to live on just bologna sandwiches. But it's not much fun cooking for one."

"No," she said, "it isn't."

It turned out to be a fine meal. She kept telling him so, and he kept insisting she was just being polite. But he was convinced when she took seconds on everything and ate almost half of the small loaf of French bread. And also did her share in finishing the bottle of burgundy.

"That was a marvelous dinner, Ernie," she said, sitting back. "I really enjoyed it."

"I did, too," he said, with his elfin grin. "A little more pepper in the meatloaf would have helped. Coffee and dessert now or later?"

"Later," she said promptly. "Much later. I ate like a pig. Can I help clean up?"

"Oh no," he said. "I'm not going to do a thing. Just leave everything right where it is. Let's relax."

They sat at the littered table, lighted cigarettes. Ernie brought out a pint bottle of California brandy and apologized because he had no snifters. So they sipped the brandy from cocktail glasses, and it tasted just as good.

She said, "It must be nice to grow up in a big family."

"Well . . ." He hesitated, touching the end of his cigarette in the ashtray. "There are some good things about it and some not so good. One of the things I hated was the lack of privacy. I mean, there was just no space you could call your own—not even a dresser drawer."

"I had my own bedroom," she said slowly.

"That would have been paradise. I shared a bedroom with one of my brothers until I went away to college. And then I had *three* roommates. It wasn't until I graduated and came to New York that I had a place of my own. What luxury! It really was a treat for me."

"Do you still feel that way?"

"Most of the time. Everyone gets lonely occasionally, I guess. I remember that even when I was living at home with my brothers and sisters, sometimes I'd be lonely. In that crowd! Of course, all my brothers were bigger. I was the runt of the litter. They played football and basketball. I was nowhere as an athlete, so we didn't have a lot in common."

"What about your sisters?" Zoe asked. "I always wished I had a sister. Did you have a favorite?"

"Oh yes," he said, smiling. "Marcia, the youngest. The baby of the family. We had a lot in common. We used to walk out of town, sit in a field and read poetry to each other. Do you know what Marcia wanted to do? She wanted to be a harpist! Isn't that odd? But of course there was no one in Trempealeau to teach her to play the harp, and my folks couldn't afford to send her somewhere else to school."

"So she never learned?"

"No," he said shortly, pouring them more brandy, "she never did. She's married now and lives in Milwaukee. Her husband is in the insurance business. She says she's happy."

"I suppose we all have dreams," Zoe Kohler said. "Then we grow up and realize how impossible they were."

"What did you dream, Zoe?"

"Nothing special. I was very vague about it. I thought I might teach for a few years. But I guess I'd thought I'd just get married and have a family. That seemed to be the thing to do. But it didn't work out."

"You told me about your mother. What is your father like?"

"Dad? Oh, he's still a very active man. He has a car agency and owns half a real estate firm, and he's in a lot of other things. Belongs to a dozen clubs and business associations. He's always being elected president of this and that. I remember he was away at meetings almost every night. He's in local politics, too."

"Sounds like a very popular man."

"I guess. I hardly saw him. I mean, I knew he was there, but he really wasn't. Always rushing off somewhere. Every time he saw me, he'd kiss me. He smelled of whiskey and cigars. But he was very successful, and we had a nice home, so I really can't complain. What was your father like?"

"Tall and skinny and kind of bent over when he got older. I think he worked himself to death; I really do. He always had two jobs. He had to with that family. Came home late and fell into bed. All us boys had jobs—paper routes and things like that. But we didn't bring home much. So he worked and worked. And you know, I never once heard him complain. Never once."

They sat in sad silence for a few minutes, sipping their brandies.

"Zoe, do you think you'll ever get married again?"

She considered that. "I don't know. Probably not—as of this moment."

He looked at her. "Were you hurt that much?"

"I was destroyed," she cried out. "Demolished. Maddie Kurnitz can hop from husband to husband. I can't. Maybe that's my fault. Maybe I'm some kind of foolish romantic."

"You're afraid to take another chance?"

"Yes, I'm afraid. If I took another chance, and *that* didn't work out, I think I'd kill myself."

"My God," he said softly, "you're serious, aren't you?"

She nodded.

"Zoe, none of us is perfect. And relationships aren't perfect."

"I know that," she said, "and I was willing to settle for what I had. But he wasn't. I really don't want to talk about it, Ernie. It was all so—so ugly."

"All rightee!" he sang out, slapping the table. "We

won't talk about it. We'll talk about cheerful things and
have dessert and coffee and laugh up a storm."

She reached out to stroke his hair.

"You're nice," she said, looking into his eyes. "I'm
glad I met you."

He caught her hand, pressed it against his cheek.

"And I'm glad I met you," he said. "And I want to
keep on seeing you as much as I can. Okay?"

"Okay," she said. "Now . . . strawberry or apple tart?
Which are you going to have?"

"Strawberry," he said promptly.

"Me, too," she said. "We like the same things."

They had dessert and coffee, chattering briskly about
books and movies and TV stars, never letting the conversation flag. Then they cleared the table and Ernest
washed while Zoe dried. She learned where his plates and
cups and saucers and cutlery were stored.

Then, still jabbering away, they sat again in the
armchairs with more brandy. He told her about his
courses in computer technology, and she told him about
the unusual problems of hotel security officers. They were
both good listeners.

Finally, about eleven o'clock, feeling a bit light-headed,
Zoe said she thought she should be going. Ernest said he
thought they should finish the brandy first, and she said if
they did, she'd never go home, and he said that would be
all right, too. They both laughed, knowing he was joking.
But neither was sure.

Ernie said he'd see her home, but she refused, saying
she'd take a taxi and would be perfectly safe. They finally
agreed that he'd go out with her, see her into a cab, and
she'd call the moment she was in her own apartment.

"If you don't phone within twenty minutes," he said,
"I'll call out the Marines."

They stood and she moved to him, so abruptly that he
staggered back. She clasped him in her arms, put her face
close to his.

"A lovely, lovely evening," she said. "Thank you so
very much."

"Thank you, Zoe. We'll do it again and again and
again."

She pressed her lips against his: a dry, warm, firm kiss.
She drew away, stroked his fine hair.

"You are a dear, sweet man," she said, "and I like you very much. You won't just drop me, will you, Ernie?"

"Zoe!" he cried. "Of course not! What kind of a man do you think I am?"

"Oh . . ." she said confusedly, "I'm all mixed up. I don't know what to think about you."

"Think the best," he said. "Please. We need each other."

"We do," she said throatily. "We really do."

They kissed again, standing and clasped, swaying. It was a close embrace, more thoughtful than fervid. There was no darting of tongues, no searching of frantic fingers. There was warmth and intimacy. They comforted each other, protective and reassuring.

They pulled away, staring, still holding to each other.

"Darling," he said.

"Darling," she said. "Darling. Darling."

He went about turning off lamps, checking the gas range, taking a jacket from a pressed wood wardrobe. Zoe went into the bathroom. Because the door was so flimsy and the apartment so small, she ran the faucet in the sink while she relieved herself.

Then she rinsed her hands, drying them on one of the little pink towels he had put out. The bathroom was as clean, tidy, and precisely arranged as the rest of his apartment.

She looked at herself in the medicine cabinet mirror. She thought her face was blushed, glowing. She felt her cheeks. Hot. She touched her lips and smiled.

She examined her hair critically. She decided she would have it done. A feather-cut perhaps. Something youthful and careless, to give her the look of a gamine. And a rinse to give it gloss.

Zoe Kohler brought morning coffee into Mr. Pinckney's office. He was behind his desk. Barney McMillan was lolling on the couch. She had brought him a jelly doughnut.

"Thanks, doll," he said; then, with a grin, "Whoops, sorry. Thank you, Zoe."

She gave him a frosty glance, went back to her own office. She could hear the conversation of the two men. As usual, they were talking about the Hotel Ripper.

"They'll get him," McMillan said. "Eventually."

"Probably," Mr. Pinckney agreed. "But meanwhile the hotels are beginning to hurt. Did you see the *Times* this morning? The first cancellation of a big convention because of the Ripper. They better catch him fast or the summer tourist trade will be a disaster."

"Come to Fun City," McMillan said, "and get your throat slit. The guy must be a real whacko. A *fegelah*, you figure?"

"That's the theory they're going on, according to Sergeant Coe. They're rousting all the gay bars. But just between you, me, and the lamppost, Coe says they're stymied. They had a police shrink draw up a psychological profile, but you know how much help those things are."

"Yeah," McMillan said, "a lot of bullshit. What they really need is one good fingerprint."

"Well . . ." Mr. Pinckney said judiciously, "prints are usually of limited value until they pick up some suspects to match them with. You know, there hasn't been a single arrest. Not even on suspicion."

"But that guy in command—what's his name? Slavin?—he keeps putting out those stupid statements about 'promising leads' and 'an arrest expected momentarily.' It's gotten to be a joke."

"If he doesn't show some results soon," Mr. Pinckney said, "he'll find himself guarding a vacant lot in the Bronx. The hotel association has a lot of clout in this town."

Then the two men started discussing next week's work schedule, and Zoe Kohler began flipping through her morning copy of *The New York Times*. The story on the Hotel Ripper was carried on page 3 of the second section, the Metropolitan Report.

The murder of Jerome Ashley, the third victim, had been front-page news in all New York papers for less than a week. Then, as nothing new developed, follow-up stories dropped back farther and farther.

That morning's *Times* had nothing to add to the story other than the mention of the first cancellation of a large convention directly attributable to the crimes of the Hotel Ripper. The story repeated the sparse description of the suspect: five feet five to five feet seven, wearing a black nylon wig.

But below the news account was an article bylined by Dr. David Hsieh, identified by the *Times* as a clinical psychologist specializing in psychopathology, and author of a book on criminal behavior entitled *The Upper Depths*.

Zoe Kohler read the article with avid interest. In it, Dr. Hsieh attempted to extrapolate the motives of the Hotel Ripper from the available facts, while admitting that lack of sufficient data made such an exercise of questionable validity.

It was Dr. Hsieh's thesis that the Hotel Ripper was driven to his crimes by loneliness, which was why he sought out hotels with their dining rooms, cocktail lounges, conventions, etc. "Places where many people congregate, mingle, converse, eat and drink, laugh and carry on normal social intercourse denied to the Ripper.

"Solitude can be a marvelous boon," Dr. Hsieh continued. "Without it, many of us would find life without savor. But there is this caveat: solitude must be by choice. Enforced, it can be as corrosive as a draft of sulfuric. To be wisely used, it must be sought and learned. And the danger of addiction lingers always. A heady thing, solitude. An elixir, a depressant. One man's triumph, another man's defeat. The Hotel Ripper cannot handle it.

"Solitude decays; mold appears; loneliness makes its sly and cunning infection. Loneliness rots the marrow, seeps through shrunken veins into the constricted heart. The breath smells of ashes, and men become desperate. The police call them 'loners,' making no distinction between those who eat alone, work alone, live alone and sleep alone by choice or through the grind of circumstances. Some desire it; some do not. The Hotel Ripper does not.

"There is a fatal regression at work here. It goes like this: Solitude. Loneliness. Isolation. Alienation. Aggression. In the penultimate stage, the happiness of others becomes an object of envy; in the final, an object of rage. 'Why should they . . . ? When I . . . ?' The Hotel Ripper is a terminal case."

Zoe Kohler put the newspaper aside and stared off into the middle distance. Try as she might, she could not recognize herself in the portrait drawn by Dr. David Hsieh.

Something new was happening to her. She had heretofore never sought to deny her responsibility for what had been done to those three men. She had planned her adventures carefully, carried them out with complete awareness of what she was doing, and reviewed her actions afterward.

She, Zoe Kohler, was the Hotel Ripper. She had not disavowed it. Never. Not for a minute. Indeed, she had gloried in it. Her adventures were triumphs. And the notoriety she had earned had been exciting.

But now she was beginning to feel a curious disassociation from her acts. She felt cleft, tugged apart. She could not reconcile the lustful images of the Hotel Ripper with the gentle memories of a woman who said, "Darling. Darling. Darling."

On May 6th, a few minutes before 6:00 P.M., Zoe Kohler entered the office of Dr. Oscar Stark. There were two patients in the reception room, which usually meant a wait of thirty minutes or so. But it was almost an hour before Gladys beckoned. The nurse led her directly to the examination room.

Zoe was weighed, then went into the lavatory with the wide-mouthed plastic cup. She handed the urine sample to Gladys and sat down, sheet-draped. Dr. Stark came bustling in a few minutes later, trailing a cloud of smoke. He set his cigar carefully aside.

"Well, *well*," he said, staring at Zoe. "What have we here? A new hairdo?"

"Yes," she said, blushing. "Sort of."

"I like it," he said. "Very fetching. Don't you like it, Gladys?"

"I told her I did," the nurse said. "I wish I could wear a feather-cut. It's so youthful."

"Maybe I should get one," the doctor said.

He pulled up his wheeled stool in front of Zoe, warmed the stethoscope on his hairy forearm. She let the sheet drop to her waist. He began to apply the disk to her naked chest and ribcage.

"Mmp," he said. "You didn't run over here from your office, did you?"

"No," Zoe said seriously, "I've been in the waiting room for almost an hour."

He nodded, then felt her pulse, something he rarely

did. He took the examination form and clipboard from Gladys and made a few quick notes. The nurse bent over him and pointed out something on the chart. The doctor blinked.

Gladys wheeled up the sphygmomanometer. Stark wrapped the cuff about Zoe's arm and pumped the bulb. The nurse leaned down to take the reading.

"Let's try that again," Stark said and repeated the process. Gladys made more notes.

The doctor sat a moment in silence, staring at Zoe, his face expressionless. Then he took the blood sample and set the syringe aside.

"Gladys," he said, "that big magnifying glass—you know where it is?"

"Right here," she said, opening the top drawer of a white enameled taboret.

"What would I do without you?" he said.

He hitched the wheeled stool as close to Zoe as he could. He leaned forward and began to examine her through the magnifying glass. He inspected her lips, face, neck, and arms. He peered at the palms of her hands, the creases in her fingers, the crooks of her elbows. He scrutinized aureoles and nipples.

"What are you doing that for?" Zoe asked.

"Just browsing," he said. "I'm a very kinky man. This is how I get my kicks. Zoe, do you shave your armpits?"

"Yes."

"Uh-huh. Open the sheet, please, and spread your legs."

Obediently, eyes lowered, she pulled the sheet aside and exposed herself. He tugged gently at her pubic hair, then examined his fingers. He had come away with a few curly hairs. He inspected them through the magnifying glass.

"Why did you do that?" she asked faintly.

He looked at her kindly. "I'm stuffing a pillow," he said, and Gladys laughed.

He handed the glass back to the nurse and began breast palpation. The pelvic examination followed. Ten minutes later, Zoe Kohler, dressed, was seated in Dr. Stark's office, watching him light a fresh cigar.

He blew a plume of smoke at the ceiling. He pushed his half-glasses atop his halo of white hair. He stared at Zoe, shaking his big head slowly. His pendulous features swung loosely.

"What am I going to do with you?" he said.

She was startled. "I don't understand," she said.

"Zoe, have you been under stress recently?"

"Stress?"

"Pressure. On your job? Your personal life? Anything upsetting you? Getting tense or excited or irritable?"

"No," she said, "nothing."

He sighed. He had been a practicing physician for more than thirty years; he knew very well how often patients lied. They usually lied because they were embarrassed, ashamed, or frightened. But sometimes, Stark suspected, a patient's lies to his doctor represented a subconscious desire for self-immolation.

"All right," he said to Zoe Kohler, "let's go on to something else . . . Are you on a diet? Trying to lose weight?"

"No. I'm eating just the same as I always have."

"You weigh almost four pounds less than you did last month."

Now she was shocked. "I don't understand that," she said.

"I don't either. But there it is."

"Maybe there's been some mistake," she said. "Maybe when Gladys—"

"Nonsense," he said sharply. "Gladys doesn't make mistakes. All right, here's what you've got . . . Your pulse is too rapid, your heart sounds like you just ran the hundred-yard dash, and your blood pressure is way up. It's still in the normal range, but very high-normal, and I don't like it. These are all signs of incipient hypertension—all the more puzzling because low blood pressure is a characteristic of your disease. That's why I asked if you've been under nervous or emotional stress."

"Well, I haven't."

"I'll take your word for it," he said dryly. "But it presents us with a small problem. A slight dilemma, you might say. You're still taking your salt tablets?"

"Yes. Two a day."

"Do you have any craving for additional salt?"

"No, not particularly."

"Well, that's something. The menstrual cramps continue?"

She nodded.

"Better, about the same, or worse?"

"About the same," she said. "Maybe a little worse last month."

"You're due—when?"

"In a few days."

He set his cigar aside. He leaned back in his chair, laced his fingers across his heavy stomach. His china-blue eyes regarded her gravely. When he spoke, his voice was flat, toneless, without emphasis.

"If you were under stress," he said, "it might account for the higher blood pressure. That would be, uh, of some concern in a woman with your condition. Increased stress—even a tooth extraction—results in higher cortisol secretion in the normal individual. But your adrenal cortex is almost completely destroyed. So if you are under stress of any kind, we should increase your cortisone intake to bring your levels up to normal."

"But I'm *not* under stress!" she insisted.

He ignored her.

"Also, while under stress, a higher amount of sodium chloride is required so that your body does not become dehydrated. You haven't been vomiting, have you?"

"No."

"Well, we'll have to wait for the blood and urine tests to come back from the lab before we know definitely that we have a cortisol deficiency. I saw minor signs of skin discoloration, which is usually a sure tip-off. A decrease in armpit and pubic hair is another indication. And there's that weight loss . . ."

"But you're not sure?" she said.

"About the cortisol deficiency? No, I'm not sure. It's the high blood pressure that puzzles me. Cortisol deficiency should be accompanied by lower blood pressure. The small problem I mentioned, the slight dilemma, is this: Ordinarily, for patients with high blood pressure, a reduced- or salt-free diet is recommended. But the nature of your disease demands that you continue to supplement your diet with sodium chloride. So what do we do? For the time being, I suggest an increased cortisone dosage.

What are you taking now?" He flipped down his glasses, searched through her file on his desk. "Here it is—twenty-five milligrams once a day. Is that correct?"

"Yes."

"When do you take it?"

"In the morning. With breakfast."

"Any stomach upset?"

"No."

"Good. I'm going to suggest you take another dose in the late afternoon. That will give you fifty milligrams a day. You may not need it, but it won't do any harm. Try to take the second dose with milk or some antacid preparation. Sometimes the cortisone affects the stomach if it's taken without food. You understand all that?"

"Yes, doctor. But I'm running short of cortisone. I need another prescription."

He pulled a pad toward him and began scribbling.

"While you're at it," Zoe Kohler said casually, "could I have another prescription for Tuinal?"

He looked up suddenly.

"You're suffering from insomnia?"

"Yes. Almost every night."

"Try a highball just before you go to bed. Or an ounce of brandy."

"I've tried that," she said, "but it doesn't help."

"Another dilemma," he mourned. "Ordinarily, with insomnia, I'd reduce the cortisone dosage. But in view of your weight loss and the other factors, I'm going to increase it until the lab tests come in and we know where we are."

"And what about the salt pills?"

He drummed his blunt fingers on the desktop, frowning. Then . . .

"Continue with the salt. Two tablets a day. Zoe, I don't want to frighten you. I've explained to you a dozen times that if you take your medication faithfully—and you must take it for the rest of your days, just like a diabetic—there is no reason why you can't live a long and productive life."

"Well, I've been taking my medication faithfully," she said with some asperity, "and now you say something's wrong."

He looked at her strangely but said nothing. He

completed the two prescriptions and handed them to her. He suggested she call in four days and he'd tell her the results of the blood test and urinalysis.

"Please," he said, "try not to worry. It might be hard not to, but worry will only make things worse."

"I'm not worried," she said, and he believed her.

After she had gone, he sat a moment in his swivel chair and relighted his cigar. He thought he knew the reason for the higher blood pressure. She was under stress, moderate to severe, but certainly acute enough to require an increase in corticosteroid therapy.

She had lied to him for her own good reasons. He wondered to what possible pressures this quiet, withdrawn, rather emotionless woman might be a victim. It wasn't unusual for female patients with her disorder to experience a weakening of the sex drive. But in Zoe Kohler's case, he suspected, the libido had been atrophied long before the onset of her illness.

So if it wasn't sexual frustration, or an emotional problem, it had to be some form of psychic stress that was demanding a higher cortisol level, burning up calories, and setting her blood pounding through her arteries. He felt like a detective searching for a motive when he should be acting like a physician seeking the proper therapy for a disorder that, untreated, was invariably fatal.

Sighing, he dug through Zoe Kohler's file for the photocopies he had made at the New York Academy of Medicine when Zoe had first consulted him. She had just come to New York and had brought along her medical file from her family doctor in Winona.

Stark thought that Minnesota sawbones had done a hell of a job in diagnosing the rare disease before it had reached crisis proportions. It was a bitch of an illness to recognize because many of the early symptoms were characteristic of other, milder ailments. But the Minnesota GP had hit it right on the nose and prescribed the treatment that saved Zoe Kohler's life.

Dr. Oscar Stark found the photocopies he sought. The main heading was "Diseases of the Endocrine System." He turned to the section dealing with "Hypofunction of Adrenal Cortex."

He began to read, to make certain he had forgotten

nothing about the incidence, pathogenesis, symptoms, diagnosis, and treatment of Addison's disease.

Her menstrual cramps began on the evening of May 7th, twenty-four hours after her visit to Dr. Stark. In addition to the low-back twinges and the deep, internal ache, there was now an abdominal pain that came and went.

She felt so wretched on the evening of May 8th, a Thursday, that she took a cab home from work, although the night was clear and unseasonably warm. After she undressed, she probed her lower abdomen gingerly. It felt hard and swollen.

She took her usual dosage of vitamins and minerals. And she gulped down a Darvon and a Valium. She wondered what physiological effect this combination of painkiller and tranquilizer might have.

She soon discovered. Soaking in a hot tub, sipping a glass of chilled white wine, she felt the cramps ease, the abdominal pain diminish. She felt up, daring and resolute.

She had been watching the hotel trade magazine for notices of conventions, sales meetings, political gatherings. It appeared to her that the activities of the Hotel Ripper had not yet seriously affected the tourist trade in New York. Occupancy rates were still high; desirable hotel rooms were hard to find.

The Cameron Arms Hotel on Central Park South looked good to her. During the week of May 4–10, it was hosting two conventions and a week-long exhibition and sale of rare postage stamps. When she had looked up the Cameron Arms in the hotel directory, she found it had 600 rooms, banquet and dining rooms, coffee shop, and two cocktail lounges, one with a disco.

Lolling in the hot tub, she decided on the Cameron Arms Hotel, and pondered which dress she should wear.

But when she stepped from the tub, she felt again that familiar weakness, a vertigo. Her knees sagged; she grabbed the sink for support. It lasted almost a minute this time. Then the faintness passed. She took a deep breath and began to perfume her body.

It took her more than an hour to dress and apply makeup. It seemed to her she was moving in a lazy glow; she could not bring her thoughts to a hard focus. When she tried to plan what she was about to do, her concentration slid away and dissolved.

An odd thought occurred to her in this drifting haze: she wondered if her adventures were habit-forming. Perhaps she was venturing out this night simply because it was something she always did just prior to her period. It was not dictated by desire or need.

She drank two cups of black decaf coffee, but no more wine and no more pills. By the time she was ready to leave, close to 9:00 P.M., her mindless euphoria had dissipated; she felt alert, sharp, and determined.

She wore a sheath of plummy wool jersey with a wide industrial zipper down the front from low neckline to high hem. Attached to the tab of the zipper was a miniature police whistle.

She transferred belongings to the patent leather shoulder bag, making certain she had her knife and the small aerosol can of Chemical Mace. As usual, she removed all identification from her wallet.

She was wearing her strawberry blond wig. Around her left wrist was the gold chain with the legend: WHY NOT?

An hour later she strode briskly into the crowded lobby of the Cameron Arms Hotel, smoking a cigarette and carrying her trenchcoat over her arm. She noticed men turning to gawk, and knew she was desired. She felt serenely indifferent and in control.

She looked in at the cocktail lounge featuring the disco, but it was too noisy and jammed. She walked down the lobby corridor to the Queen Anne Room. It appeared crowded, but dim and reasonably quiet. She went in there.

It was a somewhat gloomy room, with heavy upholstery, fake marquetry, and vaguely Oriental decoration and drapes. All the tables and banquettes were occupied by couples and foursomes. But there were vacant stools at the bar.

Zoe Kohler went into her act. She looked about as if expecting to be met. She asked the hatcheck girl the time as she handed over her trenchcoat. She made her way slowly to the bar, still peering about in the semidarkness.

She ordered a glass of white wine from a bartender dressed like an English publican of an indeterminate period: knickers, high wool hose, a wide leather belt, a shirt with bell sleeves, a leather jerkin. The cocktail waitresses were costumed as milkmaids.

She sat erect at the bar, sipping her wine slowly, looking straight ahead. On her left was a couple arguing in furious whispers. The barstool on her right was empty. She waited patiently, supremely confident.

She had just ordered a second glass of wine when a man slid onto the empty stool. She risked a quick glance in the mirror behind the bar. About 45, she guessed. Medium height, thick at the shoulders, florid complexion. Well-dressed. Blondish hair that had obviously been styled and spray-set.

His features were heavy, almost gross. She thought he looked like an ex-athlete going to fat. When he picked up his double Scotch (he had specified the brand), she saw his diamond pinkie ring and a loose chain of gold links about his hairy wrist.

The Queen Anne Room began to fill up. A party of three raucous men pushed in for drinks on the other side of the single man. He hitched his barstool closer to Zoe to give them room. His shoulder brushed hers. He said, "Pardon me, ma'am," giving her a flash of white teeth too perfect to be natural.

"Getting crowded in here," he offered a moment later.

She turned to look at him. He had very small, hard eyes.

"The conventions, I suppose," she said. "The hotel must be full."

"Right," he said, nodding. "I made my reservation months ago, or I never would have gotten in."

"Which convention are you with?"

"I'm not with any," he said, "exactly. But I came up for the meeting of the Association of Regional Airline Owners and Operators. Here . . ."

He dug into his jacket pocket, brought out a business card. He handed it to Zoe, then flicked a gold cigarette lighter so she could read it.

"Leonard T. Bergdorfer," he said. "From Atlanta, Georgia. I'm a broker. Mostly in sales of regional airlines, feeder lines, freight forwarders, charter outfits—like that. I bring buyers and sellers together. That's why I'm at this shindig. Pick up the gossip: who wants to sell, who wants to buy."

"And have a little fun with the boys?" she asked archly.

"You're so right," he said with a thin smile. "That's the name of the game."

"From Atlanta, Georgia," she said, handing back his card. "You don't talk like a southerner."

He laughed harshly.

"Hell, no, I'm no rebel. But Atlanta is where the money is. I'm from Buffalo. Originally. But I've lived all over the U.S. and A. Where you from, honey?"

"Right here in little old New York."

"No kidding? Not often I meet a native New Yorker. What's your name?"

"Irene," she said.

He had a suite on the eighth floor: living room, bedroom, bath. There was a completely equipped bar on wheels, with covered tubs of ice cubes. Liquor, wine, and beer. Bags of potato chips, boxes of pretzels, jars of salted peanuts.

"Welcome to the Leonard T. Bergdorfer Hospitality Suite," he said. "Your home away from home."

She looked around, wondering if anyone in the Queen Anne Room or on the crowded elevator would remember them. She thought not.

"All the booze hounds are at a banquet right now," he said. "Listening to a fat-ass politician give a speech on the deregulation of airfares. Who needs that bullshit?"

This last was said with some bitterness. Zoe suspected he had not been invited.

"But it'll break up in an hour or so," he went on, "and then you'll see more freeloaders up here than you can count. Stick around, Irene; you'll make a lot of friends."

She was uneasy. It wasn't going the way she had planned.

"I better not," she said. "You boys will want to talk business. I'll have a drink and be on my way."

"You don't want to be like that, honey," he said with his thin smile, "or Poppa will spank. Be friendly. I'll make it worth your while. Now then . . . let me have your coat. We'll have a drink and a little fun before the thundering herd arrives."

He hung her coat in a closet, returned to the bar. He busied himself with bottles and glasses, his back to her.

I could take him now, she thought suddenly. But it wouldn't be—wouldn't be complete.

"You married, sweetie?" he asked over his shoulder.

"Divorced. What about you, Lenny?"

"Still a bachelor," he said, coming toward her with the drinks. "Why buy a cow when milk is so cheap—right?"

She took the wine from him. When she sipped, she made certain she implanted lipstick on the rim so she could identify the glass later.

"What's this for?" he asked, fingering the small whistle hanging from the tab of her zipper.

"In case I need help," she said, smiling nervously.

"You don't look like a woman who needs help," he said with a coarse laugh. "Me, maybe. Not you, babe."

He pulled the zipper down to her waist. The dress opened.

"Hey-hey," he said, eyes glittering. "Look at the goodies. Not big, but choice." He caught up her wrist, read the legend on her bracelet. "Well . . . why not? Let's you and me go in the bedroom and get acquainted before anyone else shows up."

He grabbed her upper arm in a tight grip. He half-led, half-pulled her into the bedroom. He released her, shut the bedroom door. He set his drink and hers on the bedside table. He began to take off jacket and vest.

"Wait, Lenny, wait," Zoe said. "What's the rush? Can't we have a drink first?"

"No time," he said, pulling off his tie. "This will have to be a quickie. You can drink all you like later."

He stripped to his waist rapidly. His torso was thick, muscular. None of the fat she had imagined. His chest, shoulders, arms were furred. He sat down on the bed and beckoned, making flipping motions with his hands.

"Come on, come on," he said. "Get with it."

When she hesitated, he stood again, took one stride to her. He ripped her zipper down its full length. The front of her dress fell apart. He embraced her, hands and arms inside the opened dress, around her naked waist. He pressed close, grinding against her.

"Oh yeah," he breathed. "Oh yeah. This is something like."

His face dug into her neck and shoulder. She felt his tongue, his teeth.

"Wait," she gasped. "Wait just a minute, Lenny. Give a girl a chance. I've got to get my purse."

He pulled away, looked at her suspiciously.

"What for?" he demanded.

"You know," she said. "Female stuff. You get undressed. I'll just be a sec."

"Well, hurry it up," he growled. "I'm getting a hardon like the Washington Monument. All for you, baby."

She ran into the living room. She saw at once that she could easily escape. Grab up shoulder bag and coat, duck out the corridor door. He was half-undressed; he wouldn't follow. She could be long gone before he was able to come after her.

But she wanted to stay, to finish what she had to do. He deserved it. It was the timing that bothered her, the risk. He was expecting guests. Could she complete her job and be out of the suite before the others arrived?

Softly, she locked and chained the corridor door. She went back to the bedroom with her shoulder bag. He was pulling down his trousers and undershorts. His penis was stiffening, empurpled. It was rising, nodding at her. A live club. Ugly. It threatened.

"Be right with you," she said and went into the bathroom. Closed and locked the door. Leaned back against it, breathing rapidly. Zipped up her dress, tried to decide what to do next.

"Come on, come on," he shouted, trying the locked door, then pounding on it. "What the hell's taking you so long?"

She would never be able to lull him, get behind him. Unless she submitted to him first. But that wasn't the way it was supposed to be. That would spoil everything.

She opened the knife, placed it on the edge of the sink. Took the can of Mace from her purse. Gripped it tightly in her right hand.

"All set, Lenny!" she cried gaily.

She unlocked the door with her left hand. He slammed it open. He was close, glowering. He reached for her.

She sprayed the gas directly into his face. She kept the button depressed and, as he staggered back, followed him. She held the hissing container close to his eyes, nose, mouth.

He coughed, sneezed, choked. He bent over. His hands

came up to his face. He stumbled, fell, went down on his back. He tried to suck in air, breathing in great, hacking sobs. His fingers clawed at his weeping eyes.

She leaned over him, spraying until the can was empty.

She ran back to the bathroom, hurriedly soaked a washcloth in cold water. Held it over her nose and mouth. Picked up the knife, returned to the bedroom.

He was writhing on the floor, hands covering his face. He was making animal sounds: grunts, groans. His hairy chest was pumping furiously.

She bent over him. Dug the blade in below his left ear. Made a hard, curving slash. His body leaped convulsively. A fountain of blood. She leaped aside to avoid it. Hands fell away from his face. Watery eyes glared at her and, as she watched, went dim.

The gas was beginning to affect her. She gasped and choked. But she had enough strength to complete the ritual, stabbing his naked genitals again and again, with a mouthed, "There. There. There."

She fled to the bathroom, closed the door. She took several deep breaths of clear air. She soaked the washcloth again, wiped her eyes, cleaned her nostrils. She inspected her arms, dress, ankles, the soles of her shoes. She could find no bloodstains.

But her right hand and the knife were wet with his blood. She turned on the hot water faucet in the sink. She began to rinse the blood away. It was then she noticed the knife blade was broken. About a half-inch of the tip was missing.

She stared at it, calculating the danger. If the blade tip wasn't near him, lying on the rug, then it was probably lost in the raw swamp of his slashed throat, broken off against bone or cartilage. She could not search for it, could not touch him.

She began moving quickly. Finished rinsing hand and knife. Dried both with one of his towels. Put towel, knife, and emptied Chemical Mace can into her shoulder bag. Strode into the bedroom. The gas was dissipating now.

Leonard T. Bergdorfer lay sprawled in a pool of his own blood. Zoe looked about, but could not see the knife blade tip.

She picked up her glass from the bedside table, drained the wine. The empty glass went into her shoulder bag, too. She turned back to wipe the knobs of the bathroom door and the faucet handles with the damp washcloth. She did the same to the knobs of the bedroom door.

She put on her coat in the living room. She unlocked and opened the hallway door a few inches, peeked out. Then she wiped off the lock, chain, and doorknob with the washcloth, and tucked it into her bag. She opened the door wide with her foot, stepped out into the empty corridor. She nudged the door shut with her knee.

She was waiting for the Down elevator when an ascending elevator stopped on the eighth floor. Five men piled out, laughing and shouting and hitting each other. Men were so physical.

They didn't even glance in her direction, but went yelling and roughhousing down the corridor. They stopped in front of Bergdorfer's suite. One of them began knocking on the door.

Then the Down elevator stopped at the eighth floor, the doors slid open, and Zoe Kohler departed.

6

On April 18th, the night Zoe Kohler was sipping white wine at Harry Kurnitz's party at the Chez Ronald on East 48th Street, Edward X. Delaney was dining with reporter Thomas Handry at the Bull & Bear Restaurant, a block away.

Handry was a slender, dapper blade who looked younger than his forty-nine years. His suits were always precisely pressed, shoes shined, shirts a gleaming white. He was one of the few men Delaney had known who could wear a vest jauntily.

The only signs of inner tensions were his fingernails, gnawed to the quick, and a nervous habit of stroking his bare upper lip with a knuckle, an atavism from the days when he had sported a luxurious cavalry mustache.

"You're picking up the tab?" he had demanded when he arrived.

"Of course."

"In that case," Handry said, "I shall have a double Tanqueray martini, straight up with a lemon twist. Then the roast beef, rare, a baked potato, and a small salad."

"I see nothing to object to there," Delaney said, and to the hovering waiter, "Double that order, please."

The reporter regarded the Chief critically.

"Christ, you never change, never look a day older. What did you do—sell your soul to the devil?"

"Something like that," Delaney said. "Actually, I was born old."

"I believe it," Handry said. He put his elbows on the table, scrubbed his face with his palms.

"Rough day?" the Chief asked.

"The usual bullshit. Maybe I'm just bored. You know, I'm coming to the sad conclusion that nothing actually new ever happens. I mean, pick up a newspaper of, say, fifty or a hundred years ago, and there it all is: poverty, famine, wars, accidents, earthquakes, political corruption, crime and so forth. Nothing changes."

"No, it doesn't. Not really. Maybe the forms change, but people don't change all that much."

"Take this Hotel Ripper thing," Handry went on. "It's just a replay of the Son of Sam thing, isn't it?"

But then the waiter arrived with their drinks and Delaney was saved from answering.

They had ale with their roast beef and, later, Armagnac with their coffee. Then they sat back and Delaney accepted one of Handry's cigarettes. He smoked it awkwardly and saw the reporter looking at him with amusement.

"I'm used to cigars," he explained. "I keep wanting to chew the damned thing."

They had a second cup of coffee, stared at each other.

"Got anything for me?" Handry said finally.

"A story?" Delaney said. "An exclusive? A scoop?" He laughed. "No, nothing like that. Nothing you can use."

"Let me be the judge of that."

"I can give you some background," the Chief said. "The powers-that-be aren't happy with Lieutenant Slavin."

"Is he on the way out?"

"Oh, they won't can him. Kick him upstairs maybe."

"I'll check it out. Anything else?"

Delaney considered how much he could reveal, what he would have to pay to get the cooperation he needed.

"That last killing . . ." he said. "Jerome Ashley . . ."

"What about it?"

The Chief looked at him sternly.

"This is not to be used," he said. "N-O-T. Until I give you the go-ahead. Agreed?"

"Agreed. What is it?"

"They found nylon hairs on the rug in Ashley's hotel room."

"So? They've already said the killer wears a black nylon wig."

"These nylon hairs were a reddish blond."

The reporter blinked.

"Son of a bitch," he said slowly. "He switched wigs."

"Right," Delaney said, nodding. "And could switch again to brown, red, purple, green, any color of the goddamned rainbow. That's why nothing's been released on the strawberry blond hairs. Maybe the killer will stick to that color if nothing about it appears in the newspapers or on TV."

"Maybe," Handry said doubtfully. "Anything else?"

"Not at the moment."

"Slim pickings," the reporter said, sighing. "All right, let's hear about this research you want."

Edward X. Delaney took a folded sheet of typing paper from his inside jacket pocket, handed it across the table. Thomas Handry put on heavy, horn-rimmed glasses to read it. He read it twice. Then he raised his head to stare at the Chief.

"You say this has something to do with the Hotel Ripper?"

"It could."

The reporter continued staring. Then . . .

"You're nuts!" he burst out. "You know that?"

"It's possible I am," the Chief said equably.

"You really think . . . ?"

Delaney shrugged.

"Gawd!" Handry said in an awed voice. "What a story that would make. Well, if your game plan was to hook me, you've succeeded. I'll get this stuff for you."

"When?"

"Take me at least a week."

"A week would be fine," Delaney said.

"If I have it before, I'll let you know."

"I need all the numbers. Percentages. Rates."

"All right, all right," the reporter said crossly. "I know what you want; you don't have to spell it out. But if it holds up, I get the story. Agreed?"

Delaney nodded, paid the bill, and both men rose.

"A nightcap at the bar?" the Chief suggested.

"Sure," the reporter said promptly. "But won't your wife be wondering what happened to you?"

"She's taking a course tonight."

"Oh? On what?"

"Assertiveness training."

"Lordy, lordy," Thomas Handry said.

He went over the dossiers on the three victims again and again. He was convinced there was something there, a connection, a lead, that eluded him.

Then, defeated, he turned his attention to the hotels in which the crimes had taken place, thinking there might be a common denominator there. But the three hotels had individual owners, were apparently just unexceptional midtown Manhattan hostelries with nothing about them that might motivate a criminal intent on revenge.

Then he reviewed again the timing of the killings. The first had occurred on a Friday, the second on a Thursday, the third on a Wednesday. There seemed to be a reverse progression in effect, for what possible reason Delaney could not conceive. But if the fourth killing happened on a Tuesday, it might be worth questioning.

He never doubted for a moment that there would be a fourth murder. He was furious that he was unable to prevent it.

Sergeant Abner Boone called regularly, two or three times a week. It was he who had informed Delaney that strawberry blond hairs had been found on the rug in the third victim's hotel room. It had still not been decided whether or not to release this information to the media.

Boone also said that analysis of the bloody footprints on Jerome Ashley's rug had confirmed the killer's height as approximately five feet five to five feet seven. It had proved impossible to determine if the prints were made by a man or woman.

The sergeant reported that the scars on Ashley's hands were the result of burns suffered when a greasy stove caught fire. Boone didn't think there was any possible connection with the murder, and the Chief agreed.

Finally, the investigation into the possibility that all three murdered men were victims of the same disgruntled employee seeking vengeance had turned up nothing. There was simply no apparent connection between Puller, Wolheim, and Ashley.

"So we're back to square one," Boone said, sighing. "We're still running the decoys every night in midtown, and Slavin is pulling in every gay with a sheet or reported as having worn a wig at some time or other. But the results have been zip. Any suggestions, Chief?"

"No. Not at the moment."

"At the moment?" the sergeant said eagerly. "Does that mean, sir, that you may have something? In a while?"

Delaney didn't want to raise any false hopes. Neither did he want to destroy Boone's hope utterly.

"Well . . . possibly," he said cautiously. "A long, long shot."

"Chief, at this stage we'll take anything, no matter how crazy. When will you know?"

"About two weeks." Then, wanting to change the subject, he said, "You're getting the usual tips and confessions, I suppose."

"You wouldn't believe," the sergeant said, groaning. "We've even had four black nylon wigs mailed to us with notes signed: 'The Hotel Ripper.' But to tell you the truth, if we weren't busy chasing down all the phony leads, we'd have nothing to do. We're snookered."

Delaney went back to his dossiers and finally he saw something he had missed. Something everyone had missed. It wasn't a connection between the three victims, a common factor. That continued to elude him.

But it was something just as significant. At least he thought it might be. He checked it twice against his calendar, then went into the living room to consult one of his wife's books.

When he returned to the study, his face was stretched. The expression was more grimace than grin, and when he made a careful note of his discovery, he realized he was humming tonelessly.

He wondered if he should call Sergeant Boone and warn him. Then he decided too many questions would be asked. Questions to which he did not have the answers.

Not that he believed a warning would prevent a fourth murder.

Thomas Handry called early on the morning of April 28th.

"I've got the numbers you wanted," he said.

There was nothing in his voice that implied the results were Yes or No. Delaney was tempted to ask, right then and there. But he didn't. He realized that, for some curious reason he could not analyze, he was more fearful of a Yes than a No.

"That's fine," he said, as heartily as he could.

"I didn't have time to do any adding up," Handry continued. "No compilation, no summary. You'll have to draw your own conclusions."

"I will," Delaney said. "Thank you, Handry. I appreciate your cooperation."

"It's my story," the reporter reminded him.

The Chief wondered what that meant. Was it a story? Or just an odd sidebar to a completely different solution?

"It's your story," he acknowledged. "When and where can I get the research?"

There was silence a moment. Then:

"How about Grand Central Station?" Handry said. "At twelve-thirty. The information booth on the main concourse."

"How about a deserted pier on the West Side at midnight?" Delaney countered.

The reporter laughed.

"No," he said, "no cloak-and-dagger stuff. I have to catch a train and I'm jammed up here. Grand Central would be best."

"So be it," Delaney said. "At twelve-thirty."

He was early, as usual, and wandered about the terminal. He amused himself by trying to spot the plainclothes officers on duty and the grifters plying their trade.

He recognized an old-time scam artist named Breezy Willie who had achieved a kind of fame by inventing a device called a "Grab Bag." It was, apparently, a somewhat oversized black suitcase. But it had no bottom and, of course, was completely empty.

Breezy Willie would select a waiting traveler with a suitcase smaller than the Grab Bag, preferably a suitcase with blue, tan, or patterned covering. The traveler had to be engrossed in a book, timetable, or newspaper, not watching his luggage.

Willie would sidle up close, lower the empty shell of the Grab Bag over the mark's suitcase, and pull a small lever in the handle. Immediately, the sides of the Grab Bag would compress tightly, clamping the suitcase within.

The con man would then lift the swag from the floor, move it ten or fifteen feet away and wait, reading his own newspaper. Willie never tried to run for it.

When the mark discovered his suitcase was missing, he'd dash about frantically, trying to locate it. Breezy Willie would get only a brief glance. He looked legit, and *his* suitcase was obviously black, not the mark's blue, tan, or patterned bag. When the excitement had died down, the hustler would stroll casually away.

The Chief moved close to Breezy Willie, whose eyes were busy over the top edge of his folded newspaper.

"Hullo, Willie," he said softly.

The knave looked up.

"I beg your pardon, sir," he said. "I'm afraid you've made a mistake. My name is—"

Then his eyes widened.

"Delaney!" he said. "This is great!"

He proffered his hand, which the Chief happily took.

"How's business, Willie?" he asked.

"Oh, I'm retired now."

"Glad to hear it."

"Going up to Boston to visit my daughter. She's married, y'know, with three kids, and I figured I'd—"

"Uh-huh," the Chief said.

He bent swiftly and picked up Breezy Willie's Grab Bag with one finger under the handle. He swung the empty shell back and forth.

"Traveling light, Willie?" He laughed and set the Grab Bag down again. "Getting a little long in the tooth for the game, aren't you?"

"That's a fact," the rascal said. "If it wasn't for the ponies, I'd have been playing shuffleboard in Florida years ago. I heard you retired, Chief."

"That's right, Willie."

"But just the same," Breezy Willie said thoughtfully, "I think I'll mosey over to Penn Station. I may visit my daughter in Baltimore, instead."

"Good idea," Delaney said, smiling.

They shook hands again and the Chief watched the scalawag depart. He wished all the bad guys were as innocuous as Breezy Willie. The jolly old pirate abhorred violence as much as any of his victims.

Then he spotted Thomas Handry striding rapidly toward him. The reporter was carrying a weighted Bloomingdale's shopping bag.

"I like your luggage," Delaney said, as Handry came up.

"It's all yours," he said, handing it over. "About five pounds of photocopies. Interesting stuff."

"Oh?"

Handry glanced up at the big clock.

"I've got to run," he said. "Believe it or not, I'm interviewing an alleged seer up in Mt. Vernon. She says she saw the Hotel Ripper in a dream. He's a six-foot-six black with one eye, a Fu Manchu mustache, and an English accent."

"Sounds like a great lead," Delaney said.

The reporter shrugged. "We're doing a roundup piece on all the mediums and seers who think they know what the Hotel Ripper looks like."

"And no two of them agree," the Chief said.

"Right. Well, I've got a train to catch." He hesitated, turned back, gestured toward the bag. "Let me know what you decide to do about all this."

"I will," Delaney said, nodding. "And thank you again."

He watched Handry trot away, then picked up the shopping bag and started out of the terminal. He hated carrying packages, especially shopping bags. He thought it might be a holdover from his days as a street cop: a fear of being encumbered, of not having his hands free.

It was a bright, blowy spring day, cool enough for his putty-colored gabardine topcoat, a voluminous tent that whipped about his legs. He paused a moment to set his homburg more firmly. Then he set out again, striding up Vanderbilt to Park Avenue.

He turned his thoughts resolutely away from what he was carrying and its possible significance. He concentrated on just enjoying the glad day. And the city.

It was his city. He had been born here, lived here all his life. He never left without a sensation of loss, never returned without a feeling of coming home. It was as much domicile as his brownstone; New Yorkers were as much family as his wife and children.

He saw the city clear. He did not think it paradise, nor did it daunt him. He knew its glories and its lesions. He

accepted its beauties and its ugliness, its violence and its
peace. He understood its moods and its fancies. He was
grateful because the city never bored.

There he was, trundling north on Park Avenue, sunlight splintering off glass walls, flags snapping, men and
women scuttling about with frowning purpose. He felt the
demonic rhythm of the city, its compulsive speed and
change. It was always going and never arriving.

The city devoured individuals, deflated the lofty, allowed dreams to fly an instant before bringing them
down. New York was the great leveler. Birth, life, and
death meant no more than a patched pothole or a poem.
It was simply *there*, and the hell with you.

Edward X. Delaney wouldn't have it any other way.

He had made no conscious decision to walk home, but
as block followed block, he could not surrender. He
looked about eagerly, feeding his eyes. Never before had
the city seemed to him so shining and charged. It had the
excitement and fulfillment of a mountaintop.

And the women! What a joy. Men wore clothes;
women wore costumes. There they were, swirling and
sparkling, with wind-rosied cheeks, hair flinging back like
flame. Monica had called him an old fogy, and so he was.
But young enough, by God, to appreciate the worth of
women.

He smiled at them all, toddlers to gammers. He could
not conceive of a world without them, and gave thanks for
having been lucky enough to have found Barbara, and
then Monica. What a weasel life it would have been
without their love.

Treading with lightened step, he made his way uptown,
glorying in the parade of womankind. His face seemed set
in an avuncular grin as he saw and loved them all, with
their color and brio, their strut and sway.

Look at that one coming toward him! A princess, not
much older than his stepdaughter Sylvia. A tall, smashing
beauty with flaxen hair down to her bum. A face unsoiled
by time, and a body as pliant and hard as a steel rod.

She strode directly up to him and stopped, blocking his
way. She looked up at him with a sweet, melting smile.

"Wanna fuck, Pop?" she said.

The roiling was too much; he hadn't the wit to reply.
He crossed to the other side of Park Avenue, lumbering

now, his big feet in heavy, ankle-high shoes slapping the pavement. He climbed tiredly into the first empty cab that came along and went directly home, clutching the Bloomingdale's shopping bag.

Later, he was able to regain some measure of equanimity. He admitted, with sour amusement, that the brief encounter with the young whore had been typical of the city's habit of dousing highfalutin' dreams and romantic fancies with a bucketful of cold reality tossed right in the kisser.

He ate a sandwich of cold corned beef and German potato salad on dill-flavored rye bread while standing over the sink. He drank a can of beer. Resolution restored, he carried Handry's research into the study and set to work.

At dinner that night, he asked Monica what her plans were for the evening.

"Going out?" he said casually.

She smiled and covered one of his hands with hers.

"I've been neglecting you, Edward," she said.

"You haven't been neglecting me," he protested, although he thought she had.

"Well, anyway, I'm going to stay home tonight."

"Good," he said. "I want to talk to you. A long talk."

"Oh-oh," his wife said, "that sounds serious. Am I being fired?"

"Nothing like that," he said, laughing. "I just want to discuss something with you. Get your opinion."

"If I give you my opinion, will it change yours?"

"No," he said.

The living room of the Delaney home was a large, high-ceilinged chamber dominated by a rather austere fireplace and an end wall lined with bookshelves framing the doorway to the study. The room was saved from gloom by the cheerfulness of its furnishings.

It was an eclectic collection that appeared more accumulated than selected. Chippendale cozied up to Shaker; Victorian had no quarrel with Art Deco. It was a friendly room, the old Persian carpet time-softened to subtlety.

Everything had the patina of hard use and loving care. The colors of drapes and upholstery were warm without being bright. Comfort created its own style; the room was mellow with living. Nothing was intended for show; wear was on display.

Delaney's throne was a high-back wing chair covered in burnished bottle-green leather and decorated with brass studs. Monica's armchair was more delicate, but just as worn; it was covered with a floral-patterned brocade that had suffered the depredations of a long-departed cat.

The room was comfortably cluttered with oversized ashtrays, framed photographs, a few small pieces of statuary, bric-a-brac, and one large wicker basket that still held a winterly collection of pussy willows, dried swamp grasses, and eucalyptus.

The walls held an assortment of paintings, drawings, cartoons, posters, etchings, and maps as varied as the furniture. No two frames alike; nothing dominated; everything charmed. And there always seemed room for something new. The display inched inexorably to the plaster ceiling molding.

That evening, dinner finished, dishes done, Monica moved to her armchair, donned half-glasses. She picked up knitting needles and an Afghan square she had been working on for several months. Delaney brought in all his dossiers and the Handry research. He dropped the stack of papers alongside his chair.

"What's all that?" Monica asked.

"It's what I want to talk to you about. I want to try out a theory on you."

"About the Hotel Ripper?"

"Yes. It won't upset you, will it?"

"No, it won't upset me. But it seems to me that for a cop not on active duty, you're taking a very active interest."

"I'm just trying to help out Abner Boone," he protested. "This case means a lot to him."

"Uh-huh," she said, peering at him over her glasses. "Well . . . let's hear it."

"When the first victim, George T. Puller, was found with his throat slashed at the Grand Park Hotel in February, the men assigned to the case figured it for a murder by a prostitute. It had all the signs: An out-of-town salesman is in New York for a convention, has a few drinks, picks up a hooker on the street or in a bar. He takes her to his hotel room. They have a fight. Maybe he won't pay her price, or wants something kinky, or catches her pinching his wallet. Whatever. Anyway, they fight and she kills him. It's happened a hundred times before."

"I suppose," Monica said, sighing.

"Sure. Only there were no signs of a fight. And nothing had been stolen. A prostitute would at least have nicked the cash, if not the victim's jewelry, credit cards, and so forth."

"Maybe she was drugged or doped up."

"And carefully wiped away all her fingerprints? Not very probable. Especially after the second murder in March. A guy named Frederick Wolheim. At the Hotel Pierce. Same MO. Throat slashed. No signs of a struggle. Nothing stolen."

"The paper said the victims were mutilated," Monica said in a small voice.

"Yes," Delaney said flatly. "Stabbed in the genitals. Many times. While they were dying or after they were dead."

His wife was silent.

"Black nylon hairs were found," Delaney continued. "From a wig. Now the prostitute theory was dropped, and it was figured the killer was a homosexual, maybe a transvestite."

"Women wear wigs, too. More than men."

"Of course. Also, the weapon used, a short-bladed knife, probably a pocket knife, is a woman's weapon. It could still figure as a female, but the cops were going by probabilities. There's no modern history of a psychopathic female murderer who selected victims at random and killed for no apparent reason. Lots of male butchers; no female."

"But why does it have to be a homosexual? Why not just a man?"

"Because the victims were found naked. So Lieutenant Slavin started hassling the gays, rousting their bars, pulling in the ones with sheets, criminal records. The results have been nil. After the third murder, it was determined the killer was five-five to five-seven. That could be a shortish man."

"Or a tall woman."

"Yes. No hard evidence either way. But the hunt is still on for a male killer."

She looked up at him again.

"But you think it's a woman?"

"Yes, I do."

"A prostitute?"

"No. A psychopathic woman. Killing for crazy reasons that maybe don't even make sense to her. But she's forced to kill."

"I don't believe it," Monica said firmly.

"Why not?"

"A woman couldn't do things like that."

He had anticipated a subjective answer and had vowed not to lose his temper. He had prepared his reply:

"Are you saying a woman would not be capable of such bloody violence?"

"That's correct. Once maybe. A murder of passion. From jealousy or revenge or hate. But not a series of killings of strangers for no reason."

"A few weeks ago we were talking about child abuse. You agreed that in half the cases, and probably more, the mother was the aggressor. Holding her child's hand over an open flame or tossing her infant into scalding water."

"Edward, that's different!"

"How different? Where's the crime of passion there? Where's the motive of jealousy or revenge or hate?"

"The woman child abuser is under tremendous pressure. She was probably abused herself as a child. Now she's locked into a life without hope. Made into a drudge. The poor child is the nearest target. She can't hold her husband's hand over a flame, as she'd like to, so she takes out all her misery and frustration on her child."

He made a snorting sound. "A very facile explanation, but hardly a justification for maiming an infant. But forget about motives for a minute. Right now I'm not interested in motives. All I'm trying to do is convince you that women are capable of mindless, bloody violence, just like men."

She was silent, hands gripping the needles and wool on her lap. Her lips were pressed to thinness, her face stretched tight. Delaney knew that taut look well, but he plunged ahead.

"You know your history," he said. "Women haven't

always been the subdued, demure, gentle, *feminine* creatures that art and literature make them out to be. They've been soldiers, hard fighters, cruel and bitter foes in many tribes and nations. Still are, in a lot of places on the globe. It used to be that the worst thing that could happen to a captured warrior was to be turned over to the women of the conquering army. I won't go into the details of his fate."

"What's your point?" she snapped.

"Just that there's nothing *inherent* in women, nothing in their genes or instincts that would prevent them from becoming vicious killers of strangers if they were driven to it, if they were victims of desires and lusts they couldn't control. As a matter of fact, I would guess they'd be more prone to violence of that kind than men."

"That's the most sexist remark I've ever heard you make."

"Sexist," he said with a short laugh. "I was wondering how long it would take you to get around to that. The knee-jerk reaction. Any opinion that even suggests women might be less than perfect gets the 'sexist' label. Are you saying that women really are the mild, ladylike, ineffectual Galateas that you always claimed men had created by prejudice and discrimination?"

"I'm not saying anything of the kind. Women haven't developed their full potential because of male attitudes. But that potential doesn't include becoming mass killers. Women could have done that anytime, but they didn't. You said yourself that was the reason the police are looking for a male Hotel Ripper. Because there's no precedent for women being guilty of such crimes."

He looked at her thoughtfully, putting a fingertip to his lips.

"I just had a wild thought," he said. "It's got nothing to do with what we've been talking about, but maybe men did their best to keep women subjugated because they were afraid of them. Physically afraid. Maybe it was a matter of self-preservation."

"You're impossible!" she cried.

"Could be," he said, shrugging. "But to get back to what I was saying, will you agree women have the emotional and physical capabilities of being mass killers? That there is nothing in the female psyche that would rule against it? There *have* been women who killed many times, usually from greed, and they have always been acquainted with their victims. Now I'm asking you to make one small step from that and admit that women would be capable of killing strangers for no apparent reason."

"No," she said definitely, "I don't believe they could do that. You said yourself there are no prior cases. No Daughters of Sam."

"Right," he agreed. "The percentages are against it. That's why, right now, Slavin and Boone and all their men are looking for a male Hotel Ripper. But I think they're wrong."

"Just because you believe women are capable of murder?"

"That, plus the woman's weapon used in the murders, plus the absence of any signs of a fight, plus the fact that apparently heterosexual victims were found naked, plus the wig hairs, plus the estimated height of the killer. And plus something else."

"What's that?" she said suspiciously.

"One of the things I checked when Boone told me about the first two murders was the day of the month they had been committed. I thought there might be a connection with the full moon. You know how crime rates soar when the moon is full."

"Was there a connection?"

"No. And the third killing had no connection either. Then I looked at the intervals between the three murders. Twenty-six days between the first and second, and between the second and the third. Does that suggest anything to you?"

She didn't answer.

"Sure it does," he said gently. "Twenty-six days is a fair average for a woman's menstrual period. I checked it in your guide to gynecology."

"My God, Edward, you call that evidence?"

"By itself? Not much, I admit. But added to all the other things, it begins to make a pattern: a psychopathic female whose crimes are triggered by her monthly periods."

"But killing strangers? I still don't believe it. And you keep saying the percentages are against it."

"Wait," he said, "there's more."

He leaned down, picked up a stack of papers from the floor. He held them on his lap. He donned his reading glasses, began to flip through the pages.

"This may take a little time," he said, looking up at her. "Would you like a drink of anything?"

"Thank you, no," she said stiffly.

He nodded, went back to his shuffling until he found the page he wanted. Then he sat back.

"The probabilities are against it," he agreed. "I admit that. Going by experience, Slavin is doing exactly right in looking for a male killer. But it occurred to me that maybe the percentages are wrong. Not wrong so much as outdated. Obsolete."

"Oh?"

If she was curious, he thought mournfully, she was hiding it exceedingly well.

He looked at her reflectively. He knew her sharp intelligence and mordant wit. He quailed before the task of trying to elicit her approval of what he was about to propose. At worst, she would react with scorn and contempt; at best, with amused condescension for his dabblings in disciplines beyond his ken.

"I've heard you speak many times of the 'new woman,'" he started. "I suppose you mean by that a woman free, or striving to be free, of the restraints imposed by the oppression of men."

"And society," she added.

"All right," he said. "The oppression by individual men and a male-oriented society. The new woman seeks to control and be responsible for her own destiny. Correct? Isn't that more or less what the women's liberation movement is all about?"

"More or less."

"Feminism is a revolution," he went on, speaking slowly, almost cautiously. "A social revolution perhaps, but all the more significant for that. Revolutions have their excesses. No," he said hastily, "not excesses; that was a poor choice of words. But revolutions sometimes, usually, have results its leaders and followers did not anticipate. In any upheaval—social, political, artistic, whatever—sometimes the fallout is totally unexpected, and sometimes inimical to the original aims of the revolutionaries.

"When I was puzzling over the possibility of the Hotel Ripper being female, and trying to reconcile that possibility with the absence of a record of women committing similar crimes, it occurred to me that the new woman we were speaking about might be 'new' in ways of which we weren't aware.

"In other words, she might be more independent, assertive, ambitious, courageous, determined, and so forth. But in breaking free from the repression of centuries, she may also have developed other, less desirable traits. And if so, those traits could conceivably make obsolete all our statistics and percentages of what a woman is capable of."

"I presume," Monica said haughtily, "you're talking about crime statistics and crime percentages."

"Some," he said, "but not all. I wanted to learn if modern women had changed, were changing, in any ways that might make them predisposed to, uh, self-destructive or antisocial behavior."

"And what did you find out?"

"Well . . ." he said, "I won't claim the evidence is conclusive. I'm not even sure you can call it evidence. But I think it's persuasive enough to confirm—in my own mind at least—that I'm on the right track. I asked Thomas Handry—he's the reporter; you've met him—to dig out the numbers for me in several areas. I took the past fifteen years as the time period in which to determine if the changes I suspected in women had actually taken place."

"Why the past fifteen years?"

He looked at her stonily. "You know why. Because that period, roughly, is the length of time the modern feminist movement has been in existence and has affected the lives of so many American women. And men too, of course."

"You're blaming everything that's happened to women in the past fifteen years on women's liberation?"

"Of course not. I know other factors have been influential. But a lot of those factors, in turn, have been partly or wholly the result of feminism. The huge increase in the women's work force, for instance. Now do you or do you not want to hear what Handry discovered?"

"I'd feel a lot better if your research had been done by a woman."

He gave her a hard smile. "She would have found the same numbers Handry did. Let's start with the most significant statistics . . ."

He began speaking, consulting pages on his lap, letting them flutter to the floor as he finished with them.

"First," he said, "let's look at drugs . . . Statistics about illegal drugs are notoriously inaccurate. I'm talking now about marijuana, cocaine, and heroin. It's almost impossible to get exact tallies on the total number of users, let alone a breakdown by sex and age. But from what reports are available, it appears that men and women are about equal in illicit drug use.

"When we turn to legal drugs, particularly psychoactive drugs prescribed by physicians, we can get more accurate totals. They show that of all prescriptions issued for such drugs, about 80 percent of amphetamines, 67 percent of tranquilizers, and 60 percent of barbiturates and sedatives go to women. It is estimated that at least two million women have dependencies—addiction would be a better word—on prescription drugs. More than half of all women convicted of crimes have problems with prescription drug abuse. Twice as many women as men use Valium and Librium. Fifty percent more women than men take barbiturates regularly. They're a favored method of suicide by women."

"There's a good reason for all that," Monica said sharply. "When you consider the frustrations and—"

"Halt!" Delaney said, showing a palm. "Monica, I'm a policeman, not a sociologist. I'm not interested in the causes. Only in things as they are, and the effect they may have on crime. Okay?"

She was silent.

"Second," he said, consulting more pages, "the number of known female alcoholics has doubled since World War Two. Alcoholics Anonymous reports that in the past, one in ten members was a woman. Today, the ratio of women to men is about one to one. Statistics on alcoholism are hard to come by and not too accurate, but no one doubts the enormous recent increase of female alcoholics."

"Only because more women are coming forward and admitting their problem. Up to now, there's been such social condemnation of women drinkers that they kept it hidden."

"And still do, I imagine," he said. "Just as a lot of men keep *their* alcoholism hidden. But that doesn't negate all the testimony of authorities in the field reporting a high incidence of female alcoholism. Women make the majority of purchases in package liquor stores. Whiskey makers are beginning to realize what's going on. Now their ads are designed to attract women drinkers. There's even a new Scotch, blended expressly for women, to be advertised in women's magazines."

"When everyone is drinking more, is it so unusual to find women doing their share?"

"*More* than their share," he answered, with as much patience as he could muster. "Read the numbers in these reports Handry collected; it's all here. Third, deaths from lung cancer have increased about 45 percent for women and only about 4 percent for men. The lung cancer rate for women, not just deaths, has tripled."

"And pray, what does that prove?"

"For one thing, I think it proves women are smoking a hell of a lot more cigarettes, for whatever reasons, and suffering from it. Monica, as far as I'm concerned, alcohol and nicotine are as much drugs as amphetamines and barbiturates. You can get hooked on booze and cigarettes as easily as you can on uppers and downers."

She was getting increasingly angry; he could see it in her stiffened posture, the drawn-down corners of her mouth, her narrowed eyes. But having come this far, he had no intention of stopping now.

"All right," she said in a hard voice, "assuming more women are popping pills, drinking, and smoking—what does that prove?"

"One final set of numbers," he said, searching through the remaining research. "Here it is . . . Women constitute about 51 percent of the population. But all the evidence indicates they constitute a much higher percentage of the mentally ill. One hundred and seventy-five women for every 100 men are hospitalized for depression, and 238 women for every 100 men are treated as outpatients for depression."

"Depression!" she said scornfully. "Hasn't it occurred

to you that there's a good explanation for that? The social roles—"

"Not only depression," he interrupted, "but mania as well. They're called 'affective disorders' and it's been estimated that more than twice as many women as men suffer from them."

"As a result of—"

"Monica!" he cried desperately. "I told you I'm not interested in the causes. If you tell me that drug addiction—including alcohol and nicotine—and poor mental health are due to the past role of women in our culture, I'll take your word for it. I'm just trying to isolate certain current traits in women. The 'new women.' I'm not making a value judgment here. I'm just giving you the numbers. Percentages have no conscience, no ax to grind, no particular point to make. They just exist. They can be interpreted in a hundred different ways."

"And I know how *you* interpret them," she said scathingly. "As a result of the women's liberation movement."

"Goddamn it!" he said furiously. "Are you listening to me or are you not? The only interest I have in these numbers is as a statistical background to my theory that the Hotel Ripper is a woman."

"What the hell is the connection?"

He drew a deep breath. He willed himself to be calm. He tried to speak reasonably. She seemed to be missing the point—or perhaps he was explaining it badly.

"Monica, I'm willing to admit that the things I've mentioned about women today may be temporary aberrations. They may be the result of the social upheavals and the rapidly changing role of women in the last few years. Maybe in another ten or fifteen years, women will have settled into their new roles and learned to cope with their new problems. Then their mental health will improve and their drug dependency decrease.

"But I'm only concerned with the way things are *today*. And I think women today are capable of making irrelevant all the existing criminal data dealing with females. Those numbers were accurate for yesterday, not today. The new women make them obsolete.

"I think enough hard evidence exists to justify believing

the Hotel Ripper is a woman. I asked Handry to do this research in hopes that it might provide statistical background to reinforce that belief. I think it does.

"Monica, we have shit-all evidence of what the killer looks like. We know she's about five-five to five-seven and wears wigs. That's about it. But we can guess at other things about her. For instance, she's probably a young woman, say in the area of eighteen to forty, because she's strong enough to rip a man's throat and she's young enough to have menstrual periods.

"We also know she's smart. She plans carefully. She's cool and determined enough to carry through a vicious murder and then wash bloodstains from her body before leaving the scene. She makes certain she leaves no fingerprints. Everything indicates a woman of above average intelligence.

"This research gives us additional clues to other things she may be. Quite possibly she's addicted to prescription drugs, alcohol, or nicotine—or a combination of two or all three. The chances are good that she suffers from depression or mania, or both.

"All I'm trying to do is put together a profile. Not a psychological profile—those things are usually pure bullshit. I'm trying to give the killer certain personal and emotional characteristics that will give us a more accurate picture of the kind of woman she is."

"You think she's a feminist?" Monica demanded.

"She may be; she may not be. I just don't know and can't guess. But I do believe the great majority of women in this country have been affected by the women's liberation movement whether they are active in it or not."

Monica was silent a moment, pondering. She stared down, her eyes blinking. Then she asked the question Delaney had hoped to avoid. But, he admitted wryly, he should have known she'd go to the heart of the matter.

She looked up, directly at him. "Did Handry research current crime statistics?"

"Yes, he did."

"And?"

"The arrest rate is up for women. Much higher than that for men."

"What about murder?" she asked.

He had to be honest. "No, there's no evidence that

murder by women is increasing. But their arrests for robbery, breaking-and-entering, and auto theft are increasing at a higher rate than for men. And much higher for larceny-theft, embezzlement, and fraud. Generally, women's crimes against property are increasing faster than men's, but not in the category of violent crimes such as murder and manslaughter."

"Or rape," she added bitterly.

He said nothing.

"Well?" she questioned. "If you think your research is justification for the Hotel Ripper being a woman, wouldn't there be some evidence of murder by women being on the increase?"

"I would have thought so," he admitted.

"You *hoped* so, didn't you?" she said, looking at him narrowly.

"Come on, Monica," he protested. "It's not giving me any great satisfaction to know the Hotel Ripper is a woman."

She sniffed and rose, gathering up her knitting things.

"You don't *know* any such thing," she said. "You're just guessing. And I think you're totally wrong."

"I may be," he acknowledged.

"Are you going to tell Boone about your wild idea?"

"No. Not yet. But I'm going to call him and warn him about May seventh to May ninth. If I'm right, then there will be another killing or attempted killing around then."

She swept grandly from the room.

"You're making a damned fool of yourself!" she flung over her shoulder.

After the door slammed behind her, he kicked fretfully at the pages of research discarded on the carpet.

"Won't be the first time," he grumbled.

On the morning of May 9th, a little before 9:00 A.M., Monica and Edward X. Delaney were seated at the kitchen table, having a quiet breakfast. They were sharing a pan of eggs scrambled with lox and onions.

Since their heated debate on the significance of Thomas Handry's research, their relation had been one of careful politesse:

"Would you care for more coffee?"

"Thank you. Another piece of toast?"

"No more, thank you. Would it bother you if I turned on the radio?"

"Not at all. Would you like a section of the newspaper?"

It had been going on like that for more than a week, neither willing to yield. But on that morning, the Chief decided it had continued long enough.

He threw down his newspaper, slammed his hand on the table with a *crack* that made Monica jump.

"Jesus Christ!" he said explosively. "What are we—a couple of kids? What kind of bullshit is this? Can't we disagree without treating each other like strangers?"

"You're so damned bullheaded," she said. "You can never admit you're wrong."

"I admit I *might* be wrong," he said. "On this thing. But I haven't been proved wrong—yet. You think I'm wrong? All right, how about a bet? Put your money where your mouth is. How much? Five, ten, a hundred? Whatever you say."

"It's too serious a matter to bet money on," she said loftily.

"All right, let's make a serious bet. The windows are filthy. If I'm proved wrong, I'll wash every goddamned window in the house. If I'm proved right, you wash them."

She considered that a moment.

"Every window," she insisted. "Including basement and attic. Inside and out."

"I agree," he said and held out his big paw. They shook hands.

"Turn the radio on," she ordered.

"Pour me some more coffee," he commanded.

Things were back to normal. But they both froze when they heard the first news item.

"The body of a murdered man was discovered in a suite at the Cameron Arms Hotel on Central Park South last night around midnight. The victim has been identified as Leonard T. Bergdorfer, an airline broker from Atlanta, Georgia. A police spokesman has definitely linked the slaying with the series of Hotel Ripper murders. The death of Bergdorfer is the fourth. No further details are available at this hour."

Monica and Edward stared at each other.

"The Windex is in the cupboard under the sink," he said slowly.

She began to cry, silently, tears welling down her cheeks. He rose to put a heavy arm about her shoulders, pull her close.

"It's so awful," she said, her voice muffled. "So awful. We were joking and making bets, and all the time . . ."

"I know," he said, "I know."

"You better tell Abner," she said. "About what you think."

"Yes," he said, "I guess I better."

He went into the study, sat down heavily behind the desk. He had his hand on the phone, but then paused, pondering.

He could not understand why he had not been informed. The newscaster had said the body was discovered around midnight.

Delaney would have expected Sergeant Boone to call him as soon as it had been verified as a Ripper killing.

Perhaps Boone had been commanded by Lieutenant Slavin to stop discussing the case with Delaney. Or perhaps enough evidence had been found to wrap up the investigation with no more help from a retired cop. Or maybe the sergeant was just too busy to report. Anything was possible.

He called Boone at home, at Midtown North, and at the Cameron Arms Hotel. No success anywhere. He left messages at all three places, asking the sergeant to call him back as soon as possible.

He started a new dossier: a sheet of paper headed: "Leonard T. Bergdorfer, midnight May 8, from Atlanta, Georgia. Fourth victim. Body found at Cameron Arms Hotel." Then he went back into the kitchen to listen to the ten o'clock news. Monica was gathering a pail of water, clean rags, Windex, a roll of paper towels.

"You don't have to do the windows," he told her, smiling. "It was just a stupid joke. We'll have someone come in and do them. Besides, it looks like rain."

"No, no," she said. "I lost the bet. Also, I think I'd like to keep busy with physical work today. Therapy. Maybe it'll keep me from thinking."

"Well . . . just do the insides," he said. "Stop when you get tired."

The news broadcast added a few more facts. The victim had come to New York to attend a convention at the Cameron Arms Hotel. His body was discovered by friends who stopped by his suite for a drink and found the door unlocked.

There were indignant statements from a Deputy Mayor, from travel agents, from the president of the hotel association. All called for quick apprehension of the Hotel Ripper before tourist trade in New York dwindled to nothing.

Edward X. Delaney waited all morning in his study, but Sergeant Abner Boone never called back. The Chief concluded that his aid was no longer being sought. For whatever reason, he was being ignored.

He pulled on his raincoat, homburg, took an umbrella from the hall closet. He yelled upstairs to Monica that he was going out and would be back shortly. He waited for her shouted reply before he left, double-locking the front door behind him.

It wasn't a hard rain. More of a thick, soaking mist that fell steadily from a steely sky. And it was unpleasantly warm. There were puddles on the sidewalks. The gutters ran with filth. The day suited Delaney's mood perfectly.

His pride was hurt; he acknowledged it. He had cooperated with Boone and, through him, with Deputy Commissioner Ivar Thorsen. He had made suggestions. He had warned of the May 7–9 time period.

The only thing he hadn't passed along was his theory that the Hotel Ripper was a woman. Not a prostitute, but a psychopathic female posing as one. And he hadn't told Boone about that simply because it *was* a theory and needed more evidence to give it substance.

He thought the timing of the murder of Leonard T. Bergdorfer made it more than just a hypothesis. But if they didn't want his help, the hell with them. It was no skin off his ass. He was an honorably retired cop, and for all he cared the Department could go take a flying fuck at a rolling doughnut.

That's what he told himself.

He walked for blocks and blocks, feeling the damp creep into his feet and shoulders. His umbrella soaked through, his ungloved hands dripped, and he felt as steamed as if the city had become an enormous sauna with someone pouring water on heated rocks.

He stopped at an Irish bar on First Avenue. He had two straight whiskies, which brought more sweat popping but at least calmed his anger. By the time he started home, he had regained some measure of serenity, convinced the Hotel Ripper case was past history as far as he was concerned.

He was putting his sodden homburg and raincoat in the hall closet when Monica came out of the kitchen.

"Where have you been?" she demanded.

"Taking a stroll," he said shortly.

"Ivar Thorsen is in the study," she said. "He's been waiting almost an hour. I gave him a drink."

Delaney grunted.

"You're in a foul mood," Monica said. "Just like Ivar. Put your umbrella in the sink to drip."

He stood the closed umbrella in the kitchen sink. He felt the shoulders of his jacket. They were dampish but not soaked. He passed a palm over his iron-gray, brush-cut hair. Then he went into the study.

Deputy Commissioner Thorsen stood up, drink in hand.

"Hullo, Ivar," the Chief said.

"How the hell did you know there'd be a killing last night?" Thorsen said loudly, almost shouting.

Delaney stared at him. "It's a long story," he said, "and one you're not likely to hear if you keep yelling at me."

Thorsen took a deep breath. "Oh God," he said, shaking his head, "I must be cracking up. I'm sorry, Edward. I apologize."

He came forward to shake the Chief's hand. Then he sat down again in the armchair. Delaney freshened his glass with more Glenlivet and poured himself a healthy shot of rye whiskey. They held their glasses up to each other before sipping.

Deputy Commissioner Ivar Thorsen was called "The Admiral" in the NYPD, and his appearance justified the nickname. He was a small, slender man with posture so erect, shoulders so squared, that it was said he left the hangers in the jackets he wore.

His complexion was fair, unblemished; his profile belonged on postage stamps. His white hair, worn short and rigorously brushed, had the gleam of chromium.

His pale blue eyes seemed genial enough, but subordinates knew how they could deepen and blaze. "It's easy enough to get along with Thorsen," one of his aides had remarked. "Just be perfect."

"How's Karen?" Delaney asked, referring to the deputy's beautiful Swedish wife.

"She's fine, thanks," Thorsen said. "When are you and Monica coming over for one of her herring smorgasbords?"

"Whenever you say."

They sat in silence, looking at each other. Finally . . .

"You first or me first?" Thorsen asked.

"You," Delaney said.

"We've got problems downtown," the Admiral announced.

"So what else is new? You've always got problems downtown."

"I know, but this Hotel Ripper thing is something else. It's as bad as Son of Sam. Maybe worse. The Governor's office called today. The Department is taking a lot of flak. From the politicians and the business community."

"You know how I feel about the Department."

"I know how you *say* you feel, Edward. But don't tell me a man who gave as many years as you did would stand idly by and not do what he could to help the Department."

"Fiddle music," Delaney said. "'Hearts and Flowers.'"

Thorsen laughed. "Iron Balls," he said. "No wonder they called you that. But forget about the Department's problems for a moment. Let's talk about your problems."

Delaney looked up in surprise. "I've got no problems."

"You say. I know better. I've seen a lot of old bulls retire and I've watched what happens to them after they get out of harness. A few of them can handle it, but not many."

"I can handle it."

"You'd be surprised how many drop dead a year or two after putting in their papers. Heart attack or stroke, cancer or bleeding ulcers. I don't know the medical or psychological reasons for it, but studies show it's a phenomenon that exists. When the pressure is suddenly removed, and stress vanishes, and there are no problems to solve, and drive and ambition disappear, the body just collapses."

"Hasn't happened to me," Delaney said stoutly. "I'm in good health."

"Or other things happen," the Admiral went on relentlessly. "They can't handle the freedom. No office to go to. No beat to pound. No shop talk. Their lives revolved around the Department and now suddenly they're out. It's like they were excommunicated."

"Bullshit."

"Some of them find a neighborhood bar that becomes their office or squad room or precinct. They keep half-bagged all day and bore their new friends silly with lies about what great cops they were."

"Not me."

"Or maybe they decide to read books, visit museums, go to shows—all the things they never had time for before. Fishing and hunting. Gardening. Hockey games. And so forth. But it's just postponing the inevitable. How many books can you read? How many good plays or movies are there? How many hockey games? The day arrives when they wake up with the realization that they've got nothing to do, nowhere to go. They may as well stay in bed. Some of them do."

"I don't."

"Or become drunks or hypochondriacs. Or start following their wives around, walking up their heels. Or start resenting their wives because the poor women don't spend every waking minute with them."

Delaney said nothing.

Thorsen looked at him narrowly. "Don't tell me you haven't felt any of those things, Edward. You've never lied to me in your life; don't start now. Why do you think you were so willing to help Boone? So eager to get his reports on the Hotel Ripper case? To make out those dossiers I saw on your desk? Oh yes, I peeked, and I make no apology for it. Maybe you're not yet in the acute stage, but admit it's starting."

"What's starting?"

"The feeling that you're not wanted, not needed. No reason to your life. No aims, no desires. Worst of all is the boredom. It saps the spirit, turns the brain to mush. You're a wise man, Edward; I'd never deny it. But you're not smart enough to handle an empty life."

Delaney rose slowly to his feet, with an effort. He poured more whiskey. Glenlivet for Thorsen, rye for himself. He sat down heavily again in the swivel chair behind the desk. He regarded the Deputy Commissioner reflectively.

"You're a pisser, you are," he said. "You want something from me. You know you've got to convince me. So you try the loyalty-to-the-Department ploy. When that doesn't work, you switch without the loss of a single breath to the self-interest approach. Now I've got to do as you want if I hope to avoid dropping dead, becoming a lush, annoying my wife, or having my brain turn to mush."

"Right!" the Admiral cried, slapping his knee. "You're exactly right. It's in your own self-interest, man. That's the strongest motive of them all."

"You admit you're manipulating me—or trying to?"

"Of course. But it's in your own best interest; can't you see that?"

Delaney sighed. "Thank God you never went into politics. You'd end up owning the world. What is it, precisely, you want of me, Ivar?"

The sprucely dressed deputy set his drink aside. He leaned forward earnestly, hands clasped.

"Slavin has got to go," he said. "The man's a disaster. Releasing that black nylon wig story to the media was a blunder. We're beefing up the Hotel Ripper squad. Another hundred detectives and plainclothesmen for a start, and more available as needed. We'll put Slavin in charge of administration and scheduling of the task force. He's good at that."

"And who's going to be in command?"

Thorsen sat back, crossed his knees. He adjusted the sharp crease in his trouser leg. He picked up his drink, took a sip. He stared at Delaney over the rim of the glass.

"That's what I was doing all morning," he said. "A meeting downtown. It started at about three A.M., and went through to eleven. I've never drunk so much black coffee in my life. Everyone agreed Slavin had to go. Then we started debating who the CO should be. It had to be someone high up in the Department, to send a signal to the politicians and businessmen and public that we're giving this case top priority."

"Cosmetics," Delaney said disgustedly. "The image."

"Correct," Thorsen said levely. "When you don't know where you're going, you rush around busily. It gives the impression of action. What more could we have done? Any suggestions?"

"No."

"So we needed a top man in command. It couldn't be the Chief of Detectives. He's got a full plate even without the Hotel Ripper. He can't drop everything and concentrate on one case. Besides, we figured we needed higher brass. Someone close to the PC. No one was willing to volunteer."

"Can't say I blame them," the Chief admitted. "Too much risk for the ambitious types. Failure could break them. End their careers."

"Right. Well, we finally got one guy who was willing to stick out his neck."

"Who's the idiot?"

The Admiral looked at him steadily. "Me," he said. "I'm the idiot."

"Ivar!" Delaney cried. "For God's sake, *why?* You haven't worked an active case in twenty years."

"Don't you think I know that? I recognized the dangers of taking it on. If I flop, I might as well resign. Nothing left for me in the Department. I'd always be the guy who bungled the Hotel Ripper case. On the other hand, if I could possibly pull it off, I'd be the fair-haired boy, remembered when the Police Commissioner's chair became vacant."

"And that's what you want?"

"Yes."

"Well . . ." Delaney said loyally, "the city could do a lot worse."

"Thank you, Edward. But it wasn't just wishful thinking on my part. When I agreed to take it on, I had an ace in the hole."

"Oh? What was that?"

"*Who* was that. You."

Delaney banged his hand down on the desktop in disgust.

"Jesus Christ, Ivar, you gambled on getting me to go along?"

Thorsen nodded. "That's what I gambled on. That's why I'm here pulling out all the stops to persuade you to help me, help the Department, help yourself."

Delaney was silent, staring at the composed man in the armchair, the small foot in the polished moccasin bobbing idly up and down. Thorsen endured his scrutiny with serenity, slowly sipping his drink.

"There's one stop you didn't pull, Ivar."

"What's that?"

"Our friendship."

The deputy frowned. "I don't want to put it on that basis, Edward. You don't owe me. Turn me down and we'll still be friends."

"Uh-huh. Tell me something, Ivar—did you instruct Sergeant Boone not to call me about that killing last night, figuring to give me a taste of what it would feel like to be shut out of this thing?"

"My God, Edward, do you think I'd be capable of a Machiavellian move like that?"

"Yes."

"You're perfectly right," Thorsen said calmly. "That's exactly what I did for the reason you guessed. And it worked, didn't it?"

"Yes, it worked."

"You've got cops' blood," the Admiral said. "Retirement didn't change that. Well . . . how about it? Will you agree to work with me? Serve as an unofficial right-hand man? You won't be on active duty, of course, but you'll know everything that's going on, have access to all the papers—statements, photographs, evidence, autopsy reports, and so on. Boone will act as our liaison."

"Ivar, what do you expect of me?" Delaney asked desperately. "I'm no miracle man."

"I don't expect miracles. Just handle it as if you were on active duty, assigned to the Hotel Ripper case. If you fail, it's my cock that's on the block, not yours. What do you say?"

"Give me a little time to—"

"No," Thorsen said sharply. "I haven't got time. I need to know now."

Delaney leaned back, laced his hands behind his head.

He stared at the ceiling. Maybe, he thought, the reason for Ivar Thorsen's success in threading his way through the booby-trapped upper echelons of the New York Police Department was his ability to use people by persuading them that they had everything to gain from his manipulation.

Knowing that, the Chief still had to admit that Thorsen's sales pitch wasn't all con. There was enough truth in what he had said to consider his proposal seriously.

But not once had he mentioned a motive that cut more ice with Delaney than all the dire warnings of how retirement would flab his fiber and muddle his brain. It was a basic motive, almost simple, that would have sounded mawkish if spoken.

Edward X. Delaney wanted to stop the Hotel Ripper because killing was wrong. Not just immoral, antisocial, or irreligious. But *wrong*.

"All right, Ivar," he said. "I'm in."

Thorsen nodded, drained his glass. But when Delaney started to rise, to pour him more Glenlivet, the deputy held his hand over his glass.

"No more, thank you, Edward. I've got to go back downtown again."

"Tell me about the killing last night."

"I don't know too much about it. You'll have to get the details from Boone. But I gather it was pretty much like the others, with a few minor differences. The victim was naked, but his body was found on the floor between the bed and the bathroom. The bed hadn't been used."

"Throat slashed?"

"Yes."

"Genitals stabbed?"

"Yes."

"How old was he?"

"Middle forties. One odd thing—or rather two odd things. The body was discovered by a gang of pals who barged in for a drink. They said there was a sweet odor in the bedroom where the body was found."

"A sweet odor? Perfume?"

"Not exactly. One of the guys said it smelled to him like apple blossoms. The other odd thing was that the victim's face was burned. First-degree burns. Reddening but no blistering or charring."

"Tear gas," Delaney said. "It smells like apple blossoms in low concentrations and it can cause burns if applied close to the skin."

"Tear gas?" Thorsen said. "How do you figure that?"

"I don't. Unless the killer couldn't get behind the victim, like the others were slashed, and gassing was the only way to handle him."

"Well, they'll find out what it was in the PM. We've been promised the report tomorrow morning. Now . . . let's get back to my original question: How the hell did you know there'd be a killing last night?"

"I didn't *know*. I guessed. And I didn't specify last night; I warned Boone about May seventh to ninth. Did you put on more men?"

"Yeah," Thorsen said sourly. "As a matter of fact, we had a decoy in the Cameron Arms Hotel last night while it was going down."

"Shit," Delaney said.

"He was in a disco, figuring that would be the logical place for the killer to make contact. It didn't work out that way. Edward, we can't cover every bar, cocktail lounge, disco, dining room, and hotel lobby in midtown Manhattan. That would take an army."

"I know. Still, it burns my ass to be so close and miss it."

"You still haven't told me how you figured it might happen last night."

"It's a long story. You better have another drink."

The Admiral hesitated just a moment.

"All right," he said finally. "After what I've gone through in the last twelve hours, I've earned it."

Delaney repeated everything he had previously related to Monica: how he had slowly come to believe the Hotel Ripper might be a woman; the research he had done; and how some of it substantiated his theory.

And how the implied circumstances of the murders lent further credence: the absence of any signs of struggles; the heterosexual victims found naked; the attacks (except for the last) all made from the rear, the victims apparently not expecting sudden violence.

Midway through his recital, Delaney took two cigars from his desk humidor. Still talking, he rose and leaned forward to hand one to the Admiral, then held a match for him. He sat down again and, puffing, resumed his discourse.

He argued that only presuming the perpetrator was a woman wearing a wig—not a prostitute, but a psychopath—could all the anomalies of the murders be explained.

"She kills at regular intervals," he concluded. "In, say, twenty-five to twenty-seven-day cycles."

"During her periods?"

"Probably. Maybe a few days before or a few days after. But every month."

"Well . . ." Thorsen said with a rueful smile, "that gives us an age approximation: twelve to fifty!"

"What do you think, Ivar? About the whole idea?"

Thorsen looked down at his drink, swirling the whiskey around slowly in the glass. "Not exactly what I'd call hard evidence. A lot of shrewd guesses. And a lot of smoke."

"Oh hell yes. I admit it. But have you got any better ideas?"

"I haven't got *any* ideas. But on the basis of what you've told me, you want us to—"

"I don't want you to do a goddamned thing," Delaney said furiously. "You asked me for my ideas and I gave them to you. If you think it's all bullshit, then I—"

"Whoa, whoa!" the deputy said, holding up a hand. "My God, Edward, you've got the shortest fuse of any man I know. I don't think it's all bullshit. I think you've come up with the first new idea anyone has offered on this mess. But I'm trying to figure out what to do about it. Assuming you're right, where do we go from here?"

"Start all over again," Delaney said promptly. "They've been checking out escaped mental patients and psychos, haven't they?"

"Of course. All over the country."

"Sure they have—male crazies, and probably just homosexual male crazies. We've got to go back and do it all over again, looking for psychopathic women, escaped or recently released. And pull out all the decoys from gay bars and send them to straight places. These killings have nothing to do with homosexuals. And go back through our records again, looking for women with a sheet including violent crimes. There's a hell of a lot that can be done once you're convinced the killer is female. It turns the whole investigation around."

"You think this should be released to the media?"

Delaney pondered that a long time.

"I don't know," he admitted finally. "They're going to find out sooner or later. But publicity might frighten the killer off."

"Or spur her on to more."

"That's true. Ivar, I'd suggest keeping this under wraps as long as possible. Just to give us a little time to get things organized. But it's not my decision to make."

"I know," the Admiral said mournfully, "it's mine."

"You volunteered," the Chief said, shrugging. "You're now the commanding officer. So command."

"I'd feel a lot better about this, Edward, if you could be more positive about it. If you could tell me that, yes, you absolutely believe that the killer is definitely a woman."

"My gut instinct tells me so," Delaney said solemnly, and both men burst out laughing.

"Well," Thorsen said, rising, "I've got to get going. I'll spread the news—at least to the people who count."

"Ivar, there's no need for the media to know I'm working with you."

"I agree. But some of the brass will have to know, and some of the politicos. And Sergeant Boone, of course. Call him tomorrow morning. I'll have a system set up by then on how he's to liaise with you."

"Fine."

"Edward, I want to tell you how happy I am that you've decided to help out."

"You're a supersalesman."

"Not really. You can't sell something to someone who really doesn't want to buy. Not to someone as stubborn as you, anyway. But having you with me makes all the difference in the world. May I use your phone?"

"Of course. Want me to step outside?"

"No, no. I want you to hear this."

Thorsen dialed a number, waited a moment.

"Mary?" he said. "It's Ivar Thorsen. Put himself on, will you? He's expecting my call."

While he waited, the Deputy Commissioner winked at Delaney. Then . . .

"Timothy?" he said. "Ivar Thorsen here. All right, Timmy, I'll take the job."

He hung up and turned to the Chief.

"You bastard!" Delaney gasped. "You've got to be the biggest son of a bitch who ever came down the pike."

"So I've been told," the Admiral said.

After he had shown Thorsen out, Delaney wandered back into the kitchen. Monica was readying a veal roast for the oven, laying on thin strips of fat salt pork. The Chief took a celery stalk from the refrigerator crisper. He leaned against the sink, chomping, watching Monica work.

"I told Ivar I'd help him out on the Hotel Ripper case," he offered.

She nodded. "I thought that was probably what he wanted."

"He's in command now. I'll be working through Abner Boone."

"Good," she said unexpectedly. "I'm glad you'll be busy on something important."

"Have I been getting in your hair?"

She gave him a quick, mischievous grin. "Not any more than usual. You told Ivar you think it's a woman?"

"Yes."

"Did he agree?"

"He didn't agree and he didn't disagree. We'll check it out. He'll want to move cautiously. That's all right; his reputation and career are on the line. He wants to be Police Commissioner some day."

"I know."

"You know? How do you know?"

"Karen told me."

"And you never told me?"

"I thought you knew. Besides, I don't tell you everything."

"You don't? I tell you everything."

"Bullshit," she said, and he kissed her.

7

It wasn't so much a weakness as a languor. Her will was blunted; her body now seemed in command of all her actions. An indolence infected her. She slept long, drugged hours, and awoke listless, aching with weariness.

Each morning she stepped on the bathroom scale and saw her weight inexorably lessening. After a while she stopped weighing herself; she just didn't want to know. It was something beyond her control. She thought vaguely it was due to her loss of appetite; food sickened her: all that *stuff* going into her mouth . . .

Her monthly had ended, but the abdominal cramps persisted. Sometimes she felt nauseated; twice she vomited for no apparent reason. She had inexplicable attacks of diarrhea followed by spells of constipation. The incidents of syncope increased: more of them for longer periods.

It seemed to her that her body, that fleshy envelope containing her, was breaking up, flying apart, forgetting its functions and programs, disintegrating into chaos. It occurred to her that she might be dying. She ran into the kitchen to take a Valium.

She looked down at her naked self. She felt skin, hair, softness of fat and hardness of bone. Undeniably she was still there; warm and pulsing. Pinched, she felt hurt. Stroked, she felt joy. But deep inside was rot. She was convinced of it; there was rot. She knew more wonder than fear.

She functioned; she did what she had to do. Dropped the broken knife down a sewer grating. Wrapped the empty Mace can in a bundle of garbage and tossed it into a litter basket two blocks from her home. Inspected her body and clothing for bloodstains. She did all these things indolently, without reasoning why.

She bathed, dressed, went to work each day. Chatted with Ernest Mittle on the phone. Had lunch with Maddie Kurnitz. It was all a dream, once removed from reality. Anomie engulfed her; she swam in a foreign sea.

Once she called Sergeant Coe to ask if he was available for moonlighting. Coe's wife answered the phone and Zoe said, "This is Irene—" stopped, dazed, then said, "This is Zoe Kohler."

Something was happening to her. Something slow, gradual, and final. She let it take her, going to her fate without protest or whimper. It was too late, too painful to change. There was comfort in being a victim. Almost a pleasure. Life, do with me what you will.

On May 10th, a Saturday, she met Ernest Mittle at the entrance to Central Park at Fifth Avenue and 59th Street. It was only a few blocks from the Cameron Arms Hotel. They exchanged light kisses and, holding hands, joined the throng sauntering toward the menagerie and children's zoo.

It was more summer than spring. A high sky went on forever; the air was a fluffy softness that caressed the skin. The breeze was scarcely strong enough to raise kites; the fulgent sun cast purplish shadows.

People on the benches raised white, meek faces to the blue, happy with the new world. Coats and sweaters were doffed and carried; children scampered. Bells and flutes could be heard; the greening earth stirred.

"Oh, what a day!" Ernest exulted. "I ordered it just for us. Do you approve, Zoe?"

"It *is* nice," she said, looking about. "Like being born again."

"Would you like an ice cream? Hot dog? Peanuts?"

"No, nothing right now, thank you."

"How about a balloon?" he said, laughing.

"Yes, I'd like a balloon. A red one."

So he bought her a helium-filled balloon and carefully tied the end of the string to the handle of her purse. They strolled on, the little sun bobbing above them.

A carnival swirled about: noise, movement, color. But

they felt singularly alone and at peace, a universe of two.
It seemed to them the crowd parted to allow passage, then
closed behind them. They were in a private space and no
one could intrude.

There were other couples like them, hand in hand,
secret and serene as they. But none of them, as Ernest
pointed out, had a red balloon. They laughed delightedly
at their uniqueness.

They stared at a yak, watched a tiger pace, heard an
elephant trumpet, saw the cavortings of sea lions, listened
to the chattering of baboons, and were splashed by a
diving polar bear. Even the caged animals seemed pleased
by that blooming day.

Finally, wearying, they bought beers and sandwiches
and carried them out of the zoo to a patch of greensward
where the sounds of carnival and the cries of animals were
muted.

They sat on the warm earth, Zoe's back against the
trunk of a gnarled plane tree. They sipped their beers,
nibbled their sandwiches. A fat squirrel came close to
inspect them, but when Zoe tossed a crust, it darted off.
Two pigeons fought over the crust, divided it, waited
hopefully for more, then flew away.

Dappled light melted through the foliage above them.
The world was solid beneath them. The air was awash
with far-off cries and the faint lilt of music. They could see
joggers, cyclists, horse-drawn carriages move along a
distant road. A freshening wind brought the sweet smell
of growing things.

Ernest Mittle lay supine, his head on Zoe's lap, eyes
closed. She stroked his hair absently, looking about and
feeling they were alone on earth. The last. The only.

"I wish we could stay here forever," she murmured.
"Like this."

He opened his eyes to look up at her.

"Never go home," he said softly. "Never go to work
again. No more subways and buses and traffic. No more
noise and dirt. No violence and crime and cruelty. We'll
just stay here forever and ever."

"Yes," she said wonderingly. "Just the two of us
together."

He sat up, took her hand, kissed her fingertips.

"Wouldn't that be fine?" he said. "Wouldn't that be

grand? Zoe, I've never felt so good. Never been so happy. Why can't it last?"

"It can't," she said.

"No," he said, "I suppose not. But you're happy, aren't you? I mean right this minute?"

"Oh yes," she said. "Happier than I've ever been in my life."

He lay back again; she resumed smoothing the webby hair back from his temples.

"Did you have a lot of boyfriends, Zoe?" he asked quietly. "I mean when you were growing up."

"No, Ernie," she said, just as dreamily. "Not many."

On a lawn, beneath a tree, blue shadows mottling, they were in the world but not of it. Locked in lovers' isolation. Away from the caged and uncaged animals, and somehow protected from them by their twoness.

"My mother was strict," she said in a memory-dulled voice. "So strict. The boy had to call for me and come inside for inspection. I had to be home by eleven. Midnight on weekends, but eleven during the week."

He made a sound of sympathy. Neither moved now, fearing to move. It was a moment of fragile balance. They knew they were risking revealment. Opening up—a sweet pain. They inched cautiously to intimacy, recognizing the dangers.

"Once I went out with a boy," she said. "A nice boy. His car broke down so I couldn't get home in time. My mother called the police. Can you imagine that? It was awful."

"It's for your own good, my dear," he said in a high-pitched feminine voice.

"Yes. That's what she said. It was for my own good. But after that, I wasn't very popular."

They were silent then, and content with their closeness. It seemed to them that what they were doing, unfolding, could be done slowly. It might even cost a lifetime. All the safer for that. Knowing was a process, not a flash, and it might never end.

"I was never popular," he said, a voice between rue and hurt. "I was small. Not an athlete or anything like that. And I never had enough money to take a girl to the movies. I didn't have any real girlfriends. I never went steady."

It was so new to them—this tender confession. They were daunted by the strange world. Shells were cracking; the naked babes peered out in fear and want. They understood there was a price to be paid for these first fumblings. Involvement presaged a future they could not see.

"I never went steady either," she said, determined not to stop. "Very few boys ever asked me out a second time."

"What a waste," he said, sighing. "For both of us. I didn't think any girl could be interested in me. I was afraid to ask. And you . . ."

"I was afraid, too. Of being alone with a boy. Mother again. Don't do this. Don't do that. Don't let a boy—you know . . . get personal."

"We were robbed," he said. "Both of us. All those years."

"Yes. Robbed."

Silence again. A comfortable quiet. The wind was freshening, cooling. She looked down at him, cupped his pale face in her palms. Their eyes searched.

"But you married," he said.

"Yes. I did."

She bent, he craned up. Their soft lips met, pressed, lingered. They kissed. They kissed.

"Oh," he breathed. "Oh, oh."

She traced his face, smiling sadly. She felt his brow, cheeks, nose, lips. He closed his eyes, and lightly, lightly, she touched the velvet eyelids, made gentle circles. Then she leaned again to press her lips softly.

She straightened up. She shivered with a sudden chill.

His eyes opened, he looked at her with concern.

"Cold?"

"A little," she said. "Ernie, maybe we should think about leaving."

"Sure," he said, scrambling to his feet.

He helped her up, picked twigs from her skirt, brushed bits of bark from the back of her tweed jacket.

"What should we do with the balloon?" he asked.

"Let's turn it loose," she said. "Let it fly away."

"Right," he said, and untied the string from her purse.

He handed it to her and let her release it. The red balloon rose slowly. Then, caught by the strengthening wind, it went soaring away. They watched it fly up, pulled this way and that, but sailing higher and higher, getting smaller and smaller until it was lost in the sky.

They wandered slowly back to the paved walkway.

"Something I've wanted to ask you, Zoe," he said, looking at the ground. "Is Kohler your married name or your maiden name?"

"My married name. It was on all my legal papers and driver's license and so forth. It just seemed too much trouble to change everything. My maiden name is Spencer."

"Zoe Spencer," he said. "That's nice. Zoe is a very unusual name."

"I think it's Greek," she said. "It means 'life.' It was my mother's idea."

"What's her name?" he asked.

"Irene," she said.

Dr. Oscar Stark's receptionist had Zoe's home and office telephone numbers in her file. On the afternoon of May 13th, the doctor called Zoe at the Hotel Granger and asked how she was feeling.

She told him she felt better since her period had ended, but sometimes she felt torpid and without energy. She reported nothing about her nausea, the continued loss of weight, the increasing incidents of syncope.

He asked if she was taking the doubled cortisone dosage and the salt tablets. She said she was and, in answer to his questions, told him she suffered no stomach upset from intake of the steroid hormone and experienced no craving for additional salt.

He then said that he had received the results of her latest blood and urine tests. They seemed to indicate a slight cortisol deficiency. Dr. Stark said it was nothing to be concerned about, but nothing to disregard either. He instructed her to take her medication faithfully, and he would reevaluate the situation after her office visit on June 3rd.

Meanwhile, he wanted Zoe to stop by and pick up a new prescription. It would be left with his receptionist, so Zoe would not have to wait.

The prescription would be for two items. The first was an identification bracelet that Stark wanted Zoe to wear

at all times. It would give her name and Stark's name and
telephone number. It would also state that Zoe Kohler
suffered from an adrenal insufficiency, and in case of an
emergency such as injury or fainting she was to be
injected with hydrocortisone.

The hydrocortisone would be in a small labeled kit that
Zoe was to carry in her purse at all times. The solution
was contained in a packaged sterile syringe, ready for use.

Dr. Stark repeated all this and asked if Zoe understood. She said she did. He assured her the bracelet and
kit were merely a precautionary measure and he doubted
if they'd ever be used. He was having them made up at a
medical supply house down on Third Avenue. Zoe would
have to pay for them, but a check would be acceptable.

She copied the name and address he gave her.

On the following day, during her lunch hour, she
picked up the prescription at Dr. Stark's office, then
cabbed down to the medical supply house and purchased
the bracelet and kit. When she returned to the Hotel
Granger, she put them in the back of the bottom drawer
of her desk. She never looked at them again.

On the night of May 16th, Zoe was alone at home. She
had just showered and was wearing her old flannel robe
and frayed mules. She was curled on the couch, filing her
nails, wondering about the slight discoloration in the folds
of her knuckles, and watching *Rebecca* on TV.

A little before ten o'clock her phone rang and the
doorman reported that Mrs. Kurnitz was in the lobby and
wanted to come up. Zoe told him to let her in and went to
the door to wait.

Maddie came striding down the corridor from the
elevator. She had a soiled white raincoat over her
shoulders like a cape, empty sleeves flapping out behind
her. Her makeup was a mess, smudged and runny. Zoe
thought she had been weeping.

"Maddie," she said, "what are—"

"You got anything to drink?" Maddie demanded.
"Beer, whiskey, wine? Or cleaning fluid, lye, hemlock? I
don't give a good goddamn."

Zoe got her inside and locked the door. Maddie flung
her coat to the floor. Zoe picked it up. Maddie tried to
light a cigarette and broke it with trembling fingers. She
dropped that on the floor, too, and Zoe picked it up.

Maddie finally got a cigarette lighted and collapsed onto the couch, puffing furiously.

"I have some vodka," Zoe said, "and some—"

"Vodka is fine. A *biiig* vodka. On the rocks. No mix. Just more vodka."

Zoe went into the kitchen to pour Maddie's drink and a glass of white wine for herself. Because her supply of Valium was getting low, she took two Librium before she went back into the living room.

Maddie drained half the vodka in two throat-wrenching gulps. Zoe turned off the TV set and sat down in an armchair facing her visitor.

"Maddie," she said, "what on earth is—"

"That bastard!" Maddie cried. "That cocksucker! I should have kicked him in the balls."

"Who?" Zoe said bewilderedly. "Who are you talking about?"

"Harry. That asshole husband of mine. He's been cheating on me."

"Oh, Maddie," Zoe said sorrowfully, "are you sure?"

"Sure I'm sure. The son of a bitch told me himself."

She seemed halfway between fury and tears. Zoe had never seen her so defeated. Heavy breasts sagged, fleshy body spread. All of her appeared slack and punished. Chipped fingernails and smeared lipstick. Gaudy had become seedy.

She lighted a new cigarette from the butt of the old. She looked about vaguely.

"First time I've been up here," she said dully. "Christ, you're neat. Clean and neat."

"Yes," Zoe said. Then, when Maddie finished her vodka, she went into the kitchen again and brought back the bottle. She watched Maddie fill her glass, bottle clinking against the rim.

"It's not the cheating I mind," Maddie said loudly. "You know I play around, too. He can screw every woman in New York for all I care. We had this understanding. He could play, and I could play, and neither of us cared, and no one got hurt."

"Well then?" Zoe said.

"He wants to marry the bitch," Maddie said with a harsh bark of laughter. "Some stupid little twit in his office. He wants to divorce me and marry her. Did you ever?"

Zoe was silent.

"I met her," Maddie went on. "She was at that party you went to. A washed-out blonde with tits like funnels. A body that doesn't end and a brain that never starts. Maybe that's what Harry wants: a brainless fuck. Maybe I threaten him. Do you think I threaten him?"

"I don't think so, Maddie."

"Who the hell knows. Anyway, I'm out and she's in. God, what a bummer. What hurts is that he knows how much a divorce is going to cost him—I'm going to take the fillings right out of his teeth—but he still wants it. Like he'll pay anything to get rid of me. I even suggested we stick together and he could set her up on the side—you know? I wouldn't care. But no, he wants a clean break. That's what he said: 'a clean break.' I'd like to cleanly break his goddamned neck!"

"Uh, Maddie," Zoe said timidly, "I can understand your being upset, but you've been divorced before."

"I know, sweetie, I know. That's why I'm so down. I'm beginning to worry. What's wrong with me? Why can't I hold a guy? It lasts two or three years and then it falls apart. I get bored with him, or he gets bored with me, and off we go to the lawyers. Shit!"

"But you love—"

"Love?" Maddie said. "What the fuck is love? Having laughs together and moaning in the hay? If that's what love is, then I love Harry. A great sense of humor and a stallion in the sack. Generous with money. I had no complaints there. And he never bitched. Then *whammo!* Out of a clear blue sky he dumps on me."

"Is she younger?"

"Not all that much. If she was like nineteen or twenty, I could understand it. I'd figure he was going through a change of life and had to prove he could still cut the mustard with a young chick. But she's got to be thirty, at least, so what the hell does he see in her? I'm drinking all your booze, kiddo."

"That's all right. Take as much as you want."

"Harry dumps on me and I dump on you. I'm sorry. But I had to talk to a woman. I don't have any close women friends. A lot of guys, but all good-time Charlies.

They don't want to listen to my troubles. And they're not going to be overjoyed to hear I'm getting unhitched. Zapping a married woman is fun and games, and no problems. When you haven't got a husband, a lot of men steer clear. Too much risk."

"Is there anyone you . . . ?"

"Anyone I can snare on the rebound? No one in the picture right now. Another thing that scares me. Let's face it, luv, we're both getting long in the tooth. You've kept your body, but the rare beef and bourbon are catching up with me. Plus more than my share of one-night stands. I look like an old broad; I know it."

Zoe murmured something about going on a diet, cutting down on the drinking, buying some new clothes. But Madeline Kurnitz wasn't listening. She was staring off into the middle distance, the glass of vodka held near her lips.

"I've got to be married," she said. "Don't ask me why, but I've *got* to be. What the hell else can I do in this world? I wouldn't know how to earn a living if my life depended on it. I'm too old to peddle my ass, and just the idea of spending eight hours a day in some stinking office is enough to give me the up-chucks. I don't know how you do it."

"It's not so bad."

"The hell it isn't. While other women are having lunch at the Plaza and buying out Bonwit's . . . I couldn't stand that."

Zoe went to the kitchen again and brought back the bottle of white wine and a bowl of ice cubes for Maddie. They sat in silence for a few moments, sipping their drinks. Maddie kicked off her shoes, pulled up her feet, began picking reflectively at the silver polish on her toenails.

"You know, sweetie, my whole life has revolved around men. It really has. I mean I've depended on them. My daddy spoiled me rotten, and then I went from husband to husband like there was no tomorrow. And what have I got to show for it? A dead father and four flopped marriages. I suppose the women liberationists would say it's my fault, I should have done something with my life. Been more independent and all that horse-shit. But Goddamnit, I like men. I like to be with men.

Why the hell should I work my tuchas to a frazzle when there was always a guy ready to pick up the tab?"

"You'll find someone new."

"Yeah? I wish I could believe it. I'll take enough out of Harry's hide so that money won't be a problem. For a while at least. But I just can't live alone. I can't stand to be by myself. You can handle it, but I can't."

"Sometimes you have no choice," Zoe said.

"That's what scares me," Maddie said. "No choice. Thank God I never had any kids. Life is shitty enough without worrying about brats. Did you ever want to have kids, Zoe?"

"Once maybe. Not anymore."

"That fucking Harry sure pulled the plug on me. He's got me feeling sorry for myself—something I've never done before. That lousy turd. God, I'm going to miss him. Two years ago, for my birthday, he bought me a purple Mercedes-Benz convertible with my initials on the door."

"What happened to it?"

"I totaled it on the Long Island Expressway. I was drunk or I would have killed myself. But that's the way he was. Anything I wanted. He spoiled me rotten like my father. Oh Jesus, baby, I must be boring you senseless."

"Oh no, Maddie. I'm glad you came to me. I just wish there was some way I could help."

"You've done enough just listening to me. I don't know what—"

Suddenly Madeline Kurnitz was weeping. She cried silently, tears welling from her eyes and straggling down her powdered cheeks. Zoe went over to the couch, sat next to her, put an arm across her shoulders.

"God, God," Maddie wailed, "what am I going to do?"

Zoe Kohler didn't know. So she said, "Shh, shh," and held the other woman until she stopped crying. After a while, Maddie said, "Shit," blew her nose, took her bag and went into the bathroom.

She came out about ten minutes later, hair combed, makeup repaired. Her eyes were puffy but clear. She gave Zoe a rueful smile.

"Sorry about that, luv," she said. "I thought I was all cried out."

"Maddie, would you like to stay the night? You can

take the bed and I'll sleep out here on the couch. Why don't you?"

"No, kiddo, but I appreciate the offer. I'll have one more drink and then I'll take off. I better get home before that shithead changes the locks on the doors. I feel a lot better now. What the hell, it's just another kick in the ass. That's what life is all about—right?"

She sat again on the couch, put more ice in her glass, filled it with vodka. She stirred it with a forefinger, then sucked the finger. She bowed her head, looked up at Zoe.

"Seeing as how it's hair-down time," she said, "how about the sad story of your life? You never did tell me what happened between you and—what was his name? Ralph?"

"Kenneth. And I told you. Don't you remember, Maddie? At that lunch we had at the hotel?"

"You mean the sex thing? Sure, I remember. You never got your rocks off with him. But there's got to be more to it than that."

"Oh . . . it was a lot of things."

"Like what?"

"Silly things."

"Other people's reasons for divorce always sound silly. First of all, how did you meet the guy?"

"He was with an insurance company and was transferred to their agency in Winona. He handled all my father's business policies, and Daddy brought him home for dinner one night. He called me up for a date and we started going out. Then we began getting invited to parties and things as a couple. Then he asked me to marry him."

"Handsome?"

"I thought so. Very big and beefy. He could be very jolly and charming when there were other people around. But about six months after we were married, he quit the insurance company and my father hired him as a kind of junior partner. Daddy was getting old, slowing down, and he wanted someone to sort of take over."

"Oh-ho. And did your husband know this when he asked you to marry him?"

"Yes. I didn't know it at the time, but later, during one of our awful arguments, he told me that was the only reason he married me."

"Nice guy."

"Well . . . a handsome man says you're beautiful, and he's in love with you, and you believe it."

"Not me, kiddo. I know all he wants is to dip Cecil in the hot grease."

"I believed him. I guess I should have known better. I'm no raving beauty; I know that. I'm quiet and not very exciting. But I thought he really did love me for what I am. I know I loved him. At first."

Maddie looked at her shrewdly.

"Zoe, maybe you just loved him for loving you—or saying he did."

"Yes. That's possible."

They were subdued then, pondering the complexities of living, the role played by chance and accident, the masks people wear, and the masks beneath the masks.

"When did the fights start?" Maddie asked.

"Almost from the start. We were so different, and we couldn't seem to change. We couldn't compromise enough to move closer to each other. He was so—so *physical.* He was loud and had this braying laugh. He seemed to fill a room. I mean, I could be alone in the house, and he'd come in, and I'd feel crowded. He was always touching me, patting me, slapping my behind, trying to muss my hair right after I had it done. I told you they were silly things, Maddie."

"Not so silly."

"He was just—just all over me. He suffocated me. I got so I didn't even want to breathe the air when he was in the house. The air seemed hot and choking and smelled of his cologne. And he was so messy. Leaving wet towels on the bathroom floor. Throwing his dirty underwear and socks on the bed. I couldn't stand that. He'd have dinner, belch, and just walk away, leaving me to clean up. I know a wife is supposed to do that, but he took it for granted. He was so sure of himself. I think that's what I hated most—his superior attitude. I was like a slave or something, and had no right to question what he did or where he went."

"He sounds like a real charmer. Did he play around?"

"Not at first. Then I began to notice things: women whispering about him at parties, his going out at night after dinner. To see customers, he said. Once, when I took his black suit to the cleaners, there was a book of matches in his pocket. It was from a roadhouse out of town. It didn't, ah, have a very good reputation. So I guess he was playing around. I didn't care. As long as he left me alone."

"Oh, Zoe, was it that bad?"

"I tried, Maddie, really I did. But he was so heavy, and strong, and sort of—sort of uncouth."

"Wham, bam, thank you, ma'am?"

"Something like that. And also, he wanted to do it when he was drunk or all sweated up. I'd ask him to take a shower first, but he'd laugh at me."

"Hung?"

"What?"

"Was he hung? A big whang?"

"Uh, I don't know, Maddie. I don't have much basis for comparison. He was, uh, bigger than Michelangelo's *David*."

Madeline Kurnitz laughed. How she laughed! She bobbed with merriment, slopping her drink.

"Honey, *everyone* is bigger than Michelangelo's *David*."

"And he wanted to do disgusting things. I told him I wasn't brought up that way."

"Uh-huh."

"I told him if he wanted to act like an animal, I was sure he could find other women to accommodate him."

"That wasn't so smart, luv."

"I was past the point of worrying if what I said was smart. I just didn't want anything more to do with him. In bed, I mean. I would have kept on being married to him if he just forgot all about sex with me. Because I felt divorce would be a failure, and my mother would be so disappointed in me. But then he just walked out of the house, quit his job with my father, and left town. Lawyers handled the divorce and I never saw him again."

"Know what happened to him?"

"Yes. He went out to the West Coast. He got married again. About a week ago."

"How do you know that?"

"He sent me an invitation."

Maddie exhaled noisily. "Another prick. What a shitty thing to do."

"I was going to send a gift. Just, you know, to show him

I didn't care. But I, ah, tore up the invitation and I don't have the address."

"Screw him. Send him a bottle of cyanide. All men should drop dead."

"Oh, Maddie, I don't know . . . I guess some of it, a lot of it, was my fault. But I tried so hard to be a good wife, really I did. I cooked all his favorite foods and I was always trying new recipes I thought he'd like. I kept the house as clean as a pin. Everyone said it was a showplace. We had all new furniture, and once he got angry and ripped all the plastic covers off. That's the way he was. He'd put his feet on the cocktail table and use the guest towels. I think he did those things just to annoy me. He swore a lot—dreadful words—and wouldn't go to church. He wanted me to wear tight sweaters and low-cut things. I told him I wasn't like that, but he could never understand. He even wanted me to wear more makeup and have my hair tinted. So I guess I just wasn't the kind of woman he should have married. It was a mistake from the start."

"Oh, sweetie, it's not the end of the world. You'll find someone new."

"That's what I told you," Zoe said, smiling.

"Yeah," Maddie said, with a twisted grin, "ain't that a crock? Two old bags drinking up a storm and trying to cheer each other up. Well . . . what the hell; tomorrow's another day. You still seeing Mister Meek?"

"I wish you wouldn't call him that, Maddie. He's not like that at all. Yes, I'm still seeing him."

"Like him?"

"Very much."

"Uh-huh. Well, maybe he's more your type than Ralph."

"Kenneth."

"Whatever. You think he's interested in getting married?"

"We've never discussed it," Zoe said primly.

"Discuss it, discuss it," Maddie advised. "You don't have to ask him right out, but you can kind of hint around about how he feels on the subject. He likes you?"

"He says he does."

"Well, that's a start." Maddie yawned, finished her drink, stood up and began to gather her things together. "I've got to get going. Thanks for the booze and the talk.

You were right there when I needed you, honey, and I love you for it. Let's see more of each other."

"Oh yes. I'd like that."

After Maddie left, Zoe Kohler locked and bolted the outside door. She plumped the cushions on couch and armchair. She returned the bottles to the kitchen, washed the glasses and ashtrays. She took a Tuinal and turned off the lights. She peeked through the venetian blind but could see no sign of the watcher across the street.

She got into bed. She lay on her back, arms down at her sides. She stared at the ceiling.

Those things she had told Maddie—they were all true. But she had the oddest feeling that they had happened to someone else. Not her. She had been describing the life of a stranger, something she had heard or read. It was not her life.

She turned onto her side and drew up her knees beneath the light blanket and sheet. She clamped her clasped hands between her thighs.

He was probably trying to get his new wife to do those disgusting things. Maybe she was doing them. And enjoying them.

It was all so common and coarse . . .

There was a luncheonette near 40th Street and Madison Avenue that Zoe Kohler passed on her way to and from work. It opened early in the morning and closed early in the evening. The food, mostly sandwiches, soups, and salads, was all right. Nothing special, but adequate.

On her way home, the evening of May 21st, Zoe stopped at the luncheonette for dinner. She had a cheeseburger with French fries, which she salted liberally. A cup of black coffee and a vanilla custard.

She sat by herself at a table for two and ate rapidly. She kept her eyes lowered and paid no attention to the noisy confusion churning about her. She left a fifteen percent tip, paid her check at the cashier's counter, and hurried out.

She went directly home. Her alimony check was in the mailbox and she tucked it into her purse. In her apartment, door carefully locked, bolted, and chained, she drew the blinds and changed into a cotton T shirt and terry cloth shorts.

She took out mops, brooms, vacuum cleaner, cans of soap and wax, bottles of detergent, brushes, dustpan, pail, rags, sponges, whisks. She tied a scarf about her hair. She pulled on rubber gloves. She set to work.

In the bathroom, she scrubbed the tub, sink, and toilet bowl with Ajax. Washed the toilet seat with Lysol. Removed the bathmat from the floor, got down on her knees, and cleaned the tile with a brush and Spic and Span.

It had not been a good day. On the street, she had been pushed and jostled. In the office, she had been treated with cold indifference. Everyone in New York had a brusque assurance that daunted her. She wondered if she had made a mistake in coming to the city.

Emptied the medicine cabinet of all her makeup, perfume, medical supplies, and soap. Took out the shelves, washed them with Glass Plus and dried them. Replaced everything neatly, but not before wiping the dust from every jar, bottle, box, and tin.

The very size of the city demeaned her. It crumbled her ego, reduced her to a cipher by ignoring her existence. New York denied her humanness and treated her as a thing, no more than concrete, steel, and asphalt.

Shined the mirror of the medicine cabinet with Windex. Changed the shower curtain. Brought in a clean bathmat. Hung fresh towels, including two embroidered guest towels, although the old ones had not been used.

In the city, people paid to hear other people sing and watch other people feel. Passion had become a spectator sport supported by emotional cripples. Love and suffering were knacks possessed by the talented who were paid to display their gifts.

Emptied the wastebasket and put in a fresh plastic liner. Flushed Drano down the sink and tub drains. Changed the Vanish dispenser in the toilet tank that caused blue water to rush in with every flush. Sprayed the whole bathroom with lemon-scented Glade. Washed fingerprints from the door with Soft Scrub. Turned off the light.

Still, the anonymity of life in New York had its secret rewards. Where else but in this thundering chaos could she experience her adventures? If the city denied her humanity, it was big enough and uncaring enough to tolerate the frailties, vices, and sins of the insensate creatures it produced.

In the bedroom, she changed all the linen, replacing mattress cover, top and bottom sheets, and pillowcases. Made up the new bed with taut surfaces and sharp hospital corners. Turned down the bed, the top sheet overlapping the wool blanket by four inches.

Why had she sought adventures, and why did she continue? She could not frame a clear and lucid answer. She knew that what she was doing was monstrous, but that was no rein. The mind may reason, but the body will have its own. Who can master his appetites? The blood boils, and all is lost.

Dusted the dresser, bureau, and bedside table with Pride. Not only the top surfaces, but the front, sides, and legs as well. Cleaned the telephone with Lysol. Washed and polished the mirror with Windex. Wiped the ashtrays clean and dusted the bulbs in the lamps.

During her adventures, she quit the gallery for the stage. Never had she felt so alive and vindicated, never so charged with the hot stuff of animal existence. It was not that she donned a costume, but that she doffed a skin and emerged reborn.

Used her Eureka canister vacuum cleaner on the wall-to-wall carpeting, moving furniture when necessary. Dusted the slats of the venetian blinds. Cleaned fingerprints from the doorjambs. Lubricated the hinges of the closet with 3-in-One Oil.

Why her desire to live should have taken such a desperate form she could not have said. There were forces working on her that were dimly glimpsed. She felt herself buffeted, pushed this way and that, by powers as impersonal as the crush on city streets. The choice was hers, but so limited as to be no choice at all.

Rearranged all her clothing into precisely aligned stacks, piles, racks. Put a crocheted doily under the empty glass vase on the bedside table. Replaced the Mildewcide bags in the closet. Added more lavender sachets to the dresser and bureau drawers. Looked around. Turned off the lights.

She smiled at the theatricality of her existence. She relished the convolutions of her life. It was a soap opera! Her life was a soap opera! All lives were soap operas. At the end, just before the death rattle, a whispered, "Thank you, Proctor and Gamble."

In the kitchen, she took everything from the cupboards, cabinets, and closets. Washed the interiors with Mr. Clean. Dusted every item before putting it back. Wiped the doors. Applied Klean 'n Shine to get rid of fingerprints.

Who *was* she? The complexities defeated her. It seemed to her that she lived a dozen lives, sometimes two or more simultaneously. She turned different faces to different people. Worse, she turned different faces to herself.

Used Fantastik on the range top and refrigerator. Scrubbed away grease and splatters with Lestoil. Cleaned the stainless steel with Sheila Shine. Took all the food out of the refrigerator. Washed the interior. Put in a new open package of Arm & Hammer baking soda. Replaced the food.

Age brought not self-knowledge but a growing fear of failure to solve her mystery. Who she was, her essence, seemed to be drifting away, the smoke thinning, a misty figure lost. Her life had lost its edges; she saw herself blurred and going.

Used Bon Ami on the sink. Polished the faucets. Poured a little Drano down the drain. Threw away a sliver of hand soap and put out a fresh bar of Ivory. Replaced the worn Brillo pad. Hung fresh hand towel and dishtowel.

She wished for a shock to bring her into focus. A fatal wound or a conquering emotion. Something to which she could give. She thought surrender might save her and make her whole. She felt within herself a well of devotion untapped and unwanted.

Mopped the tiled floor with soapy water. Dry-mopped it. Mopped again with Glo-Coat. Waited until it dried, then waxed it again with Future. Looked around at the sparkle.

She wondered if love could be at once that emotion and that wound. She had never thought of herself as a passionate woman, but now she saw that if chance and accident might conspire, she could be complete: a new woman of grace and feeling.

In the living room, she dusted with an oiled rag. Used

Pledge on the tabletops. Wiped the legs of tables and chairs. Plumped pillows and cushions. Put fresh lace doilies under ashtrays and vases.

To Madeline Kurnitz, love was pleasure and laughter. But surely there was more. It might be such a rare, delicate thing, a seedling, that only by wise and willing nurture could it grow strong enough to make a world and save a soul.

Wiped picture frames and washed the glass. Ran a dry mop along baseboards. Washed fingerprints from doors and jambs. Polished a lamp with Top Brass. Cleaned the light bulb. Straightened the kinked cord.

If such a thing should happen to her, if she knew the growth, her body would heal of itself, and all the empty places in her life would be filled. She dreamed of that transfiguration and lusted for it with an almost physical want.

Vacuumed the wall-to-wall carpeting. Moved furniture to clean underneath. Replaced the furniture so the legs set precisely on the little plastic coasters. Used a vacuum cleaner attachment to dust the drapes. Another attachment on the couch and chair cushions. Another attachment to clean the ceiling molding.

Her vision soared; with love, there was nothing she might not do. The city would be created anew, she would have no need for adventures, and she would recognize herself and be content. All that by the purity of love.

Straightened the outside closet. Shook out and rehung all the garments, including her hidden gowns. Dusted the shelves. Wiped off the shoes and replaced them on the racks. Fluffed her wigs. Dusted the venetian blinds. Sprayed the whole room with Breath o' Pine.

Her penance done, she put away all the brooms, mops, vacuum cleaner, cans of soap and wax, bottles of detergent, brushes, dustpan, pail, rags, sponges, and whisks. She undressed in the bedroom while her bath was running. She went into the kitchen, swallowed several vitamin and mineral pills, capsules of this and that. A Valium. A salt tablet.

She started to pour a glass of wine, but changed her mind before opening the bottle. Instead, she poured vodka on the rocks. A big one. Like Maddie. She took that into the bathroom with her.

She eased cautiously into the hot tub. Added scented oil to the water. She floated, sipping her iced vodka. Her weariness became a warm glow. She looked down at her wavering body through half-closed eyes.

"I love you," she murmured aloud, and wondered who she addressed: Kenneth, Ernest Mittle, or herself. She decided it didn't matter; the words had a meaning of their own. They were important. "I love you."

Ernest Mittle arrived promptly at noon on Sunday, May 25th. He brought an enormous bunch of daffodils, so large that Zoe could fill vases in the living room and bedroom, with a few stalks left over for the kitchen. The golden yellow brought sunlight into her dark apartment.

She had prepared a Sunday brunch of Bloody Marys, scrambled eggs with Canadian bacon, hot biscuits, a watercress salad, and a lemon ice for dessert. She also served chilled May wine with a fresh strawberry in each glass.

They sat at the seldom used dining table, a small oval of mahogany with four ladder-back chairs set before the living room window. The china and plated silver service had been wedding gifts. Zoe had bought the crystal salad bowl and napery after she moved to New York.

Ernest complimented her enthusiastically on everything: the shining apartment, the dining table prepared just so, the excellence of the food, the fruity, almost perfumed flavor of the wine.

"Really," Zoe said, "it's nothing."

They were at ease with each other, talking animatedly of their jobs, summer clothes they were thinking of buying, TV shows they had seen.

They spoke as old friends, for already they were learning each other's habits, likes and dislikes, prejudices and fancies. And they were building a fund of mutual memories: the dinner at the Italian restaurant, the Kurnitz party, the meatloaf Ernest had made, the balloon in Central Park.

Each recollection was in itself insignificant, but made meaningful by being shared. They knew this pleasant brunch would be added to their bank of shared experience, and seemed all the more precious for that. An occasion to be savored and recalled.

After the brunch, Ernest insisted on helping Zoe clear the table. In the kitchen, she washed and he dried, and it seemed the most natural thing in the world. He even replaced all the clean dishes and cutlery in their proper racks in the correct cupboards.

Then they moved to the living room. The May wine was finished, but Zoe served vodka-and-tonics, with a wedge of fresh lime in each. She brought her little radio in from the bedroom, and found a station that was featuring Mantovani.

The dreamy music played softly in the background. They sprawled comfortably, sipping their iced drinks. They smiled at each other with satiety and ease. It seemed to them they recaptured the mood they had felt in the park: they owned the world.

"Will you be getting a vacation?" he asked casually.

"Oh yes. Two weeks."

"When are you taking it?"

"I haven't decided yet. They're very good about that. I can take off in June, July, or August."

"Me, too," he said. "I get two weeks. I usually go home for a few days. Sometimes a week."

"I do, too."

"Zoe . . ." he said.

She looked at him questioningly.

"Do you think . . . Would it be possible for us to go somewhere together? For a week, or maybe just a weekend? Don't get me wrong," he added hastily. "Not to share a room or anything like that. I just thought it might be fun to be together this summer for a while in some nice place."

She pondered a moment, head cocked.

"I think that's a fine idea," she said. "Maybe somewhere on Long Island."

"Or New England."

"There's a woman in the hotel who arranges tours and cruises and things like that. I could ask her to recommend some nice place."

"No swinging resorts," he said. "Where we'd have to dress up and all."

"Oh no," she said. "A quiet place on the beach. Where we can swim and walk and just relax."

"Right!" he said. "With good food. And not too

crowded. It doesn't have to be supermodern with chrome and glitter and organized activities."

"Nothing like that," she agreed. "Maybe just an old, family-run tourist home or motel. Where no one would bother us."

"And we could do whatever we want. Swim and walk the beach. Collect shells and driftwood. Explore the neighborhood. I'd like that."

"I would, too," she said. She took their glasses into the kitchen and brought them fresh drinks. "Ernie," she said, sitting alongside him on the couch and taking his hand, "what you said about our not sharing a room—I was glad you said that. I suppose you think I'm some kind of a prude?" .

"I don't think anything of the sort."

"Well, I'm not. It's just that going away together would be such a—such a new thing for us. And sharing a room would just make it more complicated. You understand?"

"Of course," he said. "That's exactly what I think. Who knows—if we're together for three days or a week, I might drive you batty."

"Oh no," she protested. "I think we'll get along very well and have a good time. I just don't think we should, you know, start off knowing we were going to sleep together. I'd be very nervous and embarrassed."

He looked at her with admiration.

"Just the way I feel, Zoe. We're so much alike. We don't have to rush anything or do anything that might spoil what we've got. Don't you feel that way?"

"Oh, I do, Ernie, I do! You're so considerate."

She had turned to look at him. He seemed a quiet, inoffensive man, no more exciting than she. But she saw beauty in his clear features and guileless eyes. There was a clean innocence about him, an openness. He would never deceive her or hurt her; she knew that.

"I don't want you to think I'm sexless," she said intently.

"Zoe, I could never think that. I think you're a very deep, passionate woman."

"Do you?" she said. "Do you really? I'm not very modern, you know. I mean, I don't hop around from bed to bed. I think that's terrible."

"It's worse than terrible," he said. "It just reduces

everyone to animals. I think sex has to be the result of a very deep emotional need, and a desire for honest intimacy."

"Yes," she said. "And physical love should be gentle and tender and sweet."

"Correct," he said, nodding. "It should be something two people decide to share because they really and truly love each other and want to, uh, give each other pleasure. Happiness."

"Oh, that's very true," she said, "and I'm so glad you feel that way. It's really valuable, isn't it? Sex, I mean. You just don't throw it around all over the place. That cheapens it."

"It makes it nothing," he said. "Like, 'Should we have another martini or should we go to bed?' It really should mean more than that. I guess I'm a romantic."

"I guess I am, too."

"You know what's so wonderful, dear?" he said, twisting around to face her. "It's that with both of us feeling this way, we found each other. With the millions and millions of people in the world, we found each other. Don't you think that's marvelous?"

"Oh yes, darling," she breathed, touching his cheek.

"Just think of the odds against it! I know I've never met a woman like you before."

"And I've never met a man like you."

He kissed her palm.

"I'm nothing much," he said. "I know that. I mean, I'm not tall and strong and handsome. I suppose someday I'll be making a good living, but I'll never be rich. I'm just not—not ruthless enough. But still, I don't want to change. I don't want to be greedy and cruel, out for all I can get."

"Oh no!" she cried. "Don't change, Ernie. I like you just the way you are. I don't want you different. I couldn't stand that."

They put their drinks aside. They embraced. It seemed to them they were huddling, giving comfort to each other in the face of catastrophe. As survivors might hold each other, in fear and in hope.

"We'll go away together this summer, darling," she whispered. "We'll spend every minute with each other. We'll swim and walk the beach and explore."

"Oh yes," he said dreamily. "Just the two of us."

"Against the world," Zoe Kohler said, kissing him.

Something was happening. Zoe Kohler read it in the newspapers, heard it on radio, saw it on TV. The search for the Hotel Ripper had been widened, the investigating force enlarged, the leads being followed had multiplied.

More important, the police were now discussing publicly the possibility that the killer was a woman. The "Daughter of Sam" headline was revived. Statements were issued warning visitors to midtown Manhattan of the dangers of striking up acquaintance with strangers, men or women, on the streets, in bars and cocktail lounges, in discos and restaurants.

The search for the slayer took on a new urgency. The summer tourist season was approaching; the number of canceled conventions and tours was increasing. Newspaper editorialists quoted the dollar loss that could be expected if the killer was not quickly caught.

Surprisingly, there was little of the public hysteria that had engulfed the city during the Son of Sam case. One columnist suggested this might be due to the fact that, so far, all the victims had been out-of-towners.

More likely, he added, familiarity with mass murder had dulled the public's reaction. The recent Chicago case, with more than a score of victims, made the Hotel Ripper of minor interest. There now seemed to be an intercity competition in existence, similar to the contest to build the highest skyscraper.

But despite the revived interest of the media in the Hotel Ripper case, Zoe could find no evidence that the police had any specific information about the killer's identity. She was convinced they were no closer to solving the case than they had been after her first adventure.

So what happened to her on the afternoon of May 28th came as a numbing shock.

Mr. Pinckney had originally obtained the Chemical Mace for her as a protection against muggers and rapists. She did not want to risk telling him it had been used, lying about the circumstances, and asking him to supply another container. So she said nothing. The Mace wasn't an absolute necessity; a knife was.

She had purchased her Swiss Army pocket knife at a

cutlery shop, one of a chain, in Grand Central Station. This time she determined to buy a heavier knife at a different store of the same chain. During her lunch hour, she walked over to Fifth Avenue and 46th Street.

An enormous selection of pocket knives, jackknives, and hunting knives was offered. Zoe waited patiently at the counter while the customer ahead of her made his choice. She was bemused to see that he picked a Swiss Army knife, but with more blades than the one she had owned.

While the clerk was writing up the sales check, he said, "Could I have your name and address, sir? We'd like to send you our mail-order catalog. Absolutely no charge, of course."

The customer left his name and address. Then it was Zoe's turn.

"I'd like a pocket knife as a gift for my nephew," she told the clerk. "Nothing too large or too heavy."

He laid out several knives for her inspection. She selected a handsome instrument with four blades, a horn handle, and a metal loop at one end for clipping onto a belt or hanging from a hook.

She paid for her purchase in cash, deciding that if the clerk asked for her name and address, she would give him false identity. But he didn't ask.

"I heard you offer to send that other customer your mail-order catalog," she said as the clerk was gift-wrapping her knife.

"Oh, we don't have a catalog," he said. He looked around carefully, then leaned toward her. "We're cooperating with the police," he whispered. "They want us to try and get the name and address of everyone who buys a Swiss Army knife. And if we can't get their names, to jot down a description."

Zoe Kohler was proud of her calmness.

"Whatever for?" she asked.

The clerk seemed uncomfortable. "I think it has something to do with the Hotel Ripper. They didn't really tell us."

Walking back to the Hotel Granger, the new knife in her purse, Zoe realized what must have happened: the police had identified the knife used from the tip of the broken blade found at the Cameron Arms Hotel.

But nothing had been published about it in the newspapers. Obviously the police were keeping the identification of the weapon a secret. That suggested there were other things they were keeping secret as well. Her fingerprints, perhaps, or something she had dropped at the scene, or some other clue that would lead them inevitably to her.

She should have felt dismayed, she knew, and frightened. But she didn't. If anything, she felt a sense of heightened excitement. The exhilaration of her adventures was sharpened by the risk, made more intense.

She imagined the police as a single malevolent intelligence with a single implacable resolve: to bring her down. To accomplish that, they would lie and deceive, work in underhanded and probably illegal ways, use all the powers at their command, including physical force and violence.

It seemed to her the police were fit representatives of a world that had cheated her, debased her, demolished her dreams and refused to concede her worth as a woman or her value as a human being.

The police and the world wanted nothing but her total extinction so that things might go along as if she had never been.

The evening of June 4th . . .

Zoe Kohler, alert, erect, strides into the crowded lobby of the Hotel Adler on Seventh Avenue and 50th Street. She pauses to scan the display board near the entrance. Under Current Events, it lists a convention of orthopedic surgeons, a banquet for a labor leader, and a three-day gathering of ballroom dancing teachers.

The hotel directory she had consulted listed the Adler's two restaurants, a "pub-type tavern," and a cocktail lounge. But Zoe is accosted before she can decide on her next move.

"See anything you like?" someone asks. A male voice, assured, amused.

She turns to look at him coolly. A tall man. Slender. A saturnine smile. Heavy, drooping eyelids. Olive skin. Black, gleaming hair slicked back from a widow's peak. The long fingers holding his cigarette look as if they have been squeezed from tubes.

"I don't believe we've met," she says frostily.

"We have now," he says. "You could save my life if you wanted to."

She cannot resist . . .

"How could I do that?"

"Have a drink with me. Keep me from going back into that meeting."

"What are you?" she challenges. "An orthopedic surgeon, a labor leader, or a ballroom dancing teacher?"

"A little of all three," he says, the smile never flickering. "But mostly I'm a magician."

He takes a silver dollar from his pocket, makes it flip-flop across his knuckles. It disappears into his palm. It reappears, begins the knuckle dance again. Zoe Kohler watches, fascinated.

"Now you see it," he says, "now you don't. The hand is quicker than the eye."

"Is that the only trick you know?" she asks archly.

"I know tricks you wouldn't believe. How about that drink?"

She doesn't think he is a police decoy. Too elegantly dressed. And a cop would not make the first approach—or would he?

"Where are you from?" she asks.

"Here, there, and everywhere," he says. "I've got a name you could never pronounce, but you can call me Nick. What's yours?"

"Irene," she says. "I'll have one drink with you. Only one."

"Of course," he says, plucking the silver dollar from her left ear. "Let's go, Irene."

But the cocktail lounge and the tavern are jammed. People wait on line. Nick takes her elbow in a tight grip.

"We'll go upstairs," he says, "to my room."

"One drink," she repeats.

He doesn't answer. His confidence daunts her. He pulls her along. But she cannot stop, cause a scene. No identity in her purse. But a knife with a sharpened blade.

His room looks as if he had moved in five minutes ago. Nothing to mark his presence but an unopened suitcase on a luggage rack.

He locks and chains the door behind them. He takes her coat and bag, throws them onto a chair.

"You want to see more tricks?" he says. "How about this?"

He unzips his fly, digs, pulls out his penis. It is long, dark, slender. Uncircumcised. He strokes it.

"Nice?" he says, his sardonic smile unwavering. "You like this trick?"

"I'm going," she says, reaching for her coat and bag.

He moves quickly between her and the door.

"What are you going to do?" he says. "Scream? Go ahead—scream."

She fumbles in her bag. He is there, and plucks it from her hands. She cannot believe anyone can move that swiftly. He is a blur.

He takes out her wallet, flips through it.

"No ID," he says. "That's smart."

He picks out the closed knife, dangles it by the steel loop.

"What's this for?" he asks. "Cleaning your toenails?"

He laughs, drops the knife back into the bag. He tosses it aside.

"You know the old saying," he says roguishly. "When rape is inevitable, relax and enjoy it."

"Why me?" she cries desperately.

He shrugs. "Just to pass the time. Something to do. You want to get undressed like a lady or do you want your pretty dress ripped?"

"Please," she says, "what about a drink? You promised me a drink."

"I lied," he says, grinning. "I'm always doing that."

He begins undressing. He stays between her and the door. He takes off his jacket, unknots his tie, unbuttons his shirt. He drops all his clothes onto the floor.

"Come on," he says. "Come *on*."

She takes off her clothes slowly, fingers trembling. She looks about for a weapon. A heavy ashtray. A table lamp. Anything.

"No way," he says softly, watching her. "No *way*."

She takes off shoes, dress, pantyhose. She drapes them over the back of a chair. When she looks up, he is naked. His penis is beginning to stiffen. He touches it delicately.

"Try it," he says. "You'll like it."

He takes one quick stride to her. He clamps his hands

on her shoulders. His strength frightens her. She cannot fight that power.

He pulls the strapless bra to her waist. He pinches her nipples. He strips her panties down, lifts her away from them.

"Bony," he says, "but okay. The nearer the bone, the sweeter the meat."

He presses her down. His hands on her shoulders are a weight she cannot resist. Her knees buckle. She flops onto the rug.

"I don't want to mess the bed," he says. "The floor is best. Harder. More resistance. Know what I mean?"

It is a whirl, beyond her control. Things flicker. She is swept away, protests stifled. Her puny blows on his head, arms, chest, mean nothing. He laughs throatily.

She squirms, moving by inches toward her discarded shoulder bag. But he pins her with his weight, a hard knee prying between her clamped thighs. He makes thick, huffing sounds.

She continues to writhe, and he strikes her. The open-palmed slap stings, flings her head aside. Her eyes water, ears roar. His teeth are on her throat. His body twists, pressing, pressing . . .

"What the hell is this?" he says, finding her tampon. He makes a noise of disgust. He yanks it out roughly, tosses it aside.

Then she does what she has to do, telling herself it is the only way she might survive.

Her body stills. Her punches stop. Untaloned, she begins to stroke his shoulders, his back. She moans.

"Yeah," he breathes. "Oh yeah . . ."

Her thighs ache. She thinks he will split her apart, rip her, leave steaming guts on the carpet. She feels hot tears, tastes bile.

He ramps and plunges, crying out in a language she does not recognize. His hands beneath her, gripping cruelly, pull her body up in a strained arch.

Eyes shut tightly, she sees pinwheels, whirling discs, melting blood. She wraps herself about him, feeling cold, cold. She endures the pain; within she is untouched and plotting.

His final thrusts pound her, bruise. Her moans rise in

volume to match his cries. When he collapses, shuddering, sobbing, she shakes her body in a paroxysm. She
flings her arms wide—and her fingertips just touch the
leather of her discarded shoulder bag.

She opens her eyes to slits. He props himself up, stares
down at her, panting.

"More!" she pleads. "More!"

"Wait'll I turn you over," he says, glee in his voice.
"It's even better."

He pulls away from her savagely; she feels she is being
torn inside out. He rolls onto his back, lies supine, chest
heaving.

She turns onto her side, onto hip and shoulder, pulling
herself a few inches closer to her purse. Digs toes and feet
into the rug, moving herself with cautious little pushes.

"Oh, that was so wonderful," she tells him. "So
marvelous. What a lover you are. I've never had a man
like you before."

He closes his eyes with satisfaction. He reaches blindly,
finds her vulva, squeezes and twists roughly.

"Good, huh?" he says. "The greatest, huh?"

Moving slowly, watching his closed eyes carefully, her
right hand snakes into the shoulder bag, comes out with
the knife.

"Ohh . . . I feel so good," she murmurs quietly.

Stretches up her left arm. Above her head, she opens
the big, sharpened blade. She eases it into position so it
will not click when it locks. She brings her arms gradually
down to her sides. Her right hand, gripping the knife, is
concealed behind her.

She sits up, pulling herself closer to him. She puts her
left hand on his hairless chest, toys with his nipples.

"When can we do it again?" she whispers. "I want
more, Nick."

"Soon," he says. "Soon. Just give me a chance to—"

His closed eyelids flutter. Immediately she raises the
knife high, drives the blade to the hilt into his abdomen, a
few inches below the squinched navel.

She twists the knife, yanks it free, raises it for another
blow.

But he reacts almost instantly. He rolls over completely, away from her. He springs to his feet. He stands
swaying, hands clasped to his belly.

He looks down at the blood welling from between his fingers. He raises his head slowly. He stares at her.

"You stuck me," he says wonderingly. "You *stuck* me."

He lurches toward her, claws reaching. She scrambles out of his way. She stumbles to her feet. A floor lamp goes over with a crash. One of his grasping hands comes close. She slashes it open with a backhanded swipe.

Roaring with rage and frustration, he blunders toward her unsteadily. Blood pours down his groin, his legs, drips from his flaccid penis. His slit hand, flinging, sends drops of blood flying.

An endtable is upset. An armchair is knocked over. Someone bangs on the adjoining wall. "Stop that!" a woman shouts. Still he comes on, mouth open and twisted. No sounds now but harsh, bubbling breaths. And in his eyes, terror and fury.

She trips over his discarded clothing. Before she can recover, he is on her, grappling close. His blood-slick hand finds her wrist, presses down, turns.

In a single violent movement, the naked blade edge sweeps across her right thigh, opens it up six inches above the knee. She feels the burn. Hot and icy at once.

He tries to force her down, to lean her to the floor. But his strength is leaking out, pouring, dripping, leaving pools and puddles and dribblings.

She squirms from his clutch. She whirls and begins plunging the knife into his arms, belly, face, shoulders, neck. Shoving it in, twisting it out, striking again.

She dances about him, meeting his lunges and stumbles with more blows. His life escapes from a hundred ragged wounds. His head comes lower, arms drag, shoulders sag.

He totters, goes down suddenly onto his knees. He tries, shuddering, to raise his bloodied head. Then falls, slaughtered, thumping to the floor. He rolls over once. His reddened, sightless eyes stare meekly at the ceiling.

She bends over him, hissing, and completes the ritual: throat opened wide, a blade to the clotted genitals again and again.

She straightens up, sobbing for breath, looking with dulled eyes at the butchery. His blood is smeared on her hands, arms, breasts, stomach. Worse, she feels the warm course of her own blood on leg, knee, shin, foot. She looks down. How bright it is! How sparkling!

In the bathroom, she stands naked on the tiled floor. She wipes her body clean of his blood with a dampened towel. She washes the knife and her hands with hot, soapy water. Then, using a washcloth tenderly, she cleans and examines her wound.

It is more than a scratch and less than a slash. No arteries or veins appear to be cut, but it bleeds steadily, running down to form a stain and then a shallow puddle on the tile.

She winds toilet paper around and around her thigh, making a bandage that soon soaks through. Over this, she wraps a hand towel as tightly as she can pull it. She limps back into the bedroom to retrieve Nick's necktie. She uses that to bind the towel tightly to her thigh.

She dresses as quickly as she can, leaving off her pantyhose, jamming them into her bag. She wipes her fingerprints from the sink faucets. She makes no attempt to mop up her own blood—an impossible task—and leaves the sodden towels on the floor of the bathroom.

She dons her coat, slings her shoulder bag. At the last minute, she picks up her discarded tampon from the floor. It is not stained. She puts it into her purse. She takes a final look around.

The punctured man lies slack on the floor, wounds gaping. All his magic is gone, soaking into the rug. He is emptied. Of confidence, brute strength, surging life.

She took a cab from the hotel and was back in her apartment a little after 11:00 P.M. She had worn her trenchcoat, although it was much too warm a night for it. But she feared the towel about her leg might soak through her dress.

It had; the front of her gown was stained with blood. She stripped, gently unwound the towel, pulled the wet paper away. The flow had lessened, but the thin line still oozed.

She washed it with warm, soapy water, dried it, wiped it with Q-Tips dipped in hydrogen peroxide. Then she fastened a neat bandage of gauze pads and adhesive tape. The wound throbbed, but nothing she could not endure.

Only after the bandage was secured did she go into the kitchen and, standing at the sink, drink off a double shot of iced vodka almost as quickly as she could gulp. Then she held out her right hand. The fingers were not trembling.

She took Anacin, Midol, vitamins, minerals, a salt tablet, a Darvon. She poured a fresh drink, took it back to the bathroom. She washed her face, armpits, and douched with a vinegar-water mixture. She wiped herself dry and inserted a fresh tampon. It was painful; her vagina felt stretched and punished.

Then she went into the bedroom, sat down slowly on the edge of the bed. She felt bone-weary, all of her sore, rubbed, and pulsing. Not with pain but with a kind of rawness. She felt opened and defenseless. A touch would bring a scream.

Already her adventure was fading, losing its hard, sharp outlines. She could not limn it in her memory. She had chaotic recollections of noise, violence, and the spray of hot blood. But it had all happened to someone else, in another time, another place.

She went back into the kitchen and washed down a Tuinal with the last of her second drink. She pulled on her batiste cotton nightgown with the neckline of embroidered rosebuds. She padded through her apartment to check the bolted door and turn off the lights.

She opened the bedroom window, but made certain the shade was fully drawn. The sheets felt cool and comforting, but the blanket was too warm; she tossed it aside.

As she lay awake, drugged, heart fluttering, waiting for sleep, she tried to recall those moments when she had been convinced that love would be her soul's salvation.

8

On May 10th, the Saturday afternoon Zoe Kohler and
Ernest Mittle were flying a red balloon in Central Park,
Edward X. Delaney sat in a crowded office in Midtown
North with Sergeant Abner Boone and other officers.
They were discussing the murder of Leonard T.
Bergdorfer at the Cameron Arms Hotel.

Present at the conference, in addition to Delaney and
Boone, were the following:

Lieutenant Martin Slavin, who had been relegated to a
strictly administrative role in the operations of the task
force assembled to apprehend the Hotel Ripper . . .

Sergeant Thomas K. Broderick, an officer with more
than twenty years' service in the Detective Division, most
of them in midtown Manhattan . . .

Detective First Grade Aaron Johnson, a black, with
wide experience in dealing with the terrorist fringes of
minority groups and with individual anarchists . . .

Detective Second Grade Daniel ("Dapper Dan")
Bentley, who specialized in hotel crimes, particularly
robberies, gem thefts, confidence games, etc. . . . .

Detective Lieutenant Wilson T. Crane, noted for his
research capabilities and expertise in computer technology . . .

Sergeant Boone opened the discussion by recap-
ping briefly the circumstances of Leonard Bergdorfer's
death . . .

"Pretty much like the others. Throat slashed. Multiple
stab wounds in the nuts. This time the body was found on
the floor. Take a look at the photos. The bed wasn't used.
The autopsy shows no, uh, sexual relations prior—"

BENTLEY: "Sexual relations? You mean like my sister-in-law?"

(Laughter)

BOONE: "He hadn't screwed at least twenty-four hours prior to his death. Like the others."

CRANE: "Prints?"

BOONE: "The Latent Print Unit is still at it. It doesn't look good. Two things that may help . . . The tip of a knife blade was found embedded in the victim's throat. It's a little more than a half-inch long. Lab Services is working on it now. There's no doubt it's from the murder weapon. Probably a pocket knife, jackknife, or clasp knife—whatever you want to call it."

JOHNSON: "How long was the blade do they figure?"

BOONE: "Maybe three inches long."

JOHNSON: "Sheet! A toothpick."

BOONE: "Victim suffered first-degree burns of the face, especially around the eyes and nose. The Medical Examiner's office blames phenacyl chloride used in CN and Chemical Mace. The burning indicates a heavy dose at close range."

BRODERICK: "Enough to knock him out?"

BOONE: "Enough to knock him down, that's for sure. As far as the victim's background goes, we're still at it. No New York sheet. He was from Atlanta, Georgia. They're checking. Ditto the Feds. Probably nothing we can use. And that's about it."

CRANE: "Was the Mace can found?"

BOONE: "No. The killer probably took it along. What's the law on Mace? Anyone know?"

SLAVIN: "Illegal to buy, sell, own, carry, or use in the State of New York. Except for bona fide security and law enforcement officers."

BENTLEY: "Black market? Johnson?"

JOHNSON: "You asking me 'cause I'm black?"

(Laughter)

JOHNSON: "There's some of it around. In those little purse containers for women to carry. There's not what you'd call a thriving market on the street."

BOONE: "Well, at the moment, the Mace and the knife blade tip are all we've got that's new. Before we start talking about what to do with them, I'd like you to listen to ex-Chief of Detectives Edward X. Delaney for a few

minutes. The Chief is not on active duty. At the urging of
Deputy Commissioner Ivar Thorsen and myself, he has
agreed to serve as, uh, a consultant on this investigation.
Chief?"

Delaney stood, leaning on his knuckles on the battered
table. He loomed forward. He looked around slowly,
staring at every man.

"I'm not here to give you orders," he said tonelessly.
"I'm not here to ride herd on you. I've got no official
status at all. I'm here because Thorsen and Boone are old
friends, and because I want to crack this thing as much as
you do. If I have any suggestions on how to run this case,
I'll make them to Thorsen or Boone. They can pick up on
them or not—that's their business. I just want to make
sure you know what the situation is. I'd like my presence
here to be kept under wraps as long as possible. I know
it'll probably get out eventually, but I don't need the
publicity. I've already got my pension."

They smiled at that, and relaxed.

"All right," he said, "now I want to tell you who I think
the Hotel Ripper is . . ."

That jolted them and brought them leaning forward,
waiting to hear.

He told them why he thought the killer was a woman.
Not a prostitute, but a psychopathic female. He went over
all the evidence he had presented to Monica and to
Thorsen. But this time he remembered to include the
additional detail that the person who tipped off the *Times*
could have been a woman.

He said nothing about Thomas Handry's research,
nothing about the statistics showing the increased evidence of alcoholism, drug addiction, and mental distur-
bance among women.

These men were professional policemen; they weren't
interested in sociological change or psychological motiva-
tion. Their sole concern was evidence that could be
brought into court.

So he came down heavily on the known facts about the
murders, facts that could be accounted for only by the
theory he proposed. They were facts already known to
everyone in that room, except for his suggestion that the
timing of the killings was equivalent to a woman's
menstrual period.

But it was the first time they had heard these disparate items fitted into a coherent hypothesis. He could see their doubt turn to dawning realization that the theory he offered was a fresh approach, a new way of looking at old puzzles.

"So what we're looking for," Delaney concluded, "is a female crazy. I'd guess young—late twenties to middle thirties. Five-five to five-seven. Short hair, because she has no trouble wearing wigs. Strong. Very, very smart. Not a street bum. Probably a woman of some education and breeding. Chances are she's on pills or booze or both, but that's pure conjecture. She probably lives a reasonably normal life when she's not out slashing throats. Holds down a job, or maybe she's a housewife. That's all I've got."

He sat down suddenly. The men looked at one another, waiting for someone to speak.

BOONE: "Any reactions?"

SLAVIN: "There's not a goddamned thing there we can take to the DA."

BOONE: "Granted. But it's an approach. A place to start."

JOHNSON: "I'll buy it."

BENTLEY: "It listens to me. It's got to be a twist—all those straight guys stripping off their pants."

CRANE: "It doesn't fit the probabilities for this type of crime."

DELANEY: "I agree. In this case, I think the probabilities are wrong. Not wrong, but outdated."

BRODERICK: "I'll go along with you, Chief. Let's suppose the killer is a woman. So what? Where do we go from there?"

BOONE: "First, go back and check the records again. For women with a sheet that includes violent crimes. Check the prisons for recent releases. Check the booby hatches for ditto, and for escapees. Go through all our nut files and see if anything shows up."

CRANE: "My crew can handle that."

BOONE: "Second, the knife blade . . . Broderick, see if you can trace the knife by analysis of the metal in the blade."

DELANEY: "Or the shape. Ever notice how pocket knife blades have different shapes? Some are straight, some turn up at the point, some are sharpened on both edges."

BRODERICK: "That's nice. There must be a zillion different makes of pocket knives for sale in the New York area."

BOONE: "Find out. Third, Johnson you take the business with the Mace. Who makes it, how it gets into New York. Is it sold by mail order? Can you get a license to buy it? Anyone pushing it on the street? And so forth."

BENTLEY: "And me?"

BOONE: "Pull your decoys out of the gay bars. Concentrate on the straight places, and mostly the bars and cocktail lounges in midtown hotels. And show photos of the victims to bartenders and waitresses. See if you can pick up a trail."

BENTLEY: "We've already done that, sarge."

BOONE: "So? Do it again."

DELANEY: "Wait a minute . . ."

They all turned to look at him but the Chief was silent. Then he spoke to Detective Bentley.

DELANEY: "Your squad showed photos of all the victims around in hotel bars and cocktail lounges?"

BENTLEY: "That's right, Chief."

DELANEY: "And you came up with zilch?"

BENTLEY: "Correct. That's understandable; most of the places were mobbed. What waitress would remember one customer's face?"

DELANEY: "Uh-huh. Boone, who was the victim with the badly scarred hands?"

BOONE: "The third. Jerome Ashley, at the Hotel Coolidge."

DELANEY: "Go back to the Coolidge. Don't show Ashley's photo. At first. Ask if any waitress or bartender remembers a customer with badly scarred hands. If they do, *then* show his photo."

BENTLEY: "Got it. Beautiful."

BOONE: "Any more questions?"

CRANE: "Are we releasing this to the media? About the Ripper being a woman?"

BOONE: "Thorsen says no, not at the moment. They'll decide on it downtown."

BRODERICK: "No way we can keep it quiet. Too many people involved."

BOONE: "I agree, but it's not our decision to make. Anything else?"

BENTLEY: "What color wig are my decoys looking for?"

BOONE: "Probably strawberry blond. But it could be any color."

BENTLEY: "Thank you. That narrows it down."

Laughing, the men rose, the meeting broke up. Delaney watched them go. He was satisfied with them; he thought they knew their jobs.

More than that, he was gratified by the way they had accepted, more or less, his theory as a working hypothesis. He knew how comforting it was in any criminal case to have a framework, no matter how bare. The outline, hopefully, would be filled in as the investigation proceeded.

But to start out with absolutely nothing, and still have nothing three months later, was not only discouraging, it was enervating; it drained the will, weakened resolve, and made men question their professional ability.

Now, at least, he had given them an aim, a direction. Policemen, in many ways, are like priests. No experienced cop believes in justice; the law is his bible. And Delaney had given them hope that, in this case at least, the law would not be flouted.

"Want to stay around, Chief?" Sergeant Boone asked. "Maybe you can suggest some improvements on how we're organized."

"Thanks," Delaney said, "but I better climb out of your hair and let you get to work. I think it would be smart if I stayed away from here as much as possible. Keep resentment to a minimum."

"No one resents your helping out, Chief."

Delaney smiled and waved a hand.

On his way out of Midtown North, he looked in at busy offices, squad and interrogation rooms. Most of his years of service had been spent in precinct houses older than this one, but the atmosphere was similar. The smell was identical.

He knew that most of the bustle he witnessed had nothing to do with the Hotel Ripper case; it was the daily activity of an undermanned precinct that patrolled one of the most crowded sections of Manhattan, usually the only part of New York City visited by tourists.

It would have been helpful, and probably more efficient, if the entire Hotel Ripper task force could have been accommodated in one suite of offices, or even one large bullpen. But they had to make do with the space available.

As a result, only Boone and his command squad and Slavin and his bookkeepers worked out of Midtown North. Johnson and Bentley, and their crews, were stationed in Midtown South. Broderick's men had desks in the 20th Precinct, and Lieutenant Crane's research staff had been given temporary space downtown at 1 Police Plaza.

Still, the organization creaked along, twenty-four hours a day, with three shifts of plainclothesmen and detectives turning up to keep the investigation rolling. Delaney didn't want to think about the scheduling problems involved—that was Slavin's headache.

And the paperwork! It boggled the mind. Daily reports, status updates, requests for record checks, and pleas for additional manpower were probably driving Sergeant Boone right up the wall. Delaney suspected he was sleeping on a cot in his office—when he had a chance to grab a few hours.

The Chief walked across town on 54th Street, musing on the size of the machine that had been set in motion to stop a single criminal and what it was costing the city. He didn't doubt for a moment that it was necessary, but he wondered if adding more men, and more, and more, would bring success sooner. Would doubling the task force break the case in half the time? Ridiculous.

He guessed that the size of the operation must be a matter of some pride and satisfaction to the murderer. Most mass killers had a desire for recognition of the monstrousness of their crimes. They wrote to the newspapers. They called TV and radio stations. They wanted attention, and if it came at the cost of slashed corpses and a terrorized city—so be it.

He lumbered along the city street, crowded this Saturday afternoon in spring, and looked with new eyes at the women passing by. He was as adept at observing himself as others, and he realized that his way of looking at women had changed since he became convinced that the Hotel Ripper was female.

His feelings about women had already undergone one revolution, spurred by Monica's interest in the feminist movement. But now, seeing these strange, aloof creatures striding along on a busy New York street, he was conscious of another shift in his reactions to the female sex.

He could only recognize it as a kind of wariness. It was an awareness that, for him at least, women had suddenly revealed a new, hitherto unsuspected dimension.

There was a mystery there, previously shrugged off, like most males, with the muttered comment: "Just like a woman." With no one, ever, defining exactly what was meant by that judgment, except that it was inevitably uttered in a condemnatory tone.

But now, attempting to analyze the mystery, he thought it might be nothing more complex than granting to women the humanity granted to men—with all its sins and virtues, ideals and depravities.

If one was willing to accord to women equality (superiority even!) in all the finer instincts and nobilities of which men were capable, was it such a wrench or so illogical to acknowledge also that they were capable of men's faults and corruptions?

It was a nice point, he decided, and one he would certainly enjoy debating with Monica. The first time he caught her in a forgiving mood . . .

He took an uptown bus on Third Avenue and arrived home a little before 4:00 P.M. Monica was asleep on the living room couch, a book open on her lap, reading glasses down on her nose. He smiled and closed the door quietly when he went into the kitchen.

Moving stealthily, he opened the refrigerator door and considered the possibilities. He decided on a sandwich of anchovies, egg salad, and sliced tomato on a seeded roll. Rather than eat it while leaning over the sink, he put it on a sheet of waxed paper and carried it, along with an opened beer, into the study.

While he ate and drank, he added a few additional facts to the dossier of Leonard T. Bergdorfer. Then he shuffled the files of all four victims and tried to add to his list of commonalities.

The days of the week when the crimes were committed
seemed to have no connection. Nor did the precise time of
day. The exact location of the hotels, other than being in
midtown Manhattan, suggested no particular pattern. The
victims apparently had nothing in common other than
being out-of-town males.

He threw his lists aside. Perhaps, he thought, he was
deceiving himself by believing there was a link between
the four killings that was eluding him. Maybe because he
wanted a link, he had convinced himself that one existed.

An hour later, when Monica came into the study
yawning and blinking, he was still staring morosely at the
papers on his desk. When she asked him what he was
doing, he replied, "Nothing." And that, he reflected
sourly, was the truth.

There were days when he wanted to be the lowliest of
plainclothesmen, assigned to ringing doorbells and asking
questions. Or a deskbound researcher, poring over stacks
of yellowed arrest records, looking for a name, a number,
anything. At least those men were *doing* something.

It seemed to him that his role in the Hotel Ripper case
was that of the "consultant" Boone had mentioned. He
was the kindly old uncle whose advice was solicited, but
who was then shunted aside while younger, more ener-
getic men took over the legwork and the on-the-spot
decision making.

He could not endure that inactivity. An investigation
was precisely that: tracking, observing, studying, making
a systematic examination and inquiry. A criminal investigation was a *search,* and he was being kept from the
challenge, the excitement, the disappointments and rewards of *searching.*

Deputy Commissioner Ivar Thorsen had been right; he
had cop's blood; he admitted it. He could not resist the
chase; it was a pleasure almost as keen as sex. Age had
nothing to do with it, nor physical energy. It was the
mystery that enticed; he would never be free from the lust
to reveal secrets.

His opportunity for action came sooner than expected . . .

On Friday morning, May 16th, the Delaneys sat down
to breakfast at their kitchen table. The Chief looked with

astonishment at the meal Monica had prepared: kippers, scrambled eggs, baked potatoes, sauteed onions.

"What," he wanted to know, "have you done to justify serving a magnificent breakfast like this?"

She laughed guiltily.

"It's the last meal you'll get from me today," she said. "I'm going to be busy. So I thought if you start out with a solid breakfast, it might keep you from sandwiches for a few hours. You're putting on weight."

"More of me to love," he said complacently, and dug into his food with great enjoyment. They ate busily for a while, then he asked casually, "What's going to keep you busy all day?"

"The American Women's Association is having a three-day convention in New York. I signed up for today's activities. Lectures and a film this morning. Then lunch. Seminars and a general discussion this afternoon. Then dinner tonight."

"You'll take a cab home?"

"Of course."

"Make the driver wait until you're inside the door."

"Yes, Daddy."

They ate awhile in silence, handing condiments back and forth. Delaney liked to put the buttered onions directly on his steaming potato, with a little coarsely ground black pepper.

"Where is the convention being held?" he asked idly. "Which hotel?"

"The Hilton."

He paused, holding a forkful of kipper halfway to his mouth. He gazed up in the air, over her head.

"How do you know the convention is at the Hilton?" he asked slowly.

"I got a notice in the mail. With an application blank."

"But there was no notice in the papers?"

"I didn't see any. Today is the first day. There may be stories tomorrow."

He took his bite of kipper, chewed it thoughtfully.

"But there was nothing in the papers about it?" he asked again. "No advance notice?"

"Edward, what *is* this?"

Instead of answering, he said, "What other conventions are being held at the Hilton today?"

"How on earth would I know that?"

"What conventions are being held at the Americana right now?"

"Edward, will you please tell me what this is all about?"

"In a minute," he said. "Let me finish this banquet first. It really is delicious."

"Hmph," she said, with scorn for this blatant effort to placate her. But she had to wait until he had cleaned his plate and poured each of them a second cup of black coffee.

"You don't know what conventions are at the Hilton," he said, "except for the one you're attending. I didn't know there were *any* conventions at the Hilton today. Neither of us know what conventions are being held right now at the Americana or any other New York hotel. Why should we know? We're not interested."

"So?"

"So for weeks now I've been looking for a link between the Hotel Ripper homicides. Something that ties them all together. Something we've overlooked."

She stared at him, puzzling it out.

"You mean there were conventions being held at all the hotels where the murders were committed?"

He stood, moved heavily around to her side of the table. He leaned down to kiss her cheek.

"My little detective," he said. "Thank you for a great breakfast and thank you for the lead. You're exactly right; the killings were at hotels where conventions were being held. And this was as early as the middle of February. Not precisely the height of the convention season in New York. But the killer picked hotels with conventions, sales meetings, big gatherings. Why not? She wants lots of people around, lots of single, unattached men. She wants crowds in the lobbies and dining rooms and cocktail lounges. She wants victims ready for a good time, maybe already lubricated with booze. So she selects hotels with conventions. Does that make sense?"

"It makes sense," Monica said. "In an awful way. But how does she know which hotels are having conventions?"

"Ah," he said, "good question. I've never seen a list in the daily papers. Have you?"

"No."

"But it must exist somewhere. The city's convention bureau or tourist bureau or some municipal office must keep track of these things. I know they make an effort to bring conventions to the city. Maybe they publish a daily or weekly or monthly list. And maybe the hotel association does, too. Anyway, the killer knows where the conventions are and heads for them."

"It doesn't sound like much of a clue to me," Monica said doubtfully.

"You never can tell," he said cheerfully. "You just never know. But if you do nothing, you have no chance to get lucky."

He helped Monica clean up and waited until she had departed for her first meeting at the New York Hilton. By that time he had figured out exactly how he was going to handle it.

He locked the front door, went into the study, and phoned Midtown Precinct South. He asked for Detective Second Grade Daniel Bentley, the expert on Manhattan hotels.

"Hello?"

"Bentley?"

"Yeah. Who's this?"

"Edward X. Delaney here."

"Oh, hiya, Chief. Don't tell me we got her?"

"No," Delaney said, laughing. "Not yet. How's it going?"

"Okay. I can't cover every bar and cocktail lounge, but I'm putting at least one man in every big hotel between Thirty-fourth and Fifty-ninth, river to river, between eight and two every night. You know we had a guy at the Cameron Arms when Bergdorfer was offed?"

"Yes, I heard that."

"So much for decoys," Bentley said mournfully. "But maybe next time we'll luck out."

Delaney paused, reflecting how everyone took it for granted that there would be a next time.

"About that Jerome Ashley kill at the Coolidge," Detective Bentley went on. "We checked with the bartenders and waitresses in the cocktail lounges. No one remembers a guy with scarred hands. But two of the waitresses on duty that night don't work there anymore.

We're tracking them down. Nothing comes easy."

"It surely doesn't. Bentley, I wonder if you can help me."

"Anything you say, Chief."

"I'd like to talk to a hotel security officer. Preferably an ex-cop. Are there any working in hotels now?"

"Oh hell yes. I know of at least three. Guys who took early retirement. The pay's not bad and the work isn't all that hard, except maybe in the big hotels. Why do you ask? Anything cooking?"

"Not really. I just wanted to find out how hotel security works. Maybe we can convince them to beef up their patrols or put on extra guards to help us out."

"Good idea. Here are the guys I know . . ."

He gave Delaney the names of three men, one of which the Chief recognized.

"Holzer?" he asked. "Eddie Holzer? Was he in Narcotics for a while?"

"Sure, that's the one. You know him?"

"Yes. I worked with him on a couple of things."

"He's at the Hotel Osborne. It's not a fleabag, but it's not the Ritz either."

"I'll give him a call. Many thanks, Bentley."

"Anytime, Chief."

He hung up, wondering why he had lied—well, maybe not lied, but misled Detective Bentley as to the reason why he wanted to talk to a hotel security officer. He told himself that he just didn't want to bother a busy investigating officer with a slim lead and probably a dead-end search.

But he knew it wasn't that.

He looked up the number of the Hotel Osborne and called. He was told that Mr. Holzer wouldn't be at his desk until noon.

He had no sooner hung up than the phone rang. It was Ivar Thorsen. He said he was heading for a meeting and wanted to get Delaney's thinking on two subjects . . .

"This is with the brass and their public relations men from the offices of the Mayor, the Commissioner, and the Chief of Operations," he said. "About what we give to the media. First of all, do we release the business about the Hotel Ripper switching to a strawberry blond wig?

Second, do we say we are definitely looking for a female killer? What do you think, Edward?"

Delaney pondered a moment. Then . . .

"Take the second one first . . . There's no way we can keep it quiet that we're looking for a woman. But fuzz the issue. Say the killer can be a man or a woman; we're looking for both."

"You still think it's a woman?"

"Of course. But I could be wrong; I admit it. The brass will want an out—just in case. Cover yourself on this one."

"All right, Edward; that makes sense. What about the wig?"

"Ivar, you've got to be definite on that. If the reporters print it was a blond wig, the killer will just switch to another color. That's what happened when Slavin fucked up."

"But if we don't warn tourists about a killer wearing a strawberry blond wig, aren't we endangering them?"

"Probably," Delaney said grimly. "But the decoys have got to have *something* to look for. We can't have her switching colors on us again."

"Jesus," Thorsen breathed, "if the papers find out, they'll crucify us."

"We've got to take the chance," the Chief urged. "And if the reporters dig it up, we can always say we didn't want the killer to go to another color—which is the truth."

"But meanwhile we're not warning the tourists."

"Deputy," Delaney said, his voice suddenly thick with fury, "do you want to stop this maniac or don't you?"

"All right, all right," Thorsen said hastily. "I'll try to get them to do it your way. I should be out of the meeting and uptown by late this afternoon. Can you meet me at Midtown North at, say, about four o'clock? I'll tell you how I made out and Boone can bring us up to date."

"I'll be there," Delaney said and hung up.

He was a little ashamed of himself for getting shirty with Ivar. He knew what the Admiral was up against: superior officers concerned with the image of the Department and the public relations aspects of this highly publicized case.

It was bullshit like that—image, public relations, poli-

tics—that had persuaded Edward X. Delaney it was time
for him to retire from the New York Police Department.
With his stubbornness, temper, and refusal to compromise, he knew he could never hope for higher rank.

"If you want to get along, you go along." That was
probably true in every human organization. But being
true didn't make it right. Delaney admitted he was a
maverick, always had been. But he consoled himself with
the thought that it was the mavericks of the world who got
things done. Not the yes-men and the ass-kissers.

All *they* got for their efforts, he thought morosely, were
success, wealth, and admiration.

Detective Bentley had been right; the Osborne wasn't
much of a hotel. It could have been called the Seedy
Grandeur. Located on 46th Street east of Seventh Avenue, it had a stone façade so gray and crumbled that it
seemed bearded.

It was the type of Times Square hotel that had once
hosted Enrico Caruso, Lillian Russell, and Diamond Jim
Brady. Now it sheltered Sammy the Wop, Gage Sullivan,
Dirty Sally, and others of hazy pasts and no futures.

Standing in the center of that chipped and peeling
lobby, Delaney decided the odor was compounded of CN,
pot, and ancient urinals. But the place seemed bustling
enough, all the men equipped with toothpicks and all the
women with orange hair. Tout sheets were everywhere.

Eddie Holzer was studying one, marking his choices.
His feet were parked atop his splintered desk and he was
wearing a greasy fedora. He held a cracked coffee cup in
one trembling hand. Delaney guessed it didn't contain
coffee.

Holzer glanced up when Delaney paused in the opened
door.

"Chrissake," he said, lurching to his feet, "look what
the cat drug in. Harya, Chief."

They shook hands, and Holzer brushed magazines and
old newspapers off a straight chair. Delaney sat down
cautiously. He looked at the other man with what he
hoped was a friendly smile.

He knew Holzer's record, and it wasn't a happy one.
The ex-detective had worked out of the Narcotics Division, and eventually the big money had bedazzled him.

He had been allowed to retire before the DA moved in, but everyone in the Department knew he was tainted.

Now here he was, Chief of Security in a sleazy Times Square hotel, marking up a tipsheet and sipping cheap booze from a coffee cup. For all that, Delaney knew the man had been a clever cop, and he hoped enough remained.

They gossiped of this and that, remembering old times, talking of who was retired, who was dead. The Department put its mark on a man. He might be out for years and years, but he'd be in for the rest of his life.

Finally the chatter stopped.

Holzer looked at the Chief shrewdly. "I don't figure you stopped in by accident. How'd you find me?"

"Bentley," Delaney said.

"Dapper Dan?" Holzer said, laughing. "Good cop."

He was a florid, puffy man, rapidly going to flab. His face was a road map of capillaries, nose swollen, cheeks bloomy. Delaney had noted the early-morning shakes; Holzer made no effort to conceal them. If he was a man on the way down, it didn't seem to faze him.

The Chief wasn't sure how to get started, how much to reveal. But Holzer made it easy for him.

He said: "I hear you're helping out on the Hotel Ripper thing."

Delaney looked at him with astonishment. "Where did you hear that?"

Holzer flipped a palm back and forth. "Here and there. The grapevine. You know how things get around."

"They surely do," Delaney said. "Yes, I'm helping out. Deputy Commissioner Thorsen is an old friend of mine. I hunted you down because I—because we need your help."

He had pushed the right button. Holzer straightened up, his shoulders went back. Light came into his dulled eyes.

"You need *my* help?" he said, not believing. "On the case?"

Delaney nodded. "I think you're the man. You're a hotel security chief."

"Some hotel," Holzer said wanly. "Some security chief."

"Still . . ." Delaney said.

He explained that all the Ripper slayings had occurred at hotels in which conventions were being held. He was convinced the killer had prior knowledge of exactly where and when conventions and sales meetings and large gatherings were taking place.

Eddie Holzer listened intently, pulling at his slack lower lip.

"Yeah," he said, "that washes. I'll buy it. So?"

"So how would someone know the convention schedule in midtown Manhattan? It's not published in the papers."

Holzer thought a moment.

"These things are planned months ahead," he said. "Sometimes years ahead. To reserve the rooms, you understand. Someone in the Mayor's office would know. The outfit trying to bring new business to the city. The tourist bureau. Maybe there's a convention bureau. The Chamber of Commerce. Like that."

"Good," Delaney said, not mentioning that he had already thought of those sources. "Anyone else?"

"The hotel associations—they'd know."

"And . . . ?"

"Oh," Holzer said, "here . . ."

He bent over with some effort, rooted through the stack of magazines and newspapers he had swept off Delaney's chair. He came up with a thin, slick-paper magazine, skidded it across the desk to the Chief.

"New York hotel trade magazine," he said. "Comes out every week. It lists all the conventions in town."

"This goes to every hotel?" Delaney asked, flipping through the pages.

"I guess so," Holzer said. "It's a freebie. The ads pay for it. I think it goes to travel agencies, too. Maybe they send it out of town to big corporations—who knows? You'll have to check."

"Uh-huh," Delaney said. "Well, it's a place to start. Eddie, can I take this copy with me?"

"Be my guest," Holzer said. "I never look at the goddamned thing."

The Chief stood, held out his hand. The other man managed to get to his feet. They shook hands. Holzer didn't want to let go.

"Thank you, Eddie," Delaney said, pulling his hand away. "You've been a big help."

"Yeah?" Holzer said vaguely. "Well . . . you know. Anything I can do . . ."

"Take care of yourself," Delaney said gently.

"What? Me? Sure. You bet. I'm on top of the world."

Delaney nodded and got out of there. In the rancid lobby, a man and a woman were having a snarling argument. As the Chief passed, the woman spat in the man's face.

"Aw, honey," he said sadly, "now why did you want to go and do that for?"

Pierre au Tunnel was Delaney's favorite French restaurant on the West Side. And because it was Friday, he knew they would be serving bouillabaisse. The thought of that savory fish stew demolished the memory of Monica's scrumptious breakfast.

He walked uptown through Times Square, not at all offended by the flashy squalor. For all its ugliness, it had a strident vitality that stirred him. This section was quintessential New York. If you couldn't endure Times Square, you couldn't endure change.

But there were some things that didn't change; Pierre au Tunnel was just as he remembered it. The entrance was down a flight of stairs from the sidewalk. There was a long, narrow front room, bar on the right, a row of small tables on the left. In the rear was the main dining room, low-ceilinged, walls painted to simulate those of a tunnel or grotto.

It was a relaxed, reasonably priced restaurant, with good bread and a palatable house wine. Most of the patrons were habitués. It was the kind of neighborhood bistro where old customers kissed old waitresses.

The luncheon crowd had thinned out; Delaney was able to get his favorite table in the corner of the front room. He ordered the bouillabaisse and a small bottle of chilled muscadet. He tucked the corner of his napkin into his collar and spread the cloth across his chest.

He ate his stew slowly, dipping chunks of crusty French bread into the sauce. It was as good as he remembered it, as flavorful, and the hard, flinty wine was a perfect complement. He ordered espresso and a lemon ice for dessert and then, a little later, a pony of Armagnac.

Ordinarily, lunching alone at this restaurant, he would

have amused himself by observing his fellow diners and the activity at the bar. But today, with the hotel trade magazine tucked carefully at his side, he had other matters to occupy him.

His original intention had been to take a more active role in the investigation. He had hoped that he alone might handle the search for persons with access to a list of current conventions in New York.

He saw now that such an inquiry was beyond his capabilities, or those of any other single detective. It would take a squad of ten, twenty, perhaps thirty men to track down all the sources, to make a list of all New Yorkers who might have access to a schedule of conventions.

It was a dull, routine, interminable task. And in the end, it might lead to nothing. But, he reflected grimly, it had to be done. Sipping his Armagnac, he began to plan how the men selected for the job should be organized and assigned.

He arrived at Midtown Precinct North a little after 3:30 P.M. Deputy Commissioner Ivar Thorsen was already present, and Delaney met with him and Abner Boone in the sergeant's office. Thorsen told them of the results of his meeting with the police brass.

"You got everything you wanted, Edward," he said. "I'll hold a press conference tomorrow. The official line will be that new leads are enlarging the investigation— which is true—and we are now looking for either a female or male perpetrator. Nothing will be released about the killer switching to a strawberry blond wig."

"Good," Boone said. "They picked up more blond hairs when they vacuumed Bergdorfer's suite at the Cameron Arms. What about the knife blade tip? And the Mace?"

"We'll keep those under wraps for the time being," Thorsen said. "We can't shoot our wad all at once. If the screams for action become too loud, we'll give them the investigation into the knife, and later into the tear gas. The PR guys were insistent on that. It looks like a long job of work, and we've got to hold something back to prove we're making progress."

Delaney and Boone both sighed, the Machiavellian manipulations of public relations beyond their ken.

"Edward," Thorsen went on, "we're keeping a lid on your involvement in the case for the time being."

"Keep it on forever as far as I'm concerned."

"Sergeant, all inquiries from the media will be referred to me. I will be the sole, repeat, *sole* spokesman for the Department on this case. Is that understood?"

"Yes, sir."

"Make certain your men understand it, too. I don't want any unauthorized statements to the press, and if I catch anyone leaking inside information, he'll find himself guarding vacant lots in the South Bronx so fast he won't know what hit him. Now . . . I don't suppose you have any great revelations to report, do you?"

"No, sir," Boone said, "nothing new. We're just getting organized on the knife and tear gas jobs. Lieutenant Crane's research hasn't turned up anything."

"I have something," Delaney said, and they looked at him.

He told them of his belief that the killer had prior knowledge of the location and dates of conventions held in midtown Manhattan. He listed the sources of such information and showed them the hotel trade magazine he had been given by Eddie Holzer.

"It's got to be someone connected with the hotel or convention business in some way," he argued. "We'll have to compile a list of everyone in the city who has access to the convention schedule."

Thorsen was aghast.

"My God, Edward!" he burst out. "That could be thousands of people!"

"Hundreds, certainly," Delaney said stonily. "But it's got to be done. Sergeant?"

"I guess so," Boone said glumly. "You want men *and* women listed?"

"Yes," Delaney said, nodding. "Just to cover ourselves. No use in doing the job twice. What do you figure—twenty or thirty more detectives?"

"At least," the sergeant said.

Thorsen groaned. "All right," he said finally, "you'll get them. Who's going to handle it?"

"I'll get it organized and rolling," Sergeant Boone said. "We better call in Slavin on the scheduling."

Delaney left them discussing the exact number of men

needed and the office space that would be required. He walked uptown from the precinct house until he found a telephone booth in working order.

He called Thomas Handry.

He told the reporter there would be a press conference held at police headquarters the following day. An expanded investigation would be announced and it would be stated that the killer could be either a man or a woman. Delaney said nothing about the blond wig, the knife blade tip, or the Chemical Mace.

"So?" Handry said. "What's so new and exciting? An expanded investigation—big deal."

"What's new and exciting," Delaney explained patiently, "is that actually the investigation is zeroing in on a female killer."

A moment of silence . . .

"So that research convinced you?" Handry said. "And you convinced them?"

"Half-convinced," Delaney said. "Some of them still think I'm blowing smoke."

He then went over the evidence that had persuaded him the Hotel Ripper was female. He ended by telling Handry that the timing of the homicides matched a woman's menstrual periods.

"Crazy," the reporter said. "You're sure about all this?"

"Sure I'm sure. I'm giving you this stuff in advance of the press conference for background, not for publication. I owe you one. Also, I thought you might want to prepare by digging out old stories on women killers."

"I already have," Handry said. "It wasn't hard to figure how your mind was working. I started looking into the history of mass murders. A series of homicides in which the killer is a stranger to the victims. One criminologist calls them 'multicides.'"

"Multicides," Delaney repeated. "That's a new one on me. Good name. What did you find?"

"Since 1900, there have been about twenty-five cases in the United States, with the number of victims ranging from seven to more than thirty. The scary thing is that more than half of those twenty-five cases have occurred since 1960. In other words, the incidence of multicides is increasing. More and more mass killings by strangers."

"Yes," Delaney said, "I was aware of that."

"And I've got bad news for you, Chief."

"What's that?"

"Of those twenty-five cases of multicide since 1900, only one was committed by a woman."

"Oh?" Delaney said. "Did they catch her?"

"No," Handry said.

Monica came out of the bathroom, hair in curlers, face cold-creamed, a strap of her nightgown held up with a safety pin.

"The Creature from Outer Space," she announced cheerfully.

He looked at her with a vacant smile. He had started to undress. Doffed his dark cheviot jacket and vest, after first removing watch and chain from waistcoat pockets. The clumpy gold chain had been his grandfather's. At one end was a hunter that had belonged to his father and had stopped fifty years ago. Twenty minutes to noon. Or midnight.

At the other end of the chain was a jeweled miniature of his detective's badge, given to him by his wife on his retirement.

Vest and jacket hung away, he seated himself heavily on the edge of his bed. He started to unlace his ankle-high shoes of black kangaroo leather, polished to a high gloss. He was seated there, one shoe dangling from his big hands, when Monica came out of the bathroom.

He watched her climb into bed. She propped pillows against the headboard, sat up with blanket and sheet pulled to her waist. She donned her Benjamin Franklin glasses, picked up a book from the bedside table.

"What did you eat today?" she demanded, peering at him over her glasses.

"Not much," he lied effortlessly. "After that mighty breakfast this morning, I didn't need much. Skipped lunch. Had a sandwich and a beer tonight."

"One sandwich?"

"Just one."

"What kind?"

"Sliced turkey, cole slaw, lettuce and tomato on rye. With Russian dressing."

"That would do it," she said, nodding. "No wonder you look so remote."

"Remote?" he said. "Do I?"

He bent to unlace his other shoe and slide it off. He peeled away his heavy wool socks. Comfortable shoes and thick socks: secrets of a street cop's success.

When he straightened up, he saw that Monica was still staring at him.

"How is the case going?" she asked quietly.

"All right. It's really in the early stages. Just beginning to move."

"Everyone's talking about the Hotel Ripper. At the meetings today, it came up again and again. In informal conversations, I mean; not in lectures. Edward, people make jokes and laugh, but they're really frightened."

"Of course," he said. "Who wouldn't be?"

"You still think it's a woman?"

"Yes."

He stood, began to take off tie and shirt. Still she had not opened her book. She watched him empty his trouser pockets onto the bureau top.

"I wasn't going to tell you this," she said, "but I think I will."

He stopped what he was doing, turned to face her.

"Tell me what?" he said.

"I asked people I met if they thought the Hotel Ripper could be a woman. My own little survey of public opinion. I asked six people: three men and three women. All the men said the killer couldn't possibly be a woman, and all the women I asked said it could be a woman. Isn't that odd?"

"Interesting," he said. "But I don't know what it means—do you?"

"Not exactly. Except that men seem to have a higher opinion of women than women do of themselves."

He went to shower. He brushed his teeth, pulled on his pajamas. He came out, turned off the overhead light in the bedroom. Monica was reading by the bedlamp. He got into his bed, pulled up the blanket. He lay awake, hands behind his head, staring at the ceiling.

"Why would a woman do such a thing?" he asked, turning his head to look at her.

She put down her book. "I thought you weren't interested in motives."

"Surely I didn't say that. I said I wasn't interested in *causes*. There's a difference. Every cop is interested in motives. Has to be. That's what helps solve cases. Not the underlying psychological or social causes, but the immediate motive. A man can kill from greed. That's important to a cop. What caused the greed is of little consequence. What immediate motive could a woman have for a series of homicides like this? Revenge? She mutilates their genitals. Could she have been a rape victim?"

"Could be," Monica said promptly. "It's reason enough. But it doesn't even have to be rape. Maybe she's been used by men all her life. Maybe they've just screwed her and deserted her. Made her feel like a thing. Without value. So she's getting back at them."

"Yes," he said, "that listens; it's a possibility. There's something sexual involved here, and I don't know what it is. Could she be an out-and-out sadist?"

"No," Monica said, "I don't think so. Physical sadism amongst women isn't all that common. And sadists prefer slow suffering to quick death."

"Emotional?" he said. "Could it be that? She's been jilted by a man. Betrayed. The woman scorned . . ."

"Mmm . . ." his wife said, considering. "No, I don't believe that. A woman might be terribly hurt by one man, but I can't believe she'd try to restore her self-esteem by killing strangers. I think your first idea is right: it's something sexual."

"It could be fear," he said. "Fear of sex with a man."

She looked at him, puzzled.

"I don't follow," she said. "If the killer is afraid of sex, she wouldn't go willingly to the hotel rooms of strange men."

"She might," he said. "To be attracted by what we dread is a very human emotion. Then, when she gets there, fear conquers desire."

"Edward, you make her sound a very complex woman."

"I think she is."

He went back to staring at the ceiling.

"There's another possibility," he said in a low voice.

"What's that?"

"She simply enjoys killing. *Enjoys* it."

"Oh Edward, I can't believe that."

"Because you can't feel it. Any more than you can believe that some people derive pleasure from being whipped. But such things exist."

"I suppose so," she said in a small voice. "Well, there's a fine selection of motives for you. Which do you suspect it is?"

He was silent for a brief time. Then . . .

"What I suspect is that it is not a single motive, but a combination of things. We rarely act for one reason. It's usually a mixture. Can you give me *one* reason why the Son of Sam did what he did? So I think this killer is driven by several motives."

"The poor woman," Monica said sadly.

"Poor woman?" he said. "You sympathize with her? Feel sorry for her?"

"Of course," she said. "Don't you?"

He had wanted to play a more active role in the investigation, and during the last two weeks of May he got his chance.

All the squad officers involved in the case came to him. They knew Deputy Commissioner Thorsen was in command, transmitting his orders through Sergeant Boone, but they sought out Edward X. Delaney for advice and counsel. They knew his record and experience. And he was retired brass; there was nothing to fear from him . . .

"Chief," Detective Aaron Johnson said, "I got the word out to all my snitches, but there's not a whisper of any tear gas being peddled on the street."

"Any burglaries of army posts, police stations, or National Guard armories? Any rip-offs of chemical factories?"

"Negative," Johnson said. "Thefts of weapons and high explosives, but no record of anyone lifting tear gas in cans, cartridges, generators, or whatever. The problem here, Chief, is that the Lab Services Section can't swear the stuff was Chemical Mace. But if it was carried in a pocket-size aerosol dispenser, it probably was. So where do we go from here?"

"Find out who makes it and who packages it. Get a list

of distributors and wholesalers. Trace it to retailers in this area. Slavin says it's against the law for a New Yorker to buy the stuff, but it must be available to law enforcement agencies for riot control and so forth. Maybe prisons and private security companies can legally buy it. Maybe even a bank guard or night watchman can carry it—I don't know. Find out, and try to get a line on every can that came into this area in the past year."

"Gotcha," Johnson said.

"Chief," Sergeant Thomas K. Broderick said, "look at this . . ."

He dangled a small, sealed plastic bag in front of Delaney. The Chief inspected it curiously. Inside the bag was a half-inch of gleaming knife blade tip. On the upper half was part of the groove designed to facilitate opening the blade with a fingernail.

"That's it?" Delaney asked.

"That's it," Broderick said. "Fresh from Bergdorfer's slashed throat. We got a break on this one, Chief. Most pocket knives in this country are made with blades of high-grade carbon steel. The lab says this little mother is drop-forged Swedish stainless steel. How about that!"

"Beautiful," the Chief said. "Did you trace it?"

Broderick took a knife from his pocket and handed it to the Chief. It had bright red plastic handles bearing the crest of Switzerland.

"Called a Swiss Army knife," the detective said. "Or sometimes Swiss Army Officers' knives. They come in at least eight different sizes. The largest is practically a pocket tool kit. This is a medium-sized one. Open the big blade."

Obediently, Delaney folded back the largest blade. The two men bent over the knife, comparing the whole blade with the tip in the plastic bag.

"Looks like it," the Chief said.

"Identical," Broderick assured him. "The lab checked it out. But where do we go from here? These knives are sold in every good cutlery and hardware store in the city. And just to make the cheese more binding, they're also sold through mail order. Dead end."

"No," Delaney said, "not yet. Start with midtown Manhattan. Say from Thirty-fourth Street to Fifty-ninth Street, river to river. Make a list of every store in that area that carries this knife. The chances are good the killer will try to replace her broken knife with a new one just like it. Have your men visit every store and talk to the clerks. We want the name and address of everyone who buys a knife like this."

"How is the clerk going to do that? If the customer pays cash?"

"Uh . . . the clerks should tell the customer he wants the name and address for a free mail order catalogue the store is sending out. If the customer doesn't go for that scam and refuses to give name and address, the clerk should take a good look and then call you and give the description. Leave your phone number at every store; maybe they can stall the customer long enough for you or one of your men to get there. Tell the clerks to watch especially for young women, five-five to five-seven. Got it?"

"Got it," Broderick said. "But what if we come up with bupkes?"

"Then we'll do the same thing in all of Manhattan," Delaney said without humor. "And then we'll start on Brooklyn and the Bronx."

"It looks like a long, hot summer," Detective Broderick said, groaning.

"Chief," Lieutenant Wilson T. Crane said, "we've got sixteen possibles from Records. These are women between the ages of twenty and fifty with sheets that include violent felonies. We're tracking them all down and getting their alibis for the night of the homicides. None of them used the same MO as the Hotel Ripper."

"Too much to hope for," Delaney said. "I don't think our target has a sheet, but it's got to be checked out. What about prisons and asylums?"

"No recent releases or escapes that fit the profile," Crane said. "We're calling and writing all over the country, but nothing promising yet."

"Have you contacted Interpol?"

The lieutenant stared at him.

"No, Chief, we haven't," he admitted. "The FBI, but not Interpol."

"Send them a query," Delaney advised. "And Scotland Yard, too, while you're at it."

"Will do," Crane said.

"Chief," Detective Daniel Bentley said, "we went back to the bars at the Hotel Coolidge and asked if anyone remembered serving a man with scarred hands. No one did. But two of the cocktail waitresses who worked in the New Orleans Room the night Jerome Ashley was offed, don't work there anymore. We traced one. She's working in a massage parlor now—would you believe it? She doesn't remember any scarred hands. The other waitress went out to the Coast. Her mother doesn't have an address for her, but promises to ask the girl to call us if she hears from her. Don't hold your breath."

"Keep on it," Delaney said. "Don't let it slide."

"We'll keep on it," Bentley promised.

"Chief," Sergeant Abner Boone said, "I think we've got this thing organized. The hotel trade magazine gave us a copy of their mailing list. We're checking out every hotel in the city that got a copy and making a list of everyone who might have had access to it. I've got men checking the Mayor's office, Chamber of Commerce, hotel associations, visitors' bureau, and so forth. As the names come in, a deskman is compiling two master lists, male and female, with names listed in alphabetical order. How does that sound?"

"You're getting the addresses, too?"

"Right. And their age, when it's available. Even approximate age. Chief, we've got more than three hundred names already. It'll probably run over a thousand before we're through, and even then I won't swear we'll have everyone in New York with prior knowledge of the convention schedule."

"I know," Delaney said grimly, "but we've got to do it."

From all these meetings with the squad commanders, he came away with the feeling that morale was high, the men were doing their jobs with no more than normal grumbling.

After three months of bewilderment and relative inaction, they had finally been turned loose on the chase, their quarry dimly glimpsed but undeniably *there*. No man involved in the investigation thought what he was doing was without value, no matter how dull it might be.

It was not the first time that Edward X. Delaney had been struck by the contrast between the drama of a heinous crime and the dry minutiae of the investigation. The act was (sometimes) high tragedy; the search was (sometimes) low comedy.

The reason was obvious, of course. The criminal acted in hot passion; the detective had only cold resolve. The criminal was a child of the theater, inspired, thinking the play would go on forever. But along came the detective, a lumpish, methodical fellow, seeking only to ring down the curtain.

On May 30th, all the detectives met at Midtown Precinct North. If Delaney's hypothesis was correct—and most of them now believed it was, simply because no one had suggested any other theory that encompassed all the known facts—the next Hotel Ripper slaying would take place, or be attempted, during the week of June 1–7, and probably during midweek.

It was decided to assign every available man to the role of decoy. With the aid of the hotels' beefed-up security forces, all bars and cocktail lounges in large midtown Manhattan hotels would be covered from 8:00 P.M. until closing.

The lieutenants and sergeants worked out a schedule so that a "hot line" at Midtown North would be manned constantly during those hours. In addition, a standby squad of five men was stationed at Midtown South as backup, to be summoned as needed. The Crime Scene Unit was alerted; one of their vans took up position on West 54th Street.

Monica Delaney noted the fretfulness of her husband during the evenings of June 1–3. He picked up books and tossed them aside. Sat staring for an hour at an opened newspaper without turning a page. Stomped about the house disconsolately, head lowered, hands in his pockets.

She forbore to question the cause of his discontent; she knew. Wisely, she let him "stew in his own juice." But she wondered what would happen to him if events proved his precious theory wrong.

On the night of June 4th, a Wednesday, they were seated in the living room on opposite sides of the cocktail table, playing a desultory game of gin rummy. The Chief had been winning steadily, but shortly after 11:00 P.M., he threw his cards down in disgust and lurched to his feet.

"The hell with it," he said roughly. "I'm going to Midtown."

"What do you think you can do?" his wife asked quietly. "You'll just be in the way. The men will think you're checking up on them, that you don't trust them to do their jobs."

"You're right," he said immediately and dropped back into his chair. "I just feel so damned useless."

She looked at him sympathetically, knowing what this case had come to mean to him: that his expertise was valued, that his age was no drawback, that he was needed and wanted.

There he sat, a stern, rumpled mountain of a man. Gray hair bristled from his big head. His features were heavy, brooding. With his thick, rounded shoulders, he was almost brutish in appearance.

But she knew that behind the harsh façade, a more delicate man was hidden. He was at home in art museums, enjoyed good food and drink, and found pleasure in reading poetry—although it had to rhyme.

More important, he was a virile, tender, and considerate lover. He adored the children. He did not find tears or embraces unmanly. And, unknown to all but the women in his life, there was a core of humility in him.

He had been born and raised a Catholic, although he had long since ceased attending church. But she wondered if he had ever lost his faith. There was steel there that transcended personal pride in his profession and trust in his own rightness.

He had once confessed to her that Barbara, his first wife, had accused him of believing himself God's surrogate on earth. She thought Barbara had been close to the truth; there were times when he acted like a weapon of judgment and saw his life as one long tour of duty.

Musing on the contradictions of the man she loved, she gathered up the cards and put them away.

"Coffee?" she asked idly. "Pecan ring?"

"Coffee would be nice," he said, "but I'll skip the cake. You go ahead."

She was heating the water when the phone shrilled. She picked up the kitchen extension.

"Abner Boone, Mrs. Delaney," the sergeant said, his

voice at once hard and hollow. "Could I speak to the Chief, please?"

She didn't ask him the reason for his call. She went back into the living room. Her husband was already on his feet, tugging down vest and jacket. They stared at each other.

"Sergeant Boone," she said.

He nodded, face expressionless. "I'll take it in the study."

She went back into the kitchen and waited for the water to boil, her arms folded, hands clutching her elbows tightly. She heard him come out of the study, go to the hallway closet. He came into the kitchen carrying the straw skimmer he donned every June 1st, regardless of the weather.

"The Hotel Adler," he told her. "About a half-hour ago. They've got the hotel cordoned, but she's probably long gone. I'll be an hour or two. Don't wait up for me."

She nodded and he bent to kiss her cheek.

"Take care," she said as lightly as she could.

He smiled and was gone.

When he arrived at Seventh Avenue and 50th Street, the Hotel Adler was still cordoned, sawhorses holding back a gathering crowd. Two uniformed officers stood in front of the closed glass doors listening to the loud arguments of three men who were apparently reporters demanding entrance.

"No one gets in," one of the cops said in a remarkably placid voice. "But no one. That's orders."

"The public has a right to know," one of the men yelled.

The officer looked at him pityingly. "Hah-hah," he said.

The Chief plucked at the patrolman's sleeve. "I am Edward X. Delaney," he said. "Sergeant Boone is expecting me."

The cop took a quick glance at a piece of scrap paper crumpled in his hand.

"Right," he said. "You're cleared."

He held the door open for Delaney. The Chief strode into the lobby, hearing the howls of rage and frustration from the newsmen on the sidewalk.

There was a throng in the lobby being herded by

plainclothesmen into a single file. The line was moving toward a cardtable that had been set up in one corner. There, identification was requested, names and addresses written down.

This operation was being supervised by Sergeant Broderick. When Delaney caught his eye, the sergeant waved and made his way through the mob to the Chief's side. He leaned close.

"Fifth floor," he said in a low voice. "A butcher shop. An old couple next door heard sounds of a fight. The old lady wanted to call the desk and complain; the old geezer didn't want to make trouble. By the time they ended the argument and decided to call, it was too late; a security man found the stiff. I swear we got here no more than a half-hour after it happened."

"Decoys?" Delaney asked.

"Two," Broderick said. "A hotel man in the pub, one of our guys in the cocktail lounge. Both of them claim they saw no one who looked like the perp."

The Chief grunted. "I better go up."

"Hang on to your cookies," Broderick said, grinning.

The fifth floor corridor was crowded with uniformed cops, ambulance men, detectives, the DA's man, and precinct officers. Delaney made his way through the crush. Sergeant Boone and Ivar Thorsen were standing in the hallway, just outside an open door.

The three men shook hands ceremoniously, solemn mourners at a funeral. Delaney took a quick look through the door.

"Jesus Christ," he said softly.

"Yeah," Boone said, "a helluva fight. And then the cutting. The ME says not much more than an hour ago. Two, tops."

"I'm getting too old for this kind of thing," Thorsen said, his face ashen. "The guy's in ribbons."

"Any doubt that it was the Ripper?"

"No," Boone said. "Throat slashed and nuts stabbed. But the doc says he might have been dead when that happened."

"Any ID?"

Sergeant Boone flipped the pages of his notebook, found what he was seeking.

"Get a load of this," he said. "His paper says he was

Nicholas Telemachus Pappatizos. How do you like that? Home address was Las Vegas."

"The hotel security chief made him," Thorsen said. "Known as Nick Pappy and Poppa Nick. Also called The Magician. A small-time hood. Mostly cons and extortion. We're running him through Records right now."

Delaney looked through the doorway again. The small room was an abattoir. Walls splattered with gobbets of dripping blood. Rug soaked. Furniture upended, clothing scattered. A lamp smashed. The drained corpse was a jigsaw of red and white.

"Naked," Delaney said. "But he did put up a fight."

The three men watched the Crime Scene Unit move about the room, dusting for prints, vacuuming the clear patches of carpet, picking up hairs and shards of glass with tweezers and dropping them into plastic bags.

The two technicians were Lou Gorki and Tommy Callahan, the men Delaney had met in Jerome Ashley's room at the Hotel Coolidge. Now Gorki came to the door. He was carrying a big plastic syringe that looked like the kind used to baste roasts. But this one was half-filled with blood. Gorki was grinning.

"I think we got lucky," he announced. He held up the syringe. "From the bathroom floor. It's tile, and the blood didn't soak in. And we got here before it had a chance to dry. I got enough here for a transfusion. I figure it's the killer's blood. *Got* to be. The clunk was sliced to hash. No way was he going to make it to the bathroom and bleed on the tile. Also, we got bloody towels and stains in the sink where the perp washed. It looks good."

"Tell the lab I want a report on that blood immediately," Thorsen said. "That means before morning."

"I'll tell them," Gorki said doubtfully.

"Prints?" Boone asked.

"Doesn't look good. The usual partials and smears. The faucet handles in the bathroom were wiped clean."

"So if she was hurt," Delaney said, "it wasn't so bad that she didn't remember to get rid of her prints."

"Right," Gorki said. "That's the way it looks. Give us another fifteen minutes and then the meat's all yours."

But it was almost a half-hour before the CSU men packed up their heavy kits and departed. Deputy Commissioner Thorsen decided to go with them to see what he could do to expedite blood-typing by the Lab Services Section. In truth, Thorsen looked ill.

Then Delaney and Boone had to wait an additional ten minutes while a photographer and cartographer recorded the scene. Finally they stepped into the room, followed by Detectives Aaron Johnson and Daniel Bentley.

The four men leaned over the congealing corpse.

"How the hell did she do that?" Johnson said wonderingly. "The guy had muscles; he's not going to stand there and let a woman cut him up."

"Maybe the first stab was a surprise," Bentley said. "Weakened him enough so she could hack him to chunks."

"That makes sense," Boone said. "But how did she get cut? Gorki says she bled in the bathroom. No signs of a second knife—unless it's under his body. Anyone want to roll him over?"

"I'll pass," Johnson said. "I had barbecued ribs for dinner."

"They may have fought for her knife," Delaney said, "and she got cut in the struggle. Boone, you better alert the hospitals."

"God *damn* it!" the sergeant said, furious at his lapse, and rushed for the phone.

Delaney hung around until the ambulance men came in and rolled Nicholas Telemachus Pappatizos onto a body sheet. There was no knife under the body. Only blood.

The other detectives went down to the lobby to assist in the questioning. Delaney stayed in the room, wandering about, peeking into the bathroom. He saw nothing of significance. Perhaps, he thought, because he was shaken by the echoes of violence. Tommy Callahan came back and continued the Crime Scene Unit investigation.

He pushed the victim's discarded clothing into plastic bags and labeled them. He collected toothbrush, soap, and toilet articles from the bathroom and labeled those. Then he popped the lock on the single suitcase in the room and began to inventory the contents.

"Look at this, Chief," he said. "I better have a witness that I found this . . ."

Using a pencil through the trigger guard, he fished a dinky, chrome-plated automatic pistol from the suitcase. He sniffed cautiously at the muzzle.

"Clean," he said. "Looks like a .32."

"Or .22," Delaney said. "Gambler's gun. Good for maybe twenty feet, but you'd have to be Deadeye Dick to hit your target. Find anything else?"

"Two decks of playing cards. Nice clothes. Silk pajamas. He lived well."

"For a while," Delaney said.

He left the death room and took the elevator to the lobby. The crowd had thinned, but police were still quizzing residents and visitors. Out on the sidewalk, the mob of noisy newspapermen had grown. In the street, two TV vans were setting up lights and cameras.

Delaney pushed through the throng and crossed the avenue. He turned to look back at the hotel. If she came out onto Seventh, she could have taken a bus or subway. But if she was wounded, she probably caught a cab. He hoped Sergeant Boone would remember to check cabdrivers who might have been in the vicinity at the time.

He walked over to Sixth Avenue and got a cab going uptown. He was home in ten minutes, double-locked and chained the door behind him. It was then almost 2:00 A.M.

"Is that you, Edward?" Monica called nervously from upstairs.

"It's me," he assured her. "I'll be right up."

He hung his skimmer away, then went through his nightly routine: checking the locks on every door and window in the house, even those in the vacant children's rooms. Not for the first time did he decide this dwelling was too large for just Monica and him.

They could sell the building at a big profit and buy a small cooperative apartment or a small house in the suburbs. It made sense. But he knew they never would, and he supposed he would die in that old brownstone. The thought did not dismay him.

He left a night-light burning in the front hallway, then climbed the stairs slowly to the bedroom. He was not physically weary, but he felt emptied and weak. The sight of that slaughterhouse had drained him, diminished him.

Monica was lying on her side, breathing deeply, and he thought she was asleep. She had left the bathroom light on. He undressed quickly, not bothering to shower. He switched off the light, moved cautiously across the darkened room, climbed into bed.

He lay awake, trying to rid his mind of the images that thronged. But he kept seeing the jigsaw corpse and shook his head angrily.

He heard the rustle of bedclothes. In a moment Monica lifted his blanket and sheet and slipped in next to him. She fitted herself to his back, her knees bending with his. She dug an arm beneath him so she could hold him tightly, encircled.

"Was it bad?" she whispered.

He nodded in the darkness and thought of what Thorsen had said: "I'm getting too old for this kind of thing." Delaney turned to face his wife, moved closer. She was soft, warm, strong. He held on, and felt alive and safe.

After a while he slept. He roused briefly when Monica went back to her own bed, then drifted again into a deep and dreamless slumber.

When the phone rang, he roused slowly and reached to fumble for the bedside lamp. When he found the switch, he saw it was a little after 6:00 A.M. Monica was sitting up in bed, looking at him wide-eyed.

He cleared his throat.

"Edward X. Delaney here."

"Edward, this is Ivar. I wanted you to know as soon as possible. They've run the first part of the blood analysis. You were right. Caucasian female. Congratulations."

"Thank you," Delaney said.

9

Zoe Kohler came out of the hairdresser's, poking self-consciously at her new coiffure. Her hair had been shampooed, cut and styled, and treated with a spray guaranteed to give it gloss and weight while leaving it perfectly manageable.

Now it was shorter, hugged her head like a helmet, with feathery wisps at temples and cheeks. It was undeniably shinier, though it seemed to her darker and stiffer. The hairdresser had assured her it took ten years off her life, and then tried to sell her a complete makeup transformation. But she wasn't yet ready for that.

She walked slowly toward Madison Avenue, still limping slightly although the cut in her thigh was healing nicely. Everett Pinckney had asked her about the limp. She told him that she had turned her ankle, and that satisfied him.

She passed a newsstand and saw the headlines were still devoted to the murder at the Hotel Adler. She had not been surprised to read that the victim had a police record. One columnist called him a "nefarious character." Zoe Kohler agreed with that judgment.

Two days after the homicide, the police had announced that the Hotel Ripper was definitely a woman. The media had responded enthusiastically with enlarged coverage of the story and interviews with psychologists, feminists, and criminologists.

At least three female newspaper columnists and one female TV news reporter had made fervent pleas to the Hotel Ripper to contact them personally, promising

286

sympathetic understanding and professional help. One afternoon tabloid had offered $25,000 to the Ripper if she would surrender to the paper and relate her life story.

Even more amazing to Zoe Kohler was a casual mention that in a single day, the New York Police Department had received statements from forty-three women claiming to be the killer. All these "confessions" had been investigated and found to be false.

Zoe had asked Mr. Pinckney how the police could be so certain that the Hotel Ripper was a woman. He said they obviously had hard evidence that indicated it. Bloodstains, for instance. They could do wonderful things with blood analysis these days.

Barney McMillan, who was present during this conversation, slyly suggested that another factor might have been the results of the autopsy which could show if the victim had sexual intercourse just before he was killed.

"He probably died happy," McMillan said.

Zoe Kohler wasn't particularly alarmed that the police investigation was now directed toward finding a female murderer. And she had read that plainclothesmen were now being stationed in hotel cocktail lounges in midtown Manhattan. She thought vaguely that it might be necessary to seek her adventures farther afield.

She had been fortunate so far, mostly because of careful planning. She was exhilarated by the fearful excitement she had caused. More than that, the secret that she alone knew gave her an almost physical pleasure, a self-esteem she had never felt before.

All those newspaper stories, all those television broadcasts and radio bulletins were about *her*. What she felt came very close to pride and, with her new hairdo and despite her limp, she walked taller, head up, glowing, and felt herself queen of the city.

She paused on Madison Avenue to look in the show windows of a shop specializing in clothing for children, from infants to ten-year-olds. The prices were shockingly high for such small garments, but the little dresses and sweaters, jeans and overalls, were smartly designed.

Zoe stared at the eyelet cotton and bright plaids, the crisp party dresses and pristine nightgowns. All so young, so—so innocent. She remembered well that she had been

dressed in clean, unsoiled clothing like that: fabrics fresh
against her skin, stiff with starch, rustling with their
newness.

"You must be a little lady," her mother had said. "And
look at these adorable white gloves!"

"You must keep yourself clean and spotless," her
mother had said. "Never run. Try not to become per-
spired. Move slowly and gracefully."

"A little lady always listens," her mother had said. "A
little lady speaks in a quiet, refined voice, enunciating
clearly."

So Zoe avoided mud puddles, learned the secrets of the
kitchen. She did her homework every night and was
awarded good report cards. All her parents' friends
remarked on what a paragon she was.

"A real little lady." That's what the adults said about
Zoe Kohler.

Seeing those immaculate garments in a Madison Avenue shop brought it all back: the spotlessness of her
home, the unblemished clothing she wore, the purity of
her childhood. Youth without taint . . .

On the evening of June 14th, a Saturday, Zoe had
dinner with Ernest Mittle in the dining room of the Hotel
Gramercy Park. They were surprised to find they were the
youngest patrons in that sedate chamber.

Zoe Kohler, glancing about, saw Ernest and herself in
twenty years, and found comfort in it. Well-groomed
women and respectable men. Dignity and decorum. Low
voices and small gestures. How could some people reject
the graces of civilization?

She looked at the man sitting opposite and was content.
Courtesy and kindness were not dead.

Ernest was wearing a navy blue suit, white shirt,
maroon tie. His fine, flaxen hair was brushed to a gleam.
Cheeks and chin were so smooth and fair that they
seemed never to have known a razor.

He appeared so slight to Zoe. There was something
limpid about him, an untroubled innocence. He buttered
a breadstick thoroughly and precisely and crunched it with
shining teeth. His hands and feet were small. He was
almost a miniature man, painted with a one-hair brush,
refined to purity.

After dinner they stopped at the dim bar for a Strega. Here was a more electric ambience. The patrons were younger, noisier, and there were shouts of laughter. Braless women and bearded men.

"What would you like to do, Zoe?" Ernest asked, holding her hand and stroking her fingers lightly. "A movie? A nightclub? Would you like to go dancing somewhere?"

She considered a moment. "A disco. Ernie, could we go to a disco? We don't have to dance. Just have a glass of wine and see what's going on."

"Why not?" he said bravely, and she thought of her gold bracelet.

An hour later they were seated at a minuscule table in a barnlike room on East 58th Street. They were the only customers, although lights were flashing and flickering and music boomed from a dozen speakers in such volume that the walls trembled.

"You wanted to see what's going on?" Ernest shouted, laughing. "Nothing's going on!"

But they were early. By the time they finished their second round of white wine, the disco was half-filled, the dance floor was filling up, and newcomers were rushing through the entrance, stamping, writhing, whirling before they were shown to tables.

It was a festival! a carnival! What costumes! What disguises! Naked flesh and glittering cloth. A kaleidoscope of eye-aching colors. All those jerking bodies frozen momentarily in stroboscopic light. The driving din! Smell of perfume and sweat. Shuffle of a hundred feet. The thunder!

Zoe Kohler and Ernest Mittle looked at each other. Now they were the oldest in the room, smashed by cacophonous music, assaulted by the wildly sexual gyrations on the floor. It wasn't a younger generation they were watching; it was a new world.

There a woman with breasts swinging free from a low-cut shirt. There a man with genitals delineated beneath skin-tight pants of pink satin. Bare necks, arms, shoulders. Navels. Hot shorts, miniskirts, vinyl boots. Rumps. Tits and cocks.

Grasping hands. Sliding hands. Grinding hips. Opened thighs. Stroking. Gasps and shiny grins. Flickering tongues and wild eyes. A churn of heaving bodies, the room rocking, seeming to tilt.

Everything tilting . . .

"Let's dance," Ernest yelled in her ear. "It's so crowded, no one will notice us."

On the floor, they were swallowed up, engulfed and hidden. They became part of the slough. Hot flesh poured them together. They were in a fevered flood, swept away.

They tried to move in time to the music, but they were daunted by the flung bodies about them. They huddled close, staggering upright, trying to keep their balance, laughing nervously and holding each other to survive.

For a moment, just a moment, they were one, knees to shoulders, welded tight. Zoe felt his slightness, his soft heat. She did not draw away, but he did. Slowly, with difficulty, he pulled her clear, guided her back to their table.

"Oh wow," he said, "what a crush! That's madness!"

"Yes," she said. "Could I have another glass of wine, please?"

They didn't try to dance again, but they didn't want to leave.

"They're not so much younger than we are," Zoe said.

"No," he agreed, "not so much."

They sat at their table, drinking white wine and looking with amusement, fear, and envy at the frenzied activity around them. The things they saw, flashing lights; the things they heard, pounding rhythm—all stunned them.

They glanced at each other, and their clasped hands tightened. Never had they felt so alone and together.

Still, still, there was an awful fascination. All that nudity. All that sexuality. It lured. They both felt the pull.

Zoe saw one young woman whirling so madly that her long blond hair flared like flame. She wore a narrow strip of shirred elastic across her nipples. Her jeans were so tight that the division between buttocks was obvious . . . and the mound between her thighs.

She danced wildly, mouth open, lips wet. Her eyes were half-closed; she gasped in a paroxysm of lust. Her body fought for freedom; she offered her flesh.

"I could do that," Zoe Kohler said suddenly.

"What?" Ernest shouted. "What did you say? I can't hear you."

She shook her head. Then they sat and watched. They drank many glasses of wine. They felt the heat of the dancers. What they witnessed excited them and diminished them at once, in a way they could not understand.

Finally, long past 1:00 A.M., they rose dizzily to their feet, infected by sensation. Ernest had just enough money to pay the bill and leave a small tip.

Outside, they stood with arms about each other's waist, weaving slightly. They tasted the cool night air, looked up at stars dimmed by the city's blaze.

"Go home now," Ernest muttered. "Don't have enough for a cab. Sorry."

"Don't worry about it, dear," she said, taking his arm. "I have money."

"A loan," he insisted.

She led him, lurching, to Park Avenue. When a cab finally stopped, she pushed Ernest into the back seat, then climbed in. She gave the driver her address.

"Little high," Ernest said solemnly. "Sorry about that."

"Silly!" she said. "There's nothing to be sorry for. I'll make us some black coffee when we get home."

They arrived at her apartment house. He tried to straighten up and walk steadily through the lobby. But upstairs, in her apartment, he collapsed onto her couch and looked at her helplessly.

"I'm paralyzed," he said.

"Just don't pass out," she said, smiling. "I'll have coffee ready in a jiff. Then you'll feel better."

"Sorry," he mumbled again.

When she came in from the kitchen with the coffee, he was bent far forward, head in his hands. He raised a pale face to her.

"I feel dreadful," he said. "It was the wine."

"And the heat," she said. "And that smoky air. Drink your coffee, darling. And take this . . ."

He looked at the capsule in her palm. "What is it?"

"Extra-strength aspirin," she said, proffering the Tuinal. "Help prevent a hangover."

He swallowed it down, gulped his coffee steadily. She poured him another cup.

"Ernie," she said, "it's past two o'clock. Why don't you

sleep here? I don't want you going home alone at this hour."

"Oh, I couldn't—" he started.

"I insist," she said firmly. "You take the bed and I'll sleep out here on the couch."

He objected, saying he already felt better, and if she'd lend him a few dollars, he'd take a cab home; he'd be perfectly safe. But she insisted he stay, and after a while he assented—but only if she slept in her own bed and he bunked down on the sofa. She agreed.

She brought him a third cup of coffee. This one he sipped slowly. When she assured him a small brandy would help settle his stomach, he made no demur. They each had a brandy, taking off their shoes, slumping at opposite ends of the long couch.

"Those people . . ." he said, shaking his head. "I can't get over it. They just don't care—do they?"

"No, I suppose not. It was all so—so ugly."

"Yes," he said, nodding, "ugly."

"Not ugly so much as coarse and vulgar. It cheapens, uh, sex."

"Recreational sex," he said. "That's what they call it; that's how they feel about it. Like tennis or jogging. Just another diversion. Isn't that the feeling you got, watching them? You could tell by the way they danced."

"All that bare flesh!"

"And the way they moved! So suggestive."

"I, ah, suppose they have—they make—they go to bed afterwards. Ernie?"

"I suppose so. The dancing was just a preliminary. Did you get that feeling?"

"Oh yes. The dancing was definitely sexual. Definitely. It was very depressing. In a way. I mean, then making love loses all its importance. You know? It means about as much as eating or drinking."

"What I think," he said, looking directly at her, "is that sex—I mean just physical sex—without some emotional attachment doesn't have any meaning at all."

"I couldn't agree more. Without love, it's just a cheap thrill."

"A cheap thrill," he repeated. "Exactly. But I suppose if we tried to explain it to those people, they'd just laugh at us."

"I suppose they would. But I don't care; I still think we're right."

They sat a moment in silence, reflectively sipping their brandies.

"I'd like to have sex with you," he said suddenly.

She looked at him, expressionless.

"But I never would," he added hastily. "I mean, I'd never ask you. Zoe, you're a beautiful, exciting woman, but if we went to bed together, uh, you know, casually, it would make us just like those people we saw tonight."

"Animals," she said.

"Yes, that's right. I don't want a cheap thrill and I don't think you do either."

"I don't, dear; I really don't."

"It seems to me," he said, puzzling it out, "that when you get married, you're making a kind of statement. It's like a testimonial. You're signing a legal document that really says it's not just a cheap thrill, that something more important is involved. You're pledging your love forever and ever. Isn't that what marriage means?"

"That's what it's supposed to mean," she said sadly. "It doesn't always work out that way."

She pushed her way along the couch. She sat close to him, put an arm about his neck. She pulled him close, kissed his cheek.

"You're an idealist," she whispered. "A sweet idealist."

"I guess I am," he said. "But is what I want so impossible?"

"What do you want?"

"Something that has meaning. I go to work every day, come home and fry a hamburger. I watch television. I'm not complaining; I have a good job and all. But there must be more than that. And I don't mean a one-night stand. Or an endless series of one-night stands. There's got to be more to life than that."

"You want to get married?" she asked in a low voice, remembering Maddie's instructions.

"I think so. I think I do. I've thought a lot about it, but the idea scares me. Because it's so final. That's the way I see it anyway. I mean, it's for always, isn't it? Or should be. But at the same time the idea frightens me, I can't see any substitute. I can't see anything else that would give me what I want. I like my job, but that's not enough."

"An emptiness," she said. "A void. That's what my life is like."

"Yes," he said eagerly, "you understand. We both want something, don't we? Meaning. We want our lives to have meaning."

The uncovering that had started that afternoon in Central Park had progressed to this; they both felt it. It was an unfolding, a stripping, that neither wanted to end. It was a fearful thing they were doing, dangerous and painful.

Yet it had become easier. Intimacy acted on them like an addictive drug. Stronger doses were needed. And they hardly dared foresee what the end might be, or even if there was an end. Perhaps their course was limitless and they might never finish.

"There's something I want," she said. *"Something.* But don't ask me what it is because I don't know, I'm not sure. Except that I don't want to go on living the way I do. I really don't."

He leaned forward to kiss her lips. Twice. Tenderly.

"We're so alike," he breathed. "So alike. We believe in the same things. We want the same things."

"I don't know what I want," she said again.

"Sure you do," he said gently, taking her hand. "You want your life to have significance. Isn't that it?"

"I want . . ." she said. "I want . . . What do I want? Darling, I've never told this to anyone else, but I want to be a different person. Totally. I want to be born again, and start all over. I know the kind of woman I want to be, and it isn't me. It's all been a mistake, Ernie. My life, I mean. It's been all wrong. Some of it was done to me, and some of it I did myself. But it's my life, and so it's all my responsibility. Isn't that true? But when I try to understand what I did that I should not have done, or what I neglected to do, I get the horrible feeling that the whole thing was beyond my . . ."

But as she spoke, she saw his eyelids fluttering. His head came slowly down. She stopped talking, smiled, took the empty brandy glass from his nerveless fingers. She smoothed the fine hair, stroked his cheek.

"Beddy-bye," she said softly.

He murmured something.

She got him into the bedroom, half-supporting him as he stumbled, stockinged feet catching on the rug. She sat him down on the edge of the bed and kneeled to pull off his socks. Small, pale feet. He stroked her head absently, weaving as he sat, eyes closed.

She tugged off his jacket, vest, tie, shirt. He grumbled sleepily as she pushed him back, unbelted and unzipped his trousers, peeled them away. He was wearing long white drawers, practically Bermuda shorts, and an old-fashioned undershirt with shoulder straps.

She yanked and hauled and finally got him straightened out under the covers, his head on the pillow. He was instantly asleep, didn't even stir when she bent to kiss his cheek.

"Good night, darling," she said softly. "Sleep well."

She washed the coffee things and the brandy glasses. She swallowed down a salt tablet, assorted vitamins and minerals, drank a small bottle of club soda. After debating a moment, she took a Tuinal.

She went into the bathroom to shower, her third that day. The wound on her thigh was now just a red line, and she soaped it carefully. She lathered the rest of her body thickly, wanting to cleanse away—what?

She dried, powdered, used spray cologne on neck, bosom, armpits, the insides of her thighs. She pulled on a long nightgown of white batiste with modest inserts of lace at the neckline.

She crawled into bed cautiously, not wanting to disturb Ernie. But he was dead to the world, breathing deeply and steadily. She thought she saw a smile on his lips, but couldn't be sure.

Maddie had instructed her to determine Ernest's attitude toward marriage, and she had done it. She thought that if she were a more positive woman, more aggressive, she might easily lead him to a proposal. But at the moment that did not concern her.

What was a puzzlement was her automatic response to Maddie's advice. She had obeyed without question, although she was the one intimately involved, not Maddie. Yet she had let the other woman dictate her conduct.

It had always been like that—other people pushing her this way and that, imposing their wills. Her mother's conversation had been almost totally command, molding

Zoe to an image of the woman she wanted her daughter to be.

Even her father, by his booming physical presence, had shoved her into emotions and prejudices she felt foreign to her true nature.

And her husband! Hadn't he sought, always, to remake her into something she could not be? He had never been satisfied with what she was. He had never accepted her.

Everyone, all her life, had tried to change her. Ernest Mittle, apparently, was content with Zoe Kohler. But could she be certain he would remain content? Or would the day come when he, too, would begin to push, pull, haul, and tug?

It came to her almost as a revelation that this was the reason she sought adventures. They were her only opportunity to try out and to display her will.

She knew that others—like the Son of Sam—had blamed their misdeeds on "voices," on hallucinatory commands that overrode their inclinations and volition.

But her adventures were the only time in Zoe Kohler's life when she listened to her own voice.

She turned onto her side, moved closer to Ernie. She smelled his sweet, innocent scent. She put one arm about him, pulled him to her. And that's how she fell asleep.

During the following week, she had cause to remember her reflections on how, all her life, she had been manipulated.

The newspapers continued their heavy coverage of the Hotel Ripper investigation. Almost every day the police revealed new discoveries and new leads being pursued.

Zoe Kohler began to think of the police as a single intelligence, a single person. She saw him as a tall, thin individual, sour and righteous. He resembled the old cartoon character "Prohibition," with top hat, rusty tailcoat, furled umbrella. He wore an expression of malicious discontent.

This man, this "police," was juiceless and without mercy. He was intelligent (frighteningly so) and implacable. By his deductive brilliance, he was pushing Zoe Kohler in ways she did not want to go. He was maneuvering her, just like everyone else, and she resented it—

resented that anyone would tamper with her adventures, the only truly private thing in her life.

For instance, the newspapers reported widened surveillance of all public places in midtown Manhattan hotels by uniformed officers and plainclothesmen.

Then a partial description of the Hotel Ripper was published. She was alleged to be five-seven to five-eight in very high heels, was slender, wore a shoulder-length wig, and carried a trenchcoat.

She also wore a gold link bracelet with the legend: WHY NOT? Her last costume was described as a tightly fitted dress of bottle-green silk with spaghetti straps.

These details flummoxed Zoe Kohler. She could not imagine how "police" had guessed all that about her—particularly the gold bracelet. She began to wonder if he had some undisclosed means of reading her secret thoughts, or perhaps reconstructing the past from the aura at the scene of the crime.

That dour, not to be appeased individual, who came shuffling after her told the newspaper and television reporters that the Hotel Ripper probably dressed flashily, in revealing gowns. He said her makeup and perfume would probably be heavy. He said that, although she was not a professional prostitute, she deliberately gave the impression of being sexually available.

He revealed that the weapon used in the first four crimes was a Swiss Army knife, but it was possible a different knife was used in the fifth killing. He mentioned, almost casually, that it was believed the woman involved was connected, somehow, with the hotel business in Manhattan.

It was astounding! Where was "police" getting this information? For the first time she felt quivers of fear. That dried-up, icily determined old man with his sunken cheeks and maniacal glare would give her no rest until she did what he wanted.

Die.

She thought it through carefully. Her panic ebbed as she began to see ways to defeat her nemesis.

On the night of June 24th, a Tuesday, Zoe Kohler was awakened by a phone call at about 2:15 A.M.

At first she thought the caller, a male, was Ernest
Mittle since he was sniffling and weeping; she had
witnessed Ernie's tears several times. But the caller,
between chokes and wails, identified himself as Harold
Kurnitz.

She was finally able to understand what he was saying:
Maddie Kurnitz had attempted to commit suicide by
ingesting an overdose of sleeping pills. She was presently
in the Intensive Care Unit of Soames-Phillips—and could
Zoe come at once?

She showered before dressing, for reasons she could not
comprehend. She told herself that she was not thinking
straight because of the shocking news. She gave the night
doorman a dollar to hail a cab for her. She was at the
hospital less than an hour after Harry called.

He met her in the hallway on the fifth floor, rushing to
her with open arms, his face wrenched.

"She's going to make it!" he cried, his voice thin and
quavery. "She's going to make it!"

She got him seated on a wooden bench in the brightly
lighted corridor. Slowly, gradually, with murmurs and
pattings, she calmed him down. He sat hunched over,
deflated, clutching trembling hands between his knees.
He told her what had happened . . .

He said he had returned to the Kurnitz apartment a
little before 1:30 A.M.

"I had to work late at the office," he mumbled.

He had started to undress, and then for some reason he
couldn't explain, he decided to look in on Maddie.

"We were sleeping in different bedrooms," he explained. "When I work late . . . Anyway, it was just luck.
Or maybe God. But if I hadn't looked in, the doc says she
would have been gone."

He had found her crumpled on the floor in her shortie
pajamas. Lying in a pool of vomit. He thought at first she
had drunk too much and had passed out. But then, when
he couldn't rouse her, he became frightened.

"I panicked," he said. "I admit it. I thought she was
gone. I couldn't see her breathing. I mean, her chest
wasn't going up and down or anything."

So he had called 911, and while he was waiting, he
attempted to give mouth-to-mouth resuscitation. But he

didn't know how to do it and was afraid he might be harming her.

"I just sort of blew in her mouth," he said, "but the guy in the ambulance said I didn't hurt her. He was the one who found the empty pill bottle in the bathroom. Phenobarbital. And there was an empty Scotch bottle that had rolled under the bed. The doc said if she hadn't vomited, she'd have been gone. It was that close."

Harry had ridden in the ambulance to Soames-Phillips, watching the attendant administer oxygen and inject stimulants.

"I kept repeating, 'Don't do this to me, Maddie,'" he said. "That's all I remember saying: 'Please don't do this to me.' Wasn't that a stupid, selfish thing to say? Listen, Zoe, I guess you know Maddie and I are separating. Maybe this was her way of, uh, you know, getting back at me. But I swear I never thought she'd pull anything like this. I mean, it was all friendly; we didn't fight or anything like that. No screaming. I never thought she'd . . ."

His voice trailed away.

"Maybe now you'll get back together again," Zoe said hopefully.

But he didn't answer, and after a while she left him and went in search of Maddie.

She found a young doctor scribbling on a clipboard outside the Intensive Care Unit. She asked him if she could see Mrs. Kurnitz.

"I'm Zoe Kohler," she said. "I'm her best friend. You can ask her husband. He's right down the hall."

He looked at her blankly.

"Why not?" he said finally, and again she thought of her gold bracelet. "She's not so bad. Puked up most of the stuff. She'll be dancing the fandango tomorrow night. But make it short."

Maddie was in a bed surrounded by white screens. She looked drained, waxen. Her eyes were closed. Zoe bent over her, took up a cool, limp hand. Maddie's eyes opened slowly. She stared at Zoe.

"Shit," she said in a wispy voice. "I fucked it up, didn't I? I can't do anything right."

"Oh, Maddie," Zoe Kohler said sorrowfully.

"I got the fucking pills down and then I figured I'd

make sure by finishing the booze. But they tell me I upchucked.''

"But you're alive," Zoe said.

"Hip, hip, hooray," Maddie said, turning her head to one side. "Is Harry still around?"

"He's right outside. Do you want to see him, Maddie?"

"What the hell for?"

"He's taking it hard. He's all broken up."

Maddie's mouth stretched in a grimace that wasn't mirth.

"He thinks it was because of him," she said, a statement, not a question. "The male ego. I couldn't care less."

"Then why . . . ?"

Maddie turned her head back to glare at Zoe.

"Because I just didn't want to wake up," she said. "Another day. Another stupid, empty, fucking day. Harry's got nothing to do with it. It's me."

"Maddie, I . . . Maddie, I don't understand."

"What's the point?" she demanded. "Just what is the big, fucking point? Will you tell me that?"

Zoe was silent.

"Ah, shit," Maddie said. "What a downer it all is. Just being alive. Who needs it?"

"Maddie, you don't really feel like—"

"Don't tell me what I feel like, kiddo. You haven't a clue, not a clue. Oh, Christ, I'm sorry," she added immediately, her hand tightening on Zoe's. "You got your problems too, I know."

"But I thought you were—"

"All fun and games?" Maddie said, her mouth twisted. "A million laughs? You've got to be young for that, luv. When the tits begin to sag, it's time to take stock. I just figured I had the best of it and I didn't have the guts for what comes next. I'm a sprinter, sweetie, not a long distance runner."

"Do you really think you and Harry . . . ?"

"No way. It's finished. Kaput. He had a toss in the hay with his tootsie tonight, and then came home and found me gasping my last. Big tragedy. Instant guilt. So he's all busted up. By tomorrow night he'll be sore at me for spoiling his sleep. Oh hell, I'm not blaming him. But it's all over. He knows it and I know it."

"What will you do now, Maddie?"

"Do?" she said with a bright smile. "I'll tell you what I'll do. The worst. Go on living."

Out in the corridor, Zoe Kohler leaned a moment against the wall, her eyes closed.

If Maddie, if a woman like Maddie, couldn't win, no one could win. She didn't want to believe that, but there it was.

Dr. Oscar Stark called her at the office.

"Just checking on my favorite patient," he said cheerfully. "How are we feeling these days, Zoe?"

"I feel fine, doctor."

"Uh-huh. Taking your medication regularly?"

"Oh yes."

"No craving for salt?"

"No."

"What about tiredness? Feel weary at times? All washed out?"

"Oh no," she lied glibly, "nothing like that."

"Sleeping all right? Without pills?"

"I sleep well."

He sighed. "Not under any stress, are you, Zoe? Not necessarily physical stress, but any, uh, personal or emotional strains?"

"No."

"You're wearing that bracelet, aren't you? The medical identification bracelet? And carrying the kit?"

"Oh yes. Every day."

He was silent a moment, then said heartily, "Good! Well, I'll see you on—let me look it up—on the first of July, a Tuesday. Right?"

"Yes, doctor. That's correct."

"If any change occurs—any weakness, nausea, unusual weight loss, abdominal pains—you'll phone me, won't you?"

"Of course, doctor. Thank you for calling."

She thought it out carefully . . .

Newspapers had described the Hotel Ripper as being "flashily dressed." So she would have to forget her skintight skirts and revealing necklines. Also, it was now too warm to wear a coat of any kind to cover such a costume.

So, to avoid notice by the doorman of her apartment house and by police officers stationed in hotel cocktail lounges, she would dress conservatively. She would wear no wig. She would use only her usual minimal makeup.

That meant there was no reason for that pre-adventure trip up to the Filmore on West 72nd Street to effect a transformation. She could sally forth boldly, dressed conventionally, and take a cab to anywhere she wished.

She could not wear the WHY NOT? bracelet, of course, and her entire approach would have to be revised. She could not come on as "sexually available." Her clothes, manner, speech, appearance—all would have to be totally different from the published description of the Hotel Ripper.

Innocence! That was the answer! She knew how some men were excited by virginity. (Hadn't Kenneth been?) She would try to act as virginal as a woman of her age could. Why, some men even had a letch for cheerleaders and nubile girls in middies. She knew all that, and it would be fun to play the part.

There was a store on 40th Street, just east of Lexington Avenue, that sold women's clothing imported from Latin America. Blouses from Ecuador, skirts from Guatemala, bikinis from Brazil, huaraches, mantillas, lacy camisoles—and Mexican wedding gowns.

These last were white or cream-colored dresses of batiste or crinkled cotton, light as gossamer. They had full skirts that fell to the ankle, with modest necklines of embroidery or eyelet. The bell sleeves came below the elbow, and the entire loose dress swung, drifted, ballooned—fragile and chaste.

"A marvelous summer party dress," the salesclerk said. "Comfortable, airy—and so different."

"I'll take it," Zoe Kohler said.

She read the weekly hotel trade magazine avidly. There was a motor inn on 49th Street, west of Tenth Avenue: the Tribunal. It would be hosting a convention of college and university comptrollers during June 29th to July 2nd.

When Zoe Kohler looked up the Tribunal in the hotel directory, she found it was a relatively modest hostelry, only 180 rooms and suites, with coffee shop, dining room, a bar. And an outdoor cocktail lounge that overlooked a small swimming pool on the roof, six floors up.

The Tribunal seeemed far enough removed from midtown Manhattan to have escaped the close surveillance of the police. And, being small, it was quite likely to be crowded with tourists and convention-goers. Zoe Kohler thought she would try the Tribunal. An outdoor cocktail lounge that overlooked a swimming pool. It sounded romantic.

Her menstrual cramps began on Sunday, June 29th. Not slowly, gradually, increasing in intensity as they usually did, but suddenly, with the force of a blow. She doubled over, sitting with her arms folded and clamped across her abdomen.

The pain came in throbs, leaving her shuddering. She imagined the soles of her feet ached and the roots of her hair burned. Deep within her was this wrenching twist, her entrails gripped and turned over. She wanted to scream.

She swallowed everything: Anacin, Midol, Demerol. She called Ernie and postponed their planned trip to Jones Beach. Then she got into a hot tub, lightheaded and nauseated. She tried a glass of white wine, but hadn't finished it before she had to get out of the tub to throw up in the toilet.

Her weakness was so bad that she feared to move without gripping sink or doorjamb. She was uncoordinated, stumbled frequently, saw her own watery limbs floating away like feelers. She was troubled by double vision and, clasping a limp breast, felt her heart pound in a wild, disordered rhythm.

"What's happening to me?" she asked aloud, more distraught than panicky.

She spent all day in bed or lying in a hot bath. She ate nothing, since she felt always on the verge of nausea. Once, when she tried to lift a glass of water and the glass slipped from her strengthless fingers to crash on the kitchen floor, she wept.

She took two Tuinal and had a fitful sleep thronged with evil dreams. She awoke, not remembering the details, but filled with dread. Her nightgown was sodden with sweat, and she showered and changed before trying to sleep again.

She awoke late Monday morning, and told herself she

felt better. She had inserted a tampon, but her period had not started. The knifing pain had subsided, but she was left with a leaden pressure that seemed to force her guts downward. She had a horrific image of voiding all her insides.

She dared not step on the scale, but could not ignore the skin discolorations in the crooks of her elbows, on her knees, between her fingers. Remembering Dr. Stark's test, she plucked at her pubis; several hairs came away, dry and wiry.

She called the Hotel Granger and spoke to Everett Pinckney. He was very understanding, and told her they'd manage without her for the day, and to take Tuesday off as well, if necessary.

She lay on the bed, blanket and sheet thrown aside. She looked down with shock and loathing at her own naked body.

She hadn't fully realized how thin she had become. Her hipbones jutted, poking up white, glassy skin. Her breasts lay flaccid, nipples withdrawn. Below, she could see a small tuft of dulled hair, bony knees, toes ridiculously long and prehensile: an animal's claws.

When she smelled her arm, she caught a whiff of ash. Her flesh was pudding; she could not make a fist. She was a shrunken sack, and when she explored herself, the sphincter was slack. She was emptied out and hollow.

She spent the afternoon dosing herself with all the drugs in her pharmacopeia. She got down a cup of soup and held it, then had a ham sandwich and a glass of wine. She soaked again in a tub, washed her hair, took a cold shower.

She worked frantically to revive her flagging body, ignoring the internal pain, her staggering gait. She forced herself to move slowly, carefully, precisely. She punished herself, breathing deeply, and willed herself to dress.

For it seemed to her that an adventure that night—all her adventures—were therapy, necessary to her well-being. She did not pursue the thought further than that realization: she would not be well, could not be well, unless she followed the dictates of her secret, secret heart.

It became a dream. No, not a dream, but a play in which she was at once actress and spectator. She was inside and outside. She observed herself with wonder, moving about resolutely, disciplining her flesh. She wanted to applaud this fierce, determined woman.

The Mexican wedding gown was a disaster; she knew it would never do. It hung on her wizened frame in folds. The neckline gaped. The hem seemed to sweep the floor. She was lost in it: a little girl dressed up in her mother's finery, lacking only the high-heeled pumps, wide-brimmed hat, smeared lipstick.

She put the gown aside and dressed simply in lisle turtleneck sweater, denim jumper, low-heeled pumps. When she inspected herself in the mirror, she saw a wan, tremulous, vulnerable woman. With a sharpened knife in her purse.

The rooftop cocktail lounge was bordered with tubs of natural greenery. The swimming pool, lighted from beneath, shone with a phosphorescent blue. An awning stretched over the tables was flowered with golden daisies.

A few late-evening swimmers chased and splashed with muted cries. From a hi-fi behind the bar came seductive, nostalgic tunes, fragile as tinsel. Life seemed slowed, made wry and gripping.

A somnolent waiter moved slowly, splay-footed. Clink of ice in tall glasses. Quiet murmurs, and then a sudden fountain of laughter. White faces in the gloom. Bared arms. Everyone lolled and dreamed.

The night itself was luminous, stars blotted by city glow. A soft breeze stroked. The darkness opened up and engulfed, making loneliness bittersweet and silence a blessing.

Zoe Kohler sat quietly in the shadows and thought herself invisible. She was hardly aware of the gleaming swimmers in the pool, the couples lounging at the outdoor tables. She thought vaguely that soon, soon, she would go downstairs to the crowded bar.

But she felt so calm, so indolent, she could not stir. It was the bemused repose of convalescence: all pain dulled, turmoil vanished, worry spent. Her body flowed; it just flowed, suffused with a liquid warmth.

There were two solitary men on the terrace. One, older, drank rapidly with desperate intentness, bent over his glass. The other, with hair to his shoulders and a wispy

beard, seemed scarcely old enough to be served. He was
drinking bottled beer, making each one last.

The bearded boy rose suddenly, his metal chair screech-
ing on the tile. Everyone looked up. He stood a moment,
embarrassed by the attention, and fussed with beer bottle
and glass until he was ignored.

He came directly to Zoe's table.

"Pardon me, ma'am," he said in a low voice. "I was
wondering if I might buy you a drink. Please?"

Zoe inspected him, tilting her head, trying to make him
out in the twilight. He was very tall, very thin. Dressed in
a tweed jacket too bulky for his frame, clean chinos,
sueded bush boots.

Thin wrists stuck from the cuffs of his heavy jacket, and
his big head seemed balanced on a stalk neck. His smile
was hopeful. The long hair and scraggly beard were
blond, sun-streaked. He seemed harmless.

"Sit down," she said softly. "We'll each buy our own
drinks."

"Thank you," he said gratefully.

His name was Chet (for Chester) LaBranche, and he
was from Waterville, Maine. But he lived and worked in
Vermont, where he was assistant to the president of Barre
Academy, which was called an academy but was actually a
fully accredited coeducational liberal arts college with an
enrollment of 437.

"I really shouldn't be here," he said, laughing happily.
"But our comptroller came down with the flu or something, and we had already paid for the convention
reservation and tickets and all, so Mrs. Bixby—she's the
president—asked me if I wanted to come, and I jumped at
the chance. It's my first time in the big city, so I'm pretty
excited about it all."

"Having a good time?" Zoe asked, smiling.

"Well, I just got in this morning, and we had meetings
most of the day, so I haven't had much time to look
around, but it's sure big and noisy and dirty, isn't it?"

"It sure is."

"But tomorrow and Wednesday we'll have more time
to ourselves, and I mean to look around some. What
should I see?"

"Everything," she told him.

"Yes," he said, nodding vigorously, "everything. I

mean to. Even if I stay up all night. I don't know when I'll get a chance like this again. I want to see the fountain where Zelda Fitzgerald went dunking and all the bars in Greenwich Village where Jack Kerouac hung out. I got a list of places I made out in my room and I aim to visit them all."

"You're staying here in the hotel?" she asked casually.

"Oh yes, ma'am. That was included in the convention tickets. I got me a nice room on the fifth floor, one flight down. Nice, big, shiny room."

"How old are you, Chet?"

"Going on twenty-five," he said, ducking his head. "I never have asked your name, ma'am, but you don't have to tell me unless you want to."

"Irene," she said.

He was enthusiastic about everything. It wasn't the beer he gulped down; it was him. He chattered along brightly, making her laugh with his descriptions of what life was like at the Barre Academy when they got snowed in, and the troubles he already had with New York cabdrivers.

She really enjoyed his youth, vitality, optimism. He hadn't yet been tainted. He trusted. It all lay ahead of him: a glittering world. He was going to become a professor of English Lit. He was going to travel to far-off places. He was going to own a home, raise a family. Everything.

He almost spluttered in his desire to get it all out, to explain this tremendous energy in him. His long hands made grand gestures. He squirmed, laughing at his own mad dreams, but believing them.

Zoe had three more glasses of white wine, and Chet had two more bottles of beer. She listened to him, smiling and nodding. Then, suddenly, the swimmers were gone, the pool was dimmed. Tables had emptied; they were the last. The sleepy waiter appeared with their bill.

"Chet, I'd like to see that list you made out," Zoe said. "The places you want to visit. Maybe I can suggest some others."

"Sure," he said promptly. "Great idea. We don't have to wait for the elevator. We can walk; it's only one flight down."

"Fine," she said.

She carried her glass of wine, and he carried his bottle and glass of beer. As he had said, his room was nice, big, and shiny. He showed it off proudly: the stack of fluffy towels, the neatly wrapped little bars of soap, the clean glasses and plastic ice bucket.

"And two beds!" he chortled, bouncing up and down on one of them. "Never thought I'd get to stay in a room with *two* beds! I may just sleep in both of them, taking turns. Just for the sheer luxury of it! Now . . . where's that list?"

They sat side by side on the edge of the bed, discussing his planned itinerary. Never once did he touch her, say anything even mildly suggestive, or give her any reason to suspect he was other than he appeared to be: an innocent.

She turned suddenly, kissed his cheek.

"I like you," she said. "You're nice."

He stared at her, startled, eyes widening. Then he leaped to his feet, a convulsive jump.

"Yes, well . . ." he said, stammering. "I thank you. I guess maybe I've been boring you. Haven't I? I mean, talking about myself all night. Good Lord, I haven't given you a chance to open your mouth. We could go downstairs and have a nightcap. In the bar downstairs. Would you like that? Or maybe you want to split? I understand. That's all right. I mean if you want to go . . ."

She smiled, took his hand, drew him back down onto the bed.

"I don't want another drink, Chet," she said. "And I don't want to go. Not yet. Can't we talk for a few minutes?"

"Well . . . yeah . . . sure. I'd like that."

"Are you married, Chet?"

"Oh no. No, no."

"Girlfriend?"

"Uh, yes . . . sort of. Sure, she's a girlfriend. A junior at the Academy, which is against the rules because we're not supposed to date the students. You know? But this has been going on for, oh, maybe six or seven months now. And she's been sneaking out to meet me, but vacation started last week and we've got plans to see each other this summer."

"That's wonderful. Is she nice?"

"Oh yes. I think so. Very nice. Good fun—you know? I

mean fun to be with. Alice. That's her name—Alice."

"I like that name."

"Yes, well, we usually meet out of town. I mean, the place isn't so big that people wouldn't notice, so we have to be careful. I have wheels, an old, beat-up crate, and sometimes we go to a roadhouse out of town. Sometimes, on a nice night, we'll just take a walk and talk."

"Is she pretty?"

"Oh yes. I think so. Not beautiful. I mean, she's not glamorous or anything like that. She wears glasses. She's very nearsighted. But I think she's pretty."

"Do you love her, Chet?"

He considered that a long moment.

"I don't know," he finally confessed. "I really don't know. I've given it a lot of thought. I mean, if I want to spend the rest of my life with her. I really don't know. But it's not something we have to decide right now. I mean, it's only been six or seven months. She's coming back for her senior year, so we'll have a chance to get to know each other better. Maybe it'll just, like, fade away, or maybe it'll become something. You know?"

She put her lips close to his ear, whispering . . .

"Have you had sex together?"

He blushed. "Well, ah, not exactly. I mean, we've done . . . things. But not, you know, all the way. I respect her."

"Does she have a good body?"

"Oh God—oh gosh, yes! She's really stacked. I mean, she's a swimmer and all. Doesn't smoke. Has a beer now and then. Keeps herself in very good shape. Very good. She's almost as tall as I am. Very slender with these big . . . you know . . ."

"Why haven't you had sex with her?"

"Well, uh . . . you know . . ."

She wouldn't let him off the hook. It was suddenly important to her to learn what Chet and Alice had done together.

"She wants to, doesn't she, Chet?"

"Oh yes. I think so. Sometimes we get started and it's very difficult to stop. Then we cool it. That's what we say to each other: 'Cool it!' Then we laugh, and get, uh, control again."

"You'd like to, wouldn't you?"

"Oh yes. I mean, at the moment, when we get all excited, I'd like to. I forget all my good intentions. I know that someday—some night rather—neither of us will say, 'Cool it!' And then . . ."

"Is she on the Pill?"

"Oh no! I asked her that and she said, 'What for?' I mean, she doesn't play around. She's right. Why should she take those dangerous drugs?"

"But what if you both get excited and don't say, 'Cool it,' and it happens, like you said? What if she gets pregnant?"

"No, no. I mean, I'd, uh, like take precautions. I'm not a virgin, Irene. I know about those things. I wouldn't do that to Alice."

She leaned forward, whispered in his ear again.

"Well, ah, yes," he said. "Yes, she could do that. If she wanted to. And I could, too, of course. I know about that."

"But you've never done it?"

"Well, uh, no. No, I've never done it."

"Why don't you take your clothes off?" Zoe Kohler said in a low voice. "I'd like to do it to you."

"You're kidding!"

"No, really, I want to. Don't you? Wouldn't you like the experience?"

She had said the right word. He wanted to experience everything.

"All right," he said. "But you must tell me what to do."

"You don't have to do anything," she assured him. "Just lie back and enjoy it. I have to go into the bathroom for a minute. You undress; I'll be right back."

His innocence was a rebuke to her. She was confused as to why this should be so. She didn't want to corrupt him; that would come soon enough. What she wanted to do, she decided, was to save him from corruption.

She thought this through as she undressed in the bathroom. It made a kind of hard sense. Because, despite how blameless he was now, she saw what would eventually happen to him, what he would become.

Years and the guilt of living would take their toll. He would lie and betray and cheat. His boy's body would swell at the same time his conscience would atrophy. He would become a swaggering man, bullying his way through life, scorning the human wreckage he left in his wake.

What was the worst, the absolute worst, was that he would never mourn his lost purity, but might recall it with an embarrassed laugh. He would be shamed by the memory, she knew. He would never regret his ruined goodness.

So she went back into the bedroom and slit his throat.

10

Thursday, June 5th . . .

"All right," Sergeant Abner Boone said, flipping through his notebook, "here's what we've got."

Standing and sitting around the splintered table in Midtown Precinct North. All of them smoking: cigarettes, cigars, and Lieutenant Crane chewing on a pipe. Emptied cardboard coffee cups on the table. The detritus of gulped sandwiches, containers of chop suey, a pizza box, wrappers and bags of junk food.

Air murky with smoke, barely stirred by the air conditioner. Sweat and disinfectant. No one commented or even noticed. They had all smelled worse odors. And battered rooms like this were home, familiar and comfortable.

"Nicholas Telemachus Pappatizos," Boone started. "Aka Nick Pappy, aka Poppa Nick, aka the Magician. Forty-two. Home address: Las Vegas. A fast man with the cards and dice. A small-time bentnose. Two convictions: eight months and thirteen months, here and there, for fraud and bunko. He got off twice on attempted rape and felonious assault."

"Good riddance," Detective Bentley said.

"The blood on the bathroom floor was definitely not his. Caucasian female. So it's confirmed; it's a female perp we're looking for."

"How do you figure the fight?" Detective Johnson asked.

"The PM shows sexual intercourse just before death," Boone went on, his voice toneless. "It could have been rape; he wasn't a nice guy. So after it's over, she gets her knife into him and starts cutting him up."

"That's another thing," Sergeant Broderick said. "She's obviously got a new knife. My guys are wasting their time trying to track the one that got broke."

"Right," Boone said. "Drop it; we were too late. We can use your guys on people who knew the convention schedule. We've got nearly two thousand names so far."

"Beautiful," Broderick said, but he wasn't really dismayed. No one was dismayed by the enormity of the search.

"Johnson," Boone said, "anything on the Mace?"

"Getting there," the detective said. "The stuff was sold to a lot of security outfits, armored car fleets, and so forth. Anyone who could prove a legitimate need. We're tracking them down. Every can of it."

"Keep on it. Bentley, what about that waitress from the Hotel Coolidge? The Ashley kill. His scarred hands."

"We check with her mother every day, sarge. She still hasn't called in from the Coast. Now we're tracking down her friends in case anyone knows where she is."

"As long as you're following up . . . Lieutenant? Anything new?"

"Nothing so far on the possibles. Some have moved, some are out of town, some are dead. I wouldn't say it looks promising."

"How did the decoys miss her at the Adler?" Edward X. Delaney demanded.

"Who the hell knows?" Bentley said angrily. "We had both bars in the place covered. Maybe she brought him in off the street."

"No," Delaney said stonily. "That's not her way. She's no street quiff. She knew there were conventions there. The lobby maybe, or the dining room. But it wasn't on the street."

They were all silent for a moment, trying to figure ways to stop her before she hit again.

"It should be about June twenty-ninth," Boone said, "to July second. In that time period. It's not too early to plan what more we can do. Intelligent suggestions gratefully received."

There were hard barks of laughter and the meeting broke up. Sergeant Boone drew Delaney aside.

"Chief," he said, "got a little time?"

"Sure. As much as you want. What's up?"

"There's a guy waiting in my office. A doctor. Dr. Patrick Ho. How's that for a name—Ho? He's some kind of an Oriental. Japanese, Chinese, Korean, or maybe from Vietnam or Cambodia. Whatever. With a first name like Patrick, there had to be an Irishman in there somewhere—right? Anyway, he's with the Lab Services Section. He's the guy who ran the analysis on the blood from the bathroom floor and said it was Caucasian female."

"And?" Delaney said.

Boone shrugged helplessly. "Beats the hell out of me. He tracked me down to tell me there's something screwy about the blood. But I can't get it straight what he wants. Will you talk to him a minute, Chief? Maybe you can figure it out."

Dr. Patrick Ho was short, plump, bronzed. He looked like a young Buddha with a flattop of reddish hair. When Boone introduced Delaney, he bowed and giggled. His hand was soft. The Chief noted the manicured nails.

"Ah," he said, in a high, flutey voice. "So nice. An honor. Everyone has heard of you, sir."

"Thank you," Delaney said. "Now, what's this about—"

"Your exploits," Dr. Ho went on enthusiastically, his dark eyes shining. "Your deductive ability. I, myself, would like to be a detective. But unfortunately I am only a lowly scientist, condemned to—"

"Let's sit down," Delaney said. "For a minute," he added hopefully.

They pulled chairs up to Boone's littered desk. The sergeant passed around cigarettes. The little doctor leaped to his feet with a gold Dunhill lighter at the ready. He closed the lighter after holding it for Boone and Delaney, then flicked it again for his own cigarette.

"Ah," he giggled, "never three on a light. Am I correct?"

He sat down again and looked at them, back and forth, beaming.

He was a jolly sight. A face like a peach with ruby-red lips. Tiny ears hugged his skull. Those dark eyes bulged slightly, and he had the smallest teeth Delaney had ever seen. A child's teeth: perfect miniatures.

His gestures were a ballet, graceful and flowing. His

expression was never in repose, but he smiled, frowned, grimaced, pursed those full lips, pouted, made little moues. He was, Delaney decided, a very scrutable Oriental.

"Dr. Ho," the Chief said, "about the blood . . . There's no doubt it's from a Caucasian female?"

"No doubt!" the doctor cried. "No doubt whatsoever!"

"Then what . . . ?"

Dr. Ho leaned forward, looking at them in a conspiratorial manner. He held one pudgy forefinger aloft.

"That blood," he said in almost a whisper, "has a very high potassium count."

Delaney and Boone looked at each other.

"Uh, doctor," the sergeant said, "what does that mean? I mean, what's the significance?"

Dr. Ho leaned back, crossed his little legs daintily. He stared at the ceiling.

"Ah, at the moment," he said dreamily, "it has no significance. It means only what I said: a high potassium count. But I must tell you I feel, I *know*, it has a significance, if only we knew what it was. Normal blood does not have such a high potassium level."

Edward X. Delaney was getting interested. He hitched his chair closer to Dr. Patrick Ho, got a whiff of the man's flowery cologne, and leaned hastily back.

"You're saying the potassium content of that blood is abnormal?"

"Ah, yes!" the doctor said, grinning, nodding madly. "Precisely. Abnormal."

"And what could cause the abnormality?"

"Oh, many things. Many, many things."

Again, Delaney and Boone glanced at each other. The sergeant's shoulders rose slightly in a small shrug.

"Well, doctor," Boone said, sighing, "I don't see how that's going to help our investigation."

Dr. Patrick Ho frowned, then showed his little teeth, then pouted. Then he leaned forward, began to speak rapidly.

"Ah, I have said I wish to be a detective. I am but a lowly scientist—let me speak the truth: I am but a lowly technician; nothing more—but in a way, I *am* a detective. I detect what can be learned from a drop of blood, a chip of paint, a piece of glass, a hair. And about this high-potassium blood, I have a suspicion. No, I have a—a—what is the word?"

"A hunch?" Delaney offered.

The doctor laughed with delight. "What a word! A hunch! Exactly. Something is wrong with this blood. The high potassium should not be there. So I would like to make a much more thorough analysis of this puzzling blood."

"So?" Sergeant Boone said. "Why don't you?"

Dr. Ho sighed deeply. His face collapsed into such a woebegone expression that he seemed close to tears. This time he held up two fingers. He gripped one by the tip. He talked around his shortened cigarette, tilting his head to keep the smoke out of his eyes.

"One," he said, "we are, of course, very busy. A certain amount of time must be allotted to each task. I have, at this moment, many things assigned to me. All must be accomplished. I would like to be relieved—temporarily, of course," he added hastily—"of everything but the detection of this strange blood. Second," he said, folding down one finger, switching his grip to the other, "second, I must tell you in all honesty that we do not have the equipment in our laboratory necessary for the subtle blood analysis I wish to make."

"And where is this equipment available?" Delaney asked.

"The Medical Examiner has it," Dr. Ho said sorrowfully.

"So?" Boone said again. "Ask them to do the analysis."

That expressive face twisted. "Ah," the doctor said in an anguished voice, "but then it is out of my hands. You understand?"

Delaney looked at him intently. This little man was trying to score points, to further his career. Nothing wrong with that. In fact, in the right circumstances, it might be admirable. But he also might be wasting everyone's time.

"Let me get this straight," the Chief said. "What you'd like is to be temporarily relieved of all your other duties and assigned only to the analysis of the blood found on the bathroom floor at the Hotel Adler. And then you'd like to use the machines or whatever in the Medical

Examiner's office to make that analysis. Have I got it right?"

Dr. Ho slapped his plump thigh. His eyes glowed with happiness . . . briefly.

"Exactly," he said. "Precisely." Then his face fell; the glee disappeared. "But you must understand that between my section and the Medical Examiner's office there is, ah, I would not say bad feeling, oh no, but there is, ah . . . what shall I say? Competition! Yes, there is competition. Professional jealousy perhaps. A certain amount of secrecy involved. You understand?" he pleaded.

Indeed, Edward X. Delaney did understand. It was nothing new and nothing unusual. Since when was there perfect, wholehearted cooperation between the branches of any large organization, even if their aims were identical?

The FBI vs. local cops. The army vs. the air force. The navy vs. the Marines. The Senate vs. the House of Representatives. The federal government vs. the states. Infighting was a way of life, and it wasn't all bad. Competing jealousies were a good counter for smug indolence.

"All right," the Chief said, "you want us to get you assigned full time to this analysis and you want us to get the ME's office to cooperate. Correct?"

Dr. Patrick Ho bent forward from the waist, put a soft hand on Delaney's arm.

"You are a very sympathetic man," he said gratefully.

The Chief, who hated to be touched by strangers, or even by friends, jerked his arm away. He rose swiftly to his feet.

"We'll let you know, doctor. As soon as possible."

There was a round of half-bows and handshaking. They watched Dr. Ho dance from the room.

"A whacko," Sergeant Boone said.

"Mmm," Delaney said.

They slumped back in their chairs. They stared at each other.

"What do you think, Chief?"

"A long shot."

"I think it's a lot of bullshit," Boone said angrily. "Thorsen is the only man who could give Ho what he wants, and he'd have to pull a lot of strings and crack a lot of skulls to do it. I just don't have the juice."

"I understand that."

"But if I go to Thorsen with that cockamamie story of potassium in the blood, he'll think I'm some kind of a nut."

"That's true," Delaney said sympathetically. "On the other hand, if you turn him down cold, that crazy doctor is liable to go over your head. Then, if he gets action and it turns out to be something, your name is mud."

"Yeah," the sergeant said miserably. "I know."

"It may be nothing, but I think you should move on it."

"That's easy—" Boone started to say, then shut his mouth so abruptly that his teeth clicked.

The Chief looked at him steadily.

"I know what you're thinking, sergeant—that I've got nothing to lose, but you have. I understand all that. But I don't think you can afford to do nothing. Look, suppose we do this . . . I'll call Thorsen and tell him the doctor came to see me, but you sat in on the meet. I'll recommend he gets Dr. Ho what he wants and I'll tell him you'll go along. That way the blame is on me if it turns sour. I couldn't care less. If it turns out to be something, you'll be on record as having been on it from the start."

Abner Boone thought it over.

"Yeah," he said finally. "Let's do it that way. Thanks, Chief."

Delaney tried to call Thorsen from Boone's office, but the Deputy Commissioner was in a meeting. The Chief said he'd try him later from home.

He waved so-long to the sergeant and walked home slowly through Central Park. It was a hot, steamy day, but he didn't take off his hat or doff his jacket. He rarely complained about the weather. He was constantly amazed at people who never seemed to learn that in the summer it was hot and in the winter it was cold.

As usual, Monica was out somewhere. He went upstairs to take off jacket, vest, and tie. Then he peeled off his sodden shirt and undershirt and wiped his torso cool with a soaked washcloth. He pulled on a knitted polo shirt of Sea Island cotton.

He inspected the contents of the refrigerator. On the previous night, they had had veal cutlets dredged in seasoned flour (with paprika) and then sauteed in butter with onion flakes and garlic chips. There was enough cold veal left over to make a decent sandwich.

He used white bread spread thinly with Russian dressing. He added slices of red onion and a light dusting of freshly ground pepper. He carried the sandwich and a cold can of Ballantine Ale into the study.

While he ate and drank, he searched through his home medical encyclopedia and found the section on potassium. All it said was that potassium was a chemical element present in the human body, usually in combination with sodium salts.

The section on blood was longer and more detailed. Among other things, it said that the red fluid was a very complex substance, and plasma (the liquid part of the blood) carried organic and inorganic elements that had to be transported from one part of the body to another.

The blood also carried gases and secretions from the endocrine glands (hormones) as well as enzymes, proteins, etc. Serious imbalance in blood chemistry, the encyclopedia said, was usually indicative of physiological malfunction.

He put the book aside and finished his sandwich and beer. He called Thorsen again, and this time he got through. He told the Deputy Commissioner about the visit of Dr. Patrick Ho, from the Lab Services Section.

He made it sound like the doctor had come to see him, and that Sergeant Boone was present at the meeting. He explained what it was Dr. Ho wanted and urged that they cooperate. He said Sergeant Boone agreed.

Ivar Thorsen was dubious.

"Pretty thin stuff, Edward," he said. "As I understand it, he hasn't got a clue as to why there's so much potassium in the blood or what it means."

"That's correct. That's what he wants to find out."

"Well, suppose he does find out, and the killer is popping potassium pills for some medical reason—how does that help us? My God, Edward, maybe the Hotel Ripper is a banana freak. She wolfs down bananas like mad. That would account for the potassium. So what? Are we going to arrest every woman in New York who eats bananas?"

"Ivar, I think we ought to give this guy a chance. It may turn up zilch. Granted. But we haven't got so goddamned much that we can afford to ignore anything."

"You really think it might amount to something?"

"We'll never know until we try, will we?"

Thorsen groaned. "Well . . . all right. The Lab Services Unit will be no problem. I can get this Ho assigned to us on temporary duty. The Medical Examiner's office is something else again. I don't swing much clout there, but I'll see what I can do."

"Thank you, Ivar."

"Edward," Thorsen said, almost pleading, "are we going to get her?"

Delaney was astounded.

"Of course," he said.

Newspapermen and television commentators reported no progress was being made in the investigation. SEARCH FOR RIPPER STALLED, one headline announced. The public seemed to take a ghoulish pleasure in reading how many summer conventions, hotel reservations, and tours had been canceled.

The Mayor's office took the flak from the business community and passed it along to the Police Commissioner. The PC, in turn, leaned on Deputy Commissioner Thorsen. And he, being a decent man, refused to scream at the men in his command, knowing they were doing everything that could be done, and working their asses off.

"But give me something," he begged. *"Anything!* A bone we can throw to the media."

Actually, progress was being made, but it was slow, tedious, foot-flattening labor, and didn't yield the kind of results that make headlines. The list of women who had access to the convention schedule was growing, and Detective Aaron Johnson's men were checking out every can of Chemical Mace and other tear gas delivered to the New York area.

Dr. Patrick Ho had been given what he wanted, and three days later he reported back to Sergeant Boone and Delaney. He was flushed and breathless.

"Ah, it is looking good," he said in his musical voice. "Very, very good."

"What?" Boone demanded. "What did you find out?"

"Listen to this," Ho said triumphantly. "In addition to

the high potassium content, the sodium, chloride, and bicarbonate levels are very low. Isn't that wonderful!"

Boone made a sound of disgust.

"What does that mean, doctor?" Delaney asked.

"Ah, it is much too early to say," Dr. Ho said judiciously. "But definite abnormalities exist. Also, we have isolated two substances we cannot identify. Is that not exciting?"

"Maybe it would be," the sergeant said, "if you knew what they were."

"Where do you go from here?" the Chief asked.

"There are, in this marvelous city, two excellent hospitals with splendid hematology departments. They have beautiful hardware. I shall take our slides and samples to these hospitals, and they will tell me what these unidentified substances are."

"Listen," Sergeant Boone said hoarsely, "are we going to have to pay for this?"

"Oh no," Dr. Patrick Ho said, shocked. "It is their civic duty. I shall convince them."

Delaney looked at the little man with admiration.

"You know, doctor," he said, "I think you will."

Later, Boone said, "We're getting scammed. The guy's a loser."

On June 16th, Detective Daniel Bentley arrived late for the morning meeting at Midtown Precinct North. He came striding into the room, glowing.

"Bingo!" he shouted. "We got something."

"Oh Lord," Ivar Thorsen intoned, "let it be something good."

"Twice a day," Bentley said, "we been checking with the mother of that cocktail waitress who worked the New Orleans Room at the Hotel Coolidge the night Jerome Ashley got washed. The girl went out to the Coast and she hasn't called her mother yet. So we started checking out her pals. We found a boyfriend who's on probation after doing eighteen months for B-and-E. So we could lean on him—right? He gets a call last night from this chick . . ." Here Bentley consulted his notebook. "Her name is Anne Rogovich. Anyway, she calls her old boyfriend, they talk, and she gives him her number out there. Then he calls us like he's been told. I called the girl an hour ago. It's early in the morning on the Coast and I woke her up—but what the hell."

"Get to it," Boone said.

"Yeah, she worked the New Orleans Room the night Ashley was offed. Yeah, she remembers serving a guy with badly scarred hands. She says he was sitting with a woman. Not much of a physical description: tall, slender, darkish, heavy on the makeup. Strawberry blond wig. But she remembers the clothes better. Very flashy. A green silk dress, skimpy as a slip. Skinny shoulder straps. This Anne Rogovich remembers because she really dug that dress and wondered what it cost. Also, the woman with Ashley was wearing a bracelet. Gold links. With big gold letters that spelled out WHY NOT?"

"WHY NOT?" Boone said. "Beautiful. The dress she can change, but that bracelet might be something. Broderick, how about your guys checking it out? Who makes it and who sells it. Trace it to the stores. Maybe it was bought on a charge; you never can tell."

"Yeah," Broderick said, "we'll get on it."

"Did she remember anything else?" the sergeant asked.

"That's all I could get out of her," Bentley reported. "But she was half-asleep. I'll try her again later today."

"Good, good, good," the Deputy Commissioner said, rubbing his palms together. "Can this Anne Rogovich make the woman with Ashley if she sees her again?"

"She says no," Bentley said. "The clothes, yes; the woman, no."

"Still," Thorsen said happily, "it's something. The media will have a field day with that bracelet. WHY NOT? That should keep them off our backs for a while."

"Deputy," Edward X. Delaney said, "could I see you outside for a minute? Alone?"

"Sure, Edward," Thorsen said genially. "We're all finished in here, aren't we?"

Delaney closed the door of Sergeant Boone's office. Thorsen took the swivel chair behind the desk. Delaney remained standing. Slowly, methodically, he bit the tip off a cigar, threw it into the wastebasket. Then he twirled the cigar in his lips, lighted it carefully, puffed.

He stood braced, feet spread. His hands were clasped behind him, cigar clenched in his teeth. He looked at Thorsen critically through the smoke.

"Ivar," he said coldly, "you're a goddamned idiot."

Thorsen rose from his chair slowly, his face white. Chilled eyes stared directly at Delaney. He leaned forward until his knuckles were pressing the desktop. The Admiral's body was hunched, rigid.

"You're going to release it all, aren't you?" Delaney went on. "The physical description, the clothes, the bracelet . . . You're going to go public."

"That's right," the Deputy Commissioner said tightly.

"Then I'll tell you exactly what's going to happen. As soon as this woman reads it in the papers, the next time she goes out to kill she's going to change the color of her wig or leave it off completely. She's going to dress like a schoolmarm or a librarian. And she's going to drop that bracelet down the nearest sewer."

"We'll have to take that chance," Thorsen said tonelessly.

"Goddamnit!" Delaney exploded. "You release that stuff, and we're back to square one. Who the hell are the decoys going to look for? Without the wig and flashy clothes and bracelet, she'll look like a million other women. You're making the same stupid mistake Slavin did—talking too much."

"My responsibility is to alert possible victims," Thorsen said. "To circulate as complete a description as possible so people know who to look for. My first job is to protect the public."

"Bull*shit!*" Delaney said disgustedly. "Your first job is to protect the NYPD. The money men and the media are dumping all over you, so you figure to toss them a bone to prove the Department is on the job and making progress. So for the sake of your fucking public relations, you're going to jeopardize the whole goddamned investigation."

They glared at each other, eyes locked, both pressing forward aggressively. Their friendship would survive this, they knew. Their friendship wasn't at issue. It was their wills that were in conflict—and not for the first time.

Ivar Thorsen sat down again, as slowly as he had stood up. He sat on the edge of the chair. His thin fingers drummed silently on the desk. He never took his eyes from Delaney's.

"All right," he said, "there's some truth in what you say. *Some* truth. But you're getting your ass in an uproar because you can't or won't see the value of good public relations. I happen to believe the public's perception of the Department—the image, if that's what you want to call it—is just as important as the Department's performance. We could be the greatest hotshot cops in the world, and what the hell good would that do if we were perceived as a bunch of nincompoops, Keystone Kops jumping in the air and chasing dogs? I'm not saying the image is primary; it's not. Performance comes first, and is the foundation of the image. You want more cops on the street, don't you? You want better pay, better training, better equipment? How the hell do you expect us to ask for those things if the politicians and the public see us as a disorganized mob of hopeless bunglers?"

"I'm just saying that for the sake of keeping the press off your neck for a few days, you're making it a lot tougher to break this thing."

"Maybe," Thorsen said. "And what do you think would happen if we tried to keep this Anne Rogovich under wraps and the papers got onto it somehow? How would I explain why the public wasn't alerted to what the killer looks like and what she wears? They'd crucify us!"

"Look," Delaney said, "we can go around and around on this. We have different priorities, that's all."

"The hell we do," the Admiral said. "I want to put her down as much as you do. More. But it's an ego thing with you. Isn't that right—isn't it an ego thing?"

Delaney was silent.

"You've got tunnel vision on this case, Edward. All you can see is stopping a killer. Fine. You're a cop; that's all you're supposed to be thinking about. But there are other, uh, considerations that I've got to be aware of. And the Department's reputation is one of them. You're involved in the present. I am, too. But I've also got to think about the future."

"I still say you're fucking up the investigation," Delaney said stubbornly.

Ivar Thorsen sighed. "I don't think so. Possibly making it more difficult, but I think the benefits outweigh the risks. I may be wrong, I admit, but that's my best judgment. And that's the way it's going to be."

They were silent, still staring at each other. Finally Thorsen spoke softly . . .

"By the way, I happen to know we'd never have gotten onto this Anne Rogovich if you hadn't sent Bentley's men back to question if anyone remembered a man with scarred hands. That was good work."

The Chief grunted.

"Edward," the Deputy said, "you want off?"

"No," Delaney said, "I don't want off."

"What *is* it?" Monica said. "You've been a pain in the ass all night."

"Have I?" he said morosely. "I guess I have."

They were in their beds, both sitting up, both trying to read. The overhead light was on, and the bedside lamp. The window air conditioner was humming, and would until they agreed it was time to sleep. Then it would be turned off and the other window opened wide.

Now Monica had pushed her glasses atop her head. She had closed her book, a forefinger inserted to mark her place. She had turned toward her husband. Her words might have been challenging, but her tone was troubled and solicitous.

He told her about his run-in with Ivar Thorsen, repeating the conversation as accurately as he could. She listened in silence. When he finished, and asked, "What do you think?" she was quiet a moment longer. Then:

"You really think that's what she'll do? I mean, leave off the wig and bracelet and dress plainly?"

"Monica," he said, "this is not a stupid woman. She's no bimbo peddling her ass or a spaced-out whacko with a nose full of shit. Everything so far points to careful planning, smart reactions to unforeseen happenings, and very, very cool determination. She's going to read that description in the papers—or hear it on TV—and she's going to realize we're on to her disguise. Then she'll go in the opposite direction."

"How can you be sure it *is* a disguise? Maybe she dresses that way ordinarily."

"No, no. She was trying to change her appearance; I'm sure of it. First of all, a woman of her intelligence wouldn't ordinarily dress that way. Also, she knew the chances were good that someone would see her with one of the victims and remember her. So she'd want to look as

different as possible from the way she does in everyday
life."

"What you're saying is that in everyday life she looks
like a schoolmarm or librarian—like you told Ivar?"

"Well . . . I'd guess she's a very ordinary looking lady.
Dresses conventionally. Acts in a very conservative man-
ner. Maybe even a dull woman. That's the way I see her.
Mousy. Until she breaks out and kills."

"You make her sound schizophrenic."

"Oh no. I don't think she's that. No, she knows who
she is. She can function in society and not make waves.
But she's a psychopath. A walking, functioning psychopath."

"Thank you, doctor. And why does she kill?"

"Who the hell knows?" he said crossly. "She has her
reasons. Maybe they wouldn't make sense to anyone else,
but they make sense to her. It's a completely different
kind of logic. Oh yes, crazies have a logic all their own.
And it *does* make sense—if you accept their original
premises. For instance, if you really and truly believe that
the earth is flat, then it makes sense not to travel too far
or you might fall off the edge. The premise is nutty, but
the reasoning that follows from it is logical."

"I'd really like to know her," Monica said slowly. "I
mean, talk to her. I'd like to know what's going through
her mind."

"Her mind?" Delaney said. "I don't think you'd like it
in there. Listen, when I was having that go-around with
Ivar, he said something that bothers me. That's why I've
been so grouchy all night. He said, 'It's an ego thing with
you.'"

"What did he mean by that?"

"I think he was saying that this case has become a
personal thing with me. That I'm out to prove that I'm
smarter than the Hotel Ripper. That I can plan better,
react faster, outthink her. That I'm *superior* to her."

"You mean you don't want a woman to get the better of
you?"

"Come on! Don't get your feminist balls in an uproar.
No, Ivar just meant that I see this thing as a personal
challenge."

"And is he right?"

"Oh shit," he said roughly. "Who the hell has a

coherent philosophy or a beautifully organized chart of beliefs that doesn't get daily scratching-outs and additions? Maybe the ego thing is *part* of it, but it's not *all* of it. There are other things."

"Like what?"

"Like the simple, basic belief that killing is wrong. Like the belief that the law, with all its stupidities and fuckups, is still the best we've been able to devise after all these thousands of years, and any assault on the law should be punished. And also, homicide isn't only an assault on the law, it's an attack against humanity."

"That I don't follow."

"All right, then murder is a crime against life. Does that make more sense?"

"You mean all life? Cows? And the birds and the bees and the flowers?"

"You should have been a Jesuit," he said, smiling. "But you know what I mean. I'm just saying that human life should not be taken lightly. Maybe there are more important things, but life itself is important enough so that anyone who destroys it for selfish motives should be punished."

"And you think this woman, this Hotel Ripper, has selfish motives?"

"*All* killers have selfish motives. Even those who say they were just obeying the command of God. When you get right down to it, they're just doing it because it makes them feel good."

She was incredulous. "You think this woman is killing because it makes her feel good?"

"Sure," he said cheerfully. "No doubt about it."

"That's awful."

"Is it? We all act from self-interest, don't we?"

"Edward, you don't really believe that, do you?"

"Of course I do. And what's so awful about it? The only problem is that most people spend their lives trying to figure out where their best interest lies, and nine times out of ten they're wrong."

"But I suppose you know where your best interest lies?"

"That's easy. In your bed."

"Pig."

About an hour later he turned off the air conditioner.

• • •

Delaney had no sooner settled down in the study to read his morning *Times* when the phone rang. The caller was Sergeant Abner Boone.

"Good morning, Chief."

"Morning, sergeant."

"Sorry to bother you so early, sir, but I was wondering if you were planning to drop by the precinct today."

"I wasn't, no. Should I?"

"Well, ah, I'm going to ask a favor."

"Sure. What gives?"

"I got a call from that Dr. Patrick Ho. He's got the hospital reports on the blood analysis and wants to come over to talk to me. He told me a little about it on the phone, and, Chief, I can't make any sense out of it at all. I'm up to my ass in paperwork and I was wondering if you'd be willing to talk to Dr. Ho at your place. Keep him out of my hair."

Delaney reflected that Boone was beginning to show the pressure. He was becoming increasingly dour and snappish. He should be pushing Dr. Ho for results, not trying to weasel out of talking to the man.

"You don't like him much, do you, sergeant?" he said.

"No, sir, I don't," Boone said. "He smells like a fruitcake and he treats this whole thing like some kind of scientific riddle. I still think he's just trying to make points and wasting our time in the process."

"Could be," Delaney said, thinking that maybe Boone simply wanted to disassociate himself from a loser.

"Will you deal with him, sir?"

"Sure," the Chief said genially. "Give him my address. I'll be in all morning."

Dr. Patrick Ho arrived about an hour later and made an immediate hit with Monica. She was in the kitchen, preparing a salad, and the doctor insisted on showing her how to make radish rosettes and how to slice a celery stalk so it resembled an exotic bloom.

Delaney finally got him into the study and provided him with a cup of tea. He then sat in his swivel chair, benignly watching Dr. Ho flip through a stack of papers he pulled from a battered briefcase.

"So?" the Chief said. "How did you make out with the hospitals?"

"Ah, splendid," the beaming little man said. "They were very cooperative when I explained why their aid was absolutely vital. And it was something to tell their families and friends—no? That they worked on the Hotel Ripper case."

"And were you able to identify the two unknown substances in the killer's blood?"

"Ah, yes. Where is it? Ah, here it is. Yes, yes. High potassium, low sodium, chloride, and bicarbonate, as we already knew. The two previously unidentified substances were high levels of ACTH and MSH."

He looked up at Delaney, delighted but modest, as if expecting a round of applause.

"ACTH and MSH?" the Chief asked.

"Exactly. Abnormally high levels."

"Doctor," Delaney said with great patience, "what are ACTH and MSH?"

"Pituitary hormones," Dr. Ho said happily. "They would not be present at such levels in normal blood. And something I find very, *very* interesting is that MSH is a melanocyte-stimulating hormone. I would be willing to venture the opinion that the woman whose blood this is has noticeable skin discolorations. A darkening, like a very heavy suntan, but perhaps grayish or dirty-looking."

"All over her body?"

"Oh no. I doubt that. But in exposed portions of the skin. Face, neck, hands, and so forth. Possibly on the elbows and nipples. Points of friction or pressure."

"Interesting," Delaney said, "what you can deduce from a blood analysis. Tell me, doctor, is it possible to identify an individual from an analysis of the blood? Like fingerprints?"

"Oh no," Dr. Ho said. "No, no, no. Perhaps, someday, the genetic code, but not the blood. You see, this liquid is affected by what we eat, what we drink, drugs that may be ingested, and so forth. The chemical composition of the blood is constantly changing, weekly, daily, almost minute to minute. So as a means of positive identification, I fear it would be without value. However, a complete blood profile can be a marvelous clue to the physical condition of the donor. And that is what we now have: a complete blood profile."

"Those hormones you mentioned—what were they?"

"ACTH and MSH."

"Yes. You said they were present in abnormally high levels in the killer's blood?"

"That is correct."

"Well, why is that? I mean, what would cause those high levels?"

"Illness," the doctor said with delight. "I would say that almost certainly the woman who owned this blood is suffering from some disease. Or at least some serious physiological malfunction. Chief Delaney, this is very odd blood. Very peculiar indeed."

"Would you care to make a guess as to what the illness might be?"

"Ah, no," Dr. Patrick Ho confessed, frowning sorrowfully. "That is beyond my experience and training. Also, the hematologists I consulted were unable to hazard a guess as to the illness, disease, or perhaps genetic fault that might be producing this curious blood."

"Well . . ." Delaney said, rocking back in his chair, lacing fingers across his stomach, "then I guess we're stymied, aren't we? End of the road."

Dr. Ho was horrified. His dark eyes widened, rosy lips pouted, plump hands fluttered in the air.

"Ah, no!" he protested. "No, no, no! I have obtained the names of the three best diagnosticians in New York. I will take our blood profile to these doctors and they will tell me what the illness is."

Delaney laughed. "You never give up, do you?"

Dr. Patrick Ho sobered. He looked at the Chief with eyes suddenly shrewd and piercing.

"No," he said, "I never give up. Do you?"

"No," Delaney said and stood to shake hands.

On the way out, Dr. Ho stopped at the kitchen and showed Monica how to slice raw carrots into attractive curls.

On June 25th, at the morning meeting of the Hotel Ripper task force in Midtown Precinct North, certain personnel changes were decided on.

Lieutenant Wilson T. Crane's squad was reduced to a minimum and most of his men assigned to the task of compiling and organizing the list of women who might have had access to the convention schedule. Lieutenant Crane was put in command of this group.

Detective Daniel Bentley's squad was also reduced, the men being switched to Detective Aaron Johnson's small army who were attempting to track down purchases of Chemical Mace and other tear gases in the New York area.

Detective Bentley was assigned to work with a police artist on sketches prepared from the scant description furnished by cocktail waitress Anne Rogovich.

Sergeant Thomas K. Broderick was given additional men to expedite the questioning of clerks in department stores and jewelry shops where the WHY NOT? bracelet was sold.

Everyone recognized that all these personnel shifts were merely paper changes and represented no significant breakthroughs. Still, progress was being made, and it was estimated that within a week, questioning of individual women on the convention schedule access list could begin.

And Detective Johnson reported that at the same time his men could start personal visits to the purchasers of tear gas. Every container, gun, and generator would be physically examined by Johnson's crew—or an explanation demanded for its absence.

It was decided that everyone in the task force—deskmen and street cops alike—would be on duty during the nights of June 29th through July 2nd. Midtown Manhattan would be flooded with uniformed and plainclothes officers from 8:00 P.M., to 2:00 A.M.

In addition, squad cars and unmarked vehicles would continually tour the streets of this section, and some would be parked in front of the larger hotels that were hosting conventions. The Crime Scene Unit was alerted and a command post established once again in Midtown Precinct South.

A larger number of policewomen in mufti were added to the stakeout crews in hotel bars and cocktail lounges. The reasoning here was that the women might be better able to spot suspicious behavior in another female.

It was debated whether or not an appeal should be issued asking the public to avoid the midtown area on the nights in question. It was decided the warning would be counterproductive.

"We'd have whackos flocking in from Boston to Philly," was the consensus.

When the meeting broke up, Delaney and Sergeant Boone walked out into the corridor to find a beaming Dr. Patrick Ho awaiting them. The sergeant gave the Chief a look of anguished entreaty.

"Please," he begged in a low voice, "you take him. Use my office." He hurried away.

After an exchange of polite pleasantries, during which the doctor inquired after the health of the Chief's wife, the two men went into Boone's office. Delaney closed the door to muffle the loud talk, laughter, and shouts in the hallway.

He took the swivel chair. Dr. Ho sat in a battered wooden armchair and crossed his short legs delicately, smoothing his trouser crease to avoid wrinkles.

"Well . . ." Delaney said, "I hope you have some good news to report."

"Ah, regrettably no," Dr. Ho said sadly, making his face into a theatrical mask of sorrow.

Then Delaney wondered if Boone might be right. Perhaps this busy little man was jerking them around and wanted nothing but a vacation from his regular job.

"You saw the diagnosticians?" he asked, more sharply than he had intended.

"I did indeed," the doctor said, nodding vigorously. "These are very big, important men, and they were exceedingly kind to lend their assistance."

"But no soap, eh?"

"I beg your pardon?"

"They couldn't say what the illness was?"

"Ah, no, they could not. All three agreed it is a most unusual blood profile, completely unique in their experience. Two of them refused to venture any opinion, or even a guess. They said that in the absence of an actual physical examination, they would require much more documentation: X rays, tissue samples, urinalysis, electrocardiograms, scans, sputum and feces tests, and so forth. The third man also would not offer an opinion solely on the basis of the blood profile. However, he suggested a hyperactive pituitary might be involved, but beyond that he would not go."

"Uh-huh," Delaney said. "Well, I can't really blame them. We didn't give them a whole hell of a lot to go on. So that's it? We've taken it as far as we can go?"

"Oh no!" Dr. Patrick Ho said. "No, no, no! I have more, ah, arrows in my quiver."

"I thought you might," the Chief said. "What now?"

Dr. Ho leaned forward, serious and intent.

"There are, in this marvelous country, several diagnostic computers. A fine one at the University of Pittsburgh, another at Stanford Medical, one at the National Library of Medicine, and so forth. Now these computers have stored in their memory banks many thousand symptoms and manifestations of disease. When a series of such manifestations is given to the machine, it is able, sometimes, to make a diagnosis, name the disease, and prescribe treatment."

Delaney sat upright.

"My God," he said, "I had no idea such computers existed. That's wonderful!"

"Ah, yes," the doctor said, gratified by the Chief's reaction, "I think so, too. If insufficient input is fed to the computers, they cannot always make a firm diagnosis, of course. But in such cases they can sometimes furnish several possibilities."

"And you want to send your blood profile to the computers?"

"Precisely," Dr. Ho said, blinking happily. "I would also include the sex of the subject and what physical description we have. I have prepared long telegrams telling the authorities the nature of the emergency and requesting computer time for a diagnosis."

"I don't see why not," Delaney said slowly. "Having started this, we might as well see it through."

"Ah, there is one small problem," the doctor said, almost shyly. "These telegrams will be costly. I would like official authorization."

"Sure," Delaney said, shrugging. "In for a penny, in for a pound. Send them from this phone right here. If you get any flak, say they were authorized by Deputy Commissioner Ivar Thorsen. I'll square it with him."

"Ah, thank you very much, sir. You are most understanding, and I am in your debt."

Dr. Ho rummaged through his scruffy briefcase and brought out several sheets of paper. Delaney let him have the swivel chair and the doctor prepared to phone.

"Tell me, Dr. Ho," the Chief said, "just as a matter of

curiosity . . . If the computers don't come up with a diagnosis, what will you do then?"

"Oh," the little man said cheerfully, "I'll think of something."

Delaney stared at him.

"I'll bet you will," he said.

On July 1st, a Tuesday, at 10:14 A.M., a call was received at 911 reporting a violent death at the Tribunal Motor Inn on 49th Street west of Tenth Avenue. The caller identified himself as the Tribunal's chief of security.

The alert was forwarded to Midtown North. The precinct duty sergeant dispatched a foot patrolman in the vicinity via radio, two uniformed officers in a squad car, and two plainclothesmen in an unmarked car.

He also informed commanders of the Hotel Ripper task force who were, at the time, holding their morning meeting upstairs in the precinct house. Sergeant Abner Boone sent Detectives Bentley and Johnson to check it out.

While they were waiting for the Yes or No call, the others sat in silence, smoking, sipping stale coffee from soggy cardboard containers. Edward X. Delaney rose to locate the Tribunal on a precinct map Scotch-taped to the wall. Deputy Commissioner Thorsen joined him.

"What do you think, Edward?" he asked in a low voice.

"Not exactly midtown," the Chief replied, "but close enough."

They sat down again and waited. No one spoke. They could hear the noises of a busy precinct coming from the lower floors. They could even hear the bubbling sound as Lieutenant Crane blew through his pipe stem to clear it.

When the phone rang, all the men in the room jerked convulsively. They watched Boone pick it up in a hard grip, his knuckles white.

"Sergeant Boone," he said throatily.

He listened a moment. He hung up the phone. He turned a tight face to the others.

"Let's go," he said.

They went with a rush, chairs clattering over, men pouring from offices, feet pounding down the stairs.

"What's the goddamn hurry?" Sergeant Broderick said in a surly voice. "She's long gone."

Then engines starting up, blare of horns, the wail of sirens. Delaney rode in Deputy Thorsen's car, the uniformed driver swinging wildly onto Eighth Avenue, west on 55th Street to Ninth Avenue, south to 49th Street.

"She fucked us again," the Admiral said wrathfully, and the Chief mused idly on how rarely Thorsen used language like that.

By the time they pulled up with a squeal of brakes in front of the Tribunal, the street was already choked with police vehicles, vans, an ambulance. A crowd was growing, pushed back by precinct cops until barricades could be erected.

The hotel was already cordoned: no one in or out without showing identification. Motor inn staff, residents, and visitors were being lined up in the lobby for questioning. A uniformed officer guarding the elevator bank sent them up to the fifth floor.

There was a mob in the corridor, most of them clustered about Room 508. Sergeant Boone stood in the doorway, his face stony.

"It was her all right," he said, his voice empty. "Throat slashed, stab wounds in the nuts. The clunk was Chester LaBranche, twenty-four, from Barre, Vermont. He was here for some kind of a college convention."

"A convention again," Thorsen said bitterly. "And twenty-four. A kid!"

"Did we have any decoys in the place?" Delaney asked.

"No," Boone said shortly. "The place is small and this neighborhood isn't exactly Times Square, so we didn't cover it."

The Deputy Commissioner started to say something, then shut his mouth.

Tommy Callahan came to the doorway.

"Naked," he reported. "Half-on and half-off the bed. No signs of a struggle. Looks like the early kills when she came up behind them. All the blood appears to be his. We'll scrape the bathroom drains, but it doesn't look good."

Lou Gorki shouldered him out of the way. The Crime Scene Unit man was holding a wineglass by two fingers spread wide inside. There was a half-inch of amber liquid at the bottom. The outside of the glass was whitened with powder.

"It's wine all right," Gorki said. "I dipped a finger. Chablis. Vintage of yesterday. But the kicker is that there's also a half-empty bottle of beer and a glass. No guy is going to drink beer and wine at the same time. Good prints on both. I figure this wineglass was hers."

"Check it out," Boone said.

"Sure," Gorki said. "We'll take everything downtown for the transfers. At least now we got a make if we ever pull someone in on this thing."

"Sarge," Detective Johnson said from behind them, "I think maybe we lucked onto something. I got a waiter upstairs who says he might have seen her."

They trooped after him to a staircase at the end of the corridor, closed off with a red Exit sign above the door.

"This guy's name is Tony Pizzi," Johnson said as they climbed the concrete stairs. "He's on the day shift today, but yesterday he worked from six until two. He hustles drinks in the outdoor lounge by the pool. Then, when the pool and bar closed at midnight, he went downstairs to help out in the main bar. He thinks he served LaBranche and a woman up here. Bottled beer and white wine."

Anthony Pizzi was a sleepy-eyed man, short, chunky rather than fat. He was wearing a white apron cinched up under his armpits. The apron bulged with the bulk of his belly.

He had a fleshy, saturnine face cut in half with a narrow black mustache, straight across, cheek to cheek. His teeth were almonds, and he had a raspy New York voice. Delaney figured the accent for Brooklyn, probably Bushwick.

They got him seated at a corner table and hunched around him on metal chairs. A bartender, polishing one glass, watched them intently, but a man cleaning the pool with a long-handled screen paid no attention.

"Tony," Detective Johnson said, "will you go through it again, please, for these men? When you came on duty, what you did, what you saw. The whole schmeer."

"I come on duty at six o'clock," Pizzi started, "and—"

"This was yesterday?" Boone interrupted sharply.

"Yeah. Yesterday. Monday. So I come on duty at six o'clock, and there's a few people in the pool, not many, but at that time we're busy at the bar. The cocktail crowd, y'unnerstan. Martinis and Manhattans. We got one waiter here, me, and one bartender. In the afternoon, you can buy a sandwich, like, but not after six. So's people will go down to the dining room, y'unnerstan. So the crowd thins out like till nine-ten, around there, and then we begin to fill up again, and people come up for a swim."

Sergeant Boone was the interrogator.

"What time do you close?"

"Twelve. On the dot. Then anyone he wants to keep on drinking, he's got to go down to the lobby bar. Unless he wants to drink in his room, y'unnerstan. Anyways, last night about ten-eleven, like that, a couple of people in the pool, all the tables taken . . . Not that I'm all that rushed, y'unnerstan, with the tables filled. This is a small place; look around. Mostly couples and parties of four. Two guys by theirselves and one dame. The guys are double bourbons on the rocks and bottled Millers. The dame is white wine. The bourbon guy is like maybe fifty, around there, lushing like there's no tomorrow, and the beer guy is nursing his bottles. The wine dame is sipping away, not fast, not slow."

"You allow unescorted women up here?"

"Why not? If they conduct theirselves in a ladylike manner, y'unnerstan, they can drink up a storm—who cares?"

"Describe the young guy, Tony. The one drinking beer by himself."

"He's like—oh, about twenty-five, I'd guess. Tall, real tall, and thin. He's got long blond hair, like down to his shoulders and all over his ears, and a beard. But not a hippie, y'unnerstan. He's clean and dressed nice."

"What was he wearing—do you remember?"

"Khaki pants and a sports jacket."

They looked at Boone. The sergeant nodded grimly.

"Those were the clothes he took off," he said. "That was him. What about the woman, Tony. Can you describe her?"

"I din get a good look. She's sitting over there at that small table. See? Next to the palms. At night, most of the light comes from around the pool, so she's in shadow, y'unnerstan. About forty, I'd guess, give or take."

"Tall?"

"Yeah, I'd say so. Maybe five-six or seven."

"Wearing a hat?"

"No hat. Brown hair. Medium. Cut short."

"How was she dressed?"

"Very plain. Nothing flashy. White turtleneck sweater. One of those denim things with shoulder straps."

"Was she pretty?"

"Nah. You'd never look at her once. Flat-chested. Flat heels. No makeup. A nothing."

"All right, now we got the woman by herself drinking white wine and the young blond guy by himself drinking beer. How did they get together?"

"The kid stands up, takes his bottle and glass, and goes over to her table. I'm watching him, y'unnerstan, because if she screams bloody murder, then I'll have to go over and tell him to cool it. But he talks and she talks, and I see them smiling, and after a while he sits down with her, and they keep talking and smiling, so I couldn't care less."

"Did you hear what they were talking about?"

"Nah. Who wants to listen to that bullshit? When they signal me, I bring another round of drinks. That's all I'm getting paid for. Not to listen to bullshit."

"When they left, did they leave together?"

"Sure. They were the last to go. That's how come I remember them so good. The place emptied out and I had to go over and tell them we was closing. So they paid their bill and left."

"Who paid the bill?"

"They each paid their own tabs. That was okay by me; they both left a tip so I did all right."

"Did you see where they went? To the elevators?"

"I din see. I went to the bar with the money and checks. When I come back, they was gone. My tips was on the table. Also, they took their glasses with them."

"Wasn't that unusual?"

"Nah. People staying here at the hotel, they don't finish a drink, they take it down to their rooms with them. The maids find the glasses and return them up here. No one loses."

"So they left around midnight?"

"Right to the minute."

Sergeant Boone looked at Delaney. "Chief?" he asked.

"Tony," Delaney said, "this woman—can you tell us more about her?"

"Like what?"

"Can you guess what she weighed?"

"Skinny. Couldn't have been more than one-twenty. Probably less."

"What about her voice?"

"Nothing special. Low. Polite."

"Her posture?"

"I din notice. Sorry."

"You're doing fine. You didn't happen to notice if she was wearing a gold bracelet, did you?"

"I don't remember seeing no gold bracelet."

"You said she was plain looking?"

"Yeah. A kind of a long face."

"If you had to guess what kind of work she does, what would you guess?"

"A secretary maybe. Like that."

"Did she touch the young guy?"

"Touch him?"

"His cheek. Stroke his hair. Put her hand on his arm. Anything like that?"

"You mean was she coming on? Nah, nothing like that."

"Did you ever see either of them before?"

"Never."

"Together or separately? Never been here before?"

"I never saw them."

"Did they act like they knew each other? Like old friends meeting by accident?"

"Nah. It was a pickup, pure and simple."

"When they left at midnight, would you say they were drunk?"

"No way. I could look up the bill, but I'd say he had three-four beers and she had three-four wines. But they wasn't drunk."

"Feeling no pain?"

"Not even that. Just relaxed and friendly. No trouble. When I told them we was closing, they din make no fuss."

"Do you remember the color of the woman's eyes?"

"I din see."

"Guess."

"Brown."

"Did you think they were guests here at the hotel?"

"Who knows? They come and go. Also, we get a lot of outsiders stop by for a drink. Off the street, y'unnerstan."

"Was the woman wearing perfume?"

"Don't remember any if she was."

"Anything at all you recall about her? Anything we haven't asked?"

"No, not really. She was nothing special, y'unnerstan. Just another woman."

"Uh-huh. Thank you, Tony. That's all I've got. Sergeant?"

"Thanks for your help, Tony," Boone said. "Detective Johnson will take you over to the station house and get a signed statement. Don't worry about getting docked; we'll make it right with your boss."

"Sure, I don't mind. You think this woman put him under?"

"Could be."

"She the Hotel Ripper?"

"Johnson," Boone said, gesturing, and the detective led Anthony Pizzi away.

"Good witness," Delaney said. "Those hooded eyes fooled me. He doesn't miss much. Hit him again in a day or so, sergeant. He'll be thinking about it, and maybe he'll remember more things."

"I suppose you blame me, Edward," Ivar Thorsen said.

"Blame you? For what?"

"She did what you said she'd do—left off the wig and bracelet, dressed plainly. After she read the newspaper stories."

Delaney shrugged. "Under the bridge and over the dam. Even if she had dressed up like a tart, I think she would have murdered LaBranche and walked away. Maybe it worked out for the best; now we got a firmer description of what she really looks like. Sergeant, don't forget to have Bentley take Anthony Pizzi to the police artist. Maybe they can refine that sketch."

"Do it today," Boone promised. "Anything else, Chief?"

"Nooo, not really."

"Something bothering you, Edward?"

"Up to now she's been so goddamned clever. Made sure she picked up her victims in a big, crowded place so no one would remember her. Made sure she wiped her prints clean. Now, all of a sudden, she meets the guy in a small place. Lets him pick her up in a way that people will recall. Stays late until they're the only two left. The waiter was sure to remember. Then carries her wineglass down to his room and leaves it there with prints all over it. Stupid, stupid, stupid! I can't understand it. It's just not like her."

"Maybe," Ivar Thorsen said slowly, "maybe she wants to be caught."

Delaney looked at him. "You think so? It's possible, but that's a fancy-schmancy explanation. Maybe the reason is simpler than that. Maybe she's just tired."

"Tired?"

"Weary. Fatigued. Can you imagine what the stress must be like? Picking up these strangers, any one of whom could be a sadistic killer himself. Then going up against them with a pocket knife. Killing them and destroying any evidence that would point to her. My God, the strain of doing all that, month after month."

"You think she's falling apart?" Boone asked.

"It makes sense, doesn't it? Especially when she reads the papers and realizes that little by little we're getting closer. I think the tension is beginning to get to her. She's not thinking straight anymore. She's forgetting things. The pressure is building up. Yes, sergeant, I think she's cracking."

"Is there anything more we could be doing?" Thorsen asked anxiously.

"Finish that sketch," Delaney said, "and get it out to all the newspapers and TV stations. Better put extra men on to handle the calls. Start immediately on individual interviews with every woman between the ages of, say, twenty-five and fifty, on the convention schedule access list. Get Johnson's men started on the physical examination of every tear gas container sold in New York."

"Right," Sergeant Boone said. "We'll put on the heat."

"You better," Delaney said drily. "We've only got another twenty-six days."

"I'm not sure I'll be around then," Deputy Commissioner Thorsen said.

They looked at him and realized he wasn't joking.

Delaney left the motor inn, pushed through the crowd on the street, and caught a cab going uptown on Tenth Avenue. He sat crossways on the back seat, stretching out his legs.

He thought of Thorsen's last comment. He reckoned the Admiral might weather this latest unsolved killing, but if there was another late in July, Thorsen would be tossed to the wolves and a new commander brought in.

It would be a hard, cruel thing to do, and would put an effective end to the Deputy's career in the NYPD. But Ivar knew the risk when he accepted the job of stopping the Hotel Ripper. Delaney could imagine the man's fury with this "plain looking, nothing special" woman whose fate was linked with his.

Monica met him in the hallway and put a hand on his arm. She had evidently heard the news on the radio, for she looked at him with shocked eyes.

"Another one?" she said.

He nodded.

"Edward," she said, almost angrily, "when is this going to stop?"

"Soon," he said. "I hope. We're getting there, but it's slow work. Ivar won't—"

"Edward," she interrupted, "Dr. Ho is waiting for you in the living room. I told him I didn't know when you'd be back, but he said he had to see you."

"All right," Delaney said, sighing. "I'll see what he wants now."

He hung his skimmer away in the hall closet, then opened the door to the living room.

The moment he appeared, Dr. Patrick Ho bounced to his feet. His eyes were burning with triumph. He waved a sheaf of yellow telegrams wildly.

"Addison's disease!" he shouted. "Addison's disease!"

11

July 1st; Tuesday . . .

There had been a brief, hard summer squall just before
Zoe Kohler left work. When she came out onto Madison
Avenue, the pavement was steaming, gutters running with
filth. The clogged air bit and stank of wet char.

She walked down to the office of Dr. Oscar Stark. She
passed a liquor store, saw in the window a display of
wines. She thought of the wineglass she had left in the
hotel room of Chester LaBranche.

It was not a serious oversight—her fingerprints were not
on file, anywhere—but the slipup bothered her. In many
ways—in the Hotel Granger office, in the clean order of
her home—she was a perfectionist. She knew it and found
pride in it.

So this minor error annoyed her. It was the first mistake
she could not blame on chance or accident. It depressed
her because it tainted her adventure, made it bumbling
happenstance instead of a clear statement of her will.

"Did you hear about the new murder?" the receptionist
asked excitedly. "The Hotel Ripper again."

"I heard," Zoe Kohler said. "It's awful."

"Just awful," the woman agreed.

When Dr. Stark came into the examination room,
preceded by a plume of cigar smoke, the first thing he said
was, "Where's your bracelet?"

Her heart surged, then settled when she realized he was
not referring to the gold links with the WHY NOT? legend,
but to her medical identification strap stating she was a
victim of Addison's disease.

"Uh, I took a shower this morning," she said, "and forgot to put it back on."

"Oh sure," he said. "But the kit's in your purse, isn't it?" Then, when she didn't answer, he said, "Zoe, Zoe, what am I going to do with you?"

He scanned the clipboard Gladys handed him. Then he commanded Zoe to stand and drop the sheet. He hitched the wheeled stool closer until his face was only inches from her sunken abdomen.

"Look at you," he said wrathfully. "Skin and bones! And look at this . . . and this . . . and this . . ."

He showed her the bronzy discolorations on her knees, elbows, knuckles, nipples. Then he plucked at her pubic hair, displayed what came away.

"See?" he demanded. "See? You're taking your medication?"

"Yes, I am. Every day."

He grunted. The remainder of the examination was conducted in silence. Because she was having her period, the pelvic probing and Pap smear were omitted.

It seemed to Zoe that he was not as gentle as usual. He was rough, almost savage, in his handling of her body. He ignored her gasps and groans.

"I'll see you in my office," he said grimly, picking up his cigar and stomping out.

He seemed a little calmer when she sat down facing him across his littered desk. He was, she saw, writing rapidly in her file.

Finally he tossed the pen aside. He relit his cold cigar. He pushed his glasses atop the halo of billowing white hair. He talked to the ceiling . . .

"Weight down," he said tonelessly. "Blood pressure up. Pulse rapid. Hyperpigmentation pronounced."

He brought his gaze down to stare into her eyes.

"Have you injured yourself?"

"No. Just that little cut on my leg. I told—"

"Have you been fasting? Have you stopped eating completely?"

"Of course not."

"Then you must be under some severe emotional or psychological stress that is affecting your body chemistry."

She was silent.

"Zoe," he said again in a kindlier tone, "what am I going to do with you? You come to me for advice and help. To assist you when you're ill or, better yet, to keep you healthy. Am I correct? For this, you pay me a fee, and I do my best. A nice relationship. But how can I do my job when you lie to me?"

"I don't lie to you," she said hotly.

He held up a palm. "All right, you don't lie. A poor choice of words. I apologize. But you withhold information from me, information I need to do my job. How can I help you if you refuse to tell me what I need to know?"

"I answer all your questions," she said.

"You don't," he said furiously. "You never tell me what I need to know. All right now, let's calm down, let's not get excited. We'll try again, very quietly, very logically. You are still taking the prescribed amount of cortisol?"

"Yes."

"And the salt tablets?"

"Yes."

"Do you have a craving for additional salt?"

"No."

"Your diet is well-balanced? You aren't on some faddish diet to lose weight fast?"

"No. I eat well."

"Any vomiting?"

"No."

"Nausea? Upset stomach?"

"No."

"Weakness?"

"Only during my period."

"Diarrhea or constipation?"

"No."

"When I probed your abdomen, you groaned."

"You hurt," she said.

"No," he said, *"you* hurt. The abdomen is tender?"

"I'm having my period," she protested.

"Uh-huh. And you're not wearing your bracelet or carrying your emergency kit?"

She didn't answer.

"Zoe," he said gently, "I want to put you in the hospital."

"No," she said immediately.

"Only for tests," he urged. "To find out what's going on here. I don't want to wait for your blood and urine tests; I want you in the hospital now. The last thing in the world we want is an Addisonian crisis. Believe me, it's no fun. We can prevent that if you go into the hospital now, and we can make tests I can't do here."

"I don't want to go into a hospital," she said. "I don't like hospitals."

"Who does? But sometimes they're necessary."

"No."

He sighed. "I can't knock you on the head and drag you there. Zoe, I think you should consult another physician. I think you may be happier with another doctor."

"I won't be happier. I don't want another doctor."

"All right, then *I'll* be happier. You won't tell me the truth. You won't follow my advice. I've done all I can for you. I really do think another physician will be better for both of us."

"No," she said firmly. "You can refuse to treat me if you want, but if you do, I won't go to anyone else. I just won't go to *any* other doctor."

They stared at each other. Something like a fearful wariness came into his eyes.

"Zoe," he said in a low voice, "I think there is a problem here. I mean a special problem that is not physical, that has nothing to do with Addison's, but is fueling the disease. You won't tell me about it, that's plain. I know a good man, a psychiatrist—will you talk to him?"

"What for? I don't have a special problem. Maybe I just need more medicine. Or a different medicine."

He drummed fingers on the desktop, looking at her reflectively. She sat quietly, legs crossed at the ankles, hands placidly clasped in her lap. She was expressionless, composed. Spine straight, head held high.

"I'll tell you exactly what I'm going to do," he said quietly. "I am going to wait until I have the results of your blood tests and urinalysis. If they show what I expect, I am going to call you and ask you once again to go into the hospital for further tests and treatment. If, at that time, you again refuse, I am going to call or wire your parents in Minnesota. I have their names and address in your file. I will explain the situation to them."

"You wouldn't," she said, gasping.

"Oh yes," he said, "I would, and will. At that time, the decision will be yours, and theirs. I'll have done everything I can possibly do. After that, it's out of my hands."

"And you'll just forget all about me," she said, beginning to weep.

"No," he said sadly, "I won't do that."

She stumbled home in the waning light of a summer night. The sky as bronzed as the tainted patches on her flesh. She saw, with dread, how ugly people were. Snout of pig and fang of snake.

It was a city of gargoyles, their lesions plain as hers. She could almost hear the howls and moans. The city writhed. "Special problems" everywhere. She was locked in a colony of the damned, the disease in or out, but festering.

Those answers she had given to Dr. Stark's questions—they were not lies, exactly.

She was aware of everything: her weakness, nausea, vertigo, salt craving, diarrhea. But she sloughed over these things, telling herself they were temporary, of no consequence. To admit them to Dr. Stark would give them an importance, a significance she knew was unwarranted.

And when he asked about emotional and psychological stress—well, that was simply prying into matters of no concern to him. She knew what he was doing, and was determined to block him. Her adventures were hers alone, private and secret.

Still, she was saddened by his threat to turn her away. Rejection again. Just as Kenneth had rejected her. And her father. He had rejected by ignoring her, but it was all the same.

She was still musing about rejection and how men did it with a sneer or a laugh, spurning something tender and yearning they could not appreciate and did not deserve, when Ernest Mittle called her soon after she returned home.

Ernie hadn't rejected her. He phoned almost every night, and they saw each other at least once a week and sometimes twice. She thought of him as a link, her only anchor to a gentle world that promised. No gargoyles or cries of pain in that good land.

He knew she had gone to the doctor for her monthly

checkup, and asked how she made out.

She said everything was fine, she had passed with flying colors, but the doctor wanted her to eat more and put on a little weight.

He said that was marvelous because he wanted her to come down to his place on Saturday night for dinner. He was going to roast a small turkey.

She said that sounded like fun, and she would bring some of those strawberry tarts he liked. Then she asked him if he had heard anything about Maddie and Harry Kurnitz.

He said he had learned nothing new, but Mr. Kurnitz was still seeing the blonde, and was very irritable lately, and had Zoe heard about the latest Hotel Ripper killing, and wasn't it horrible?

She said yes, she had heard about it, and it was horrible, and had Ernie definitely scheduled his summer vacation?

He said he'd know by next week, and he hoped Zoe could get the same vacation time, and who was she going to vote for?

So it went: a phone conversation that lasted a half-hour. Just chatter, laughs, gossip. Nothing important in the content. But the voices were there. Even in talking about the weather, the voices were there. The soft tones.

"Good night, darling," he said finally. "I'll call you tomorrow."

"Good night, dear," she said. "Sleep well."

"You, too. I love you, Zoe."

"I love you, Ernie. Take care of yourself."

"You, too. I'll see you on Saturday, but I'll speak to you before that."

"Tomorrow night?"

"Oh yes, I'll call."

"Good. I love you, Ernie."

"I love you, sweetheart."

"Thank you for calling."

"Oh Zoe," he said, "be happy."

"I am," she said, "when I talk to you. When I'm with you. When I think of you."

"Think of me frequently," he said, laughing. "Promise?"

"I promise," she said, "if you'll dream of me. Will you?"

"I promise. Love you, darling."

"Love you."

She hung up, smiling. He had not rejected her, would not. Never once, not ever, had he criticized the way she looked, what she did, how she lived. He loved her for what she was and had no desire to change her.

"Mrs. Ernest Mittle." She spoke the title aloud. Then tried, "Mrs. Zoe Mittle."

He was not an exciting man, nor was he a challenge. There was no mystery to him. But he was caring and tender. She knew she was stronger than he, and loved him more for his weakness.

She would not have him different. Oh no. Never. She had her fill of male bluster and swagger. Maddie might call him "Mister Meek," but Maddie was incapable of seeing the sweet innocence of meekness, the scented fragility, as an infant is fragrant and vulnerable, shocked by hurt.

Zoe Kohler showered before she went to bed, not looking at her knobbed, discolored body. In bed, she dreamed that with Ernie at her side, always, as husband and helpmate, she might no longer have need for adventures.

Then the void would be filled, the ache dissolved. She would regain her health. She would blossom. Just blossom! They would create a world of two, and there would be no place for the cruel, the ugly, or the brutish.

July 2nd; Wednesday . . .

"Goddamn it!" Abner Boone shouted, and slapped a palm on the desktop. "Then you're not certain it definitely is this Addison's disease?"

Dr. Patrick Ho blinked at the sergeant's violence.

"Ah, no," he said regretfully. "Not certain. Not definite. But Addison's was first on the lists of possibilities from all computers queried. When a definite diagnosis cannot be computed because of lack of sufficient input, a list of possibilities is given with probability ratings. Addison's had the highest rating on all the lists."

"What probability?" Boone demanded. "What percentage?"

"Ah, a little above thirty percent."

"Jesus Christ!" the sergeant said disgustedly.

They were jammed into Boone's cramped office: the sergeant, Dr. Ho, Delaney, and Deputy Commissioner Thorsen.

"Let me get this straight," Thorsen said. "There's a thirty percent possibility that our killer is suffering from Addison's disease. Is that correct?"

"Ah, yes."

The Admiral looked at Delaney. "Edward?"

"Dr. Ho," the Chief said, "what is the possibility rating of the second highest ranked diagnosis?"

"Less than ten."

"So Addison's disease has three times the probability of the second diagnosis?"

"Yes."

"But still only about one chance in three of being accurate?"

"That is so."

"Mighty small odds to move on," Boone said glumly.

"Even if it was only one percent," Delaney said, "we'd have to move on it. We've got no choice. Doctor, I think you better tell us a little more about Addison's disease. I don't believe any of us knows exactly what it is."

"Ah, yes," Dr. Patrick Ho said, beaming. "Very understandable. It is quite rare. A physician might practice for fifty years and never treat a case."

"Just how rare?" Delaney said sharply. "Give us some numbers."

"Ah, I have been studying the available literature on the disease. One authority states the incidence is one case per hundred thousand population. Other estimates are slightly higher. There is, you understand, no registry of victims. I would guess, in the New York metropolitan area, possibly two hundred cases, but closer to one hundred. I am sorry I cannot be more precise, but there is simply no way of knowing."

"All right," Delaney said, "let's split the difference and say there are a hundred and fifty cases, with maybe thirty or forty in Manhattan. That's rare enough. Now, what exactly is this Addison's disease?"

Dr. Ho stood immediately and unbuttoned the jacket and vest of his natty tan poplin suit. A soft belly bulged over his knitted belt. Enthusiastically, he dug the fingers of both hands into an area below the rib cage.

"Ah, here," he said. "Approximately. Near the kidneys. Two glands called the adrenals. I will try to keep this as nontechnical as possible. These adrenal glands have a center portion called the medulla, and a covering or rind called the cortex. All right so far?"

He looked around the room. There were no questions from the other three men, so the doctor rebuttoned his vest and sat down again. He crossed his little legs slowly, adjusting the trouser crease with care.

"Now," he went on, "the adrenals secrete several important hormones. The medulla secretes adrenaline, for instance. You have heard of adrenaline? The cortex secretes cortisol, which you probably know as cortisone. The adrenals also secrete sex hormones. Of sex, of course, you have probably also heard."

The doctor giggled.

"Get on with it," Sergeant Boone growled.

"Ah, yes. Sometimes the cortex, the covering of the adrenal glands, is damaged, or even destroyed. This can be the result of tuberculosis, a fungal infection, a tumor, and other causes. When the cortex of the adrenals is damaged or destroyed, it cannot produce cortisol. The results can be catastrophic. Weakness, weight loss, nausea and vomiting, low blood pressure, abdominal pains, and so forth. If untreated, the course of the disease is invariably fatal."

"And if it's treated?" Delaney asked.

"Ah, there is the problem. Because it is such a rare disorder, and because so few doctors are familiar with the symptoms, the disease is sometimes not diagnosed correctly. The early manifestations, such as weakness, nausea, constipation, and so forth, could simply indicate a viral infection or the flu. But as the disease progresses, one symptom appears that is almost a certain clue: portions of the body—the elbows, knees, knuckles, the lips and creases of the palms—become discolored. These can be tan, brown, or bronze patches, like suntan. Sometimes they are bluish-black, sometimes gray. The reason for this discoloration is very interesting."

He paused and looked about brightly. He had their attention; there was no doubt of that.

"There is a small gland in the brain called the pituitary, sometimes known as the 'master gland.' It produces secretions that affect almost all functions of the body. The pituitary and the adrenals have a kind of feedback relationship. The pituitary produces two hormones, ACTH and MSH, which stimulate the adrenal cortex to produce cortisol which, in turn, helps keep the ACTH and MSH at normal levels. But when the adrenal cortex is damaged or destroyed, the levels of ACTH and MSH build up in the blood. That is what has happened to our killer. Now, MSH is a melanocyte-stimulating hormone. That is, it controls the melanin in the skin. Melanin is the dark brown or black pigmentation. So when there is an abnormally high level of MSH, there is an accumulation of melanin, which causes discoloration of the skin and is an indication to diagnosticians that the patient is suffering from adrenal cortical insufficiency, or Addison's disease."

Dr. Patrick Ho ended on a triumphant note, as if he had just proved out a particularly difficult mathematical theorem. QED.

"All right," Delaney said, "I've followed you so far. I think. And the high potassium level and the other stuff?"

"Also classic indications of Addison's disease. Especially the low sodium level."

"Tell me, doctor," Thorsen said, "if someone has Addison's disease, can you tell by looking at them? Those skin discolorations, for instance?"

"Ah, no," Dr. Ho said. "No, no, no. With proper medication and diet, an Addisonian victim would look as normal as any of us. They are somewhat like diabetics in that they must take synthetic cortisol for the remainder of their lives and watch their salt intake carefully. But otherwise they can live active lives, exercise, work, have sex, raise families, and so forth. There is no evidence that Addison's disease, adequately treated, shortens life expectancy."

"Wait a minute," Delaney said, frowning. "Something here doesn't jibe. Assuming our killer has Addison's disease and is being treated for it, her blood wouldn't show all those characteristics, would it?"

"Ah-ha!" Dr. Ho cried, slapping his palms together gleefully. "You are absolutely correct. One possibility is that the killer is in the primary stages of Addison's and has not yet sought treatment. Another possibility is that she has sought treatment, but her disease has not been correctly diagnosed. Another possibility is that her disorder has been properly diagnosed and prescribed for, but she is not taking the proper medication, for whatever reason."

"That's a helluva lot of possibilities," Boone grumbled.

"Ah, yes," the doctor said, not at all daunted. "But there is yet another possibility. Addisonian crisis may be brought on by acute stress such as vomiting, an injury, an infection, a surgical procedure, even a tooth extraction. And, I venture to say, by a prolonged period of severe mental, emotional, or psychic stress."

They stared at him, slowly grasping what he was telling them.

"What you're saying," Delaney said, "is that you believe the Hotel Ripper is suffering from Addison's disease. That she is being treated for it. But the treatment isn't having the effect it should have because of the stress of ripping open the throats of six strangers in hotel rooms. Is that it?"

"Ah, yes," Dr. Ho said placidly. "I believe that is a definite possibility."

"That's crazy!" Sergeant Boone burst out.

"Is it?" the doctor said. "What's so crazy? Surely you will not deny the influence of mental and emotional attitudes on physical health? The close relationship has been firmly established. You can will yourself to live and will yourself to die. All I am saying is that the physical health of this woman could be adversely affected by the strains and fear connected with her horrible activities. There may be a psychological factor at work here as well. If she acknowledges the evil of what she is doing, sees herself as a worthless individual not fit for society, that too might affect her health."

"Look," Deputy Thorsen said, "let's not go off into left field trying to figure out the emotional and psychological quirks of this woman. We'll leave that to the psychiatrists after we've caught her. But let's just stick to what we've got. You think she's suffering from Addison's disease, and either it's not being adequately treated or she's ignoring the treatment, and the stress of these murders is killing her. That sounds silly, but it's what you're saying, isn't it?"

"Approximately," Dr. Ho said in a low voice.

"So?" the Admiral said. "Where do we go from here? How do we begin finding everyone in New York City suffering from Addison's disease?"

They stared at each other a moment.

"Go to all the doctors?" Sergeant Boone questioned. "Ask them if they're treating anyone with the disease?"

Edward X. Delaney wagged his big head, side to side.

"Won't work, sergeant," he said. "You know the laws of confidentiality regarding privileged information between doctor and patient. The doctors will tell us to go screw and the courts will back them up."

"Edward," Thorsen said, "suppose we go to all the doctors in the city and instead of demanding the names of any patients they're treating for Addison's disease, we just ask a general question, like, 'Are you treating anyone for Addison's'?"

Delaney thought a moment before he answered:

"If a physician wants to cooperate with the cops, I think he could answer a general question like that without violating the law or his code of ethics. But what the hell good would it do? If a doctor answered, 'Yes,' then our next question would have to be, 'What is the patient's name and address?' Then he'd tell us to get lost and we'd be right back where we started."

They sat in silence, staring at their hands, the walls, the ceiling, trying to come up with *something*.

"Dr. Ho," the Chief said, "in answer to one of the Deputy's questions, you said an Addisonian victim would not have those skin discolorations if she was receiving the proper treatment. Right?"

"That is correct."

"But our killer obviously isn't getting the proper treatment or, for whatever reason, it isn't working the way it should. Her blood is all fucked up. Does that mean she would have the skin discolorations?"

"Ah, I would say possibly. Even probably, judging by the high MSH level."

"Could the discolorations be seen? On the street, I mean, if she was dressed in everyday clothes? Would a witness notice the blotches?"

"Ah, I would say no. Not on the elbows, knees, palms of the hands, etcetera. If it spread heavily to hands and face, then of course it would be noticeable. But by that time the victim would probably be hospitalized."

"How do the laws of privileged information apply to hospitals?" Boone asked.

"Same as to physicians," Delaney said. "In hospitals, patients are under a doctor's care. All information is privileged."

"Shit," Boone said.

"Perhaps," Dr. Ho said tentatively, "the Mayor would be willing to make a personal appeal to all the doctors of the city, asking for their cooperation in this civic emergency."

The Deputy Commissioner looked at him pityingly.

"I don't believe the Mayor would care to put himself in the position of urging physicians publicly to break the law. He had enough trouble just getting that offer of a fifty-thousand-dollar reward past the Council. No, doctor, don't expect any help from the politicos. They have their own problems."

They all went back to staring into the middle distance.

"The problem here is identification," the Chief said. "How do we identify all the victims of Addison's disease in New York?"

"Wait," Dr. Patrick Ho said, holding up a plump palm. They looked at him.

"A problem of identification," the doctor mused. "All the papers I read on Addison's were written for physicians, and gave the history of the disease, symptoms, treatment, and so forth. Without fail, every author recommended the Addisonian victim be instructed to wear a medical identification bracelet stating that he suffered from the disease. Also, the bracelet carries his name and address, and the name, address, and phone number of his doctor. This is in case of emergency, you understand. An automobile accident, sudden injury, or fainting."

"Go on," Delaney said, hunching forward on his chair. "This is beginning to sound good."

"Also, the patient should carry a small kit at all times. In the kit is a sterile syringe containing a hydrocortisone solution ready for injection in an emergency, with instructions for use."

"Better and better," Delaney said. "And where do you get a bracelet and kit like that?"

"Ah, I do not know," Dr. Ho confessed. "But I would guess the sources are limited. That is, you could not walk into just any drugstore in the city and expect to buy such specialized equipment. It would have to be a medical supply house, I would think, or a pharmacy that handles rare and difficult prescriptions."

"There can't be many places like that in the city," Sergeant Boone said slowly.

"Edward," Thorsen said, "do the laws of privileged information apply to prescriptions in drugstores?"

"I'd say not," the Chief said. "I think you take a prescription in and then it's between you and the pharmacist. It's out of the doctor's hands, and the pharmacist can reveal the names of the patient and the doctor who wrote the prescription."

"I better get a legal ruling on it," the Deputy said.

"Good idea," Delaney said. "Meanwhile, sergeant, I think you better organize a crew to track down the places that sell those medical identification bracelets and kits to people with Addison's disease."

"Long shot," Boone said doubtfully.

"Sure it is," Delaney said. "And that convention schedule access list is a long shot. And the list of tear gas customers is a long shot. But every list makes the odds shorter. We get enough lists, and crosscheck them, we're going to come up with some good possibles."

"Oh, I love this work!" Dr. Patrick Ho cried, his dark eyes gleaming.

They looked at him.

July 7–8; Monday and Tuesday . . .

Zoe Kohler sat primly at her desk in the security section of the Hotel Granger. She had finished four letters for Everett Pinckney, placed the neatly typed pages and envelopes on his desk. She had completed a tentative summer vacation schedule, requesting August 11–22 for herself since those were the weeks Ernest Mittle would be off.

She leafed idly through the pages of the current issue of the hotel trade magazine. The lead article reported that the New York association had raised its reward for capture of the Hotel Ripper. That brought the total of rewards offered to more than $100,000.

Mr. Pinckney came in with the signed letters and handed them to her for mailing.

"Perfect job, Zoe," he said. "As usual." He noticed the magazine on her desk and snapped his fingers. "I've been meaning to tell you," he said, "and it keeps slipping my mind. Last week a detective came by the manager's office and got a list of everyone in the hotel who sees that magazine."

"A detective, Mr. Pinckney? From the police department?"

"That's what his ID said. He wouldn't tell us what it was all about, just wanted the names of everyone who saw the magazine. Said they were checking the entire mailing list of the publisher."

"That's odd," Zoe said, her voice toneless.

"Isn't it?" Pinckney said. "I guessed it might have something to do with the Hotel Ripper case, but he wouldn't say. Can you imagine how big a job that will be? Why, we get six copies ourselves, and I suppose thousands are distributed. The list of people who read it must be endless."

"It's certainly a strange thing to do," Zoe said.

"Well," Pinckney said, shrugging, "I suppose they have their reasons. Whatever it is, I haven't heard any more about it."

He went back into his office and a moment later she heard the sound of his desk drawer being opened and the clink of bottle and glass.

She sat there staring down at the journal. She wondered if Mr. Pinckney's guess was correct, that the detective's request had something to do with the Hotel Ripper case. She could not conceive what the connection might be. As he said, thousands of people had access to the magazine.

Still, the incident was unsettling; it left her feeling

uneasy and somehow threatened. She had a sense of the initiative slipping from her hands. Once again in her life she was being moved and manipulated by forces outside herself.

She had the same feeling of being pushed in directions she did not wish to go when, late in the afternoon, Dr. Oscar Stark phoned.

"Zoe," he said without preamble, "I want you in the hospital as soon as possible. Your tests are back and the results are even more disturbing than I thought they'd be. I talked over your case with a friend of mine, a very capable endocrinologist, and he agrees with me that you belong in a hospital before we have an Addisonian crisis."

"I won't go," she said flatly. "I don't need a hospital. I'm perfectly all right."

"Now you listen to me, young lady," he said sharply. "You are not perfectly all right. You are suffering from a pernicious disease that requires constant treatment and monitoring. All your vital signs point to a serious deterioration of your condition. We've got to find out why. I'm not talking about an operation; I'm talking about tests and observation. If you refuse, I can't be responsible for the consequences."

"No," she said, "I won't go to a hospital."

He was silent a moment.

"Very well," he said. "The only thing left for me to do is contact your parents. Then, unless you change your mind, I must ask you to consult another physician. I'm sorry, Zoe," he said softly before he hung up.

She could not have said exactly why she was being so obdurate. She did not doubt Dr. Stark's expertise. She supposed he was correct; she was seriously ill and her health was degenerating rapidly.

She told herself she could not endure the indignity of a hospital, of being naked before unfeeling strangers, to be poked and prodded, her body wastes examined critically, her flesh treated as a particularly vile and worthless cut of meat.

And there was also a secret fear that, somehow, in a hospital, she might be restored to perfect health, but in the process be deprived of those private pains and pleasures that were so precious to her.

She did not fully comprehend how this might happen, but the alarm was there, that hospital treatment would mollify those surges of insensate strength and will she felt during her adventures. They would reduce her to a dull, enduring beast and quench the one spark that set her above the animal people who thronged the city's streets.

She was special in this way only. She had excited the dread of millions, had caused fury and confusion in the minds of the police, had influenced the course of events of which, heretofore, she had been merely another victim.

A hospital might end all that. It might rob her of her last remaining uniqueness. It might, in fact, destroy the uncommon soul of Zoe Kohler.

That evening, on the way home, she stopped for a light dinner at the Madison Avenue luncheonette she frequented. She had a salad of cottage cheese and fresh fruit slices. She sat at the counter, drank an iced tea, and dabbed her lips delicately with a paper napkin.

By the time she reached her apartment, she had put the whole idea of hospitals from her mind, just as she was able to ignore the now obvious manifestations of her body's growing decrepitude. She took her pills and nostrums automatically, with the vague hope that she might wake the following morning cured and whole.

But a new shock awaited her on Tuesday. She was seated at her desk, sipping coffee and leafing through *The New York Times*. There, on the first page of the second section, was a headline: POLICE RELEASE NEW "RIPPER" SKETCH.

Beneath the legend was a two-column-wide drawing in line and wash. The moment Zoe Kohler saw it, she looked about wildly, then slapped another section of the paper over the sketch.

Finally, when her heart stopped thudding and she was able to breathe normally, she uncovered the drawing again and stared at it long and hard.

She thought it was so *like*. The hair was incorrectly drawn, her face was too long and thin, but the artist had caught the shape of her eyebrows, straight lips, the pointed chin.

The more she stared, the more the drawing seemed to resemble her. She could not understand why hotel employees did not rush into her office, crowd around her desk, point at her with accusing fingers.

Surely Mr. Pinckney, Barney McMillan, or Joe Levine would note the resemblance; they were trained investigators. And if not them, then Ernest Mittle, Maddie Kurnitz, or Dr. Stark would see her in that revealing sketch and begin to wonder, to question.

Or, if none of her friends or acquaintances, it might be a passerby, a stranger on the street. She had an awful fantasy of a sudden shout, hue and cry, a frantic chase, capture. And possibly a beating by the maddened mob. A lynching.

It was not fear that moved her so much as embarrassment. She could never endure the ignominy of a public confrontation like that: the crazed eyes, wet mouths, the obscenities. Rather die immediately than face that humiliation.

She read the newspaper article printed beneath the drawing, and noted the detailed description of the clothing she had worn to the Tribunal Motor Inn. She supposed that she had been seen having a drink with that boy, and witnesses had told the police.

There was even mention that she drank white wine, though nothing was said about fingerprints. But the police suggested the woman they sought spoke in a low, polite voice, wore her hair quite short, dressed plainly, and might be employed as a secretary.

It was fascinating, in a strange way, to read this description of herself. It was like seeing one's image in a mirror that was a reflection of an image in another mirror. Reality was twice removed; the original was slightly distorted and wavery.

There was no doubt it was Zoe Kohler, but it was a remote woman, divorced from herself. It was a likeness, a very good likeness, with her hair, face, body, clothes. But it was not her. It was a replica.

Carefully she scissored the drawing from the newspaper, folded it, put it deep in her purse. Then, thinking that someone might notice the clipped page, she carried the whole newspaper to the trash room and dug it into a garbage can.

She hurried home from work that evening, keeping her head lowered, resisting an urge to hold her purse up in front of her face. No one took any notice of her. As usual, she was the invisible woman.

Safe in her apartment, she sat with a glass of iced vodka and inspected that damning sketch again. It seemed incredible that no one had recognized her.

As she stared at the drawing, she felt once again the sensation of disorientation. Like the printed description, the portrait was her and yet it was not her. It was a blurred likeness. She wondered if her body's rot had spread to her face, and this was a representation of dissolution.

She was still inspecting the drawing, eagerly, hungrily, trying to find meaning in it, when her parents called from Minnesota.

"Baby," her father said, "this is Dad, and Mother is on the extension."

"Hello, Dad, Mother. How are you?"

"Oh, Zoe!" her mother wailed, and began weeping noisily.

"Now, Mother," her father said, "you promised you wouldn't. Baby, we got a call from a doctor there in New York. Man named Stark. He your doctor?"

"Yes, Dad."

"Well, he says you're sick, baby. He says you should be in a hospital."

"Oh, Dad, that's silly. I was feeling down for a few days, but I'm all right now. You know how doctors are."

"Are you telling the truth, Zoe?" her mother asked tearfully.

"Mother, I'm perfectly all right. I'm taking my medicine and eating well. There's absolutely nothing wrong with me."

"Well, you certainly sound all right, baby. Are you sure you don't want me or Mother to come to New York?"

"Not on my account, Dad. There's just no need for it."

"Well, uh, as Mother wrote you, we were planning a trip to Hawaii this summer, but we can . . ."

"Oh, Dad, don't change your plans. I'm really in very good health."

"What do you weigh, Zoe?"

"About the same, Mother. Maybe a pound or two less, but I'll get that back."

"Well, why the hell did that New York doctor call us,

baby? He got me and your mother all upset."

"Dad, you know how doctors are; the least little thing and they want to put you in the hospital."

"Have you missed work, Zoe?"

"Not a single day, Mother. That proves I'm all right, doesn't it?"

"Listen, baby, we're not going to Hawaii until late in July. Do you think you'll be able to get out here on your vacation?"

"I don't know when my vacation is, Dad. When I find out, I'll write you, and maybe we can work something out, even if it's only for a few days."

"Have you met anyone, Zoe?" her mother asked. "You know—a nice boy?"

"Well, there's one fellow I've been seeing. He's very nice."

"What does he do, baby?"

"I'm not sure, Dad. I know he's taking courses in computers."

"Computers? Hey, sounds like a smart fellow."

"He is, Dad. I think you'd like him."

"Well, that's fine, baby. I'm glad you're getting out and, uh, socializing. And it's good to hear you're feeling okay. That damned doctor scared us."

"I'm feeling fine, Dad, really I am."

"Now listen to me, Zoe," her mother said. "I want you to call us at least once a week. You can reverse the charges. All right, Dad?"

"Of course, Mother. Baby, you do that. Call at least once a week and reverse the charges."

"All right, Dad."

"You take care of yourself now, y'hear?"

"I will. Thank you for calling. Goodbye, Mother. Goodbye, Dad."

"Goodbye, Zoe."

"Goodbye, baby."

She hung up, and when she looked at her hands, they were trembling. Her parents always had that effect: made her nervous, defensive. Made her feel guilty. Not once during the call had she said, "I love you." But then, neither had they.

She ate a sandwich of something she couldn't taste. She

drank another vodka, and swallowed vitamins, minerals, two Anacin, and a Valium. Then she took a shower, pulled on her threadbare robe.

She sat on the living room couch, drained by the conversation with her parents. It had taken energy, even bravado, to speak brightly, optimistically, to calm their fears and forestall their coming to New York and seeing her in her present state.

She supposed that when they thought of her, they remembered a little girl in a spotless pinafore. White gloves, knee-length cotton socks, and shiny black shoes with straps. A cute hat with flowers. A red plastic purse on a brass chain.

Zoe Kohler opened her robe, looked down, and saw what had become of that little girl. Tears came to her eyes, and she wondered how it had happened, and why it had happened.

As a child, when balked, scolded, or ignored, she had wished her tormentor dead. If her mother died, or her father, or a certain teacher, then Zoe's troubles would end, and she would be happy.

She had wished Kenneth dead. Not *wished* it exactly, but dreamed often of how her burdens would be lightened if he were gone. Once she had even fantasized that Maddie Kurnitz might die, and Zoe would comfort the widower, and he would look at her with new eyes.

All her life she had seen the death of others as the solution to her problems. Now, looking at her spoiled flesh, she realized that only her own death would put a stop to . . .

She was sick, and she was tired, and that thin, sour man she saw as "police" was stalking closer and closer. She wished *him* dead, but knew it could not be. He would persevere and . . .

That drawing was so accurate that it was only a matter of time until . . .

She might return to her parents' home and pretend . . .

Thoughts, unfinished, whirled by so rapidly that she felt faint with the flickering speed, the brief intensity. She closed her eyes, made tight fists. She hung on until her mind slowed, cleared, and she was able to concentrate on what she wanted to do, and find the resolve to do it.

She phoned Ernest Mittle.

"Ernie," she said, "do you *really* love me?"

July 11–12; Friday and Saturday . . .

Detective Sergeant Thomas K. Broderick and his squad had been assigned the task of tracing the WHY NOT? bracelet worn by the Hotel Ripper, but it was proving to be another dead end. Too many stores carried the bracelet, too many had been sold for cash; it was impossible to track every one.

So Broderick and his crew were pulled off the bracelet search and given the task of finding victims of Addison's disease who had purchased a medical identification bracelet and emergency kit in New York.

Broderick decided to start with the island of Manhattan, and the Yellow Pages were the first place he looked for names and addresses of medical supply houses.

Then he talked to police surgeons and to a small number of physicians who were police buffs or "groupies" and who were happy to cooperate with the NYPD as long as they weren't asked to violate the law or their professional ethics.

From these sources, Broderick compiled a list of places that might conceivably sell the things he was trying to trace. Then he divided his list into neighborhoods. Then he sent his men out to pound the pavements.

Most of the pharmacists they visited were willing to help. Those who weren't received a follow-up visit from Broderick or Sergeant Abner Boone. Both men were armed with opinions from the Legal Division of the NYPD, stating that the courts had held that communications to druggists and prescriptions given to them by customers were not confidential and not protected from disclosure.

"Of course," Boone would say, "if you want to fight this, and hire yourself a high-priced lawyer, and spend weeks sitting around in court, then I'll have to get a subpoena."

Cooperation was 100 percent.

As the names and addresses of Addisonian victims began to come in, Broderick's deskmen put aside the obviously masculine names and compiled a list only of the women. This list, in turn, was broken down into separate files for each borough of New York, and one for out-of-town addresses.

"It's all so mechanical!" Monica Delaney exclaimed.

"Mechanical?" the Chief said. "What the hell's mechanical about it? How do you think detectives work?"

"Well, maybe not mechanical," she said. "But you're all acting like bookkeepers. Like accountants."

"That's what we are," he said. "Accountants."

"Wise-ass," she said.

They were having dinner at P. J. Moriarty on Third Avenue. It was a fine, comfortable Irish bar and restaurant with Tiffany lampshades and smoke-mellowed wood paneling. For some unaccountable reason, a toy electric train ran around the bar on a track suspended from the ceiling.

They had started with dry Beefeater martinis. Then slabs of herring in cream sauce. Then pot roast with potato pancakes. With Canadian ale. Then black coffee and Armagnac. They were both blessed with good digestions.

"The greatest of God's gifts," Delaney was fond of remarking.

During dinner, he had told her about Dr. Ho's report on Addison's disease, and exactly how Sergeant Broderick's men were going about the search for Addisonian victims in New York.

"He says his list should be completed by late today," he concluded. "Tomorrow morning I'm going down to the precinct. We'll crosscheck the lists and see if we have anything."

"And if you don't?"

He shrugged. "We'll keep plugging. Every murder in the series has revealed more. Eventually we'll get her."

"Edward, if you find out who it is—what then?"

"Depends. Do we have enough evidence for an arrest? For an indictment?"

"You won't, uh . . ."

He looked at her, smiling slightly.

"Go in with guns blazing and cut her down? No, dear, we won't do that. I don't believe this woman will be armed. With a gun, that is. I think she'll come along quietly. Almost with relief."

"Then what? I mean, if you have enough evidence for an arrest and an indictment? What will happen to her then?"

He filled their coffee cups from the pewter pot.

"Depends," he said again. "If she gets a smart lawyer, he'll probably try to plead insanity. Seems to me that slitting the throats of six strangers is pretty good prima facie evidence of insanity. But even if she's adjudged capable of standing trial and is convicted, she'll get off with the minimum."

"Edward! Why? After what she's done?"

"Because she's a woman."

"You're joking?"

"I'm not joking. Want me to quote the numbers to you? I don't need Thomas Handry's research. The judicial system in this country is about fifty years behind the times as far as equality between men and women goes. Almost invariably females will receive lighter sentences than males for identical or comparable crimes. And when it comes to homicide, juries and judges seem to have a built-in bias that works in favor of women. They can literally get away with murder."

"But surely not the Hotel Ripper?"

"Don't be too sure of that. A good defense attorney will put her on the stand dressed in something conservative and black with a white Peter Pan collar. She'll speak in a low, trembling voice and dab at her eyes with a balled-up Kleenex. Remember when we were first arguing about whether the Hotel Ripper could be a woman, and you asked people at one of your meetings? All the men said a woman couldn't commit crimes like that and all the women said she could. Well, an experienced defense lawyer knows that, even if he doesn't know why. If he's got a female client accused of homicide, he'll try to get an all-male jury. Most of the men in this country still have a completely false concept of women's sensibilities. They think women are inherently incapable of killing. So they vote Not Guilty. That's why I think there should be an ECA."

"An ECA?"

"Sure," he said innocently. "To go along with the

ERA, the Equal Rights Amendment. ECA, the Equal Conviction Amendment."

"Bastard," she said, kicking him under the table.

They walked home slowly through the warm, sticky summer night.

"Edward," Monica said, "back there in the restaurant you said you thought the killer would surrender quietly, with relief. Why relief?"

"I think she's getting tired," Delaney said, and explained to his wife why he believed that. "Also, Dr. Ho thinks that emotional stress could be triggering an Addisonian crisis. It all ties in: a sick woman coming to the end of her rope."

"Then you believe she *is* sick?"

"Physically, not mentally. She knows the difference between right and wrong. But the laws regarding insanity and culpability are so screwed-up that it's impossible to predict how a judge or jury might decide. They could say she's usually sane but killed in moments of overwhelming madness. Temporary insanity. It's really not important. Well, it is important, but it's not the concern of cops. Our only job is to stop her."

"Good luck tomorrow morning," Monica said faintly. "Will you call me?"

He took her arm.

"If you want me to," he said.

Edward X. Delaney slept well that night. In the morning he was amused to find himself dressing with special care for the meeting at Midtown Precinct North.

"Like I was going to a wedding," he mentioned to Monica. "Or a funeral."

He wore a three-piece suit of navy blue tropical worsted, a white shirt with starched collar, a wide cravat of maroon rep. His wife tucked a foulard square into the breast pocket of his jacket, one flowered edge showing. Delaney poked the silk down the moment he was out of the house.

As many men as possible crowded into the conference room upstairs at Midtown Precinct North. Lieutenant Crane, Sergeant Broderick, Boone, Bentley, Delaney, and Thorsen got the chairs. The others stood against the walls. Men milled about in the corridor outside, waiting for news. Good or bad.

"Okay, Tom," Sergeant Boone said to Broderick, "it's all yours."

"What I got here first," the detective sergeant said, "is an alphabetical list of female victims of Addison's living in Manhattan. Sixteen names."

"Right," Lieutenant Wilson T. Crane said, shuffling through the stack of typed lists in front of him. "What I have is a list of females who work or reside in Manhattan and who, one way or another, have access to a schedule of hotel conventions. Let's go . . ."

"First name," Broderick said, "is Alzanas. A-l-z-a-n-a-s. Marie. That's Marie Alzanas."

Lieutenant Crane pored over his list, flipped a page.

"No," he said, "haven't got her. Next?"

"Carson, Elizabeth J. That's C-a-r-s-o-n."

"Carson, Carson, Carson . . . I've got a Muriel Carson."

"No good. This one is Elizabeth J. Next name is Domani, Doris. That's D-o-m-a-n-i."

"No, no Domani."

"Edwards, Marilyn B. E-d-w-a-r-d-s."

"No Marilyn B. Edwards."

The roll call of names continued slowly. The other men in the room were silent. The men in the hallway had quieted. They could hear noises from downstairs, the occasional sound of a siren starting up. But their part of the building seemed hushed, waiting . . .

"Jackson," Sergeant Broderick intoned. "Grace T. Jackson. J-a-c-k-s-o-n."

"No Grace T. Jackson," Lieutenant Crane said. "Next?"

"Kohler. K-o-h-l-e-r. First name Zoe. Z-o-e. That's Zoe Kohler."

Crane's finger ran down the page. Stopped. He looked up.

"Got her," he said. "Zoe Kohler."

A sigh like a wind in the room. Men slumped, expressionless. They lighted cigarettes.

"All right," Sergeant Boone said, "finish the list. There may be more than one."

They waited quietly, patiently, while Sergeant Broderick completed his list of names. Zoe Kohler was the only name duplicated on Crane's convention schedule access list.

"Zoe Kohler," Delaney said. "Where did you find her, Broderick?"

"She bought a medical ID bracelet for Addison's disease and an emergency kit at a pharmacy on Twenty-third Street."

"Crane?" the Chief asked.

"We've got her listed at the Hotel Granger on Madison and Forty-sixth Street. Access to the hotel trade magazine that publishes the convention schedule every week."

They stared at each other, looks going around the room, no one wanting to speak.

"Sergeant," Delaney said to Abner Boone, "is Johnson down at Midtown South?"

"If he's not there, one of his guys will be. The phone is manned."

"Give him a call. Ask if the Hotel Granger, Madison and Forty-sixth, is on the list of tear gas customers."

They all listened as Boone made the call. He asked the man at the other end to check the list for the Hotel Granger. He heard the reply, grunted his thanks, hung up. He looked around at the waiting men.

"Bingo," he said softly. "The security chief at the Granger bought the stuff. Four pocket-size spray dispensers and three grenades."

Sergeant Broderick pushed his chair back with a clatter.

"Let's pick her up," he said loudly.

Delaney whirled on him furiously.

"What are you going to do?" he demanded. "Beat a confession out of her with a rubber hose? What kind of a garbage arrest would that be? She's got Addison's disease, she reads a hotel trade magazine, and the place where she works bought some tear gas. Take that to the DA and he'll throw your ass out the window."

"What do you suggest, Edward?" Thorsen asked.

"Button her up. At least two men on her around the clock. Better include a policewoman in the tail, in case she goes into a john. Put an undercover man where she works. Broderick, where does she live?"

The sergeant consulted his file.

"Thirty-ninth Street, east. The address sounds like it would be near Lex."

"Probably an apartment house. If it is, get an under-cover man in there as a porter or something. Find a friendly judge and get a phone tap authorization. Around the clock. I mean, know exactly where she is every minute of the day and night. Where she goes. Who her friends are. It'll give us time to do more digging."

"Like what, Chief?" Boone said.

"A lot of things. How did she get hold of the tear gas, for instance. Get a photo of her with a long-distance lens and show it to that waiter at the Tribunal and to the cocktail waitress out on the Coast."

"I've got her doctor's name and address," Sergeant Broderick offered.

"It's a possibility," Delaney said. "He probably won't talk, but it's worth a try. The important thing is to keep this woman covered until she proves out, one way or the other. Meanwhile, Broderick, I suggest you check the rest of your lists against Lieutenant Crane's. There may be more duplications."

Deputy Thorsen, Delaney, and Boone left the con-ference room and went into the sergeant's office. The men in the corridor had heard the news and were talking excitedly.

"Sergeant," the Chief said, "you're going to have your hands full keeping a lid on this. If Zoe Kohler's name gets to reporters, and they print it, we're finished. She'll go back into the woodwork."

"Wait a minute, Edward," Thorsen said. "What are you figuring—that she'll try another kill, and we catch her at it?"

"It may come to that," Delaney said grimly. "I hope not, but it may turn out to be the only way we can make a case. She's due again late this month."

"Jesus," Sergeant Boone breathed, "that's a dangerous way to make a case. If we fuck it up, we'll have another stiff on our hands and we'll all be out on the street."

"It may be the only way," Delaney insisted stubbornly. "I don't like it any more than you do, but we may have to let her try. Meanwhile, make sure your men keep their mouths shut."

"Yeah," Boone said, "I better give them the word right now."

"And while you're at it," the Chief said, "call Johnson again. Tell him not to send a man to check out that tear gas at the Hotel Granger until we figure out how to handle it and give him the word."

"Right," Boone said. "I'll take care of it."

He left the office.

"Edward," Thorsen said nervously, "are you serious about letting that woman try another killing?"

"Ivar," Delaney said patiently, "it may turn out to be the only way we can step on her. You better be prepared for it. Right now, at this moment, we haven't got enough for a clean arrest, let alone an indictment. Believe me, nothing makes a stronger case than 'caught in the act.'"

"If we catch her in time," the Deputy said mournfully.

Delaney shrugged. "Sometimes you have to take the risk. But it may not come to that. We've got two weeks before she hits again. If she follows the pattern, that is. We can do a lot in two weeks. With the round-the-clock tail and the phone tap, we may be able to make a case before she tries again."

"We've *got* to," Thorsen said desperately.

"Sure," Delaney said.

July 13; Sunday . . .

She was weary of gnarled thoughts and knotted dreams. There came a time when only surrender seemed feasible. Peace at any price.

She could endure no more. Those attractive, smartly dressed, *happy* women she saw on the streets . . . The men who whispered dreadful things or just glanced at her derisively . . . It was a city of enemies, a foreign place. Sickened by her own substance, she wanted to be gone.

"You look so solemn," Ernest Mittle said. "I feel so good, and you look so sad."

"Do I?" she said, squeezing his hand. "I'm sorry. Just thinking."

"When you called me the other night, you sounded so *down.* Is something wrong, darling?"

"Not a thing," she said brightly. "I'm just fine. Where are we going?"

"It's a secret," he said. "Do you like secrets?"

"I love secrets," she said.

He had met her in the lobby of her apartment house. She saw at once that he was jangling with nervous excitement, almost dancing with eagerness. And he was dressed in his best summer suit, a light blue, pin-striped seersucker. He wore a dark blue polka-dotted bowtie and, in his buttonhole, a small cornflower.

He insisted on taking a taxi, showing the driver an address scrawled on a slip of paper. In the back seat of the cab, he held her hand and chattered about the weather, his job, the plans he was making for their vacation together.

The cab headed downtown and then across Manhattan Bridge. Laughing delightedly, Ernie confessed that they were going for Sunday brunch at a restaurant built on a barge moored on the Brooklyn waterfront.

"The food is supposed to be good," he said, "and the view of the Manhattan skyline is fantastic. Okay?"

"Of course," she said. "I just hope it isn't too expensive."

"Oh well," he said, bowing his head, "it's sort of, uh, you know, an occasion."

They weren't able to get a window table in the restaurant, but from where they sat they had a good view of the East River, the sweep of the Brooklyn Bridge and, in the background, the swords of Manhattan slashing the pellucid sky.

They had Bloody Marys to start, and then scrambled eggs with ham steaks, toasted English muffins with guava marmalade, and a small green salad. Black coffee and raspberry sherbet for dessert.

The food was good, and the service efficient but too swift; they were finished and handed their check in less than an hour. On their way out, they passed a growing crowd of customers waiting hopefully behind a chain.

"A popular place," Ernie said when they were outside. "Well, the food is all right, and the prices are reasonable. First time I've ever eaten on a boat."

"It's different," Zoe said, "and I enjoyed it. Thank you, dear."

The restaurant had set up a number of park benches

facing the Manhattan shore. Zoe and Ernie sat on the bench closest to the water. They watched a red tugboat push a string of barges upriver against the current.

The sun was bright and hot, but a salt-tanged breeze washed the air. A few small clouds, scoops of vanilla ice cream, drifted lazily. Smoke-colored gulls perched atop wharf pilings, preening their feathers.

And there in the distance, shimmering, were the golden spires of Manhattan. They gave back the sun in a million gleams. The city burned, prancing, a painted backdrop for a giant theater, a cosmic play.

"Oh, Zoe," Ernest Mittle breathed, "isn't it lovely?"

"Yes," she said, but she lowered her eyes. She didn't want to admit that the city could have beauty and grace.

He turned on the bench so he could face her. He took both her hands between his. She raised her eyes to look at him. His vivacity had vanished. Now he seemed solemn, almost grave.

"Uh," he said in a low voice, "there's something I want to talk to you about."

"What is it, dear?" she said anxiously. "Is something the matter? Is it something I did?"

"Oh no, no," he protested. "No, nothing's the matter. Uh, darling, I've been thinking about you a lot. Every minute. I mean, at work and walking down the street and when I'm home alone and before I go to sleep. I think about you all the time. And, uh, well, I've decided I want to be with you all the time. Forever." He finished with a rush: "Because I love you so much, and I want to marry you, Zoe. Darling . . . Please?"

She looked into his eyes and blinked to keep from weeping.

"Oh, Ernie—" she started.

"Listen a minute," he said hoarsely. He released her hands, swung back to face the river, hunched over on the bench. "I know I'm not so much. I mean, I have a good job and all, and I'm not afraid of hard work, and I think I'll do better. But I'm not much to look at, I know—not exactly every woman's dream. But I do love you, Zoe. More than I've ever loved anyone or anything, and I want to spend the rest of my life with you. I've thought this over very carefully, and I'm sure this is what I want to do.

You're in my mind all the time, and I love you so much that sometimes it almost hurts, and I feel like crying. I know that's silly, but that's the way I feel."

"Oh, Ernie," she said again. She took him by the shoulders, turned him to her. She hugged him close, his face pressed into her neck. She held him tightly, stroking his fine, flaxen hair. She moved him away, saw tears in his eyes.

She kissed his soft lips tenderly and put her palm to his cheek.

"Thank you, darling," she said. "Thank you, thank you, thank you. You don't know how much that means to me, knowing how much you care. It's the nicest, sweetest thing that's ever happened to me, and I'm so proud."

"We could make a go of it, Zoe," he pleaded. "Really we could. We'd have to work at it, of course, but I know we could do it. When I finish my computer course, I'll get a better job. And I have some money in the bank. Not a lot, but *some*. So we wouldn't starve or anything like that. And you could move into my place. For the time being, I mean, until we can find a bigger place. And I have—"

"Shh, shh," she whispered, putting a finger on his lips. "Let me catch my breath for a minute. It isn't every day a girl . . ."

They sat immobile. She held his face between her palms and stared into his brimming eyes.

"You love me that much, darling?" she said in a low voice.

"I do, I do!" he declared. "I'd do anything for you, Zoe, I swear it. Except leave you. Don't ask me to do that."

"No," she said, smiling sadly. "I won't ask you to do that."

"There's no one else, is there?" he asked anxiously.

"Oh no. There's no one else."

"Zoe, I can understand that you might feel . . . Well, you know, having been married once and it didn't work out, you might feel, uh, very careful before you marry again. But I'd try very hard, darling, really I would. As hard as I can to be a good husband and make you happy."

"I know you would, Ernie. You're a dear, sweet man, and I love you."

"Then . . . ?"

"Oh, darling, I can't answer right now, this minute. I'm in a whirl. You'll have to give me time to think about—"

"Of course," he said hastily, "I understand. I didn't expect to sweep you off your feet or anything like that. But you will think about it, won't you?"

"Oh sweetheart, of course I will."

"Well . . ." he said, giggling nervously, "just to keep reminding you, I bought you this . . ."

He fumbled in the side pocket of his jacket, brought out a little velvet-covered ring box. He opened it.

"World's smallest diamond," he said, laughing. "But it's pretty, isn't it, Zoe? Isn't it pretty?"

"It's beautiful," she said, looking down at the twinkling stone set in a silver band. "Just beautiful."

"Try it on," he urged. "I didn't know your size, so it may be too tight or too large. But the man said it can be adjusted or even exchanged for a different size."

She slipped the ring onto her bony finger. It hung loosely.

"Too large," she said regretfully. She took off the ring and placed it carefully back into the box.

"It can be fixed," he assured her. "Zoe, your fingers are so thin. And what's this brown stain here?"

"I burned myself," she said swiftly. "On a hot pan. It'll clear up."

"Better see about it. Does it hurt?"

"Oh no. It's nothing. It'll go away."

She tried to return the ring box to him, but he wouldn't take it.

"You keep it, dear," he said. "Put it someplace where you'll see it every day and think about what I asked you. Will you do that, Zoe?"

"I don't need the ring to remind me," she said, smiling. "Oh, Ernie, it was so kind of you. And the ring is lovely. It truly is."

"You like it? Really?"

"It's the most beautiful ring in the world, and you're the most beautiful man."

"Say Yes, darling. Think it over, remember how much I love you, and say Yes."

That night, alone in her apartment, Zoe Kohler put the

ring on her finger again, making a fist so it wouldn't slip
off. Staring down at that shining circlet, she became
aware of happiness as a conscious choice, hers for the
taking.

She would call Dr. Stark and agree to enter a hospital.
She would do whatever was necessary, endure any mor-
tification to regain her health. She would throw out all her
unnecessary pills and capsules. She would stop drinking,
eat only good, nutritious food.

She would fill out, and her skin would become smooth
and pure. She would make her body beautiful, slender
and willowy. Her breath would be sweet and her monthly
cramps would vanish as she grew content.

She would end her adventures because there would no
longer be a need for them. The police would grow tired of
the search, and the Hotel Ripper would fade from the
headlines. In a few weeks or months the whole thing
would be forgotten.

She would marry Ernest Mittle. Yes, and send an
announcement to her ex-husband! Ernie would move in
with her because her apartment was larger. She would
keep her job at the Hotel Granger until Ernie was
launched on a successful career in computers.

They would take turns cooking, and hurry home each
night just to be together and talk to each other. They
would go on wonderful vacations together, walk deserted
beaches and swim in an endless sea.

They would make love gently, tenderly, and find bliss.
Then they would sleep in each other's arms and wake to
make love again, with smiles. They would find joy in each
other's body, in their shared passion. They would not do
anything ugly.

Their closeness would keep the brutal city at bay,
would defend against the world's cruelty. *They* would be
the world, a world of two, and nothing would daunt or
defeat them.

Then they would have a child. Perhaps two. They
would create a family of their own. With their clean,
bright children, they would defy the darkness.

She replaced the ring in its box and hid it far back in the
bureau drawer, next to the WHY NOT? bracelet. She went
to sleep smiling, still living her dream.

It all seemed possible.

July 15–18; Tuesday to Friday . . .

Detective Daniel ("Dapper Dan") Bentley was given responsibility for the physical surveillance of Zoe Kohler. He used three crews, each on duty for eight hours. Each team consisted of two male and one female police officers.

Most of their time was spent in an unmarked police vehicle parked outside the subject's apartment house on East 39th Street or the Hotel Granger on Madison Avenue. The car was changed every day in an effort to prevent easy recognition by the suspect.

When Zoe Kohler walked to work, went to lunch, or just went shopping or on an innocent errand, one of the surveillance team tailed her on foot, keeping in touch with the stakeout car by walkie-talkie.

In addition to this close physical watch, a court order for a wiretap was obtained. With the cooperation of the owner of Zoe's apartment house, a tap and tape recorder were installed in the basement, hooked up to her telephone terminal. Two-man crews were on duty around the clock.

Gradually, a description of the subject and a time-habit pattern were assembled in the command post at Midtown Precinct North. The existence of Ernest Mittle and Madeline Kurnitz was established by phone call traces, and investigation begun of their relationship with the suspect.

Also, by means of a collect call made by the subject, the names and address of her parents were obtained. Following Zoe when she visited her bank resulted in an examination of her bank account and credit rating.

Slowly, the profile of the subject was filled in, with a complete physical description, personal history, her present job, employment record, friends, habits, etc. None of this, of course, added to or subtracted from her validity as a suspect, but it did give substance to the woman. In Midtown North, they began to speak familiarly of her as "Zoe." A friend of the family.

Photographs were taken from the surveillance car by a police photographer using a telephoto lens. Blowups of the best pictures were flown to the Coast by a New York detective and shown to Anne Rogovich, the former cocktail waitress. The result was negative; she could not identify the suspect as the woman she had seen with the late Jerome Ashley.

The same disappointment resulted when the photos were shown to Anthony Pizzi, the waiter at the Tribunal Motor Inn. So Mr. Pizzi was installed in the surveillance car and given an actual look at the subject. He still could not provide positive identification.

But not all inquiries were fruitless . . .

A long, involved discussion was held on how best to determine the disposition of tear gas purchased by Everett Pinckney, security chief of the Hotel Granger.

"The problem here," Delaney said, "is that if he gave her a can of the stuff, or she pinched it, then questions about it are sure to spook her. If she still has the can—maybe it's half-full—she's sure to dump it. And if she's already gotten rid of it, the questions will give her a chance to frame a story."

"Maybe we can tell this Pinckney to keep his trap shut," Sergeant Boone said.

"You can tell him," the Chief said, "but don't take it to the bank." He thought a moment, then: "Look, let's handle this in a conventional way. Just go in, verify the purchase with Pinckney, and say we'll be back in a week or so for a physical count of the containers he bought. Treat it very casually. If he mentions it to her, it may scare her into doing something foolish. Johnson, can you handle it?"

"I'll do it personally," the detective said. "No sweat. I want to get a look at the lady anyway."

So Detective Aaron Johnson visited Security Chief Everett Pinckney at the Hotel Granger. His cover story was that he was investigating a wholesale burglary of Chemical Mace and was tracing the serial numbers of every can sold in the New York area.

"The good news," he reported later, "is that this Pinckney admits the purchase, and says he handed out the spray dispensers to his assistants, including Zoe. He's got the grenades right there in his office and says he'll collect the spray cans from the others for examination. The bad news is that I didn't get to see her; she was out to lunch or some such."

That, at least, proved Zoe's access to a can of tear gas. It was a plus but, as Sergeant Boone said, "a little bitty plus."

More important was the result of a search of Zoe Kohler's apartment, a completely illegal enterprise. It was planned at a meeting attended only by Delaney, Boone, and Detective Bentley. Deputy Commissioner Ivar Thorsen was deliberately not informed of the plan; the Chief wanted to shield him from guilty knowledge.

"We can get a man in there easy," Abner Boone explained to Bentley. "The owner will go along. Our guy will be a maintenance man, porter, repairman, or whatever—in case any of the tenants spot him and ask questions. He'll go in when she's at work; we'll verify that with the tails."

"The problem," Delaney said, "is that he'll have to pick the lock. We don't want to ask the owner for a passkey. The fewer people who know about this, the better. Also, we need a fast guy, someone who'll get in, toss the place, and be out in, say, an hour or less."

"Got just the guy," Bentley said promptly. "Ramon Gonzales, a PR. Naturally, we call him 'Speedy.' He's a fast man on locks and he'll be in and out of there so quick and so slick no one will notice a thing. What does he look for?"

"A spray dispenser of tear gas," Boone said. "A pocket knife, or jackknife, switchblade—anything like that. Also, a gold link bracelet with the words WHY NOT? on it. And clothes, flashy clothes. A dark green dress with skinny straps. High-heeled shoes. She wore those to the Ashley kill. And a white turtleneck sweater and a denim thing with shoulder straps. The stuff she was wearing when she wasted the LaBranche boy. Anything else, Chief?"

"Yes," Delaney said. "Tell him to look for nylon wigs. Black and strawberry blond. Tell this Speedy Gonzales to wear gloves and to touch as little as possible, move things as little as possible. And don't, for God's sake, bring anything out with him. Leave everything exactly where it is."

"She'll never know she had a visitor," Bentley assured them.

Two days later, he was back with a report. He

consulted a notebook, flipping the pages as he talked . . .

"No problems," he said. "Speedy didn't see anyone except the guy on the lobby desk who talked a minute or two but didn't ask any questions. The owner had told him to expect a guy who was going to make an estimate on cleaning the hallway rugs. Speedy got into Zoe's apartment with no trouble. He says the locks were a joke. He was inside less than an hour, gave the place a complete toss. He found that WHY NOT? bracelet and the dark green dress with thin shoulder straps. Her clothes are mostly plain and dull, but the fancy stuff is hidden in the back of a closet. A lot of hooker's dresses there, Speedy says. He didn't find any knife or can of tear gas."

"The wigs?" Delaney asked.

"Oh yeah. Black and blond. Both nylon. In the same closet with the whore's duds. High-heeled shoes in there, too. And in a dresser drawer, way in the back, black lace underwear and fancy shit like that."

"Did he say anything about what the apartment was like?" the Chief said.

"Very neat," Bentley reported. "Very clean. Spotless."

"That figures," Delaney said.

Late on Friday afternoon, July 18th, the Chief met with Deputy Commissioner Thorsen at a back table in a seedy tavern on Eighth Avenue. There were only a few solitary drinkers at the bar. The waitress, wearing a leotard and black net hose, brought their Scotch-and-waters and left them alone.

"How's it going, Edward?" Thorsen asked.

Delaney flipped a palm back and forth. "Some good, some bad," he said.

"But is it *her?*" the Deputy said.

"No doubt about that. It's her, all right."

"But you still don't want to pick her up?"

"Not yet."

"We've got about a week, Edward. Then she's due to hit again."

"I'm aware of that, Ivar."

The Admiral sat back, sighing. He lifted his glass around on the Formica tabletop, making damp interlocking circles.

"You're a hard man, Edward."

"Not so hard," Delaney said. "I'm just trying to make a case for you."

"Since when has any case been airtight?"

"I didn't say an airtight case. Just a strong case that has a chance in the courts."

Thorsen stared at him reflectively.

"Sometimes I think you and I are—well, maybe not on opposing sides, but we see this thing from different viewpoints. All I want to do is stop these killings. And you—"

"That's all I want," Delaney said stolidly.

"No, that's not all you want. You want to squash the woman."

"And what do you want—to let her walk away whistling? That's exactly what will happen if we pull her in now."

"Look," Thorsen said, "let's get our priorities straight. You're convinced she's the killer?"

"Yes."

"All right, now suppose we pull her in, even charge her, and eventually she walks. But she's not going to kill again, is she? She's going to behave, knowing we'll keep an eye on her. So the killings will end, won't they? Even if she walks?"

"And what about George Puller, Frederick Wolheim, Jerome Ashley, and all the rest? Just tough titty for them—right?"

"Edward, our main job is crime prevention. And if pulling her in now can prevent a crime, then I say let's do it."

"Prevention is only part of the job. Another part is crime detection and punishment."

"Let's have another drink," Ivar Thorsen said, signaling the waitress and pointing at their empty glasses.

They were silent while they were being served. Then Thorsen tried again . . .

"On the basis of what we know now," he said, "we can probably get search warrants for her apartment and office. Agreed?"

"Probably. But unless you find the weapon used, with her prints on it and stains of blood from her last kill, what have you got?"

"Maybe we'll find that WHY NOT? bracelet."

"Hundreds of them were sold. Probably thousands. It would mean nothing."

"The tear gas container?"

"Even if we find it, there's no proof it was the one used on Bergdorfer. Ditto the clothes she wore. And the wigs. Ivar, that's all the sleaziest kind of circumstantial evidence. A good defense attorney would make mincemeat of a prosecution based on that."

"She's got Addison's disease."

"So have fifteen other women living in Manhattan. I know you think we've got a lot on her. We have. Enough to convince me that she's the Hotel Ripper. But it's been a long time since you've testified in court. You've forgotten that there's a fucking big gap between knowing and proving. We have enough to know we have the right perp, but we have shit-all when it comes to proving. I tell you frankly that I don't think the DA will go for an indictment on the basis of what we've got. He's looking for good arrests and convictions. Like everyone else, he's not particularly enamored of lost causes."

"I still say we have enough to bring her in for questioning. Even if we don't find anything new in her apartment or office, we can throw the fear of God into her. She won't slit any more throats."

"You're sure of that? Positive? That she won't leave the city, move somewhere else, change her name, and take up her hobby again?"

"That's some other city's problem."

Delaney grunted. "Ivar, you're all heart."

"You know what I mean. I volunteered for this job because I figured if anyone could find the Hotel Ripper, you could. All right, you've done it, and I want you to know how much I appreciate what you've done. But the whole point of the thing was to bring this series of homicides to an end. It seems to me that we can do that now by picking her up and telling her what we know. Trial and conviction are secondary to stopping her."

"Then it's bye-bye, birdie," Delaney said. "That's not right."

Ivar Thorsen slapped his palms on the table.

"No wonder they called you 'Iron Balls,'" he said.

"You've got to be the most stubborn, opinionated man I've ever met. You just won't give."

"I know what's right," Delaney said woodenly.

The Admiral took a deep breath.

"I'll give you another week," he said. "That's, uh, Friday the twenty-fifth. If we have nothing more on her by then, I'm bringing her in anyhow. I just can't take the risk of letting her try another slashing."

"Shit," Delaney said.

He strode home through the sultry twilight. He went through Central Park, trying to walk off his anger. Intellectually, he could understand the reasoning behind Ivar Thorsen's decision. But that didn't make it any better. It was all political.

"Political." What a shifty word! Political was everything weak, sly, expedient, and unctuous. Political was doing the right things for the wrong reasons, and the wrong things for the right reasons.

Ivar had his career and the Department's reputation to think about. In that connotation, he was doing the "right" thing, the political thing. But he was also letting a murderess stroll away from her crimes; that was what it amounted to.

Delaney planned how they could smash her. It would be an audacious scheme, but with foresight and a bit of luck, they could pull it off.

Not letting her out on the prowl to pick up some innocent slob, going with him to his hotel room, and then ripping his throat. With the cops tailing her and breaking in at the last minute to catch her with the knife in her hand and the victim-to-be still alive. That would never work.

It would have to be a carefully plotted scam, using a police decoy. The guy selected would have to be a real cowboy, with quick reflexes and the balls to see it through. He'd have charm, be physically presentable, and have enough acting ability to play the role of an out-of-town salesman or convention-goer.

He would have a room in a midtown hotel, and they would wire it like a computer, with mikes, a two-way mirror, and maybe a TV tape camera filming the whole thing. A squad of hard guys in the adjoining room, of course, ready to come on like Gangbusters.

She'd be tailed to the hotel she selected and the cowboy would be alerted. He'd make the pickup or let her pick him up. Then he'd take her back to his hotel room. The pickup would be the dicey part. Once the cowboy made the meet, the rest should go like silk.

It would be important that even the appearance of entrapment be avoided, but that could be worked out. With luck they'd be able to grab her in the act, with her trusty little jackknife open and ready. Let her try to walk away from that!

Delaney admitted it was a chancy gamble, but God-damnit, it *could* work. And it would cut through all the legal bullshit, all the court arguments about the admissibility of circumstantial evidence. It would be irrefutable proof that Zoe Kohler was a bloody killer.

But the politicians said No, don't take the risk, all we want to do is stop her, and start booking conventions again, and if she walks, that's too bad, but we stopped her, didn't we?

Edward X. Delaney made a grimace of disgust. The law was the law, and murder was wrong, and every time you weaseled, you weakened the whole body of the law, the good book it had taken so many centuries to write.

By God, if he was on active duty and in command, he would smash her! If the cowboy didn't succeed, then Delaney would try something else. She might kill again, and again, but in the end he'd hang her by the heels, and the best defense attorney in the world couldn't prevent those words: "Guilty as charged."

By the time he arrived home, he was sodden with sweat, his face reddened, and he was puffing with exhaustion.

"What happened to you?" Monica asked curiously. "You look like you've been wrestling with the devil."

"Something like that," he said.

July 22; Tuesday . . .

She did not wake pure and whole—and knew she never would. The abdominal pains were constant now, almost as severe as menstrual cramps. Weakness buckled her knees; she frequently felt giddy and feared she might faint on the street.

She continued to lose weight; her flesh deflated over her joints; she seemed all knobs and edges. The discolored blotches grew; she watched with dulled horror as whole patches of skin took on a grayish-brown hue.

Everything was wrong. She felt nausea, and vomited. She suddenly had a craving for salt and began taking three, four, then five tablets a day. She tried to eat only bland foods, but was afflicted first with constipation, then with diarrhea.

Her dream of happiness, on the night following Ernest Mittle's proposal of marriage, had vanished. Now she said aloud: "I am sick and tired of being sick and tired."

When Madeline Kurnitz called to ask her to lunch, Zoe tried to beg off, not certain she had the strength and fearful of what Maddie might say about her appearance.

But the other woman insisted, even agreeing to lunch in the dining room of the Hotel Granger.

"I want you to meet someone," Maddie said, giggling.

"Who?"

"You'll see!"

Zoe reserved a table for three and was already seated when Maddie arrived. With her was a tall, stalwart youth who couldn't have been more than twenty-two or twenty-three. Maddie was hanging on to his arm possessively, looking up at his face, and whispering something that made him laugh.

She hardly glanced at Zoe. Just said, "Christ, you're skinny," and then introduced her escort.

"Kiddo, this stud is Jack. Keep your hands off; I saw him first. Jack, this is Zoe, my best friend. My only friend. Say, 'Hello, Zoe, how are you?' You can manage that, can't you?"

"Hello, Zoe," Jack said with a flash of white teeth, "how are you?"

"See?" Maddie said. "He can handle a simple sentence. Jack isn't so great in the brains department, luv, but with what he's got, who needs brains? Hey, hey, how's about a little drink? My first today."

"Your first in the last fifteen minutes," Jack said.

"Isn't he cute?" Maddie said, stroking the boy's cheek. "I'm teaching him to sit up and beg."

It was the other way around; Zoe was shocked by *her* appearance. Maddie had put on more loose weight, and it bulged, unbraed and ungirdled, in a straining dress of red silk crepe, with a side seam gaping and stains down the front.

Her freckled cleavage was on prominent display, and she wore no hose. Her feet, in the skimpiest of strap sandals, were soiled with street dirt. Her legs had been carelessly shaved; a swath of black fuzz ran down one calf.

It was her face that showed most clearly her loss: clown makeup wildly applied, powder caked in smut lines on her neck, a false eyelash hanging loose, lipstick streaked and crooked.

There she sat, a blob of a woman, all appetite. It seemed to Zoe that her voice had become louder and screakier. She shouted for drinks, yelled for menus, laughing in high-pitched whinnies.

Zoe hung her head as other diners turned to stare. But Maddie was impervious to their disapproval. She held hands with Jack, popped shrimp into his mouth, pinched his cheek. One of her hands was busy beneath the tablecloth.

". . . so Harry moved out," Maddie chattered on, "and Jack moved in. A beautiful exchange. Now the lawyers are fighting it out. Jack, baby, you have a steak; you've got to keep up your strength, you stallion, you!"

He sat there with a vacant grin, enjoying her ministrations, accepting them as his due. His golden hair was coiffed in artful waves. His complexion was a bronzed tan, lips sculpted, nose straight and patrician. A profile that belonged on a coin.

"Isn't he precious?" Maddie said fondly, staring at him with hungry eyes. "I found him parking cars at some roadhouse on Long Island. I got him cleaned up, properly barbered and dressed, and look at him now. A treasure! Maddie's own sweet treasure."

She was, Zoe realized, quite drunk, for in addition to her usual ebullience, there was something else: almost an hysteria. Plus a note of nasty cruelty when she spoke of the young man as if he were a curious object.

Either he did not comprehend her malicious gibes or chose to ignore them. He said little, grinned continuously, and ate steadily. He poked food into an already full mouth and masticated slowly with heavy movements of his powerful jaw.

"We're off for Bermuda," Maddie said, "or is it the Bahamas? I'm always getting the two of them fucked up. Anyway, we're going to do the tropical paradise bit for a month, drink rum out of coconut shells, and skinny-dip in the moonlight. How does that scenario grab you, kiddo? What does a thirsty gal have to do to get another drink in this dump?"

She ate very little, Zoe noted, but she drank at a frantic rate, gulping, wiping her mouth with the back of her hand when liquid trickled down her chin. But never once did she let go of Jack. She hung on to his arm, shoulder, thigh.

Zoe, remembering the brash bravado of a younger Maddie, was terrified by the woman's dissolution. Frightened not only for Maddie but at what it presaged for her own future.

For this woman, as a girl, had been the best of them. She was courageous and independent. She swaggered through life, dauntless and unafraid. She *lived,* and never feared tomorrow. She dared and she challenged, and never asked the price or counted the cost.

Now here she was, drunk, wild, feverish, her flesh puddled, holding on desperately to a handsome boy young enough to be her son. Behind the bright glitter of her mascaraed eyes grew a dark terror.

If this woman could be defeated, this brave, free, indefatigable woman, what hope in life was there for Zoe Kohler? She was so much weaker than Madeline Kurnitz. She was timid and fearful. She was *smaller.* When giants were toppled, what chance was there for midgets?

They finished their hectic meal and Maddie threw bills to the waiter.

"The son of a bitch cut off my credit cards," she muttered.

She rose unsteadily to her feet and Jack slid an arm about her thick waist. She tottered, staring glassily at Zoe.

"You changing jobs, kiddo?" she asked.

"No, Maddie. I haven't even been looking. Why do you ask?"

"Dunno. Some guy called me a few days ago, said you had applied for a job and gave me as a reference. Wanted to know how long I had known you, what I knew about your private life, and all that bullshit."

"I don't understand. I haven't applied for any job."

"Ah, the hell with it. Probably some weirdo. I'll call you when I get back from paradise."

"Take care of yourself, Maddie."

"Fuck that. Jack's going to take care of me. Aren't you, lover boy?"

She watched them stagger out, Jack half-supporting the porcine woman. Zoe walked slowly back to her office, dread seeping in as she realized the implications of what Maddie had said.

Someone was making inquiries about her, about her personal history and private life. She knew who it was—that stretched, dour man labeled "police," who would not give up the search and would not be content until Zoe Kohler was dead and gone.

She slumped at her desk, skeleton hands folded. She stared at those shrunken claws. They looked as if they had been soaked in brine. She thought of her approaching menstrual period and wondered dully if blood could flow from such a desiccated corpus.

"Hello there!" Everett Pinckney said brightly, weaving before her desk. "Have a good lunch?"

"Very nice," Zoe said, trying to smile. "Is there something I can do for you, Mr. Pinckney?"

He beamed at her, making an obvious effort to focus his eyes and concentrate on what he wanted to say. He leaned forward, knuckles propped on her desk. She could smell his whiskey-tainted breath.

"Yes," he said. "Well, uh . . . Zoe, remember that tear gas I gave you? The spray can? The little one for your purse?"

"I remember."

"Well, have you got it with you? In your purse? In your desk?"

She stared at him.

"Silly thing," he went on. "A detective was around. He's investigating a burglary and has to check the serial numbers of all the cans sold in New York. I asked McMillan and Joe Levine to bring theirs in. You still have yours, don't you? Didn't squirt anyone with it, did you?" He giggled.

"I don't have it with me, Mr. Pinckney," she said slowly.

"Oh. It's home, is it?"

"Yes," she said, thinking sluggishly. "I have it at home."

"Well, bring it in, will you, please? By Friday? The detective is coming back. Once he checks the number, you can have the can again. No problem."

He smiled glassily and tottered into his own office.

Stronger now, it returned: the sense of being moved and manipulated. Events had escaped her power. They were pressing her back into her natural role of victim. She had lost all initiative; she was being controlled.

She thought wildly of what she might do. Claim an attack by a would-be rapist whom she had repulsed with tear gas? Defended herself against a vicious dog? But she had already told Mr. Pinckney she had the dispenser at home.

Finally, she decided miserably, she could do nothing but tell him she had lost or misplaced the container.

Not for a moment did she believe the detective's claim of investigating a burglary. He was investigating *her,* and what would happen when he was told Zoe Kohler had "lost or misplaced" her dispenser, she didn't wish to imagine. It was all so depressing she could not even wonder how they had traced the tear gas to her.

That evening, when she returned to her apartment, she did something completely irrational. She searched her apartment for the tear gas container, knowing she had disposed of it. The worst thing was that she *knew* she was acting irrationally but could not stop herself.

Of course she did not find the dispenser. But she found something else. Or rather, several things . . .

When she had placed Ernest Mittle's engagement ring far in the back of the dresser drawer, she had paused a moment to open the box and take a final look at the pretty stone. Then she had shoved the box away, but remembered very well that it opened to the front.

When she found it, the box was turned around in its hiding place. Now the hinge was to the front, the box opened from the rear.

When she had put away her nylon wigs, wrapped in

tissue, the blond wig was on top, the black beneath. Now they were reversed.

The stacks of her pantyhose and lingerie had been disturbed. She always left them with their front edges neatly aligned. Now the piles showed they had been handled. They were not messy; they were neat. But not the way she had left them.

Perhaps someone less precise and finicky than Zoe Kohler would never have noticed. But she noticed, and was immediately convinced that someone had been in her apartment and had searched through her possessions.

She went at once to her front window. Drawing the drape cautiously aside, she peeked out. She did not see the white-shirted watcher in the shadows of the apartment across the street. She did not see him, but was certain he was there.

She made no connection between the voyeur and the search of her personal belongings. She knew only that her privacy was once again being cruelly violated; people wanted to know her secrets. They would keep trying, and there was no way she could stop them.

When Ernest Mittle called, she made a determined effort to sound cheerful and loving. They chatted for a long time, and she kept asking questions about his job, his computer classes, his vacation plans—anything to keep him talking and hold the darkness back.

"Zoe," he said finally, "I don't, uh, want to pressure you or anything, but have you been thinking about it?"

It took her a moment to realize what he meant.

"Of course, I've been thinking about it, darling," she said. "Every minute."

"Well, I meant every word I said to you. And now I'm surer than ever in my own mind. This is what I want to do. I just don't want to live without you, Zoe."

"Ernie, you're the sweetest and most considerate man I've ever met. You're *so* considerate."

"Yes . . . well . . . uh . . . when do you think you'll decide? Soon?"

"Oh yes. Soon. Very soon."

"Listen," he said eagerly, "I have classes Friday night. I get out about eight-thirty or so. How's about my picking up a bottle of white wine and dropping by? I mean, it'll be

Friday night and all, and we can talk and get squared away on our vacation. Okay?"

She didn't have the strength to object. Everyone was pushing her—even Ernie.

"Of course," she said dully. "Friday night?"

"About nine," he said happily. "See you then. Take care of yourself, dear."

"Yes," she said. "You, too."

He hung up and she sat there staring at the phone in her hand. Without questioning why, she called Dr. Oscar Stark. She got his answering service, of course. The operator asked if she'd care to leave a message.

"No," Zoe Kohler said, "no message."

She wandered into the kitchen. She opened the cabinet door. She stared at the rows and rows of pills, capsules, ampules, powders, medicines. They all seemed so foolish. Toys.

She closed the door without taking anything. Not even her cortisol. Not even a salt tablet. Nothing would make her a new woman. She was condemned to be her.

She thought vaguely that she should eat something, but just the idea of food roiled her stomach. She poured a glass of chilled vodka and took it into the living room.

She slouched on the couch, staring into the darkness. She tried to concentrate and feel the workings of her body. She felt only deep pain, a malaise that sapped her spirit and dulled her senses.

Was this the onset of death—this total surrender to the agony of living? Peace, peace. Something warm and comfortable. Something familiar and close. It seemed precious to her, this going over. The hurt ended . . .

She was conscious that she was weeping, surprised that her dried flesh could squeeze out that moisture. The warm, thin tears slid down her cheeks, and she did not wipe them away. She found a glory in this evidence of her miserableness.

"Poor Zoe Kohler," she said aloud, and the spoken words affected her so strongly that she gasped and sobbed.

What she could not understand, would never understand, was what she had done to deserve this wretchedness.

She had always dressed neatly and kept herself clean. She had never used dirty words. She had been polite and kind to everyone. Whom had she hurt? She had tried, always, to conduct herself like a lady.

There may have been a few times, very few, when she had forgotten herself, denied her nature, and acted in a crude and vulgar manner. But most of her life had been above reproach, spotless, obeying all the rules her mother had taught her.

She had moved through her days refined and gentle, low-voiced, and thoughtful of the feelings of others. She had worked hard to succeed as dutiful daughter and loving wife.

And it had all, *all,* come to this: sitting in the darkness and weeping. Smelling her body's rot. Hounded by unfeeling men who would not stop prying into things of no concern of theirs.

Poor Zoe Kohler. All hope gone, all passion spent. Only pain remained.

July 23–24; Wednesday and Thursday . . .

Delaney had to *see* her; he could not help himself.

"You can learn a lot about people by observing them," he explained to Monica. "How they walk, how they gesture. Do they rub their eyes or pick their nose? How they light a cigarette. Do they wait for a traffic light or run through traffic? Any nervous habits? How they dress. The colors and style. Do they constantly blink? Lick their lips? And so forth."

His wife listened to this recital in silence, head bowed, eyes on the mending in her lap.

"Well?" he demanded.

"Well what?"

"I just thought you might have a comment."

"No, I have no comment."

"Maybe it'll help me understand her better. Why she did what she did. Clues to her personality."

"Whatever you say, dear," she said.

He looked at her suspiciously. He didn't trust her complaisant moods.

He told Abner Boone what he wanted to do, and the sergeant had no objections.

"Better let Bentley know, Chief," he suggested. "He

can tell his spooks you'll be tailing her too. In case they spot you and call out the troops."

"They won't spot me," Delaney said, offended.

But he spotted *them:* the unmarked cars parked near the Hotel Granger and Zoe Kohler's apartment house, the plainclothes policewomen who followed the suspect on foot. Some of the shadows were good, some clumsy. But Zoe seemed oblivious to them all.

He picked her up on 39th Street and Lexington Avenue at 8:43 on Wednesday morning and followed her to the Granger. He hung around for a while, then wandered into the hotel and inspected the lobby, dining room, cocktail bar.

He was back at noon, and when she came out for lunch, he tailed her to a fast-food joint on Third Avenue, then back to the Granger. At five o'clock he returned to follow her home. He never took his eyes off her.

"What's she like?" Monica asked that night.

"So ordinary," he said, "she's outstanding. Miss Nothing."

"Pretty?"

"No, but not ugly. Plain. Just plain. She could do a lot more with herself than she does. She wears no makeup that I could see. Hair a kind of mousy color. Her clothes are browns and tans and grays. Earth colors. She moves very slowly, cautiously. Almost like an invalid, or at least like a woman twice her age. Once I saw her stop and hang on to a lamppost as if she suddenly felt weak or faint. Sensible shoes. Sensible clothes. Nothing bright or cheerful about her. She carries a shoulder bag but hangs on to it with both hands. I'd guess the knife is in the bag. When she confronts anyone on the sidewalk, she's always the first to step aside. She never crosses against the lights, even when there's no traffic. Very careful. Very conservative. Very law-abiding. When she went out to lunch, I thought I saw her talking to herself, but I'm not sure."

"Edward, how long are you going to keep this up—following her?"

"You think it's morbid curiosity, don't you?"

"Don't be silly."

"Sure you do," he said. "But it's not. The woman fascinates me; I admit it."

"That I believe," Monica said. "Does she look sad?"

"Sad?" He considered that a moment. "Not so much sad as defeated. Her posture is bad; she slumps; the sins of the world on her shoulders. And her complexion is awful. Muddy pale. I think I was right and Dr. Ho was right; she's cracking."

"I wish you wouldn't do it, Edward—follow her, I mean."

"Why not?"

"I don't know . . . It just seems indecent."

"You are a dear, sweet woman," he told her, "and you don't know what the hell you're talking about."

He went through the same routine on Thursday. He maneuvered so he walked toward her as she headed up Madison Avenue on her way to work. He passed quite close and got a good look at her features.

They seemed drawn and shrunken to him, nose sharpened, cheeks caved. Her lips were dry and slightly parted. The eyes seemed focused on worlds away. There was a somnolence about that face. She could have been a sleepwalker.

No breasts that he could see. She appeared flat as a board.

He was there a few minutes after 5:00 P.M., when she exited from the Hotel Granger and turned downtown on Madison. Delaney was behind her. Bentley's policewoman was across the avenue.

The suspect walked south on Madison, then went into a luncheonette. Delaney strolled to the corner, turned, came back. He stood in front of the restaurant, ostensibly inspecting the menu Scotch-taped inside the plate glass window.

Zoe Kohler was seated at the counter, waiting to be served. Everyone in the place was busy eating or talking. No one paid any attention to the activity on the street, to a big, lumpy man peering through the front window.

Delaney walked on, looked in a few shop windows, came back to the luncheonette. Now Zoe had a plate before her and was drinking a glass of something that looked like iced tea.

If he had been a man given to theatrical gestures, he would have slapped his forehead in disgust and dismay. He had forgotten. They all had forgotten. How could they have been so fucking *stupid*?

He loitered about the front of the luncheonette. He looked at his watch occasionally to give the impression of a man waiting for a late date. He saw Zoe Kohler pat her lips with a paper napkin, gather up purse and check, begin to rise.

He was inside immediately, almost rushing. As she moved toward the cashier's desk, he brushed by her.

"I beg your pardon," he said, raising his hat and stepping aside.

She gave him a shy, timorous smile: a flicker.

He let her go and slid onto the counter stool she had just left. In front of him was most of a tunafish salad plate and dregs of iced tea in a tall glass. He linked his hands around the glass without touching it.

A porky, middle-aged waitress with a mustache and bad feet stopped in front of him. She took out her pad.

"Waddle it be?" she asked, patting her orange hair. "The meat-loaf is good."

"I'd like to see the manager, please."

She peered at him. "What's wrong?"

"Nothing's wrong," he said, smiling at her. "I'd just like to see the manager."

She turned toward the back of the luncheonette.

"Hey, you, Stan," she yelled.

A man back there talking to two seated customers looked up. The waitress jerked her head toward Delaney. The manager came forward slowly. He stood at the Chief's shoulder.

"What seems to be the trouble?" he asked.

"No trouble," Delaney said. "This iced tea glass here— I've got a dozen at home just like it. But my kid broke one. I'd like to fill out the set. Would you sell me this glass for a buck?"

"You want to buy that glass for a dollar?" Stan said.

"That's right. To fill out my set of a dozen. How about it?"

"A pleasure," the manager said. "I've got six dozen more you can have at the same price."

"No," Delaney said, laughing, "just one will do."

"Let me get you a clean one," the porky waitress said, reaching for Zoe Kohler's glass.

"No, no," Delaney said hastily, protecting the glass with his linked hands. "This one will be fine."

Waitress and manager looked at each other and shrugged. Delaney handed over a dollar bill. Touching the glass gingerly with two fingers spread inside, he wrapped it loosely in paper napkins, taking care not to wipe or smudge the outside.

He had to walk two blocks before he found a sidewalk phone that worked. He set the wrapped glass carefully atop the phone and called Sergeant Abner Boone at Midtown Precinct North. He explained what he had.

"God *damn* it!" Boone exploded. "We're *idiots!* We could have had prints from her office or apartment a week ago."

"I know," Delaney said consolingly. "It's my fault as much as anyone's. Listen, sergeant, if you get a match with that wineglass from the Tribunal, it's not proof positive that she wasted the LaBranche kid. It's just evidence that she was at the scene."

"That's good enough for me," Boone said grimly. "Where are you, Chief? I'll get a car, pick up the glass myself, and take it to the lab."

Delaney gave him the location. "After they check it out, will you call me at home and let me know?"

"Of course."

"Better call Thorsen and tell him, too. Yes or no."

"I'll do that," Abner Boone said. "Thank you, sir," he added gratefully.

Delaney was grumpy all evening. He hunched over his plate, eating pork roast and applesauce in silence. Not even complimenting Monica on the bowl of sliced strawberries with a sprinkle of Cointreau to give it a tang.

It wasn't until they had taken their coffee into the air-conditioned living room that she said: "Okay, buster, what's bothering you?"

"Politics," he said disgustedly, and told her about his argument with Ivar Thorsen.

"He was right and I was right. Considering his priorities and responsibilities, picking the woman up and getting her out of circulation makes sense. But I still think going for prosecution and conviction makes more sense."

Then he told Monica what he had just done: obtaining Zoe Kohler's fingerprints for a match with the prints found on the wineglass at the Tribunal Motor Inn.

"So I handed Ivar more inconclusive evidence," he said wryly. "If the prints match, he's sure to pick her up. But he'll never get a conviction on the basis of what we've got."

"If you feel that strongly about it," Monica said, "you could have forgotten all about the prints."

"You're joking, of course."

"Of course."

"The habits of thirty years die hard," he said, sighing. "I had to get her prints. But no one will believe me when I tell them that even a perfect match won't put her behind bars. Her attorney will say, 'Sure, she had a drink with the guy in his hotel room—and so what? He was still alive when she left.' Those prints won't prove she slashed his throat. Just that she was there. And another thing is—"

The phone rang then.

"That'll be Boone," Delaney said, rising. "I'll take it in the study."

But it wasn't the sergeant; it was Deputy Commissioner Ivar Thorsen, and he couldn't keep the excitement out of his voice.

"Thank you, Edward," he said. "Thank you, thank you. We got a perfect match on the prints. I had a long talk with the DA's man and he thinks we've got enough now to go for an indictment. So we're bringing her in. It'll take all day tomorrow to get the paperwork set and plan the arrest. We'll probably take her Saturday morning at her apartment. Want to come along?"

Delaney paused. "All right, Ivar," he said finally. "If that's what you want to do. I'd like a favor: will you ask Dr. Patrick Ho if he wants to be in on it? That man contributed a lot; he should be in at the end."

"Yes, Edward, I'll contact him."

"One more thing . . . I'd like Thomas Handry to be there."

"Who's Thomas Handry?"

"He's on the *Times*."

"You want a *reporter* to be there?"

"I owe him."

Thorsen sighed. "All right, Edward, if you say so. And thank you again; you did a splendid job."

"Yeah," Delaney said dispiritedly, but Thorsen had already hung up.

He went back into the living room and repeated the phone conversation to Monica.

"So that's that," he concluded. "If she keeps her nerve and doesn't say a goddamn word until she gets a smart lawyer, I think she'll beat it."

"But the murders will end?"

"Yes. Probably."

She looked at him narrowly.

"But that's not enough for you, is it? You want her punished."

"Don't you?"

"Of course—if it can be done legally. But most of all I want the killings to stop. Edward, don't you think you're being vindictive?"

He rose suddenly. "Think I'll pour myself a brandy. Get you one?"

"All right. A small one."

He brought their cognacs from the study, then settled back again into his worn armchair.

"Why do you think I'm being vindictive?"

"Your whole attitude. You want to catch this woman in the act, even if it means risking a man's life. You want, above all, to see her punished for what she's done. You want her to suffer. It's really become an obsession with you. I don't think you'd feel that strongly if the Hotel Ripper was a man. Then you'd be satisfied just to get him off the streets."

"Come on, Monica, what kind of bullshit is that? The next thing you'll be saying is that I hate women."

"No, I'd never say that because I know it's not true. Just the opposite. I think you have some very old-fashioned, romantic ideas about women. And because this particular woman has flouted those beliefs, those cherished ideals, you feel very vengeful toward her."

He took a swig of brandy. "Nonsense. I've dealt with female criminals before. Some of them killers."

"But none like Zoe Kohler—right? All the female murderers in your experience killed from passion or greed or because they were drunk or something like that. Am I correct?"

"Well . . ." he said grudgingly, "maybe."

"You told me so yourself. But now you find a female killer who's intelligent, plans well, kills coldly with no apparent motive, and it shatters all your preconceptions about women. And not only does it destroy your romantic fancies, but I think it scares you—in a way."

He was silent.

"Because if a woman can act in this way, then you don't know anything at all about women. Isn't that what scares you? Now you've discovered that women are as capable as men. Capable of evil, in this case. But if that's true, then they must also be as capable of good, of creativity, of invention and art. It's upsetting all the prejudices you have and maybe even weren't aware of. Suddenly you have to revise your thinking about women, all your old, ingrained opinions, and that can be a painful process. I think that's why you want more than the killings ended. You want revenge against this woman who has caused such an upheaval in all your notions of what women are and how they should act."

"Thank you, doctor, for the fifty-cent analysis," he said. "I'm not saying you're completely wrong, but you *are* mistaken if you think I would have felt any differently if the Hotel Ripper was a man. You have to pay for your sins in this world, regardless of your sex."

"Edward, how long has it been since you've been to church."

"You mean for mass or confession? About thirty-five years."

"Well, you haven't lost your faith."

"The good sisters beat it into me. But my faith, as you call it, has nothing to do with the church."

"No?"

"No. I'm for civilization and against the swamp. It's as simple as that."

"And that is simple. You believe in God, don't you?"

"I believe in a Supreme Being, whatever you want to call him, her, or it."

"You probably call it the Top Cop."

He laughed. "You're not too far wrong. Well, the Top Cop has given us the word in a body of works called the law. Don't tell me how rickety, inefficient, and leaky the law is; I know better than you. But it's the best we've been able to come up with so far. Let's hope it'll be improved as the human race stumbles along. But even in the way it exists today, it's the only thing that stands between civilization and the swamp. It's a wall, a dike. And anyone who knocks a hole in the wall should be punished."

"And what about understanding? Compassion? Justice?"

"The law and justice are not always identical, my dear. Any street cop can tell you that. In this case, I think both the law and justice would be best served if Zoe Kohler was put away for the rest of her life."

"And if New York still had the death penalty, you'd want her electrocuted, or hanged, or gassed, or shot?"

"Yes."

July 25; Friday . . .

Her pubic hair had almost totally disappeared; only a few weak wisps survived. And the hair on her legs and in her armpits had apparently ceased to grow. She had the feeling of being *peeled,* to end up as a skinless grape, a quivering jelly. Clothing rasped her tender skin.

She took a cab to work that morning, not certain she had the strength to walk or push her way aboard a crowded bus. In the office, she was afraid she might drop the tray of coffee and pastries. Every movement was an effort, every breath a pain.

"Did you bring it in, Zoe?" Everett Pinckney asked.

She looked at him blankly. "What?"

"The tear gas dispenser," he said.

She felt a sudden anguish in her groin. A needle. She knew her period was due in a day, but this was something different: a steel sliver. But she did not wince. She endured, expressionless.

"I lost it," she said in a low voice. "Or misplaced it. I can't find it."

He was bewildered.

"Zoe," he said, "a thing like that—how could you lose it or misplace it?"

She didn't answer.

"What am I going to do?" he asked helplessly. "The cop will come back. He'll want to know. He'll want to talk to you."

"All right," she said, "I'll talk to him. I just don't have it."

He was not a man to bluster. He just stood, wavering . . .

"Well . . ." he said, "all right," and left her alone.

The rest of the day vanished. She didn't know where it went. She swam in agony, her body pulsing. She wanted to weep, cry out, claw her aching flesh from the bones. The world about her whirled dizzily. It would not stop.

She walked home slowly, her steps faltering. Passersby were a streaming blur. The earth sank beneath her feet. She heard a roaring above the traffic din, smelled scorch, and in her mouth was a taste of old copper.

She turned into the luncheonette, too weak to continue her journey.

"Hullo, dearie," the porky waitress said. "The usual?"

Zoe nodded.

"Wanna hear somepin nutty?" the waitress asked, setting a place for her. "Right after you was in here last night, a guy comes in and buys the iced tea glass you drank out of. Said he had glasses just like it at home, but his kid broke one, and he wanted to fill the set. Paid a dollar for it."

"The glass I used?"

"Crazy, huh? Din even want a clean one. Just wrapped up the dirty glass in paper napkins and rushed out with it. Well, it takes all kinds . . ."

"Was he tall and thin?" Zoe Kohler asked. "With a sour expression?"

"Nah. He was tall all right, but a heavyset guy. Middle sixties maybe. Why? You know him?"

"No," Zoe said listlessly, "I don't know him."

She was still thinking clearly enough to realize what had happened. Now *they* had her fingerprints. *They* would compare them with the prints on the wineglass she left at the Tribunal. *They* would be sure now. *They* would come for her and kill her.

She left her food uneaten. She headed home with stumbling steps. The pains in her abdomen were almost shrill in their intensity.

She wondered if her period had started. She had not inserted a tampon and feared to look behind her; perhaps she was leaving a spotted trail on the sidewalk. And following the spoor came the thin, dour man, nose down and sniffing. A true bloodhound.

At home, she locked and bolted her door, put on the chain. She looked wearily about her trig apartment. She had always been neat. Her mother never had to tell her to tidy her room.

"A place for everything and everything in its place," her mother was fond of remarking.

She slipped shoes from her shrunken feet. She sat upright in a straight chair in the living room, hands folded primly on her lap. She watched dusk, twilight, darkness seep into the silent room.

Perhaps she fainted, dozed, dreamed; it was impossible to know. She saw a deserted landscape. Nothing there but gray smoke curling.

Then, as it thinned to fog, vapor, she saw a cracked and bloodless land. A jigsaw of caked mud. Craters and crusted holes venting steam. A barren world. No life stirring.

How long she sat there, her mind intent on this naked vision, she could not have said. Yet when her telephone rang, she rose, quite sane, turned on the light, picked up the phone. The lobby attendant: could Mr. Mittle come up?

She greeted Ernie with a smile, almost as happy as his. They kissed, and he told her she was getting dreadfully thin, and he would have to fatten her up. She touched his cheek lovingly, so moved was she by his concern.

The white wine he carried was already chilled. She brought a corkscrew and glasses from the kitchen. They sat close together on the couch. They clinked glasses and looked into each other's eyes.

"How do you feel, darling?" he asked anxiously.

"Better now," she said. "You're here."

He groaned with pleasure, kissed her poor, shriveled fingers.

He prattled on about his computer class, his job, their vacation plans. She smiled and nodded, nodded and smiled, searching his face. And all the time . . .

"Well," he said briskly, slapping one knee as if they had come to the moment of decision in an important business haggle, "have you thought about it, Zoe? Will you marry me?"

"Ernie, are you sure . . . ?"

He rose and began to stalk about the dimly lighted room, carrying his wineglass.

"I certainly am sure," he said stoutly. "Zoe, I know this is the most important decision of my life, and I've considered it very carefully. Yes, I'm sure. I want to spend the rest of my life with you. No two ways about *that!* I know I don't have a great deal to offer you, but still . . . Love—you know? And a promise to work hard at making you happy."

"I have nothing to offer," she said faintly. "Less than nothing."

"Don't say that," he cried.

He sat down again at her side. He put his glass on the cocktail table. He held her bony shoulders.

"Don't say that, darling," he said tenderly. "You have all I want. You *are* all I want. I just don't want to live without you. Say Yes."

She stared at him, and through his clear, hopeful features saw again that sere, damned landscape, the gray smoke curling.

"All right," she said in a low voice. "Yes."

"Oh, Zoe!" he said, clasped her to him, kissed her closed eyes, her dry lips. She put her arms softly about him, felt his warmth, his aliveness.

He moved her away.

"When?" he demanded. "When?"

She smiled. "Whenever you say, dear."

"As soon as possible. The sooner the better. Listen, I've been thinking about it, planning it, and I'll tell you what I think would be best. If you don't agree, you tell me—all right? I mean, this is just my idea, and you might have some totally different idea on how we should do it, and if you do, I want you to tell me. Zoe? All right?"

"Of course, Ernie."

"Well, I thought a small, quiet wedding. Just a few close friends. Unless you want your parents here?"

"Oh no."

"And I don't want my family. Mostly because they can't afford to make the trip. Unless you want to go to Minnesota for the wedding?"

"No, let's have it here. A few close friends."

"Right," he said enthusiastically. "And the money we

save, we can spend on the, uh, you know, honeymoon. Just a small ceremony. If you like, we could have a reception afterward at my place or here at your place. Or we could rent a room at a hotel or restaurant. What do you think?"

"Let's keep it small and quiet," she said. "Not make a big, expensive fuss. We could have it right here."

"Maybe we could have it catered," he said brightly. "It wouldn't cost so much. You know, just a light buffet, sandwiches maybe, and champagne. Like that."

"I think that would be plenty," she said firmly. "Keep it short and simple."

"Exactly," he said, laughing gleefully. "Short and simple. See? We're agreeing already! Oh Zoe, we're going to be so happy."

He embraced her again. She gently disengaged herself to fill their wineglasses. They tinked rims in a solemn toast.

"We've got so much to do," he said nervously. "We've got to sit down together and make out lists. You know— schedules and who to invite and the church and all. And when we should—"

"Ernie," she said, putting a palm to his hot cheek, "do you really love me?"

"I do!" he groaned, turning his face to kiss her palm. "I really do. More than anything or anyone in my life."

"And I love you," Zoe Kohler said. "You're the kindest man I've ever known. The sweetest and nicest. I want to be with you always."

"Always," he vowed. "Always together."

She brought her face close, looked deep into his eyes.

"Darling," she said softly, "do you remember when we talked about—uh—you know—going to bed together? Sex?"

"Yes. I remember."

"We agreed there had to be love and tenderness and understanding."

"Oh yes."

"Or it was just nothing. Like animals. We said that, Ernie—remember?"

"Of course. That's the way I feel."

"I know you do, dear. And I do, too. Well, if we love

each other and we're going to get married, couldn't we . . . ?"

"Oh Zoe," he said. "Oh my darling. You mean now? Tonight?"

"Why not?" she said. "Couldn't we? It's all right, isn't it?"

"Of course it's all right. It's wonderful, marvelous, just great. Because we do love each other and we're going to spend the rest of our lives together."

"You're sure?" she said. "You won't be, uh, offended?"

"How can you think that? It'll be sweet. So sweet. It'll be right."

"Oh yes," she breathed. "It will be right. I feel it. Don't you feel it, darling?"

He nodded dumbly.

"Let's go into the bedroom," she whispered. "Bring the wine. You get undressed and get into bed. I have to go into the bathroom for a few minutes, but I'll be right out."

"Is the front door locked?" he said, his voice choked.

"Darling," she said, kissing his lips. "My sweetheart. My lover."

She took her purse into the bathroom. She closed and locked the door. She undressed slowly. When she was naked, she inspected herself. She had not yet begun to bleed.

She waited a few moments, seated on the closed toilet seat. Finally she rose, opened the knife, held it in her right hand. She draped a towel across her forearm. She did not look at herself in the medicine cabinet mirror.

She unlocked the door. She peeked out. The bedside lamp was on. Ernest Mittle was lying on his back, hands clasped behind his head. The sheet was drawn up to his waist. His torso was white, hairless, shiny.

He turned his head to look toward her.

"Darling," she called with a trilly laugh, "look away. I'm embarrassed."

He smiled and rolled onto his side, away from her. She crossed the carpeted floor quickly, suddenly strong, suddenly resolute. She bent over him. The towel dropped away.

"Oh lover," she breathed.

The blade went into soft cheese. His body leaped frantically, but with her left hand and knee she pressed him down. The knife caught on something in his neck, but she sawed determinedly until it sliced through.

Out it went, the blood, in a spray, a fountain, a gush. She held him down until his threshings weakened and ceased. Then he just flowed, and she tipped the torn head over the edge of the bed to let him drain onto the rug.

She rolled him back. She pulled the sodden sheet down. She raised the knife high to complete her ritual. But her hand faltered, halted, came slowly down. She could not do it. Still, she murmured, "There, there, there," as she headed for the bathroom.

She tossed the bloodied knife aside. She inspected herself curiously. Only her hands, right arm, and left knee were stained and glittering.

She showered in hot water, lathering thickly with her imported soap. She rinsed, lathered again, rinsed again. She stepped from the tub and made no effort to wash away the pink tinge on the porcelain.

She dried thoroughly, then used her floral-scented cologne and a deodorant spray. She combed her hair quickly. She powdered neck, shoulders, armpits, the insides of her shrunken thighs.

It took her a few moments to find the Mexican wedding dress she had bought long ago and had never worn. She pulled it over her head. The crinkled cotton slid down over her naked flesh with a whisper.

The gown came to her blotched ankles, hung as loosely as a tent. But it was a creamy white, unblemished, as pure and virginal as the pinafores she had worn when she was Daddy's little girl and all her parents' friends had said she was "a real little lady."

Ernest Mittle's engagement ring twisted on her skinny finger. Working carefully, so as not to cut herself, she snipped a thin strip of Band-Aid. This she wound around and around the back part of the ring.

Then, when she worked it on, the fattened ring hung and stuck to her finger. It would never come loose.

She went into the kitchen, opened the cabinet door. In her pharmacopeia she found a full container of sleeping pills and a few left in another. She took both jars and a bottle of vodka into the bedroom. She set them carefully on the floor alongside the bed.

She checked the front door to make certain it was locked, bolted, and chained. Then she turned out all the lights in the apartment. Moving cautiously, she found her way back to the bedroom.

She sat on the edge of the bed. She took four of the pills, washed them down with a swallow of vodka. She didn't want to drink too much, remembering what had happened to Maddie Kurnitz.

Then she stripped the soaked sheet from the bed and let it fall at the foot. She got into bed alongside Ernest Mittle, wearing her oversized wedding gown and taped ring. She moved pills and vodka onto the bedside table. She took four more pills, a larger swallow of vodka.

She waited . . .

She thought it might come suddenly, blackness descending. But it did not; it took time. She gulped pills and swallowed vodka, and once she patted Ernie's cooling hip and repeated, "There, there . . ."

The scene she had been seeing all night, the blasted landscape, came back, but hazed and softened. The pitted ground slowly vanished, and only the curling smoke was left, the fog, the vapor.

But soon enough that was gone. She thought she said something aloud, but did not know what it meant. All she was conscious of was that pain had ceased.

And for that she was thankful.

July 26; Saturday . . .

"Surveillance reported ten minutes ago," Sergeant Abner Boone said, consulting his notes.

"Is she still there?" Thorsen said sharply.

"Yes, sir. Got home about six-forty last night. Hasn't been out since."

"Any phone calls?" Delaney asked.

"One," Boone said. "About nine o'clock last night. The deskman in the lobby, asking if Ernest Mittle could come up."

"Mittle?" Detective Bentley said. "He's the boy-friend."

"He didn't leave," Boone said. "He's still up there."

"Shacking up?" Sergeant Broderick said.

"He never did that before," Detective Johnson said.

"Well, apparently both of them are still up there."

"Maybe he's closer to this than we figured," Broderick said. "Maybe he's been in on it all along."

"We'll soon find out," Boone said.

"How do we do this?" Ivar Thorsen asked.

"Maybe I've overplanned it," Boone said, "but rather be safe than sorry. Two cars at Lex and Third to block off her street. Precinct men for crowd control. The two guys on the wiretap will cover the basement. One man posted at each end of her hallway. Then we'll go in."

"What if she doesn't open up?" Thomas Handry said.

"We'll get the lobby man to use his passkeys," Boone said. "He's got them; I checked. Deputy, you, the Chief and I go in first. Uh, and Dr. Ho and Handry. Bentley, Johnson, and Broderick to follow. We got a floor plan of her apartment from the owner, and those guys will spread out fast to make sure she doesn't have a chance to dump anything. Sound okay?"

They all looked at Delaney.

"I don't think she'll try to run," he said, "but it won't do any harm to have a man on the roof."

"Right," Boone said, "we'll do it." He looked at his watch. "Coming up to ten o'clock. Let's get this show on the road."

Delaney, Dr. Patrick Ho, Sergeant Boone, and Thorsen rode in the Deputy's car.

"Ah, will there be any shooting?" Dr. Ho asked nervously.

"God forbid," Boone said.

"I want this to go down quickly and quietly," the Admiral said.

"Get her and the boyfriend out of there as soon as possible," Delaney advised. "Then you can tear the place apart."

"You have the warrants, sergeant?" Thorsen asked.

Boone tapped his breast pocket. "Right here, sir. She's signed, sealed, and delivered."

Thorsen remarked on the beauty of the morning; a bare sun rising in a strong sky. He said the papers had predicted rain, but at the moment it looked like a perfect July day.

It went with a minimum of confusion. The screening

cars sealed off the block. Two uniformed officers were posted at the outer door of the apartment house. Precinct men began to set up barricades.

The others piled into the lobby. Uniformed men went first, hands on their holstered revolvers. The lobby attendant looked up, saw them coming. He turned white. Sergeant Boone showed the warrants. The man couldn't stop nodding.

They waited a few moments for the roof and corridor men to get in position. Then they crowded into the elevators, taking the lobby attendant along with them.

They gathered outside her door. Boone waved the others aside, then knocked on the door with his knuckles.

No response.

He banged on the door with his fist, then put his ear to the panel.

"Nothing," he reported. "No sounds at all." He gestured to the lobby attendant. "Open it up."

The man's hands were shaking so hard he couldn't insert the passkeys. Boone took them from him, turned both locks. The door opened a few inches, then caught on the chain.

"I've got a bolt-cutter in my car," Sergeant Broderick said.

"Wait a minute," Delaney said. He turned to the attendant. "Gas or electric ranges?" he asked.

"Gas."

The Chief stepped close, put his face near the narrow opening, sniffed deeply.

"Nothing," he reported and stepped aside.

Sergeant Boone took his place.

"Police officers," he yelled. "We've got a warrant. Open up."

No answer.

"They've got to be in there," Thorsen said nervously.

"Should I get the bolt-cutter?" Broderick asked.

Boone looked to Delaney.

"Kick it in," the Chief said curtly.

The sergeant stood directly in front of the door. He drew up his leg until his knee almost touched his chin. He drove his foot forward at the spot where the chain showed. Wood splintered, the chain swung free, the door slammed open.

They rushed in, jostling each other. The searchers spread out. Thorsen, Delaney, Dr. Ho, Handry, and Boone stood in the living room, looking around.

"Clean and neat," the Chief said, nodding.

"Sarge!" Johnson yelled from the bedroom. "In here!"

They went in, clustered around the bed. They stared down. The drained man with his raw throat gaping wide. The puttied woman wrapped in cloth as thin as a shroud.

"Shit," Sergeant Boone said bitterly.

Delaney motioned to Dr. Ho. The little man stepped close, put two fingers to the side of Zoe Kohler's neck.

"Ah, yes," he said gently. "She is quite, quite deceased."

He peered closely at the empty pill bottles but did not touch them. The vodka bottle was on its side on the rug, a little clear liquid left.

"Barbiturates?" Handry asked Dr. Ho.

"Ah, I would say so. And the liquor. Usually a lethal combination."

Ivar Thorsen took a deep breath, hands on his hips. Then he turned away.

"You'll have to clean up this mess, sergeant," he said. "Do what you have to do."

Thorsen and Delaney took the elevator down together.

"She killed him?" the Deputy said. "Then did the Dutch?"

"Looks like it."

"How do you figure it?"

"I don't," Delaney said.

Outside, on the sidewalk, a crowd was beginning to gather. They pushed their way through. They walked slowly to the Deputy's car.

"I'll have to call a press conference," Thorsen said, "but I could use a drink first. How about you, Edward?"

"I'll pass."

"I'll buy," the Deputy offered.

"Thanks, Ivar," Edward X. Delaney said, smiling briefly. "Some other time. I think I'll go home. Monica is waiting for me."